Sign up for our newsletter to hear
about new and upcoming releases.

www.ylva-publishing.com

Books in the Series
Cops and Docs

Blurred Lines

Crossing Lines
(Book #2; Coming Spring 2016)

BLURRED LINES

 **KD WILLIAMSON**

Dedications

To my Michelle—She stuck around all this time, so I must be a pretty okay person…weird but okay.

To my mother and the rest of my family—I've always stuck out, but you fostered my idiosyncrasies.

Acknowledgments

I would like to thank the gang at Ylva Publishing for making my transition back into the world of writing almost seamless. Special thanks to Jove Belle who pushed and pushed…and pushed until I was ready to jump over the cliff and be better. Last, but certainly not least, big thanks to my friend and writing buddy, Maria Bennet. Without you kicking me in the ass, this story would have never been what it turned into.

CHAPTER 1

Kelli McCabe blinked her eyes rapidly, trying to see through the gray haze that filled her vision. There was a coppery taste in her mouth. Kelli swallowed and realized it was her own blood. She beat down panic and clung to consciousness with both hands. Her own special brand of stubbornness kept the darkness at bay. This wasn't the first time that trait had served her well, and it sure as fuck wasn't going to be the last. The sound of gunfire echoed in her ears, but the roar of her own heartbeat took precedence, blocking out everything else. It reminded her that those assholes had failed. She had to live. Pure and simple. It was the best sort of *fuck you* to send out to the universe and the gunmen who had shot her.

Gradually, Kelli focused on the medical personnel. They were making too much goddamned noise so she didn't really have a choice. Two EMTs prodded her at the same time, seemingly everywhere at once. They spoke to her and each other, but Kelli couldn't understand a word. The one thing she knew for sure was this shit hurt. Pain twisted her insides, and she fought against it. Kelli smacked away the hands that poked at her. "Stop…no fucking touching." She growled, impressed that she could speak through the crapload of pain.

"She's coming out of it," one of the EMTs said.

"What's she saying?"

"Uh, I think she's cursing at us." He paused. "Listen, we're trying to help you," he said slowly.

"Then…stop poking…your fingers in me…shit," Kelli countered even slower.

"I know it hurts. You've been shot. We're almost at the hospital."

Everything came back to her in a rush of jumbled images. The gray haze turned to blood-red anger, and it left her tired as hell.

"Travis." Kelli screamed his name, but all that came out was a raspy whisper.

"What?" the EMT asked.

"Travis," she mumbled, a little louder than before.

"I think she said Travis, but I'm not sure. She's fading."

"Doesn't matter. We're here."

The doors to the ambulance opened with a loud creak, drowning out Kelli's next attempt to speak. They moved her abruptly and jostled her, causing a burst of pain to jolt through her chest. She groaned. Bright light and a tangle of voices flooded her senses, and put her in overload. Kelli flinched. Everything already hurt, and all that other shit was just too much.

"What do we have?"

"White female. GSW to the chest and right thigh. Diminished breath sounds. BP is seventy over fifty-five and falling," a familiar voice answered.

She had to get them to listen. Kelli's pain and desperation fueled her. "Travis!" She tried to sit up but was pushed back down.

"Weak my ass! There is no way she should be awake. Let's get her to trauma one."

An eternity later, Kelli was lifted and moved to a different bed. Pain slapped her in the face. She cried out, "Dammit."

"Miss? Can you tell me your name?"

It was getting harder to breathe, but Kelli held on. The room began to swim, turning the person looking down at her into a blur. "Shit."

"Let's try it again."

"Fuck…Kel-li."

"Okay, I'm Dr. Rader, Kelli. You're at Seattle Memorial. We're trying to take care of you. Is Travis your husband?"

"Partner."

"I'm sure he's being taken care of," Dr. Rader said dismissively.

It pissed her off all over again. "Fuck you. I need to know. Go check on him."

"Kelli, I need you to calm down. Let us do our job."

Kelli wanted to scream. Why wouldn't these dumbasses listen to her? She was alive. She knew that because she hurt everywhere, but she had no idea what happened to Travis. "Fuck that. He wasn't moving. Go fix him."

"Kel? Kelli?"

Kelli turned toward the sound of her name. She blinked, bringing her brother into focus. She couldn't remember ever feeling that relieved.

"Sean…Travis…he…"

Sean moved closer. She wanted to reach out to him. "Let them take care of you. I'll find out what's going on with him."

"Sir, you can't be in here. Family—"

"She's my sister." Sean cut him off.

"Sorry. If you can calm her down…"

Ignoring the others around her, Kelli concentrated on her brother. "They got him in the back, Sean. He…wasn't moving. Please—"

"I've got this. Mom's on her way. I'm sure Bruce will be here soon too."

His voice was soft. It soothed her.

"Just do what they say. I got this," he repeated.

Kelli wanted to believe him. A crushing pain fluttered through her chest, making it even harder to breathe. Kelli gasped as everything went dim.

"What do we have?" Dr. Nora Whitmore asked as she entered.

Dr. Rader stiffened visibly. "Dr. Whitmore, there was no need—"

"What do we have?" Nora stared at Rader, demanding his cooperation. He remained still and silent as the rest of his team worked diligently. Nora lost her patience. "You can urinate all over your territory later if that's what you need to do, Dr. Rader. For now, though, I don't communicate telepathically so…" She paused for a few seconds to give herself a moment to calm down and assess the patient for herself. "GSW to the leg and chest." She glanced at a nurse. "Breath sounds?"

"Some, but they are wet and decreasing."

"Get her to surgery before she bleeds out," Dr. Whitmore ordered. "I'm going to go check on our other gunshot victim."

Rader nodded as he helped to wheel Kelli from the room.

Nora glanced at the remaining occupant as she made her exit.

He followed her. "I'm Kelli's brother, Sean. I think you were talking about her partner, Gerald Travis Jr. Is he okay?"

She walked briskly toward the next patient's room. "I'm not sure who it is, but I'll know more about his prognosis momentarily."

Sean nodded and stepped away as she entered another trauma room. She looked over her shoulder. Sean was still there, looking through the window. This was obviously his friend.

The heart monitor beeped loudly in concert with the IV pump. The sounds centered Nora and brought her patient's needs into focus. The cervical collar around his neck inhibited movement to prevent any additional injury. She had taught her residents well.

"Dr. Simmons should be here momentarily. I'm here to help. Talk to me," Nora said. The staff looked her way.

"GSW, probably trauma to the spine, plus significant blood loss. Abdomen is rigid indicating an internal bleed. His extremities aren't responding to stimulation, and his blood pressure is dropping." Dr. Fuller, a third-year resident, responded immediately, and Nora was surprised that she was the resident to take lead. Dr. Fuller's performance had been subpar recently, but Nora approved of her initiative.

The electrocardiograph whined. The patient's blood pressure bottomed out, and he went into ventricular fibrillation.

"He's coding."

"You know what to do." Nora disliked giving unnecessary direction.

Dr. Fuller placed the defibrillator pads on his chest.

The door to the trauma room banged against the wall and the young police officer entered. "Gerry!"

"Someone escort him out." Nora maintained her focus. "Twenty joules."

"Charging."

The defibrillator bleeped in readiness.

"Clear," Nora said.

Infused with electrical current, Gerald Travis arched upward.

Nora stared at the monitor, mentally ordering it to respond. When it didn't, she changed tactics. He was her patient. She refused to give up easily and was confident she could stabilize his vitals. "Push an amp of epi and bump it to forty joules."

Nora waited patiently for the defibrillator.

"Clear."

The patient was shocked again, and seconds later, his heart returned to a normal sinus rhythm. *Perfect.* Now, she could focus on the other challenges his battered body faced.

Nora peeled the defibrillator pads from the patient's chest.

"Vitals are stabilizing." Dr. Fuller stated the obvious.

The door burst open as Dr. Simmons entered. He bent over slightly as he tried to catch his breath. "Sorry," he muttered. "Sorry."

Instead of responding to his apologies, Nora relayed information on Gerald Travis Jr.

Dr. Simmons stood, nodded, and asked for forgiveness once more.

"Get him to an OR." Nora removed her gloves and stepped to the side.

Last to leave, Nora walked out behind the gurney. Sean McCabe met her at the door. His police uniform was wrinkled, and he held his hat in a white knuckled grip. He watched as they wheeled his friend down the hall.

"This is so messed up. It's hard to see him like this. He's usually smirking or saying something stupid." Sean turned toward Nora. "Thank you for what you did in there."

Uncomfortable with being praised for doing her job, Nora nodded and chose her words carefully, intent on ending the interaction as soon as possible. "He's sta—"

"I know. I get it." Sean nodded, looking dejected.

"I'm sorry, officer. I know this is difficult." Platitudes were easy. She had plenty of them on standby. Nora used them so she would appear to care while still remaining detached. She did her best to comfort the young man, but it was time to move on. "If you'll excuse me, I need to get to a previously scheduled surgery. Another surgeon will be operating on your friend. They'll contact you as soon as they know more."

She nodded stiffly and started down the corridor. This scenario was her least favorite part of being a doctor. She hated not having answers for loved ones. She hated that the most she could do was imitate empathy. Most of all, she hated handing off patient care to another surgeon because of prior obligations. It prevented her from being able to offer assurances about the quality of care a patient would receive. Not that the other surgeons weren't capable. They were all fine doctors. They just weren't Nora Whitmore. And she may be a lot of things that weren't desirable, but she was the best at her job. None of her peers could compete with her success rates.

As she moved quickly toward the elevator, she justified leaving the officer without the comfort he so clearly needed. Any time she spent consoling him was time taken away from saving lives. That wasn't a sacrifice she would make.

"I fucking hate hospitals," Sean whispered.

Despite his lowered volume, Nora overheard every word as the elevator doors slid shut.

CHAPTER 2

Kelli pushed through her grogginess, and bit by bit, she became more aware.

The first thing she felt was white-hot pain. It was a shitty way to wake up, but there wasn't a damn thing she could do about it.

Second, her nose felt weird. There was a tube forcing air into her nostrils. That moved things even higher on the weird scale, even though it made breathing easier. Some machine hissed in the background. Momentary anxiety grabbed hold of her, but the feeling passed quickly when she figured out that the tubes didn't reach her throat.

Third, Kelli did her best to case the environment. She strained to hear over the noise of the hospital equipment, but finally, her mother's and brother's voices became clearer. She forced her heavy eyelids to open. The room came in to blurry focus, but she could see people moving around her. When she blinked again, Kelli saw a nurse walking out of the room. The effort to concentrate took just about everything she had. She could barely keep her eyes open. So, she didn't fight it. This sucked *hard*. Fuck it. At least she could hear what was going on. That was better than nothing.

"She doesn't even look like herself. I've never seen her like this."

"I know it's scary, Mom, but she's here."

"I know. You're right." Her mother sighed. "Why isn't Antony here? He should be here."

"I tried to call him, but his phone was disconnected," Sean said.

"I don't understand that boy. I'll never understand him." Carina sounded tired. More tired than Kelli could remember hearing before.

"I don't either, Mom." Sean sounded almost as weary as their mother.

A warm, soft hand stroked Kelli's cheek. It felt good to be touched, especially by her mother. Kelli didn't allow it often, but if this wasn't a fucking exception, she didn't know what was. She leaned into the caress and whispered, "Mom."

Her mother sobbed loudly. "Kelli? Baby?"

Kelli swallowed thickly. Her throat felt like it was lined with glass, but she kept trying. "Mom?" She opened her eyes again and was determined to hang on. It was time for her second wind, whether it wanted to come or not.

"I'm here Kelli. Sean is too." Her mother's fingers tangled with her own.

"Hey, sis." Sean grasped the other hand.

Kelli wanted to cry. Their words rushed over her and settled in deep. She felt clear enough to recognize she was missing something, but didn't know what exactly. "Travis?" That's when it hit her. Bone rattling panic. She tried to sit up but the instant jolt of pain cut through her. "Shit."

"Whoa, Kelli. Calm down. You gotta calm down."

She heard Sean's words, but they didn't matter. Kelli had one goal, and it didn't involve calming down. No matter how crappy she felt, she needed to know about Travis. Sean tried to put his arms around her. She pushed them away. "Travis." Her brother and mother peered at each other. Warning bells went off like a siren in her head. "Dammit, no." Kelli managed to whisper. She was a goddamn lion. Lions roar. And all she could manage was a few words. Pathetic. Getting shot had made her pathetic.

"They had to take him back to surgery," Carina said.

Back to surgery. Yes, Travis was alive, but she was sure nothing good ever came from going *back* to surgery. Kelli couldn't stop fear from creeping over her, no matter how much she wanted to beat the shit out of it. To make matters worse, she was stuck here. Too weak. Too broken to do anything to help. She couldn't even go see him for herself. "Check on him. Please."

Sean nodded. Kelli didn't have to push hard because he was just as worried. Travis was family. She tracked Sean as he made his way out of the room and down the hall. After Sean left, Kelli felt her mother watching her. She turned her head slightly and met her gaze. Carina was upset and her distress was big enough to fill the whole room. It made it even harder for Kelli to breathe.

Kelli didn't look away. Her mom's eyes were filled with worry and relief.

"You can't leave me." Carina gripped Kelli's hand.

The weight of the words crashed down on Kelli's shoulders. Cheating death was a promise she wouldn't always keep—not in her line of work. She sure as hell was going to try. It was strange to be face to face with her own mortality. The possibility of dying brought up all kinds of emotions that she didn't want to name. Instead, Kelli pushed the feelings away.

"I'm fine, Mom. Not going anywhere." Her words were a lie, but it was a one of the good ones. The kind that made her mother smile.

It seemed like hours had passed in just a few minutes, and her body started to protest once more. Kelli's eyelids fluttered as the feeling of weightlessness took over.

"It's okay. Don't fight it. We'll be here when you wake up."

The words washed over her and provided her a sense of safety as she drifted back into sleep.

Nora studied her patient's peritoneum. There was enough blood filling it to be life threatening no matter how many units were transfused into him. With steady hands and a discerning eye, she searched. This is what she lived for—following clues and solving mysteries.

"Suction."

Dr. Sanford vacuumed out the fluid, but she didn't thank him. She didn't want to be thanked for doing her job, why would he? The music of Branford Marsalis surrounded her, swelling to a crescendo.

This part excited her the most. It was a combination of pure logic, science, and instinct. This man was dying. There was always a reason behind it, information to be collected, collated, and quantified, and *this* was where Nora excelled. She was the one who put all the pieces together. If she had been present for the first surgery, there would have been no need for a second. The sloppy work of the previous surgeon and his team continued to annoy her even though she had already discussed the incident with Dr. Simmons. Incompetence. She didn't tolerate it in herself and found it unforgiveable in others. Unfortunately, Nora couldn't be everywhere at once.

"Suction."

Her team was quiet because they knew she preferred it that way. She disliked forced niceties and idle conversation under normal circumstances and even more so in her operating room. She worked with professionals who were very capable, and that created the level of trust needed to save lives.

Nora studied his spleen closely and saw only mild inflammation. She scanned his liver just as carefully. "Suct—there it is."

Dr. Sanford cleansed the area.

"Clamp." With quick, sure fingers, and the added help of other precise tools, Nora closed the tear. Well done. Dr. Sanford siphoned out the remaining blood and irrigated the surgical site. Nora examined the area for several seconds but knew she'd done the repair properly.

"Dr. Sanford?" Nora said.

His gaze met hers. He had been a quick, quiet resident who learned to anticipate her moves without instruction. "Yes ma'am?"

"You may close." Without another word, she left the operating room. When she reached the prep area, Nora began her post-surgery ritual. She removed her gloves and surgical cap. Then, she loosened her habitual ponytail and let her hair hang freely. As she washed her hands, she watched Dr. Sanford engage the others. She heard laughter as the tension that held them in check just a few moments ago seemed to dissipate. For a second, Nora experienced a pang of longing in her chest. The feeling passed just as quickly as it came. Nora dried her hands and moved toward the exit.

The intercom buzzed as she walked by. "Dr. Whitmore? I'm sorry to bother you, but your surgical nurse told me you were done."

Nora pressed the button. "Yes?"

"There is a Sean McCabe who's demanding a report on Mr. Travis's condition."

"I'll be there momentarily." Sometimes people needed the truth delivered bluntly, no matter how uncomfortable it was. Sean McCabe struck her as one of those people. And Nora didn't know any other way to say what needed to be said. She wasn't one to pull her punches.

When Nora entered the waiting area, his back was to her. "Mr. McCabe?"

Sean spun around. A shock of sandy-brown hair fell over his forehead, and his features were stricken and drawn. It didn't distract from his boyish good looks. "H-how is he? You don't have to sugarcoat anything. I can take it."

Nora almost smiled. "The bullet caused swelling in his spinal column. As I hope you were informed earlier by his previous surgeon, true damage, if any, can't be assessed until the swelling subsides." She waited for him to acknowledge her, and he nodded. Nora continued, "Apparently, there was also damage to his liver, which I just repaired with no further complications." Since Mr. Travis was incapacitated and he had no other family present, Nora deemed it necessary to pass along pertinent information regarding his prognosis.

Sean's eyes widened. "That wasn't caught the first time?"

"No, it was not. Compared to the other internal damage, it was a small tear but still dangerous." Nora offered no further explanation. She knew to be cautious in a potential lawsuit situation.

He wiped a hand over his face. "God. So all the talk about possible paralysis was true?"

"Unfortunately, yes it is."

Sean sighed. "I knew it, but I was hoping—"

"I understand." Nora nodded, and in a way, she did. "Will there be anything else, Mr. McCabe?"

"Sean. Call me Sean. I kind of feel like we're old friends after all this." His smile was soft, crooked. His expression was sincere.

Nora cringed internally. She refused to engage in that level of familiarity. "While I understand your reasoning, I don't think that would be appropriate."

He deflated a bit, and his shoulders slumped.

"I can understand that. I'm a cop. We all have procedures. Professional boundaries."

The conversation had gone on long enough to make her uneasy. It was time to go. "Is there anything else—"

"Can you just come take a look at my sister? I know she's alive and all, but I just want to make sure—"

"Dr. Rader hasn't been in yet?"

"Not this morning, no."

The man was exasperating but well liked at Seattle Memorial and not just by the female staff. Nora couldn't figure out why. "Yes, I can do that."

Nora followed him even though she knew the way. As she entered the room, a petite, dark-haired woman stood to greet her. She looked to be in her mid fifties. "Good morning, doctor."

Nora nodded. "Whitmore. It's Dr. Whitmore. I'm the attending."

Though the woman looked confused, she continued to smile. "Carina McCabe."

In reply, Nora picked up Kelli McCabe's chart. She flipped through the pages and glanced at the woman in question. Kelli was sleeping soundly. It wasn't a pretty sight. Her mouth was open, and her features were pinched like she smelled something sour. It probably had more to do with discomfort caused by her injuries. Kelli's short auburn hair stuck up at odd angles but still fanned out on the stark white pillow, highlighting a slight paleness to her olive-toned skin which was similar to her mother's.

"She looks so weak right now. That's just not her."

"She suffered significant injuries and blood loss, but her pallor and strength will return with time," Nora said.

"That's not what she means. Kelli is a badass. Wait 'til she feels better. I guarantee she's going to be the worst patient you ever had."

Nora glanced from Sean to Carina, then she peered at Kelli and evaluated her carefully. The woman was tall, stocky yet covered in a lean layer of muscle. Her face was aesthetically pleasing, but she appeared to be nothing more than an average woman. There was nothing special about her. Nora looked at Sean skeptically.

"Trust me," he said.

Nora moved toward the head of the bed to check the surgical sites. She started with the most severe. Kelli's eyelashes flickered, and she groaned. "Fuck."

Well. *That* was unexpected. Nora was taken aback by the language. Kelli's voice was deep and gravely, which somehow made the utterance more powerful.

Sean laughed suddenly, startling Nora. She turned to see mother and son smiling and holding hands.

So, it was obviously common for her to start every interaction with cursing. "Ms. McCabe? Can you hear me?"

"What?" Kelli mumbled.

"Can you hear me?" Nora asked once more.

"Yes, fuck. What do you want?"

She cursed twice in a matter of minutes. Nora definitely sensed a pattern. "I'm Dr. Whitmore. I'm going to check your surgical sites for signs of infection. This may be uncomfortable."

Kelli opened her eyes completely. The telltale post-surgery haze cleared gradually until Kelli stared back at her with sharply focused green eyes.

"Okay." Kelli rumbled. "Travis, my partner—"

"He's in recovery. He has a significant spinal injury."

"Fuck."

That made three. Nora sighed internally. "Yes. When the inflammation recedes, we will know more."

"Okay."

Kelli's green eyes darkened, and Nora was captivated by the intensity of her stare. She felt odd. Unnerved by the scrutiny, Nora continued with Kelli's examination. When she glanced up again, Kelli's eyes were thankfully closed.

Nora stepped back and turned to Sean and Carina McCabe. "Everything looks as it should. She will be in a fair amount of pain. The bullet to her leg didn't hit bone, but some rehabilitation will be needed to return the muscle to full functionality."

Carina smiled. "Thank you, Dr. Whitmore."

Nora returned the smile. "You're welcome."

The McCabe family seemed to be genuinely kind, something they extended to everyone who came into their radius, and she didn't understand why. Why be nice to someone who isn't in return? Nora brushed the thought aside and left the room in pursuit of something less emotional and a lot safer. Surgery was the first thing—the *only* thing—to spring to mind, but it would have to wait.

Nora marched down the hall to the elevator and pushed the button to call it to her floor. After a few seconds, she heard laughter coming from inside. It stopped when the doors slid open.

Several of the occupants were part of the medical staff. They looked everywhere except at her. Nora stepped in anyway. She was used to the whispers and the stares from the residents and other hospital employees. Sometimes, they called her "iceberg princess." Other times, it was "queen mean." Nora refused to be bothered by it. Besides, any reaction would just be fodder for gossip, and Nora had no intensions of feeding that beast.

When the elevator reached her destination, Nora stepped out and left the others to continue their rumormongering. She made an educated guess as to Dr. Rader's location, the senior resident's lounge was where he usually spent his perceived downtime, mingling with the other residents. She pushed against the lounge door. Strangely, it was locked. Undeterred, Nora took out her keys and opened it.

Dr. Rader cursed and scrambled from the couch.

Dr. Reed, one of the residents, gasped and struggled to cover herself. As she quickly dressed and made her way to the door, she avoided eye contact completely.

Obviously, mingling was not a strong enough word.

"It's not what it…" His voice trailed off.

Nora stared at him. He was more intelligent than that, but Nora knew pedigree wasn't the same as having common sense. In most cases, it was a completely separate concept. "Shouldn't you be making rounds?"

His face reddened. "I was. I—"

"Yes, I see."

He glowered at her. "You really don't care, do you?"

"About?" Nora asked.

"Us."

"There is no—"

"Us! I know that. How can you not care? Do you know what you did to me?"

"This conversation is moot as well as redundant." They were done. It was a simple fact, yet he refused to accept it.

"The hell it is. I had sex with you, and my whole life fell apart. I couldn't think about anything else." He walked toward her. He was a decidedly handsome man. With blond hair and chiseled features, he was a prime representation of the male of the species. "And all you were doing was scratching an itch."

Sex with him had been a mistake. Nora knew this, but he had been willing, presumably unattached, and had promised to be discreet. "Is there some reaction I can mimic that will satisfy you and end this?"

"My fiancé—"

Yes, that. If she'd known that a fiancé existed, none of this would have happened. Her lack of information concerning Rader's relationship was a direct drawback of not being social. This was a lesson learned, and even though she dismissed a majority of gossip, Nora was more aware of the happenings inside the hospital now. Regardless, he was definitely not the man he pretended to be. Aggravated with his dramatics, Nora cut him off. "That was your doing, not mine."

He closed his mouth, and a muscle ticked in his jaw. "What do you want, Nora?"

"You inspire incompetence all around you, James. The residents worship you, but that doesn't equate to actual skill."

"What are you talking about?"

"Gerald Travis Jr."

"Dr. Simmons was there to assist, but Taylor was more than ready to do this on her own—"

"Was that according to you or your genitalia?"

He turned away without giving an answer.

"She missed the liver lac. It was small but enough to kill him."

James turned his head fast enough to cause whiplash. "What? But, Simmons was there. You should be chewing him out too."

"I discussed it with him, and now, because you're chief resident, she is mainly your responsibility so I'm bringing it to your attention as well." Nora didn't elaborate further. It wasn't unnecessary. "I trust that this won't happen again?"

James's face darkened to a deep red, and Nora assumed his expression was fueled by shame. He nodded.

As far as she was concerned, this discussion was over on every level. Not sparing him another glance, Nora exited the lounge. Rader didn't deserve any more of her time, and she refused to give it. She looked at the board detailing the surgical rotation, then at the clock. The tension drained from Nora's shoulders. She tingled with anticipation. There was nothing better than this. It was time to scrub in.

CHAPTER 3

Kelli tried to catch Sean's attention when he walked into her room. He glanced in her direction but didn't meet her gaze. There were no smirks, no jokes. Maybe she was reading too much into it because she was already on high alert because of their train wreck of a brother, Tony. He was the youngest of the three of them, and sometimes he acted like it. She hadn't really seen him much the last couple of weeks. His bulb never shined too brightly, but lately something was even more off than normal. Kelli didn't even want to think about what that meant.

So, to round everything out nicely, Sean was throwing off weird vibes too. He was hiding something. She felt it deep down in her gut. When they were kids, the only time he acted like this was when he lied or had taken something of hers. At the moment, she didn't have shit to take.

She studied him just like she did Antony a few minutes earlier. And just like Tony, Sean stood with his arms crossed and tried to pretend that she was invisible.

"Tony not here?" Sean asked.

Their mother smiled. "He could only stay for a minute. He had to get to work. He's starting a new job today." Carina shook her head. "I wish he would come work at the deli. It would be easier for him. I just don't understand it. I could change it to McCabe and Son. Your father would have loved that."

Kelli continued to watch her brother. Finally, he looked her in the eye. He grinned, but it was bogus as hell. He wasn't fooling anyone. She wanted to smack him in the back of the head. Maybe it would knock some sense into him. Tony deserved much of the same, but Kelli swallowed the impulse instead. She didn't have the energy to deal with his—or anybody else's—shit. She had a hole in her chest for fuck's sake.

Sean cleared his throat. "I have to get outta here too, but I have some news."

He smiled for real this time, and Kelli wanted in on it. She needed the distraction. She hated being cooped up. "Good news? Because if it's not, I won't be held responsible," Kelli informed him.

"Travis is awake."

Kelli shifted her focus from Tony to Travis. "Really?"

"Yeah, went to see him after giving Tony your room number. Not a damn thing wrong with his mouth. He's still a smartass."

Kelli chuckled. "I have to find a way to go see him."

"Or you could just call his room for right now until you're able to get around better," Sean said.

Kelli caught the worry in Sean's eyes before he covered it with one of his phony-ass smiles.

"That's a good idea," Carina said.

Kelli stared at her brother, but his expression was unreadable. Hesitantly, she agreed. "Yeah, I can go with that for a while, I guess."

Sean looked away, moved toward their mother, and kissed her on the cheek. Then he had the balls to lean over Kelli and pucker his lips.

Kelli glared.

He smirked and squeezed her shoulder instead. "Later, Big Red."

"Really? That's what you guys did? Come up with a pissy nickname for me?"

"Yep." Sean pulled the door open.

"Asshole," Kelli yelled after him. He didn't even turn around, but she got the last word. That was all that mattered.

Mindful of her wounds, Kelli moved carefully as she tried to find a more comfortable position in the bed—if it could be called a bed. The thing felt more like she was lying on a box spring covered with blankets. She subtracted points just for that shit alone. It definitely wasn't her mattress, so that was even more points deducted. The pillows, brought by her mother on the first day, were way too soft even though they were better than what the hospital had to offer. Kelli had almost requested the bedding from her own place, but she hadn't wanted to get on her mother's nerves too soon. That ended up being an idiot move. Her comfort was way more important.

This wasn't her space, and every day, that fact pissed her off more and more. This whole thing sucked ass, and she hated fucking hospitals. After seeing her father lying there lifeless in a bed just like this, it was easy to feel that way. She knew they helped people here. Hell, they'd saved her, but sometimes hospitals were like sponges. Places like this…they sucked the life out of people and left behind a shitload of misery. Mix that lingering funk with her boredom and loneliness and it resulted in her craptastic state of mind. *Craptastic.* Her picture needed to go in the urban dictionary right beside the definition.

A nurse entered, a stern-looking older woman who Kelli had seen way more than she wanted. The woman didn't smile. Kelli was sure they were supposed to at least *try* to look happy. A few butterflies and cartoon birds wouldn't hurt either. Maybe it would have helped Kelli's mood. Instead, she shoved a thermometer in Kelli's face. That took some fucking audacity—way, *way* too much of it. Kelli glared.

"Open, please."

Kelli turned away.

The nurse sighed and rolled her eyes. "What are you? Two?"

"What are you? Eighty? Didn't you get the memo? Retirement age is sixty-five." Kelli didn't have anything against folks working as long as they wanted, but she wasn't above taking the easy shot when it presented itself.

"I can do this anally. It's a more accurate reading anyway." The nurse held the thermometer up, an evil smile on her face.

"Touch my ass, lady, and they will be fitting you for a prosthetic." Kelli evaluated the nurse. Even laid up like this, she was pretty sure she could take her.

"Ms. McCabe, I need your vitals. That's all. It doesn't have to be difficult."

"I'm alive. Can't you tell?" Kelli asked. "Maybe you should try coming in here with a smile on your face and treating me like a human."

The nurse curled her lips upward in a garish attempt at a smile.

Kelli snorted. "No sale, lady."

The nurse stared.

"What?" Kelli crossed her arms.

"We're really doing this?"

"Well, you're not doing anything at the moment, but if you want to bring me lunch, I'd be good with that." Kelli grinned. She wasn't going to sing show tunes, but Kelli was a little less irritated. Tormenting the nurse was fun.

The nurse's mouth fell open.

"We can try this again later. Hopefully, you'll come back with a better fucking attitude." Kelli couldn't help tossing out one last parting shot.

The woman's face turned red, but instead of responding, she turned and left.

"Make sure you tell your friends."

Alone again, Kelli flipped through TV channels. Unfortunately, there was nothing on. She sighed and decided that sleep was a better option anyway.

The sound of voices dragged Kelli from a deep sleep. She frowned and tried to tune them out.

"Patient's name is Kelli McCabe. She had multiple GSWs. There was one to the chest and upper thigh."

That voice sounded vaguely familiar. It was refined, dulcet, and a bit imperial.

"She's healing rapidly, but complications can still occur. What might those entail?"

"Infection." The young man sounded unsure. A few chuckles followed.

"I have a mosquito bite that is several days old. It could become infected as well, but why state the obvious?"

Somebody gasped.

"It was rhetorical, Dr. Simpson."

"Dr. Whitmore?"

"Yes, Dr. Bridges?"

"There is a chance of total lung collapse or scarring. She is also a bit too muscular. Should we check for steroid usage?"

"Steroid usage would compromise the healing process." Another voice added an opinion into the fray.

Kelli had heard enough. She opened her eyes. "Now that's just rude. This isn't the morgue. I'm a pretty light sleeper, and I could hear everything you were saying. I guarantee you this is all real." She recognized a few of the doctors, including Dr. Whitmore.

Dr. Whitmore cleared her throat. "Now, Ms. McCabe—"

"Dr. Whitmore," Kelli countered teasingly.

The doctor looked a bit frazzled. She tucked a strand of honey-blond hair behind her ear and continued. "This is a teaching hospital. While you may hear some indelicate things—"

"Like being a 'roidhead?"

"Yes, well, I assure you—"

"I have curves too. Nobody looks good in these shitty gowns." Kelli plucked at the edges of the hospital gown.

The residents laughed again.

"Ms. McCabe!" Dr. Whitmore sounded pissed.

"Dr. Whitmore." Kelli deliberately sang her name and grinned. Dr. Whitmore's tawny-brown eyes flashed with irritation. Plus, there was something about the way the good doctor said her name as if she ate something that tasted bad. Kelli loved it.

"It seems your brother was correct in his assessment."

Kelli narrowed her eyes. "I'm not sure what you're talking about, but that sounded really close to an insult."

"That is something you can discuss with him on his next visit." Dr. Whitmore turned, seemingly intent on ending the conversation.

"Hold on! I was just kidding." Kelli rolled her eyes. "I'm bored as shit. I need a little fun."

"Ms. McCabe." Dr. Whitmore pursed her full lips and red seeped into her cheeks. This just pushed Kelli further.

"Call me Kelli." She grinned, but somehow she knew Dr. Whitmore wouldn't use her first name. This day was getting better and better.

"I will not, that's highly inappropriate."

Kelli read the doctor's name tag. "Uh-huh. So what's the N stand for Dr. Whitmore?"

Except for the sound of whirring machines, things went quiet. Kelli looked around her. The students looked alarmed. Some of them even seemed afraid. "Okay," she muttered. "Party's over, huh?"

No one answered.

Dr. Whitmore addressed her students. "Wait in the hallway please. I'll be there shortly."

Kelli blinked. As the students filed out, she suddenly felt like she was in the principal's office. "Am I in trouble?" She raised a brow. "I really don't think you can expel me."

Dr. Whitmore sighed, and her lips thinned. "I do apologize if you found this encounter rude. If you wish to lodge a complaint against me or—"

"What? No! Lady, I said I was just kidding. Jesus." Kelli interrupted.

"Nora?" Dr. Rader stepped into the room.

They both looked toward the door.

The tension went from a hundred to about a thousand really fast. Kelli was stunned, but at least it was interesting. She thought this lady had been mad before, but clearly that was wrong. Now, she wouldn't have been surprised if Dr. Whitmore's eyes started to glow and Dr. Rader's head exploded.

"Please wait in the hall with the rest of the residents, Dr. Rader."

Dr. Rader's expression morphed into the same silent, alarmed look as the other doctors.

"So…Nora, I like that."

"Ms.—"

"Kelli." She corrected Nora just to needle her. So far, the fallout had been fucking fascinating.

"No." Nora looked even more flustered.

"Well, I'm gonna call you Nora no matter what you call me."

"How nice for you."

"Especially if I know it aggravates you. Are you aggravated? Because you look that way." Kelli might have been enjoying this a little too much.

"Is that your aim?"

Kelli shook her head. "No, not when I woke up this morning."

"Then boredom changed your mind?"

"Exactly." Kelli nodded sagely.

"Why am I participating in such nonsense?"

"Because I grow on people, Nora."

"Like the proverbial fungus?" Nora didn't wait for a reply. "No one enjoys fungus, Ms. McCabe." She backed away from the bed. "Have a nice day." Then, she was gone.

Kelli stared at the door. She wasn't so bored anymore. She was intrigued and a little offended, but most importantly, she was amused. Kelli smirked. Dr. Nora Whitmore had been better entertainment than the nurse from earlier.

Then, she remembered. Travis was awake. She could call him. Damn medication. It made her drowsy and fucked with her memory. She could have talked to him hours ago. Instead, she'd fallen asleep.

She dialed his room. On the fourth ring, she was about to give up.

"Yeah?" Travis sounded even more tired than Kelli felt. She didn't know that was possible.

"Yeah, yourself." Kelli smiled. It was good to hear his voice.

"Kelli?"

"No, it's Big Red," she deadpanned.

Travis chuckled, but it was brief and pained. "You don't like it?"

"No comment until you can see my face."

He laughed again, followed by a groan.

"Take it easy." The sounds he was making scared her.

"Stop."

"Stop what?" She had an idea what he was alluding to, but she didn't call for a pep talk.

"Kelli, you aren't responsible for every single thing that goes wrong."

Kelli sighed. "I didn't say—"

"Listen to me." Travis spoke slowly, clearly, leaving no room for misunderstanding. "Everything bad that happens isn't because Kelli McCabe didn't do something to stop it."

"I don't think that."

"You do about the people you care about." He knew her too damn well.

"I'm allowed." She could be overprotective at times, and that was a fact. She couldn't stop everything, but it never kept her from trying.

"Okay, tell me how this is your fault? Somehow you're psychic? You just knew our perps would kill someone who was just a potential witness? We barely had any leads, Kelli. No one could have figured that shit out."

Kelli pressed her lips together and breathed through her nose. "I really hate when people ask me a question and then answer it themselves."

"Well, I hate those little sperm-like things attached to egg yolks. The universe can't make every fucker happy."

"Bitch." Kelli shot back. Sometimes, he just made her ass itch.

"Twat waffle." Apparently, Travis was ready for her.

"Are we having a moment?"

"Possibly. Mark it with ten seconds of silence and let it pass."

Kelli smirked because it was easy to do with him. As she thought about all that had happened, all that could have happened, her smirk gave way to a frown. "I was really worried about you," she said softly—seriously.

"Yeah, well ditto white girl. But it's going to work out."

"White girl? I think of myself as an ethnic mix. Irish and Italian. Now *that* is a potent combination."

"I'm just as complicated…Korean and black. It shows just a little more on me. Don't you think?" Travis countered.

"You could have a point there. By the way, Sean told me your Dad is stuck overseas? That's shitty."

Travis grunted. "Life of a civilian contractor, I guess. It took him a week to get back after mom's car crash. He was in Saudi Arabia that time."

"No offense, but I really don't like that man. His priorities are screwed up."

"I don't like him sometimes myself." Travis agreed.

"I'm here. You know that, right? *We're* your family." Kelli knew that Travis knew that already, but if ever there was a time to reinforce it, this was it.

"I know you are. Don't get me wrong. I love my dad, but man, I miss my mom right now. I wish…" His voice trailed off.

"I know what you mean." The loss of her father left a hole big enough for her to walk through. It didn't seem to want to close anytime soon.

"She had this way of making all the bad shit go away. I was seven maybe eight when my dad found religion. He took us to an all-black church. Me and my mom stuck out. I mean, really. If you don't look too close, I can pass for black. That wasn't the case for my mom. I've never had anybody stare at us like that. She would pull me close and say something to make me laugh. Then, it was like nothing else mattered." Travis sighed. "Damn."

"Yeah." This was some heavy shit, and for both their sakes, Kelli needed to lighten the mood. "Did you hear? One of the shooters is dead and the other is in pretty bad shape. Probably right here in the ICU."

"I did. You'd be surprised what people say when they think you're unconscious." Travis sounded less hesitant and emotional.

Kelli smiled again. "No, I would not." She paused. "We can find out his room number and drown him in his bedpan."

"I'm not touching that thing."

Kelli rolled her eyes. "Think of the imagery…a piece of shit dying in shit."

"You can't drown in that," Travis said.

"God, never mind."

"Something is seriously wrong with you." Travis's voice was weak.

"True. I'd like to hear your theories later." Kelli continued the banter as long as possible. Even though she knew it would be short lived, it felt familiar.

As predicted, Travis yawned and went quiet.

"You need to go?" Kelli asked.

"Yeah, I probably should." He already sounded half asleep.

"Okay."

Kelli hung up the phone. She listened to the activity around her—beeping machines, low murmuring voices, and ringing telephones. Kelli didn't mind being alone, but she hated the feeling of loneliness. If she wasn't moving…if she wasn't laughing…if she wasn't working…it caught up with her, sneaking in from behind to almost overpower her. She didn't like being overwhelmed, especially by her feelings. Emotions usually fucked things up all the way to hell and back. Kelli was a good detective because she was detached enough to see the big picture, but her love life was screwed up for that exact same reason. At least her friends were fellow cops, so they knew the score. Her family was a different story. Things with them were always messy. All the time. Times ten.

Family. Maybe times ten wasn't strong enough.

Sean was hiding something and not very well. If she was up to full speed, she'd already know what it was. But she wasn't, and apparently he'd decided his balls had dropped enough to wear his big boy shorts now. Despite her irritation, she was almost proud. But it was shitty of him to keep things from her.

Then, there was Antony. Kelli closed her eyes. She wasn't ready to think about whatever mess he was in. She needed to move. She needed to laugh. Where was Dr. Nora Whitmore when she needed her?

The night was still and humid. Nora smoothed a hand over her pale silk blouse and unfastened another button to reveal more of her cleavage. The matching black Dolce and Gabbana skirt hugged her voluptuous curves, and the Louboutin's added to her five-foot-eight-inch frame. Her appearance was perfect, just as she wanted it to be. Nora handed her keys to the valet. Her heels tapped loudly against the stairs as she made her way up. She was flustered and exasperated. Her lack of professionalism today had been unnerving. Engaging with a patient like that was inappropriate. Her behavior was out of character, and she still did not understand how she let that McCabe woman get to her. She didn't have the answers, but she needed to start clean the next day. Then, there was James. He assumed a level of familiarity with her that he hadn't earned. It was very irritating. She was his superior, not only at the hospital, but in many other ways as well.

Throughout the rest of the day, she'd let work guide her. Now, she wanted sexual release. Sex was a necessity. The need for it—the oblivion it provided—was nothing to be ashamed of. Nora pursued it with the same single-mindedness that she used during surgery.

Tonight she craved a softer touch. A woman's touch.

She entered the building and walked briskly down the long hallway. A lone man stood at the end by the elevator. Nora nodded, and he stepped aside.

She'd been here several times, so it stood to reason that he recognized her from previous visits. The elevator moved quickly, preventing her from thinking about anything else. The doors opened, and semi-darkness and smooth jazz greeted her. This was an exclusive club that only catered to those who could afford it. She walked around the smattering of tables to the bar, aware of the gazes that followed her. Nora slid onto a stool. She flicked her hair over her shoulder as she waited for the bartender. She didn't have to wait long.

"Martini. Dirty."

The bartender nodded and smiled.

The gazes of the other patrons burned into her skin, teasing over her heightened senses. She studied her first suitor from the periphery. The woman was a compact brunette, and her hands shook as she shredded her napkin. She muttered to herself and wiped at her face. No, not this one. She didn't have the patience to deal with someone else's nerves. The brunette turned to finally speak, but Nora ignored her.

A few minutes later, another prospect appeared. Nora sipped her drink, aware of the other woman studying her. She was bold and had potential. Better. Much better. Nora turned slightly. The woman was tall and curvy, and blond hair spilled over her shoulders in waves.

"Tina." The woman's smile was slow and positively wicked. She held out a hand in greeting.

Nora took it. Her skin was soft, warm. Nora's anticipation grew. "Nora."

"That's so tragically plain. It doesn't fit you at all."

Nora smiled slightly.

Tina chuckled. "You're right that line really missed its mark. Should I try another?" She leaned forward, invading Nora's space. "Or should we just discuss all the things I'd like to do to you instead?"

Nora's back slammed against the door, and pleasure sharp enough to cut sliced through her. A moan rumbled in her chest, but she refused to make a sound. She controlled the venue. She controlled the pace. She controlled every aspect.

Nora glanced up at the hanging light fixtures that adorned her living room ceiling before she dropped her gaze to the woman between her thighs. Nora's skirt was bunched up around her waist, and her lingerie had been pushed aside to allow access. Nora tangled her hand in Tina's hair and encouraged each brush of Tina's tongue with a roll of her hips. The tension left her body with each thrust. Her final release was silent, unassuming. She pulled roughly at Tina, forcing her to stand.

Allowing a strategic meeting of lips, Nora walked them deeper into the living room. She stopped when they hit the arm of the couch. She spun Tina around, pushed her face first over the side of the sofa, and removed her underwear. Tina moaned as Nora plunged three fingers inside her. Phineas, her kunekune, ambled past them. Weighing over two hundred pounds, the pig made slow, but determined progress through the house. Nora smiled and rustled the fingers of her free hand through the black and white hairs covering his back. He paused and glanced at her for a moment before huffing and continuing his journey.

Tina gasped and looked at Phineas with confusion in her eyes. Nora twisted her fingers and burrowed deeper still, bringing Tina's attention back where it belonged.

CHAPTER 4

They walked up the sidewalk toward the witness's home. Kelli looked around. Everything was tinted different shades of red, from the color of blood to a darker crimson, even the sky and grass.

Travis bumped her shoulder. "There's this new bar, The Armory, that just opened. You wanna go tonight after work?"

Kelli smiled, nodded, and tried to ignore the weirdness around her. As they got closer, her guts churned—not a good sign. Something was way the fuck off. Her heartbeat slowed, but the sound echoed like a base drum in her ear. Kelli tried to push the feeling away, but as they climbed the stairs, it went up a notch.

It hurt to breathe. She knew there was a reason, but she couldn't quite remember. The thought was there, just out of her reach. All of this was way too familiar. She had to warn him. "Travis…I—"

Gunshots rang out from inside the house. It sounded like the Fourth of July. Or a battlefield.

They both pulled their weapons, hunkered down to avoid the windows at all cost. Travis watched her. She mouthed, "Call it in."

He nodded, and did just that.

"ETA five minutes. There's a car in the vicinity," Travis whispered.

Kelli scanned the nearby houses. Thank Christ no one came out to be nosy. "Find some good cover. We'll wait for backup." Kelli watched as he jumped the hedge, leading to the neighbor's house. She could barely see him through the thick greenery. He continued to waddle toward their car.

Kelli started to do the same.

The sound of running footsteps made them both move faster. They needed to find cover. Now. Then, everything happened in slow motion. Someone was shooting at them, and Kelli watched helplessly as a bullet caught Travis and sent him flying face first into the concrete. Blood as black as pitch pooled around him.

He didn't move.

Rage and fear gripped her and propelled her forward. Kelli could almost feel the hot breath of the shooter rippling down her neck. She ran and laid down suppressive fire as she moved toward the car. White-hot pain seared her upper thigh, and she dropped to the ground. She stared at her leg. Black liquid oozed from the wound. Kelli's body flooded with adrenaline and gave her just enough energy to drag herself across the lawn. She tried to get to cover…to get to Travis. Before she could make it, someone grabbed her injured leg. Kelli nearly blacked out from the pain. One man kicked her gun away as another pulled her back toward the house. Kelli yelled and cursed in defiance.

Behind black masks, they laughed as she struggled.

Then, they stopped. She glanced up to see a nine millimeter pointed at her head. Fear lanced through her but the rage overpowered it. "Do it!" she yelled. "They're gonna take you down so fucking hard—"

The sound of approaching sirens cut through what Kelli thought was her final *fuck you.*

"We need to go. Now," one of them yelled. They released her and ran toward a car across the street. Kelli pulled herself up only to be launched backward once again as a bullet slammed into her chest.

Kelli awoke with a gasp and tried to sit up in bed. The dull ripple of pain reminded her that her body was shit. She looked around the room to get used to being back in reality. It was nice and boring…all white and sterile. Perfect, which was just what she needed after coming out of that fucked-up Salvador Dali-esqe dream. Her hands shook as she wiped sweat from her forehead. Her pajamas were wet and clammy and stuck to her body. Kelli closed her eyes and waited to get off the tilt-o-whirl. When she opened them again, there was still a little tremor left in her hands, but it was a big improvement. Kelli inhaled as deep as she could and for once appreciated the hospital tang in the air.

Sounds filtered in through the open door. For some reason, the noises calmed her. It was a coping skill she developed when her nightmares first started. Voices, laughter, phones ringing, they all wove around her body and soothed her like a comfortable blanket, grounding her in the moment.

She shook her head and ordered her memories to leave her the hell alone. The dream world wasn't a place she wanted to go back to anytime soon, but she knew she would. Kelli wanted to blame the painkillers, but after being in the hospital just over a week, she told the nurses the higher dosage wasn't needed anymore—total bullshit. But Kelli didn't like being fuzzy headed. She could blame her confinement, but that was a crap excuse at best. This wasn't the first time she had been hurt, but it was the worst.

After all that sweating, her throat was bone dry. She reached for the pitcher of water on the night stand, and a stab of pain stopped her from grabbing it. All she wanted was a shitty glass of water. Kelli ignored the mounting ache in her chest. She growled and muttered curses, but the McCabe stubborn streak refused to let her give up. Helplessness was not her thing.

"Kelli what the fuck are you doing? Why didn't you just call a nurse?" Sergeant Bruce Williams, her ex-partner, asked as he walked into the room. He filled a paper cup and handed it to her.

Kelli glared, but took the drink. He was a good man and knew her well, but there was a huge difference between Travis and him. Travis would have pushed the pitcher closer instead of doing it for her. To Kelli, this made all the difference in the world. She crumpled the cup in her hand, throwing it across the room.

"Fuck! I hate this. I fucking hate this!" Kelli blew up. She could barely breathe, but that was beside the point. She needed to get out of this bed. She needed to see Travis with her own eyes. Maybe that would keep the damn nightmares away.

Williams was a bear of a man with broad shoulders and a barrel chest, but he was soft around the middle, kind of like the Michelin Man. His caramel-colored skin was lined more with experience than age, set off by distinguished, well-groomed gray eyebrows, mustache, and bald head. He watched her. The usual teasing glint in his eyes was missing. As she ranted, he sat there quietly.

"Say something!"

His eyebrows shot up. "You done?"

Kelli sighed and rolled her eyes. "Yeah," she answered softly, deceptively. He was about to piss her off. She just knew it.

"Good. Because you could be dead."

She ground her back teeth together. "I know that."

"Do you? Do you really? Because I see pity party written all over your face."

Her anger flared to life. The feeling was simple, base. She could do anger all day long. "Stop trying to get in my head," Kelli demanded. Goddamn him. The man saw everything.

"Why? Because you don't like being in there? Can't always hide behind jokes and a husky voice."

"Whatever."

"I know you better than most, Kelli."

Kelli snorted. Her thoughts pushed her back to the past. Right now, it was easier to reopen old wounds than to deal with newer, more fucked-up ones, and something about the way he said her name caught her by the throat. The words just fell out of her mouth. "Not anymore, old man."

Williams's eyebrows formed a nice little "V" right above his nose. There was a flash of hurt in his eyes, followed by surprise. "I thought all of that was water under the bridge."

"It is, but it doesn't keep it from stinging every once in a while."

"I'm calling you on your shit. What's done is done. It happened. I can't take it back. You didn't want to be my partner anymore because of it. You got your space. That's a long time to hold a grudge."

"You were part of my family." Kelli paused. "He was barely gone a month, Williams." He understood the point. There was no need to continue.

He had on his poker face. She couldn't tell what he was thinking. Williams sighed. "You know why, and it's been almost two years. It's petty to bring it up now." He narrowed his eyes and studied her for several seconds.

Kelli squirmed. She didn't like to be observed like some bug under a glass.

"You're deflecting," Williams said.

"That's ridiculous bullshit." Kelli glared. Goddamn bullet wounds kept her from walking away like she wanted to.

"Uh-huh. You haven't changed that much. Something's going on in that head of yours, and this old crap is a lot easier to deal with." He stood.

Kelli's stomach twisted, and for a moment she regretted letting anyone in that deep. Meanwhile, there was another part of her that relished it. In the past, he'd been there to drag her out of any dark hole she fell into.

"I was going to stay, visit for a little while, but now, that's shot all to hell." He paused and sighed again. "Listen, when and if you want to talk, I'm here. Just because I don't watch your back anymore doesn't mean I don't have it."

Kelli looked at him sharply. She knew he would listen, but there were times when her shit was just her shit. She nodded slightly.

"Good. See you later."

She watched him go without calling him back. Kelli pressed the controls on the bed to make the incline sharper. This angle gave her a better view of the open door. Williams was right. There was no need to wallow. There was no need to let a harmless dream strangle her with the fucking lights on.

She stared out the door for what seemed like hours, watching the hustle and bustle. Her mind was calmer, but she still didn't want to be stuck inside her thoughts. Her brain wasn't the most pleasant place to be. She blinked as a large section of white paper floated in front of the entrance. The writing on it made her grin like an idiot. *Luck of the Irish.*

The sign stayed there for a few seconds before a face she hadn't seen in a while peeked out from around the corner. "I see I put a smile on your face so my job is pretty much done." Booker sniffed and tipped the brim of the tattered Sonics cap in her direction. He was an older black man with skin the color of toffee. He had definite swagger even in the old jeans and tattered T-shirt he wore. "They must be taking good care of you because you are looking *good.*" He sat in one of the chairs by the bed, making himself comfortable.

Kelli smirked.

Booker leaned forward and studied her. "What…a nurse got your tongue?"

Kelli chuckled. These nurses would rather flog her. "Nope. Not at all. I'm just a little shocked."

"You shouldn't be. You're my girl. I wouldn't be living if it wasn't for you. Of course I'm gonna come check on my favorite detective. I wanted to give you some time, but I was sitting at home bored. Figured you would be too. So, here I am."

"Thanks, but you didn't have to, Booker. Don't feel obligated. It's been years since—"

"You wound me," Booker interrupted. "I know how long it's been…six years, and it's actually been two since I've seen you. Don't mean I forgot anything. You saved my life McCabe. You were the best thing that happened to the drug enforcement unit. Anybody else would have left my ass in the gutter. When I heard about what happened, I had to see for myself. Had to see that you were okay."

Kelli's face flushed with heat. "Well, I've seen better days."

"I'm sure, but in no time you'll be rocking those pantsuits and looking deadly."

Kelli laughed. It rumbled in her chest and was out of her mouth before she could do a thing about it. The sound increased in volume and depth without her permission. She winced in reaction. No matter the pain, it was good to really laugh again.

Booker grinned.

"Thanks, Booker. I really needed—" The familiar flash of a white lab coat and blond hair caught her attention. "Nora!"

Seconds ticked by, and Kelli wondered if Nora heard her or if she was ignoring her. She smirked. After their last meeting, it had to be the latter.

"Ms. McCabe, if you need assistance, the red button connects you to the nurses' station." Nora Whitmore appeared in the doorway.

"No shit? I thought it just made the toilet flush."

Booker snorted.

Nora's face reddened, and her mouth fell open. Kelli smiled. It had been a few days since Kelli had seen her. A little light teasing couldn't hurt.

"Ms. McCabe, I don't have time for games." Her expression changed from stunned to stern as she narrowed her honey-brown eyes.

Booker leaned in and said, "Damn she says your name like you stink."

Kelli glanced at him knowingly.

"I won't stand here and be insulted by your vagrant—"

Kelli bristled. The annoyance that was bubbling underneath the surface seeped out of her pores. She was going to make sure she got the last word this time.

Booker whirled around. "Listen here, lady. Don't judge a book by its cover. What you see isn't always what you get, in my case especially. I don't know about yours."

Kelli's gaze bounced between the two of them. Nora's face turned almost purple, and she pressed her lips so tightly together that they looked like they weren't there at all. Kelli got a strange sense of satisfaction from that. "Well, I guess he told you."

Nora opened and closed her mouth several times. "I assure you. I didn't mean—"

Kelli waved, dismissing the comment to clear the way for a different approach. "People say crazy shit when they're flustered, especially when I do the flustering."

Nora's eyes darkened. "Your arrogance…how is there room for it all?"

"I have a big head?"

Booker chuckled.

"Something has to occupy the space. Common sense has obviously defected."

Kelli glanced at Booker and pointed at Nora. "That's what flustered looks like."

He nodded.

"Is this how you are going to pass the time during your convalescence?"

"If you keep falling for it, yes."

"My time is more valuable than this encounter will ever be. Please don't waste it."

Kelli disagreed. This was priceless. "All I can promise is, while you're in here with me, you'll be kept on your toes."

"Is that what you're calling it?" Nora asked.

"Yep. Got something better?"

"I have better things to attend to, and your—"

"Vagrant?" It felt good to throw the word back in her face. After everything that had been beating her up the past few hours, it felt even better to play this game with Nora.

The blush returned to Nora's face. "No! *Your friend* should be the one to entertain you."

"Is that your way of apologizing for being rude?"

"I didn't intend to be offensive. I was…" She glanced from Kelli to Booker.

"Flustered?" Kelli interrupted and offered helpfully.

"You can't be this insufferable."

"Yes, I can."

Nora blinked and just stared before she turned and left the room. Kelli was disappointed. She'd hoped for more.

Booker whistled. "She's way more high-strung than you'll ever be, but I see what you did there. Thanks."

Kelli nodded, but felt a flash of guilt. She'd been a little harsh.

They talked and laughed for several more minutes before Booker stood.

"Okay, I won't keep you, but don't worry, this won't be my last visit."

※

Nora entered one of the residents' lounges and was exceedingly grateful to be alone. She pressed the back of her hand to her face and could still feel the heat emanating from her skin in waves. She was appalled at her behavior and didn't understand how her brain, which was always functioning at the highest level, would allow her to say such things. The situation was very off-putting. Nora couldn't remember anyone who had ever talked to her that way. So without reserves or history to pull from, her mind misfired every time she saw Kelli McCabe. Embarrassment found a home on her shoulders, weighing her down and forcing Nora to sit. Her professionalism had abandoned her again, and for a moment, human decency had as well.

She had insulted a stranger.

Nora searched herself, taking a long moment for introspection. She didn't enjoy contemplating her emotions. In Nora's opinion, the act was a waste of energy. She simply could not figure out what it was about that woman that provoked this kind of reaction. Guilt gnawed at her, and she felt awful. The person who had stood in that doorway was not her, at least not a version of herself that she was used to. Nora had to admit, however, there were some aspects of this other side of her personality that fascinated her.

Determined to make amends for her behavior, she rose from the chair and exited quickly. When she arrived at the nurses' station, she noticed a sudden hush in the chatter. Even after all this time, Nora was unsure if people's reaction to her was out of fear or just some strange byproduct of idle gossip. Part of her hoped that their silence was out of respect, but she knew better.

The nurse looked at her expectantly from behind the counter. "Yes, Dr. Whitmore?"

"Would you see to it that Ms. McCabe is escorted via wheelchair to her partner's room?" Nora paused. "I would also appreciate if you kept my involvement anonymous."

The nurse looked puzzled. "Are you asking me—"

"Yes." Nora interrupted. "Provided that her pain is tolerable enough to be transported in that manner."

The nurse nodded. "We'll be careful. Not being able to see him has been a recent complaint of hers…along with other things."

"She is somewhat of an acquired taste." Nora nodded tightly. That was a severe understatement.

The nurse smiled as if they were sharing a moment. "Very true."

Feeling suddenly awkward, Nora fidgeted. Instead of speaking, she dipped her head in acknowledgement. Nora watched and listened discreetly as she absently flipped through a chart. Kelli's room was only two doors down, after all. She then peered at the white board behind the desk like it was the most interesting thing in creation as some of the staff attended to their newly assigned duties. Two CNAs entered the room hesitantly. She waited for some sort of loud response either due to their appearance or the message they were delivering.

"What? You're shitting me?" Kelli's voice carried out into the hall.

Nora sighed. The woman's language really was atrocious. She was obviously more intelligent than her vocabulary suggested.

"I'm not going to argue then. Let's go."

Several minutes passed before they exited the room. Kelli appeared pale, but the smile on her face could not be denied. Nora curled her lips slightly at the sight. Nora turned away from Kelli's sharp gaze, glad she had been able to offer some solace but not ready to acknowledge the reasons behind it.

Kelli swallowed and wiped her hands on her pajamas. Her leg throbbed and the right side of her chest ached. None of that mattered. She wanted to see him, but she couldn't shake the feeling of dread. The nurses stopped the wheelchair just outside his door and ducked inside without her. Kelli found that odd, but she didn't know dick about hospital procedure.

Less than a minute later, they wheeled her in. Travis's dark-brown eyes crinkled as he smiled at her. She'd missed that grin. Travis had grown a beard since the last time she saw him. His whiskers were thin and still had spots that needed to fill out, but, regardless, it was damn good to see him. Kelli released a shaky breath and tried to return his greeting with a smirk of her own. Tears prickled her eyes instead. She wasn't prepared for this moment to affect her like this. She was relieved. Kelli looked down at her hands. She tried to hide the tears and pull herself together.

Gerry Travis didn't say a word.

When Kelli glanced up again, they were alone. "I think part of me was convinced that your voice was just some recorded message."

Travis rolled his eyes, but his expression was soft, understanding. "No one could do me as well as…me." He finished lamely and winced outwardly at his own awful joke.

Kelli laughed and wiped at her eyes. "That's your problem. You have to learn to give directions. Let those girls know what you need." She smirked.

He rolled his eyes again. "Left myself open, didn't I?"

"Yup."

"Yeah, I need to come up with some new material. I'm using all my best stuff on the nurses." He grinned. "They just love you."

"Well, what's not to love?"

"You are kidding, right?" Travis asked.

"If you're going to insult me, at least wait until my ass can walk so I can smack you in the head," Kelli said.

He paled.

It bothered Kelli. "You okay? You need me to get a nurse?"

"Nah, I'm okay. It'll pass."

She watched him carefully for a few seconds before nodding in acquiescence. "You look like shit. Aren't Asian men supposed to look distinguished at all times?" she teased affectionately. "I like the whiskers though. Kinda."

Travis snorted lightly. "I may not look good, but I'm clean. Giving me a sponge bath is the nurses' favorite part of the day. Heard they tried to drown you a few times." He grinned.

"Please, they don't touch me. My moth—"

"Yeah, it's best you don't finish that."

Kelli sneered, but she couldn't stop looking at him. He seemed slighter somehow, hidden underneath hospital sheets. "You got everything you need? Sean can—"

"He already did. I'm keeping the beard. It'll be a good look for me when it fills out. Makes me a little mysterious."

Kelli nodded and fell silent. The banter between them was customary, but this…*this* was hard. "You'll have your first scars." Kelli winced because it came out all wrong. "To go along with the beard, I mean. Something to show the ladies."

"Kelli?" There was something in his voice. It let her know that he could see past her words to the emotion stunting her.

She looked around the room before letting her gaze rest on him once more. "Yeah?"

"I'm here and in one piece."

Kelli scoffed. "You said that over the phone, and I can see that."

"Good." He could have said so much more, making things uneasy, making things more emotional than they already were, but he didn't.

"Your mom been washing your hair too? There's this thing they have now. Shit's called conditioner."

Kelli burst out laughing. She cradled her chest and grimaced at the pain. Still, she continued to laugh. "Fuck you."

"You trying to call me a pussy?"

"No, but you are an asshole."

A nurse breezed in. She gave Kelli a wide birth and smiled at Travis. "Just doing my rounds. Pretend that I'm not here."

Travis smiled and nodded. A few seconds later he mumbled groggily, "Damn this is some good shit."

She didn't have to be a detective to get that his pain killers had been electronically dispensed. "I know right? Medicine on a timer. Don't have to worry about a thing." Kelli didn't want to leave, but she understood. "I guess I should go."

"Later then?" Travis asked with an apologetic smile.

"Maybe in the morning?" Kelli glanced at the nurse hopefully.

"I'd say you pretty much have a green light," the nurse answered.

"Great. Uh, I'm gonna need some help back to my room when you get done."

***

Nora took a deep breath and tried to relax. She was glad that her shift was ending soon because she was engaged in her least favorite activity, charting. Paperwork for any job was a necessary evil, and she treated it as such, going through each one with thorough efficiency. Her pager beeped and vibrated, causing it to dance across the desk. She peered at the message and picked up the nearby phone, calling the ICU nurses' station.

"Dr. Whitmore."

"Dr. Whitmore, I'm sorry to disturb you, but Kelli McCabe is insisting that she see you."

An uneasy feeling filled her, but it was chased by something new. Anticipation? Nora did not like this at all. "I'm not her doctor. I'm sure Rader—"

"She's being very adamant about it. Is it possible for you to give her a few minutes before the end of your shift?"

Nora was at a loss. She couldn't deny the request in case a complaint was being made. Not after what occurred earlier. She was the attending, and she had responsibilities. "I'll allot a few minutes to visit before I leave."

"Thank you." The nurse sounded relieved.

Nora immediately returned to the chart featuring a colon resection, but she couldn't stay focused. She had done quite a few things today that were completely out of character, and Kelli was the catalyst for it all, both good and bad. Nora again tried to concentrate. No good would come out of dwelling on the issue. After several minutes, she realized that she had been staring at the same word the entire time.

Scoffing at her own idiotic efforts, she closed the chart and mumbled to herself. "Obviously, she needs to be dealt with first." Nora stood and steeled herself for another encounter with that woman. She strengthened her resolve. No insults, and Nora wouldn't allow herself to get upset. Ms. McCabe was just like any other patient, and that's the way Nora was going to treat her. She stepped out into the hallway.

The elevator doors open, revealing one lone occupant, Dr. Rader. Nora stood back mentally and admired the irony in the moment. She could take care of two issues within minutes of each other. She stepped in, and the doors closed behind her.

"What floor?" he asked.

Nora ignored him and pushed the button for the seventh floor.

He sighed. "I could have done that for you, Nora."

"What is the definition of an attending as opposed to chief resident, Dr. Rader?"

He turned and looked at her as if she'd spoken some unknown language. "You're kidding, right?"

"Not at all, because you seem to have forgotten it. We are not friends. We are not lovers, and from this point on, you will show me the proper respect in front of our colleagues and patients by referring to me as Dr. Whitmore."

His face grew red and blotchy. "Got it," he grumbled.

"Are you sure?" Nora held his gaze steadily.

"Jesus fucking Christ. I said yes. How about I just put my balls in a paper sack for you?"

"That won't be necessary." The elevator dinged. Nora glanced at the number and stepped out.

"Fucking cunt."

Turning slowly, she peered at James and refused to be cowed by his insults. "No, not anymore." Nora walked away with her head held high. Someone grabbed her elbow. She spun around to find Rader a few inches away.

"Release me, Dr. Rader."

He tightened his grip and gazed murderously at her.

"Now," Nora commanded. *He* had the audacity to look upset? She was the one being violated.

Within seconds, his expression changed to meek, ashamed. "Look, I didn't mean it. You just do something to me, you know? I didn't mean what I said. Can't we just start over? I want to be something to you. I'm not sure I care what that is right now." He pleaded with his eyes and loosened his grip.

Nora pulled her elbow away. People were watching, their gazes heavy with interest. Nevertheless, she had to finish this. "It was a sexual liaison, James, nothing more. Your antics helped it to spiral out of control. I do not engage in friendships or love affairs, so please do not hold out hope for either," She whispered harshly.

He looked stricken but nodded anyway. "I'm…sorry."

She turned away, done with the conversation. She had respected this man once, as a doctor and as a person. The respect dwindled as of late and was now nonexistent. Nora needed this moment. It felt as if her equilibrium had been restored. She was ready for Ms. McCabe.

She walked briskly toward room 708 and entered with confidence. Kelli was sitting up with the remote raised toward the television.

"How may I help you Ms. McCabe?" Her words were clipped and professional.

Kelli scratched at her chin. She pursed her full lips and looked everywhere except at Nora. After a moment, she said, "Uh…look."

Kelli looked…contrite. She expected sarcasm and teasing. This abrupt change caused alarms to jangle in Nora's head, warning her that she was not as ready as she thought. She licked her lips. "Yes?"

"I'm sorry for being such an asshole earlier." Kelli's words were said in a rush, but were still understandable. "I was having a very shitty day, but it got better. So, I figured apologizing was the right thing to do."

Nora was speechless. She felt somewhat deflated, but at the same time reassured. Maybe she was wrong about this woman. She was arrogant, stubborn, and rude. Seemingly, there were other layers as well. It intrigued her and left her even more at a loss for words.

"I wasn't that bad, was I?" Kelli asked.

Ordering her brain to respond, Nora stammered, "I'm not sure what to say."

"What? No one ever apologized to you for something before?"

Nora searched her mind. There had to be at least once instance of sincere apology. Dr. Rader's didn't count at all. "I'm not sure."

"Are you gonna accept my apology?"

"I suppose…" Nora took a breath to calm her racing heart. "I should apologize as well." The words tumbled out of her mouth without permission. She hardly recognized herself.

"Hmm, yeah about that? The way I figure, you already have. It wasn't very inconspicuous hiding at the nurses' station. It had to be you that made that visit happen." Kelli smirked, but her tone was sincere. "Thank you."

Nora felt the blush coming. There was nothing she could do to hide it.

There was a glint in Kelli's gaze. "Did I fluster you again, Nora?"

Nora had the strong urge to roll her eyes. She just barely resisted. "This was just…unexpected."

"Mmm, well we still won't be braiding each other's hair and listening to Justin Bieber."

Nora blinked in confusion. "Who?"

"Oh dear God. You're not in touch with the outside world at all are you?" Kelli asked teasingly.

"Are you referring to pop culture?"

"Why yes, yes I am."

"Is sarcasm going to be your answer to everything?" Nora felt like she was on more familiar ground now.

"Why yes, yes it is." Kelli replied.

Exasperation took hold of Nora and refused to let go, which was the exact opposite of where she was when she first walked in. How was that possible? "I'm honored." she said snidely.

Kelli shrugged.

"I can empathize with your frustration at being stationary, but this… juvenile behavior is some sort of release for you, isn't it?" Then again, maybe it was a release for her as well.

"Don't judge. I get mine where I can. How do you get yours?" Kelli mocked.

Nora felt the flush of heat return to her face. The constant reoccurrence was disconcerting. "I assure you that it's none of your business. Is that all, Ms. McCabe?"

"Mmm, I guess." Kelli tilted her head to the side. "So you have to come if I ask for you?"

There were those warning bells again. "I have charts to complete, Ms. McCabe. Have a nice night."

As Nora exited, she heard Kelli's chuckle. The sound followed her to the elevator. Once inside, she leaned against the far wall. She was beginning to think that there was nothing that could prepare her for that woman, but she had to admit there was a part of her—a very small one—that was beginning to enjoy the skirmishes with Kelli.

CHAPTER 5

Nora pressed the soft, fluffy towel to her chest to soak up some of the perspiration that lingered, before she wiped it across her brow. She was pleasantly winded and enjoyed the slight burn in her muscles resulting from her morning Pilates. She pushed herself harder this morning in hopes of relieving some stress. The exercise helped a bit, but probably not enough to last throughout the day. She peered out the French doors at the fiery orange sky of the new day. For a few seconds, she enjoyed the sight before silently moving on. Nora grimaced in mild discomfort. Even though the Zella workout gear was designed to absorb moisture, the clothing still clung to her torso and thighs unpleasantly. In response, she plucked at the sleek black material as she wrapped the towel around her neck. Nora left the workout room and headed for the master bath.

The walls of the bathroom were a warm sage which complemented the sink and other essentials included by Spanish designer Ramon Soler. This added to the room's sleek, monochromatic appearance. She undressed quickly and put her soiled clothing and her towel in the hamper. When she turned on the shower, hot water blasted from all sides and filled the room with steam. She stepped in and sighed as glorious rivulets of water massaged her heavily exerted muscles.

Nora was a person of routine. The expensive furniture, appliances, and the art that peppered the walls remained the standard, carried over from childhood. Beautiful things had always surrounded her. These trinkets were all she'd had when her parents were away. They were all she'd had when her parents returned as well. The Whitmore's were never overly attentive, never fawning. They were never much of anything.

Why did she choose this morning to wallow in the past? Nora didn't have an answer. She got dressed and brushed away the pang of insecurity caused by her memories and old wounds. Nora reminded herself that she looked flawless in the green high-waisted Gucci pencil skirt and matching cream-colored blouse. No one was privy to her thoughts and feelings anyway. When Nora entered the kitchen, the well-timed espresso machine had already done its work. She opened the refrigerator and reached for the fresh fruit, as well as Greek yogurt. She ate quickly, mechanically, and left her home at seven-fifteen, the same time she did each morning during the week.

When she finished her story, Kelli threw her head back and roared with laughter. This was where she wanted to be, and this was how she liked it, hanging out with two of the people she cared about the most. They were loud, teasing, and completely inappropriate, and Kelli didn't give a damn that they were in the hospital. Sean laughed so hard his face was red and sweaty, but Gerry Travis was something else altogether. That high-pitched squeal he had going on made it sound like he'd sprung a leak.

"Shit. You should have seen the way she looked at me. I was sure she was gonna drag me out of bed." Kelli shrugged. "I thought it was clever while it lasted. Whoever came up with that phrase needs to be rich. It doesn't even spell out the exact word, just sounds like it," Kelli murmured.

Travis snorted. "I got it the first time you used it, and I didn't like being called a cunt either. 'You're a real *see you next Tuesday*.' You've gotten so sloppy. Nobody is that stupid!"

"Yeah, she's a freakin' nurse. She's no dummy. She was definitely gonna catch on," Sean added.

"At least I didn't just come out and say it! I don't wanna wake up with a bedpan as a pillow," Kelli said.

"That's what you're worried about? Man, they probably control *everything* in the hospital by punching a couple of buttons. To be safe, you better check the apple juice before you drink it next time," Sean said.

Kelli glared and waved it all away. "It's not that serious."

Travis raised a brow. "Oh, you don't think so?"

"She had it coming! I'm the one that's stuck in this place. She doesn't have to be rude."

Gerry shook his head. "You've been biting their heads off. I'm surprised *any* of them talk to you at all with the way you've been treating them."

"You can be a dick. I swear! How could any woman want you?" Sean asked.

Kelli shrugged. "Hey, I have charm."

"Whatever. You just show them your tits." Sean nodded knowingly.

"You'd better straighten up. They're going to be burning Kelli dolls in effigy on the hospital steps."

Kelli rolled her eyes at her partner. "This is a whole new set of nurses. It's gonna take more than one incident. I'm not in ICU anymore, remember?"

"This is a hospital. Word travels fast." Travis looked at her as if she were an especially slow child.

She sneered. "So you're saying nurses are like black people? They all know each other?"

"Ooooh," Sean muttered. "Shit just got real."

Travis's eyes narrowed. "I don't remember. I've been hanging out with Italians the past couple of years watching *GoodFellas* and eating spaghetti every fucking weekend."

Sean snickered.

"That didn't keep you from eating my mom's cannoli."

A nurse entered the room and glared at Kelli as she moved past her wheelchair.

Travis and Sean looked at each other, breaking into laughter all over again. The nurse silently checked his IV and left.

"In effigy." Travis said it in this low creepy voice.

"Yeah, yeah. I just hate this fucking place. It doesn't feel right being here. I don't have my gun, my badge. I'm not doing anybody any good." Just like that, Kelli stepped from behind the humor and subterfuge because, with these two, she was safe enough to do so.

"So, misery really does love company?" Travis asked. "These are some really nice people, Kelli."

She felt suitably admonished. He was right. "I know," Kelli mumbled. She knew she could be an asshole, and she accepted it, but Kelli had to admit that she'd gotten a little out of control.

Travis tilted his head toward her. "What was that?"

"You heard me."

Sean leaned forward in his chair and shook his head, smiling. "I swear to God, you have some kind of super power to get this one to back down or admit anything." Sean snapped his fingers. "What do they call those guys who can calm down horses and shit?"

"I'm not a damn horse." Kelli growled.

"Whisperers?" Travis asked.

"Yeah." Sean nodded. "Whisperers. That's it."

Travis made a face. "Oh hell no. She needs to find a woman to do that."

Two more nurses filed into the room. "Time to take a ride, Mr. Travis."

Travis nodded, and they watched silently as the nurses readied his bed for transport.

Out of concern, Kelli asked, "Where are you taking him?"

Neither nurse answered her.

Kelli sighed.

Travis chuckled. "I'm guessing radiology." He waved. "Later, guys."

Kelli waited for Sean to get behind her. She looked up at him and saw something shadowed in his eyes. The weird feeling in her belly returned—dread. Kelli had to admit that it had never left. It whispered to her and told her to pay attention to the little things going on around her. "He's okay, right? I know it was serious, and they have to monitor his injury."

Sean held her gaze for a few seconds before he turned his attention to the brake on the wheelchair. "He'll be fine."

Kelli continued to stare at her brother. That didn't really answer the question, but she didn't press. Maybe deep down, she wasn't ready for the actual answers anyway. This was dangerously close to running from the truth, from fucked-up reality, but Kelli did it anyway. Running made her feel weak and alone, even though there was life, love all round her.

<hr />

Kelli flipped through the channels on the television, but found nothing that interested her. She dropped the remote. It hung from the cable that attached it to the bed frame and banged uselessly against the side of the bed. There had to be something to keep her occupied. She didn't want to think. She didn't want to feel, and anxiety shifted just under skin, leaving her uncomfortable and twitchy. Kelli was made up of rough, jagged pieces. In the past, they had cut into others, but oftentimes, they pierced her even more. There were no dark secrets or hidden monsters that could explain it all away. This was how she worked best. This was who she was. Kelli delved deep to get into a murderer's mind. Sometimes touched the shadows and kept a little for herself. The subject of her own mortality and forced immobility had become triggers of sorts, and her emotions churned inside her, growing darker by the day.

Kelli stared at the crutches leaning against the foot of her bed. She wanted to ignore the pain in her torso and use those evil pieces of metal to get moving again, even if it was only throughout the hospital. She'd tried, but it hurt too fucking much. The crutches sat there, taunting her with the possibility of getting away from the images of violence, brutality, and blood that came to her every time she closed her eyes. It made total sense that she couldn't sleep. Kelli didn't like asking for a sedative, but the medicine was the only thing that helped her rest and kept her from dreaming.

Kelli felt like she was in some kind of alternate universe where everything looked shiny and normal, but underneath something brewed. Absolutely nothing seemed right. She had great instincts, and they were screaming for her ass to pay attention. It was her own fault. She hadn't been asking the right questions about Travis and Tony. She avoided when he should have confronted, but shit, she could only deal with so much.

"How are we doing this afternoon, Ms. McCabe?"

The sudden sound of Dr. Rader's voice startled her. She hid it well. "Same as I was yesterday."

Dr. Rader closed the door and stepped farther into the room. Kelli glanced at him as he flipped through her chart. He was pleasant enough, but it felt as though he was trying too hard. He was phony, and that made her uneasy. Rader was pretty much a shell with a TV doctor poured into it, which was the complete opposite of Nora. Something simmered inside Nora, hiding behind those incredible eyes. That something challenged Kelli at times and irked her during others. Nora was unique. She smirked at the thought. There was only one Dr. Whitmore.

"You tried the crutches?" He didn't look at her as he asked the question.

"I did. Hurt like fuck or did you forget I have a chest injury?"

Dr. Rader chuckled. "I did not, but you're healing nicely. The crutches are a motivator of sorts. I think it's time for some physical therapy so we can start discussing plans to get you out of here."

Kelli's heart thudded. "Seriously? Now you're talking. I figure I'll be as good as new in a few days—"

"No, not that soon. Someone with your type of wounds is usually incapacitated for well past a month. We'll be over the three-week mark when I re-evaluate you for possible discharge, which is remarkable. Not to mention, you've had no complications. Even then, you won't be ready for anything except desk duty."

Kelli deflated. Another week and a half. The churning in her stomach drowned out the rest of his words. The only thing she could do was nod.

Williams poked his head in. "Do I need to come back in a few minutes?"

The idea of company actually perked Kelli up a few degrees.

"No, if she's okay with it, I am too." Dr. Rader smiled and glanced from Kelli to Williams, who was still waiting at the door.

Kelli rolled her eyes and motioned him in.

"I'm just going to check her injuries and then be out of your hair."

Williams stopped and turned around as the doctor lifted Kelli's shirt. "My tits don't bite, Williams."

"Yeah, well I still don't want to see them."

Kelli chuckled. The doctor pressed around the wound. She sucked in a pained breath.

"Good. Tenderness is decreasing. By the way, I love your pajamas. I'm a huge Seahawks fan myself." He grinned, and Kelli was surprised his teeth didn't sparkle.

Kelli didn't believe him. Why the hell would anyone lie about the Seahawks? She rolled her eyes. "Uh-huh." She glanced at Williams only to see his back was still turned.

"Now, let's check the leg." Dr. Rader did more of the same, pressing around the wound. "I'll send PT to get you in about an hour, and tomorrow they are going to start a daily regimen with you."

Nodding, Kelli rolled her shorts back down and covered herself with the thin sheet.

"Okay," Dr. Rader patted her on the knee. "All done here." He winked. "You can turn around now. Your friend is decent."

The comment annoyed Kelli, but right now, just about everything did.

Williams snorted but said nothing else as he moved to the chair beside Kelli's bed. They stared at each other.

He tilted his head to the side and continued to look at her. "Anything else from the past you want to bring up while I'm comfortable?"

Kelli sighed. "Probably not."

"You sure?" He looked skeptical.

"Yes, dammit."

"Your mom needed a shoulder. Things got out of hand. I'm not holding some type of torch for her, but you know all of this. It's not your business now, just like it wasn't your business then, despite your reaction to it. Nobody meant for you to walk in on it."

Kelli's mumbled. "I know that." At least everything she saw was above the waist.

Williams slapped a hand on his knee. "We're good? No more bullshit?"

She glared at him. "We'll see."

He chuckled. "So, ready to come out of your skin yet?"

Kelli's shoulders sagged with relief. It felt good to think someone knew exactly how she felt. "A little bit, yeah."

"Must piss you off that things still hurt."

Kelli blinked and waited for him to continue. There was more. With him, there always was.

"I may not have been injured on the job, but I was in the armed forces, Kelli. Remember?"

"Forgot you were old as fuck. You don't really look it," Kelli said.

"Thanks, I think."

"You're welcome."

For several seconds, Williams was silent. He watched her and waited. Kelli felt herself squirming under his scrutiny once more. "Will you stop that? Just say what you have to say."

"Okay." He held up his hands in a placating gesture. "Nightmares start yet?"

Kelli sucked in a breath. She didn't need this right now especially when her emotions were so raw. Damn his fucking eyes.

"I guess that's my answer."

"Williams," she said his name as a warning.

Again, he held up a hand. "I'm not going to press you on this. Just know that it doesn't go away by itself, Kelli."

This conversation needed to be over. Tension coiled through her and made her muscles clench. She could handle the pain. It centered her. "I'm not doing this."

"I'm not asking you to, but it's happening. That's all I'm saying on the subject." Williams paused. "How's everything else?"

Kelli shook her head. "I don't know. I'm missing something, and it's right in front of me. I...I don't want to talk about that either."

Williams gazed at her. "Travis seems fine to me."

"Yeah, I guess. It's not just him—" Kelli looked away.

He cut her off. "Kelli—"

"Dammit, Williams. Stop pushing me."

He raised his hands for a third time. "All right, I wasn't trying to." Williams stood.

Kelli didn't want him to leave, but she didn't want him to stay either. Not if it meant he was going to stay on this topic.

"You need anything?" he asked.

Kelli ground her teeth at the reminder that she was still pretty much useless. "No." It was strange how he could know her so well one minute, and the next it was something completely different.

Williams sighed. "I'll go visit the kid, then. I'll try not to wear out my welcome so quickly next time."

Their gazes met. Kelli nodded and watched him go.

Nora peered at the white board behind the trauma desk. There had to be something interesting to fill her time. She ignored the large contingent of residents and pressed her way forward. They seemed mostly oblivious to her anyway. She caught bits and pieces of conversation. Some were louder than others.

"I like Mistress of Kink. It has pizazz."

Gossip was a childish activity, and she was not surprised that Dr. Fuller was involved in it.

"Shhh!"

"Please, she has a one-track mind. She's not paying attention to us." Taylor didn't even bother to lower her voice.

"Threesomes are not all that kinky unless you bring out the whips and chains."

"I'm sure she does that too. Never thought she would be the clingy type, though. Rader wants nothing to do with her, and she's still hanging on. It's pathetic." Dr. Fuller sounded almost gleeful.

Nora straightened her shoulders. She held no illusions about who they were talking about. The new rumors were trite, not very inventive, and an obvious attempt for Rader to save face. He had a reputation to uphold, and thanks to him, so did she. She refused to let her anger and irritation show. Nora was better than this, but there were times when she didn't want to be.

"Dr. Fuller?" Nora interrupted.

"Taylor, I told you she heard you!" Dr. Crowder whispered harshly.

"I can hear you as well, Dr. Crowder," Nora said with authority. "Since neither of you have anything more productive to do—"

"Oh, I'm on Rader's service." Dr. Fuller pointed at the board.

Nora's lips twitched. "I'm sure you are."

Taylor reddened and glanced away.

Nora felt emboldened by Dr. Fuller's reaction. Taylor responded as the immature girl that she was. While, as a woman in her stride, Nora met it head on. She stepped away from the desk. "Follow me…both of you."

Walking through the hall, Nora slowed as they neared the free clinic. The angry hushed murmurs coming from behind let her know that this was the right decision. She turned and nearly bumped into them. "You will spend your day lancing boils, removing foreign objects from patients, and adhering band aids, since a surgical rotation isn't challenging enough for you."

Taylor's blue eyes widened. "It is. There must be some kind of mis—"

"If it were, you would have time for nothing else." Nora smiled politely. "Have a productive day," she said as she strolled away.

Nora had many dissenters for one reason or another. They wanted her small and cowed, but she had hardened herself against such attacks. No cracks remained for anything to seep through. So, what she did to Dr. Fuller wasn't retribution. It was a calculated move. Nora peered down at her watch and almost smiled. She had a Whipple procedure to remove lesions from a patient's pancreas and small intestines scheduled to start in an hour.

***

A pleasant weariness settled on Nora's shoulders. The Whipple was a success, and at this point, the patient needed continuous monitoring for any complications. She checked charts. Then, she did her final rounds to check the residents' work and see to the welfare of their patients before retiring for the night.

Nora neared Kelli's room. There was really no reason for her to go inside. She was healing without complications or setbacks, but still, Nora stopped just outside the entrance. Curiosity got the better of her, but she knew it went deeper. The conversations, the sparring they'd engaged in had been her most genuine interactions in a very long time. After her confrontation with the residents earlier, Nora knew that this association, however brief, would be like cleansing her palate of all pretense.

She stepped inside. Light flickered from the muted television, illuminating the room every few seconds and highlighting the empty bed. Nora stared at the rumpled sheets, confused. Kelli was essentially immobile. Nora scanned the room. Her gaze stopped at the light shining from underneath the closed bathroom door. She moved toward it, hearing the unmistakable sound of a running shower.

A muffled, metallic crash came from the bathroom. Alarmed, Nora called out. "Ms. McCabe?"

A loud groan was her answer.

Based on that alone, Nora made her decision. "Ms. McCabe, I'm coming in."

Nora did not hesitate as she entered the bathroom. She expected billowing steam. She expected…she did not expect this. Kelli leaned against the wall of the tiny shower with a metal crutches at her feet.

Kelli's hair was plastered to her head, and her eyes were wide open and wild with pain. Her face was pale except the blotchy red patches on her cheeks and the blue tint of her lips. Her whole body trembled. Kelli was soaked and the Seahawks pajamas clung to her.

Nora was shaken to find Kelli like this, and she schooled her features to her habitual calm so Kelli wouldn't detect her alarm. Her heart thudded against her chest, but she ignored it. She stepped forward, and Kelli, fraught with visible tension, shriveled back even further. Nora was not a master of social cues and interaction, but through the years, she'd learned to recognize fear and anxiety when she saw it. Now, was not the time to be formal. "Kelli."

Kelli's gaze finally met hers. Nora held up a hand. "I would like to make the water warmer."

Kelli gave a jerky nod of her head. She watched Nora's every move. Nora turned the knob and held her fingers under the spray until it increased to a desirable temperature. Then, she moved back to a safer distance.

She glanced down at Kelli's feet. "You lost your crutches. Would you like me to get them for you so you can get back to bed?" Nora spoke with a slow, measured tone. Despite Kelli's obvious pain, Nora wanted to give her a chance to assert some autonomy before she offered additional help.

"Can't. Hurts." Kelli licked her lips. "I…just wanted it to stop."

Nora instinctively knew that "it" had nothing to do with physical pain, but she still had no idea what 'it' was. That, however, was not the point. "Did it?" She asked softly.

Kelli shook her head vehemently and croaked, "No."

A pang of sympathy reverberated through Nora. It was an odd, peculiar feeling, and very much a shock to her system. She felt lightheaded, breathless, but continued to defy the emotions bombarding her. "Would you like something to help you sleep?"

Kelli looked away. She seemed ashamed. "I guess…I need to."

"I'll call a nurse—"

"No! They—"

"No nurse." Nora interrupted, seeing the distress.

"You get it," Kelli pleaded.

Nora swallowed as she held Kelli's gaze. Something passed between them. A moment of trust that she hadn't really earned, but it was there nonetheless. "If I bring a wheelchair, will you allow me to help you to get cleaned up and back to bed?"

Kelli's eyes closed briefly, and the tension in her body dissipated. "Yes."

Nora didn't wait. She left immediately to gather what she needed. The on-duty nurses watched her warily but said nothing. Re-entering the room, she searched the small chest of drawers, and found another set of pajamas. Her hands were shaking. She looked down and tried to understand why. There wasn't time to ponder.

Back in the bathroom, Kelli stood unmoving. Her eyes were still closed, her brow was wrinkled in misery, and water trickled around her.

"Kelli," Nora murmured.

Kelli opened her eyes slowly.

"I'm going to turn the water off now."

Kelli was silent as Nora twisted the knobs. The water stopped.

"Can you come toward me?"

Kelli shook her head and muttered, "No."

Without another word, Nora moved forward into the shower away from Kelli's injured side. "Lean on me."

Kelli did so without hesitation. Her body was heavy, solid, but not unmanageable. Nora moved quickly. Within a few minutes, Kelli was dry and back in her bed. Nora picked up the syringe she'd left on the bedside table and administered it quietly.

Kelli lay there and her discomfort was obvious. Her eyes were closed again and her face was frozen in a grimace.

"The injection should ease the pain as well."

Kelli didn't offer any kind of acknowledgement that she'd heard what Nora said. As the silence stretched, Nora began to feel ill at ease. She backed away, intending to leave.

"Nora."

Her name was a whispered husk, but it stopped her progress toward the door. Nora turned back toward the bed, and swallowed her momentary discomfort. "I'm here."

Kelli gazed at her from under lowered lashes. "Stay…until I fall asleep?"

Nora nodded slowly and lowered herself into the chair near the bed. She cringed. Her clothing was damp. Their entire exchange…this entire situation was strange, but she felt compelled to see it through to completion. There would be time for analysis later.

CHAPTER 6

Nora's kitchen was a staged and sterile environment. She used it regularly but cleaned it even more. The stainless steel gleamed and granite countertops glinted in the muted rays of sunshine that filtered in through the windows. Remnants from her meager breakfast remained on the counter, marring the otherwise pristine surface. It was an easy fix, however, to rid the counter of a coffee cup and a bowl that still had yogurt swirled around the edges. Yet, Nora stood immobile, staring blankly into something that only she could see. The latest incident with Kelli left her decidedly off kilter. She waited just like she had all week for unidentified emotions to either disappear or to make themselves known. It was a pointless endeavor.

Nora didn't regret helping Kelli. That, in itself, was a ridiculous notion. She was a doctor, after all. It was the disintegration of formality that she disliked. Her response was necessary in the moment, but Nora had the distinct impression that she had seen more of Kelli that night than a stranger—or even her friends—were normally allowed to see. That's what had shaken Nora. Before that night, she didn't know she even possessed the level of gentleness she'd offered Kelli. And she did it without thought or hesitation. That disturbed her to the very core.

Nora blinked and checked the slim Rolex on her right wrist. It was 7:27 a.m.—twelve minutes off her normal routine. Nora was going to be even later than she was yesterday. Still, she stood with her hands on the counter, as if to brace herself against the onslaught of alien emotions. She heard her front door close. Her latest sexual liaison, which lasted well into the night, had been serviceable but offered only an ounce of respite. This situation obviously required more than a sexual release to return her to a more balanced state of mind.

The sound of a light trot caught her attention. Phineas was making his way toward his food dish, which teemed with fresh vegetables and grass pellets. The visitors who learned of his existence often expressed shock and disgust that she had a pig as a companion.

It was true that Phineas was different from the average pet, but he was loyal and more intelligent. Nora was sure he understood her, while no one else took the time to try. Affection snared her and, for a moment, so did envy. He was an affable creature and often kept to himself. Then, there were the times when he actually sought her out. He'd nudge her to garner attention. He led an uncomplicated existence.

Nora longed for something similar. At times, she even worked toward it, but there were hurdles in her path that slowed her progress. Rumors were one such obstacle. Perpetuated by residents who had their own messy lives to contend with, but that didn't stop them from trying to pull Nora down with them. They never succeeded, and Nora wasn't going to let them. It was almost easy. The whole thing had become utterly predictable.

However, Nora could not use that word to describe Kelli or her reaction to the woman. In fact, she spent too much time pondering the situation, and too many emotions still swirled inside her. All of this had to stop. Nora had avoided Kelli's room and further interaction, but that wasn't the answer. She tried analysis. She tried evasion. Nora saw only one other avenue—confrontation. Something had to work.

Nora glanced at her watch again. It was 7:38 a.m. She had devoted too much time to woolgathering…to Kelli McCabe. It was time for her to return to status quo.

"Bullshit. You weren't fired. Bet you didn't have a job in the first place, Tony."

"Kelli." Her mother said her name as though she were a step away from getting her ass kicked.

"Oh come on, Mom. That pretty-face thing he does really shouldn't work for you anymore."

Carina threw her hands up. "He's your brother."

"I know that, and that's why I'm not coddling his ass."

"He's trying. Can't you see that?"

Kelli glared at her mother. "You really don't wanna know what I see."

Through it all, Antony stood there with his head bent, staring at his shoes.

This made Kelli even angrier. "Nothing to say for yourself, or are you just gonna keep letting everyone else speak for you?"

Antony shrugged. "Don't matter. You're gonna always think I'm a fuck-up. You and Sean."

Kelli glanced in her other brother's direction. He sat away from them with his police cap in his hands. For some reason, this made her even more suspicious of him than she was before. "You don't have anything to say about this, Sean?"

Sean glanced up. "What's the point?"

Carina gasped. "I can't believe the way you two are treating your brother."

"It's okay, Mom. They have reason," Antony said.

Kelli couldn't look away from Tony. He held his body rigid, and a muscle in his jaw flexed. She wiped a hand over her face. She was too damn tired for this shit. Her dreams kept her from sleeping and no matter how hard Kelli tried, she couldn't make them go away. She wasn't a fucking magician. She finally caught Antony's gaze, but only for a few seconds before he looked away. Kelli opened her mouth to demand answers.

"I'm not gonna stand for this crap." Carina raised her voice. She officially crossed the line from speaking to yelling. "I didn't raise you to be assholes."

Kelli inhaled deeply. She ignored the tightness in her chest and released her breath slowly, hoping for a moment of calm, a moment of peace. She stared out at the open door as life went on around her and wished she were moving with it.

"Do you hear me?" her mother asked.

Kelli blinked as a familiar figure appeared in the doorway.

"While this isn't ICU, hospital policy dictates that noise be kept at a minimum." Nora entered the room. "Since a majority of the nurses categorically refused to deliver the message for me…" She looked at Kelli. Their refusal was her fault after all. "I decided to deliver it myself."

Kelli swallowed and glanced away. Nora had seen enough the other night. She didn't want to show her any more.

"I don't care who you are, lady. This is a family discussion." Her mother was on a roll.

"This is a hospital. While Ms. McCabe may be the center of your universe, she can't be the center of mine. So, in the interest of other patients, please lower your voices."

Carina's face grew red and blotchy, but she didn't say another word.

Kelli was impressed. Not many people could silence her mother.

Sean stood. "I was about to leave anyway." He nodded in Nora's direction. "Doc." He gave Kelli his fake smile and left.

"I guess I need to go too." Her mother reached out and squeezed Kelli's hand, and she held her gaze for a few seconds. Kelli could see her disappointment even though she tried to look away. "C'mon, Tony."

Antony followed his mother dutifully. He paused when they neared Nora but a well-placed swat to the back of his head got him moving again.

Kelli almost chuckled. Nora was indeed worth the stop. Assuming that she was now alone, she closed her eyes. Maybe pretending to sleep would somehow trick her body into actually doing it.

"The nurses tell me that you haven't asked for a sedative at all this week. Why? You obviously need it."

Startled, Kelli opened her eyes and turned toward Nora.

As the seconds passed, stillness enveloped them. Breaking it, Nora brushed a strand of hair behind her ear. Kelli wondered if it was a nervous gesture. Or was it something Nora did only around her? Kelli swallowed. She felt open, exposed.

Nora repeated her question.

Then, they both went quiet.

Nora looked as unsure as Kelli felt. She squirmed as if she was uncomfortable. Nora moved deeper into the room. Kelli licked her lips, but she had no idea what to say.

"Kelli?"

Well, shit. Were they friends now? Kelli didn't expect Nora to say her first name. She had just gotten used to Ms. McCabe. A few nights ago, she hadn't expected Nora to be kind and gentle either. She hadn't expected her to stay as the drugs pulled her under, but Nora had. "That's the third time you've said my first name. It has to be a record or something."

Nora took a step back. "I must apologize. That was very unprofessional of me."

Nora was flustered again, and Kelli had barely said a word. Nora's change in demeanor placed them in recognizable waters. Kelli could navigate them safely without even trying. "Well, you have seen me naked."

Nora face turned the brightest red Kelli had ever seen. "It was only momentary. I assure you, I—"

Kelli couldn't help herself. She laughed. It felt good. "Nora, God, lighten up."

Nora blinked.

Kelli sighed.

"Let your hair down…relax." Kelli brought her thumb and forefinger together. "You're a little bit uptight."

"There is nothing wrong with trying to keep our interactions professional."

"I never said it's wrong. It's just boring as all hell."

"I prefer—"

"To be boring?" Kelli lifted a brow in question.

Nora was silent. She tilted her head to the side and studied Kelli.

Suddenly, very aware of the inspection and made uncomfortable by it, Kelli glanced down. She picked at her tank top. "What? Did a nipple slip or something?" Humor was always, and would forever be, the perfect cover. Lately, she needed it more and more.

"You neglected to answer my initial question. Is all of this…subterfuge?" Nora refused to be distracted.

Kelli's breath caught. This woman saw a lot more than Kelli gave her credit for. "Sub what? I don't even know what that means."

Nora scoffed. "That is completely untrue. I'm sure intelligence lies behind the foul language you insist on using."

Kelli's mouth dropped open. She closed it slowly. "Did you just give me a compliment?"

"No. I was simply pointing out the obvious, and you're doing it again."

"Doing what?"

"Attempting to divert the conversation. I assure you this is unpleasant for me as well."

"Then let's not go there. I like butting heads with you a whole lot better than talking about other shit. Don't you?"

"Yes, but—" Nora's eyes widened, and she reddened even more.

Kelli chuckled. "It's okay to admit it."

Nora's lips thinned. Then, a thoughtful look passed over her face. "Just as it's okay to admit the need for a sedative."

Kelli slammed her mouth shut so hard that she nearly bit her tongue. "What does that matter to you?" Kelli demanded. Nora was about to overstep the line that Kelli kept drawn in the sand.

Nora broke their gaze. "I'm not sure. This conversation hasn't progressed the way I thought it would."

Doing a mental double take, Kelli asked, "What?" She'd gone from teetering on the edge of fight mode to completely confused.

"I'm not your assigned physician. Dr. Rader is, and yet I find myself involuntarily entwined in your situation. I'm not even sure why I engage you in conversation." The words spilled from Nora's mouth. "You're crass—"

Then, out of the blue, Nora's words made sense. It was like someone slapped her in the back of the head. "You…like me." Kelli interrupted. She was floored.

Nora looked stricken, pale. "That is ridiculous. I don't—"

"Like people?"

"Well…no," Nora said.

"That's strange given what you do, but I did tell you I would grow on you."

Nora's eyes narrowed in response.

Kelli chuckled and shrugged. "I'm still not listening to Justin Bieber with you. I'm more of a rock-alternative kinda girl."

"I still have no idea who this Justin Bieber is."

"Doesn't matter. Maybe I'll introduce you to Metallica one day."

"What a horrid name for a person—"

Kelli sighed again. "It's the name of a band."

Nora took another step backward as if preparing to bolt at any second.

"You don't wanna like me, do you, Nora?"

Nora looked away.

"It's okay. You're not the type I usually hang out with either." Kelli had no idea what she was doing. Nora was one more person who had seen her weakened. At the beginning of this conversation, Kelli was leaning toward intentional cruelty, but this woman had returned no matter how much she had insulted her. And she held her own. This woman had stayed by her side when she didn't have to. This woman, Kelli realized, had earned the benefit of the doubt. "That doesn't have to mean anything, though."

Nora gazed back at Kelli, her features now placid, completely void of emotion. She had an awesome poker face. "You're pale, Ms. McCabe, and the discoloration beneath your eyes are a typical sign of exhaustion. You're not sleeping well." Nora paused and then murmured softly, "I've prescribed a mild sedative to go along with your other medications. Will that suffice?" Nora looked at her with compassion, but something else was there. Kelli just didn't know what it was.

Kelli smirked, and for the moment, let her pride go. "Yeah."

Nora turned to leave, but Kelli refused to let her, at least not yet.

"Nora?"

She looked back at Kelli expectantly but with an air of uncertainty.

"I'm different. I challenge you. That's why you like me." Kelli meant it as a question, but the words didn't come out as one. She sounded arrogant, but she didn't mean to be. People seemed to cower around Nora or carry with them a distinct aura of dislike. Kelli had seen it, felt it, and she was none of those things.

Nora's expression was void, but Kelli was sure she saw a little something in her eyes.

"Have a good day, Ms. McCabe."

The elevator dinged as it stopped and opened. Nora walked quickly. Her vision was tunneled, ignoring the chatter and the smattering of people around her. A sense of relief invaded her as she turned down the long hallway that led to the on-call rooms. With a trembling hand, she turned the knob on the first room she reached, but it was locked. She tried two more, only to find the same. Nora could have used her keys, but her ability to handle whatever she might find behind those locked doors was currently a bit compromised.

Finally, there was success. Nora entered, not bothering with the light. She leaned heavily against the closed door and relaxed in the darkness. Kelli's words seeped into her. *You…like me.* Nora brought a hand to her chest in hopes of calming her racing heart. Liking Kelli McCabe was not possible. She was rude, crass, insufferable, and unpredictable, but Nora sighed in reluctant acceptance that Kelli was also so much more. She had to be in order to crash through the walls Nora had spent a lifetime building. How was that even possible?

Throughout her years in college, medical school, and her residency at Seattle Memorial, she'd met people that she'd developed a healthy respect for with regard to their insight, work ethic, and attention to detail. It had been a simple transference for Nora to admire what she herself held dear, but her response and feelings concerning Kelli sent her into a tailspin.

Did she like her? Yes, she did. The answer explained everything so succinctly. She didn't understand how one emotion could cause so much chaos. Her routine was affected and so was her concentration. That much was obvious, and those feelings were wholly responsible for what just occurred in Kelli's room. The words Nora prepared and practiced to end their more personal interactions fled as soon as they were alone. She despised this loss of control, this intrusion into simplicity. The feeling left her disconcerted. Yet, somehow she felt more alive, more alert than ever before, and Nora *liked* that. Yes, she liked it a lot. Something in her stomach fluttered warmly. It tickled her insides in an effort to escape, and she bit her bottom lip as she tried to rein it in. Slowly, Nora let herself smile.

Kelli didn't bother with small talk as the nurse wheeled her down the hall. That ship had sailed, and she had decided that it was okay for the nurses to think she was the consummate asshole. There was no way to turn back now.

As the nurse wheeled her into Travis's room, Kelli heard snatches of conversation.

"Fuck…just fuck. This isn't right," Sean murmured. His voice was thick and full of emotion.

"I know. I'm scared as shit." Travis's voice trembled.

They stopped talking as soon as she entered.

Her brother was seated on Travis's bed. The air was heavy, almost stifling. This just added to the tension she'd already picked up on. Kelli's stomach twisted.

Sean wiped his eyes with the back of his hand, but Kelli saw the tears.

Travis didn't look at her at all. His shoulders sagged, and there was a noticeable hitch in his breathing.

"Someone talk to me…please?" Kelli pleaded.

No one spoke.

A muscle in Kelli's jaw ticked. "I knew something…" She exhaled shakily. "Just tell me."

Sean studied her for a moment. His eyes were red rimmed. His expression was listless. Kelli tried to swallow down the fear that gripped her. He tore his gaze away and glanced in Travis's direction. "It should be you."

"Ye—"

"Spit it the fuck out," Kelli's words were harsh, demanding. The situation called for a softer touch, but she didn't have it in her.

Travis looked at her then. The sadness in his eyes was crushing. "I didn't want to say anything until all the swelling went down. I was hoping it was gonna be good news, but I…I'm paralyzed, Kelli."

Kelli gasped. "No."

"Kelli," Travis whispered.

"No, this can't be happening. You can't…"

"It is ha…happening." Travis's voice broke, and he wiped at his tears.

"We didn't mean to lie to you. We just thought you needed to concentrate on yourself for a while," Sean said.

Kelli looked away, completely overwhelmed. She couldn't stay that way for long. She forced herself into action. With a grunt of pain, she wheeled forward. When she was close enough, Kelli reached out. Travis did the same. They clasped hands.

Stillness surrounded them, but strength did as well.

CHAPTER 7

"Ms. McCabe, you remember Dr. Fuller?"

Kelli grunted in response and continued to look out the window. She was damn near fascinated by the tiny specks of dust caught in the light that streamed in from outside. It was better than dealing with this…whatever he was.

"She's sitting in the dark. Are we sure she's lucid?" Dr. Fuller asked.

Kelli rolled her eyes.

"Yes," Dr. Rader answered. "She isn't the most demonstrative."

Kelli smirked.

Dr. Rader sighed. "Okay, well." He flipped through her chart. "Everything is looking good Ms. McCabe. We're looking at a discharge date of next Wednesday. You'll need to continue your PT after that point until you reach full mobility."

Kelli turned to face them and nodded. It was about damn time, but that was still a week away. She was knee-deep in the present. Right now, she needed to pace herself to keep from getting overwhelmed. She had a lot of shit to sift through. It was hard to wrap her head around the whole thing. Kelli shifted her thoughts to Travis. She wasn't a doctor but she knew she could provide him with something they couldn't—support and strength. Everything she was feeling—fear, sadness, anger—needed to take a backseat. He couldn't see her like that. It was selfish, and Travis needed a hell of lot more from her.

"I thought you would be happier with the news." Rader smiled.

Kelli eyed him warily. He was trying way too hard. "I am." She bared her teeth in a parody of a grin. It seemed like days since she'd actually smiled.

Dr. Rader chuckled and shook his head. "We're sure going to miss you around here, especially the nurses."

Kelli glared.

He raised his hands in supplication. "Although, I've heard relations have improved."

Dr. Fuller snorted. Kelli's gaze zeroed in on her. The other doctor's eyes widened, and she looked away.

For a moment, Kelli was somewhat amused.

"Oh."

They all turned toward the sound coming from the open doorway.

Kelli blinked. Nora stood at the entrance in her usual purple scrubs and lab coat. Honey-blond tresses were piled at the top of her head instead of hanging free. Nora had the tiniest ears, but that wasn't a bad thing. They were cute. But it was the elegant line of her neck that caught Kelli's eye. The wisps of hair that dangled around her face made Nora look soft and approachable. There was a woman underneath all the arrogance and ten dollar words. Nora's femininity was undeniable. Kelli had somehow missed it before, but there was no way she going to make that mistake again. She swallowed. Her throat was dry, and she wasn't sure why.

That was a lie. Kelli knew.

"I didn't mean to interrupt." Nora glanced at the residents before looking Kelli's way.

Kelli blinked again. She was confused. Nora didn't normally care who was in her room. She always came in anyway, but all that happened before realizations and…well stuff. Kelli smiled. She couldn't help herself. "Nora."

As if it were an invitation, Nora stepped farther into the room. She ignored the other doctors until she was closer to the bed.

Dr. Rader and Dr. Fuller watched them. Kelli was fascinated by the abrupt increase in tension. Hell, she could stab it with a fork and eat it like a steak.

Nora nodded stiffly toward the other doctors. "Still on Dr. Rader's… service, Dr. Fuller?"

They younger woman turned a very interesting shade of red and left like her ass was on fire.

Dr. Rader was pissed off. Kelli could see it in his eyes. She could damn near feel it. It rivaled the tension for space in the room.

Nora just stood there glaring at him as if daring him to say something. This lady had balls. Kelli liked that. She almost smiled.

Kelli's gaze went from one to the other. It was like watching an intense game of tennis. Kelli knew there was some weird shit between them, but this was like a soap opera on acid. She waited for someone to cue the dramatic music.

Dr. Rader turned and looked at Kelli. His smile was tight and fake. He left quietly. What choice did he have? Nora just cut him off at the knees in ten words or less. When they were alone, Nora seemed to physically relax. Her shoulders dropped.

"Gee, you really know how to clear a room. I wanna learn that trick," Kelli teased.

Nora's expression warmed when she met Kelli's gaze.

"Good morning to you too, Ms. McCabe." Nora sat down in the chair by the bed.

Kelli quirked an eyebrow. "Ms. McCabe. We're back to that?"

"We are."

"Mmm."

Nora's eyes twinkled.

"I'm not your patient."

"You are a patient in this hospital, however."

"So, when I see you after next Wednesday you can call me Kelli?"

Nora paused. "I don't think so."

"I won't be a patient anymore."

"You'll be an outpatient. Therefore—"

Kelli laughed. "You're a hard sell. I like that."

"I'm glad you're pleased."

It felt good to do this—talk, laugh, and trade snarky comments. It was a release of sorts. "You've graced my door twice in twenty-four hours, doc. Isn't that some kind of record for us?"

Nora released a long breath. "That is partly due to Mr. Travis."

"You're his doctor?" Kelli had a hunch she was right. Otherwise, why bring up Travis at all?

"Due to HIPAA, I can't confirm or deny. But I did what I thought was best."

"I'm gonna assume that's a yes." Kelli wasn't irritated by the omission. She was relieved. Her partner seemed to be in good hands.

"If that helps." Nora inclined her head slightly.

"Okay. That will have to do." Maybe a change in conversation would help since the subject was closed for now, and she just wasn't ready to talk or think about the clusterfuck with Travis today. Not yet. "I'm not complaining, mind you, but what's the other reason you're here?"

"Pardon?"

"You said it was partly because of Travis."

"Oh." Nora looked a little lost. "I'm not sure."

Kelli snorted, but it was without humor. "Aren't we just peas in a pod? I'm not sure what the hell I'm doing either."

They stared at each other.

"He's very important to you…Mr. Travis?" Both Nora's words and her expression were hesitant.

Kelli was confused by the display. "Of course he is. He's my partner. Hell, he's like one of my brothers really. What kind of quest…" Kelli's question died as she figured it out. "You don't have brothers or sisters?"

"No, I'm an only child."

"Why? Your parents realized they could only handle one of you?" Kelli teased.

"I don't know. They never told me why."

"You should ask. Tell them inquiring minds want to know."

Nora shook her head. "I can't ask them. That's impossible."

"You're parents are gone?"

Nora nodded, but she looked unaffected.

"I'm sorry."

Nora didn't even blink.

"I didn't mean to offend you." Kelli said because she simply didn't know what to say.

"You didn't."

Things had taken an odd turn. "Mmkay, so why are you asking me about Travis?" As she waited for answers, Kelli pulled all the strange pieces of the conversation together to get the bigger picture. "You don't have anyone…do you?" That was pitiful. Kelli couldn't understand it. All a person had to do was take the time. Nora was way too interesting to just brush off. "No friends?"

Nora's gaze wandered.

Kelli knew she had pushed a little too far. "You're uncomfortable. I can change the subject if you want."

Nora just looked at Kelli. Her eyes were unreadable. "I didn't have friends. Even the socialites were an acquired taste, or, more accurately, thought I was. I don't have any now either."

"Well shit. It's their fucking loss. Fuck them, all I say."

Nora just continued to stare.

"Uh, sorry about the language."

"No you're not." Nora almost smiled. Kelli could see the beginnings of it tugging at the corners of her mouth.

Kelli smirked. "That's beside the point. I'm sorry if I made you uncomfortable."

"I thought you liked me that way."

"There's a difference between uncomfortable and flustered, at least in my dictionary." Kelli tilted her head to the side and gave Nora a full-blown smile.

Nora's eyes widened, and her cheeks turned pink.

"That's flustered."

Nora cleared her throat. "I see."

"Mmm, so about that subject change?" Kelli asked.

"Yes, please."

"Uh, you don't like Dr. Rader."

"I won't disparage a fellow doctor," Nora said.

"You don't have to. He looked like he was going to piss himself." Kelli grinned. "It was kinda hot."

Nora sighed. "Ms. McCabe—"

"Okay, fine, but the shit was hilarious. And that girl you said was sleeping with him—"

"I said no such thing." Nora shook her head, her body inching closer to Kelli as if to make her point.

"Alluded to or insinuated, whatever you want to call it."

Nora's lips thinned.

"Do you ever smile?" It wasn't what she was about to ask, but it's what came out.

Nora's gaze sharpened.

Kelli chuckled. "Let's hold on to that one."

"Let's," Nora agreed.

"So, you and twinkle toes have a history?"

"History is far from the correct term."

Nora was sharing. In the couple minutes Nora'd been in the room, Kelli learned more about her than she had during all her other visits combined. Kelli wanted to know more. "Do tell."

"When I find an adequate descriptor, I'll be sure to let you know."

"Deal, but I'm gonna let you in on something. I don't like him either," Kelli whispered. "Not sure why yet, but I'll figure it out."

"Indeed."

"Yep." Kelli's gaze wandered toward the window again. Her thoughts went to Travis. "How is he?"

Nora took a moment to respond. "I don't have a satisfactory answer for that."

Kelli closed her eyes, and she could see Travis's anger and his tears as clear as day. "I still can't fucking believe this." She exhaled shakily. "I knew something wasn't right, but I didn't expect this."

"His paralysis was kept from you?"

"Yeah, they were trying to protect me. Can you believe it? Protect *me*."

Nora stayed quiet, and it was exactly what Kelli needed.

"If I could just get away from all this for a few minutes. Gain some perspective…gain something. I can't do a damn thing in this bed except wallow in it."

Nora stood, a thoughtful look on her face. "I'll be back."

Kelli watched her go, but she was left wondering. Nora was a mystery, but Kelli couldn't help herself. She wanted to put the pieces together and see what it made.

A few minutes later, Nora came back with a wheelchair in tow.

"I can't see him feeling like this."

"We're not going to ICU," Nora countered.

"Then where?"

"Outside, Ms. McCabe."

Kelli's breath caught. She didn't know what to say, but she got another piece of the Nora puzzle. Kelli just didn't know where to put it.

⁂

Nora blinked as the mid-morning sun shined in her eyes, but her vision adjusted quickly. The landscape around them looked almost alien even though she'd seen it a thousand times or more in passing. It was different to actually make time to peruse the well-kept greenery. Well, it was different to actually make time for anything other than surgery. The topiaries were severely pruned into symmetrical designs. The lines were clean, precise. Nora took a moment to admire the view because it was a perfect foil for the messiness that churned inside her.

Despite the emotional upheaval of the prior day, Nora was sure that her epiphany would provide a sense of peace. Maybe she was being naïve to think she could simplify and categorize all these new, foreign emotions into nothingness. Today, Nora woke up floundering even more than she had before. Thankfully, she was able to pull herself together enough to leave her home by eight.

When Nora had entered the hospital this morning, she immersed herself in the familiar. Routine acted as a warm, comfortable blanket and settled on her shoulders. The sense of peace lasted through the monthly departmental meeting which she detested because it was more about the bottom line than patient care. To her, they were formal affairs, and she always looked the part with a high-end pantsuit and properly coiffed hair to show an elevated level of professionalism. The easy calm ended abruptly when she spoke with Gerald

Travis Jr. He mentioned his partner with such deference that Nora allowed her own growing regard for Kelli to seep through. It produced a warmth of a different kind, and she let the feeling take her where it wanted to go. Her destination was obvious, but still she was just as bewildered as Drs. Rader and Fuller when she'd entered Kelli's room. What was happening to her? Better yet, why was it happening?

Nora glanced downward. Kelli's spiky auburn tresses moved softly with the breeze. She swallowed. Kelli brought with her a level of excitement and chaos that Nora found herself drawn to despite her internal warnings. She had no idea how to stop it, and at the moment, Nora wasn't sure she wanted to.

Nora turned the wheelchair along the pattern of the sidewalk. She enjoyed the continued silence between them. It seemed to fit. People hurried past them, but they moved slowly.

"I don't want this for him." Kelli looked up and over her shoulder.

Nora let her speak.

Kelli gripped the arms of the chair. "I don't want him trapped in something like this. I feel helpless letting other people push me around…I can't even imagine what it would be like not having the choice."

Nora stopped at a nearby bench. She pulled Kelli to the side and sat down. Nora didn't know what to do with her hands so she placed them in her lap. More than anything else, she wanted to make sure Kelli knew she was listening. She may not know what to say, but at least there was this. Nora felt awkward at first. She wasn't good at this kind of thing, but she pushed her uncertainty aside. She looked at Kelli and waited.

"I dream about the shooting every night," Kelli whispered. "Every time I try to sleep, really."

The sudden admission momentarily made Nora breathless, but there was something else as well. The warmth was back. The feeling was becoming a regular occurrence when they were together, but sharing was still a horribly unfamiliar concept to her. Nora felt privileged that Kelli was able to open up to her. "The medication helps."

Kelli nodded and briefly looked away. A muscle spasmed in her jaw. "I can't stay on them forever, but I know it'll pass given some time." She paused and a peculiar expression took over her features. "I don't even know you, Nora, not really. So why the hell am I spilling my guts to you?"

"I'm definitely not the right person to ask." Nora continued to marvel at the changes in her own demeanor. Kelli's admission helped her to know that she wasn't the only one.

Kelli smirked and shook her head. "Williams, my old partner, has been trying like hell to get me to talk. You've barely said a word…" She finished the sentence with a chuckle. "This is weird."

Nora was in total agreement. This situation…this tenuous connection between them was…odd.

Their gazes met, and Nora found she was unable to look away.

Kelli pushed a trembling hand through her hair. "He's not dead. I keep telling myself that, but…he's a cop. He's a detective, and that's all he wanted to be. Without his legs—"

"He'll still be alive." Nora interrupted. The words fell from her lips, and they felt right. This entire interaction was surreal, but Nora felt the pull like a gravitational force, and she had no desire to be free of it. She just wanted to understand.

"Yeah. I know you can't share everything with me, but I have a feeling that if I ask you, you'll be straight with me."

"I can only speak in generalities. Are you asking?"

Kelli gazed at her warily. "Yeah."

"His injuries are significant and the odds aren't in his favor. It's as straight as I can be without violating HIPAA." Nora wanted her words to be less clinical and dry. Kelli at least deserved that. Nora continued, "I wish I could say more, and I didn't mean to sound—"

"No, I understand. As for the rest of it, I needed a dose of reality." Kelli reached out, but her hand stopped inches away from Nora's arm before Kelli pulled back.

Nora was intrigued by the action. She couldn't remember the last time someone touched her without pretense or sexual intent, and suddenly, Nora wanted to know what that felt like.

"I need to separate all my shit from his. I have to. Anything else would be selfish." Kelli stared at her. "I'm usually good at that, but this time…how the hell do I do it?"

Kelli's gaze was heavy. Nora decided that she could handle the weight. "You're asking me?"

Kelli's mouth opened and closed a couple of times. "I guess I am."

As Kelli continued to stare, Nora was sure that she could see through her and into the little compartments where she kept aspects of her life. "You just do."

"Is that what you do?" Kelli asked softly.

Nora's heart fluttered in her chest. It was strange for someone to actually see her and try to understand. "Yes."

Nora felt raw, exposed, and she figured that Kelli did as well. When she stood, Kelli glanced up at her. The look in her eyes confirmed Nora's suspicions. Without a word, Nora steered her toward the hospital entrance.

As the elevator doors closed, Nora hit the button for Kelli's floor.

"I don't wanna go back yet. Take me to the chapel please?" Kelli held her hands tightly together in her lap.

Surprised by the request, Nora asked. "Are you religious?"

"Not really. Not after all the things I've seen in my line of work. We were raised in the Catholic Church. It was a two-pronged attack. My Dad was Irish, and my mother's Italian. We went to mass whether we liked it or not. They kind of loosened the reins when we got older. I guess they saw we were all going our own way. You could say they were probably more progressive than most."

"If you don't believe, why would you—"

Kelli shrugged. "I don't know. Maybe if I use His direct line, He'll be more likely to listen."

A few minutes later, Nora eased into the last pew and watched as Kelli lit several candles. The chapel was quiet, solemn. It was understandable why some lingered here looking for peace. Minutes passed. Kelli glanced over her shoulder. "I changed my mind. Can you take me to see him?"

Kelli's gaze was stormy with emotion, and Nora had somehow learned to recognize the determined glint in her eyes. Nora nodded in agreement.

She wheeled Kelli into Travis's room. Despite what had just occurred between them, Nora felt like an intruder. She left silently but stood just outside the doorway.

"Hey," Kelli's voice was rougher than normal.

"Hey, yourself—"

"We need to kick this paralysis shit in the ass." Kelli interrupted.

A strained chuckle was his response. "We do. It's a real twat. Not liking it at all."

"Good, but either way, you know I…"

"I know," Travis finished for her.

"Do you?"

"Yeah, you're here for me."

"Yes, I am."

Nora was moved by what she heard. The lure of friendship was powerful, and for the first time, she understood the need for it. Maybe some part of her longed for it as well.

As she walked down the hall, Nora tried to move her thoughts toward her upcoming procedures. "Nora." Instinctually, she turned. It didn't matter that James was the one calling her.

Dr. Rader jogged toward her. Nora came to her senses and started walking in the other direction.

"Nora, wait!"

He grabbed her elbow. Nora jerked her arm away. His very presence hampered the clarity she'd just found.

His eyes were soft, needy. "Thanks for stopping."

"It was an involuntary action. I assure you." Nora moved away quickly, intent on avoiding the interaction.

James stayed with her. "You're in a hurry. I can understand that. I just need a minute."

Nora stopped abruptly. She prepared her words carefully. "Can you understand that we have nothing to discuss? This is getting dangerously close to harassment. This *will* stop while there's some semblance of a professional relationship between us. You won't like my next course of action."

His mouth opened and worked frantically, but no words escaped.

Pity leaked into her voice. "You're an intelligent human being. Surely, this type of behavior is beneath you?"

James's eyes widened to comical proportions. His face contorted and turned a purplish hue. Anger emanated from him, but Nora decided that it could only be a good thing. She had grown tired of the simpering.

"Are you even human?" His tone was menacing. James took a step forward. "I mean, do you really have to be so hateful about this…about us? You can't just treat me like this, Nora. You cut me down whenever you get the chance, even in front of my patients and the other residents. I'm warning you—"

Nora held her ground. The man was delusional. The audacity it took to blame her for all of this had to be astounding. She wasn't afraid of him, and he needed to understand that. "Cause and effect, Dr. Rader." Nora interrupted. "My treatment of you is the consequence of your continued actions. If you were mature enough, I'm sure you'd accept responsibility for your behavior and just move on."

"Did you just tell me to grow up?"

"How very astute of you."

"What did I see in you in the first place?" He paused. "Oh yeah, the way you sucked my cock." James sneered.

Nora wasn't fazed by his crude remarks. She repeated the words that she'd said to him outside the elevator days ago. "Not anymore."

James's jaw dropped. Nora assumed from his shocked expression that he was expecting more of a reaction. How unfortunate. He stood in the middle of the hallway as still as a statue. Nora walked around him. She would not let him be an obstacle. She had a much better road ahead of her.

CHAPTER 8

Nora entered her kitchen and paused at the chill the stainless steel brought to the room. The area lacked nuance, and for some reason, this morning that disturbed her. The only splash of color was the deep blue of Phineas's food bowl. For the first time, her environment felt foreign. There was little she could do to fix it at the moment. She opened the refrigerator and automatically reached for the strawberries and Greek yogurt, intent on her habitual morning faire. At the last moment, Nora decided that the blueberries were a better choice.

She glanced at her watch. She was still a few minutes behind her usual schedule. It would have to do. She always greeted a day at the hospital with detached anticipation, mentally going through the list of patients on her rounds as well as the surgeries scheduled. Recently, however, there was an addition. Kelli had become part of her routine. Nora was not sure how any of this happened, but she adjusted her activities to include several visits with Kelli throughout the day. A different type of anticipation surged through her. The feeling was even warmer than what she had become accustomed to. Kelli accepted her and genuinely seemed to like her presence. Nora wasn't merely tolerated, and she had no idea it would feel this good.

Change had swept into Nora's life quickly, bombarded her defenses, and broke through before she could fortify herself. She had no choice but to adapt efficiently before another piece of her armor came tumbling down. Her lack of filter regarding Kelli troubled her, just not as much as it had before. Nora had to acknowledge that change was happening with or without her permission, and maybe it was time to admit that the minute loss of control was stimulating. Not as stimulating as Kelli, but Nora doubted anything was.

Nora rinsed her used dishes and put them in the dishwasher for later. She glanced at her watch again. It was 7:19 a.m. This was a vast improvement over the previous day. Nora stopped abruptly. Her life with Kelli in it felt as if it were a step closer to her previous routine, relatively speaking. Nora wondered how long this current stint of normalcy would last. Feelings were unpredictable and messy, as were the circumstances surrounding them. This lull in activity might be the calm before everything imploded. With a deep breath, Nora placed the uncertainty in its own compartment and exited the kitchen. Surely, Kelli couldn't be that dangerous?

Kelli released a loud grunt, caused more by soreness than pain.

"Move the knee toward your chin as far as you can."

Kelli wiped at the sweat on her forehead and glared at the physical therapist. "Dan, no offense, you're a nice guy and all, but I fucking hate your voice."

Dan chuckled. "A little farther. You can do it."

Kelli huffed. "You remind me of that artist guy on with the curly fro, always painting happy trees. He was on PBS."

Dan shrugged. "No idea."

Kelli searched her memory. When it hit her, she smirked. "Bob Ross."

"You can call me whoever you want if it helps. Now, I want you to stand unaided and lower yourself into the wheelchair. It's time to really get to work."

Kelli's legs trembled, and sweat continued to trickle down her face and back. She brought herself to a sitting position and ignored the pull of her still healing chest muscles.

Dan stepped away. He left the wheelchair two feet from her bed. Kelli's socked feet touched the ground. Slowly, she applied pressure and weight to ease herself through the soreness and her body's protest. She was fucking doing this no matter what.

Kelli stood.

She led with her good leg, gritted her teeth, and shuffled the other one forward. "Fuck, yeah."

"Good. Good!"

"Fuck you, Bob," Kelli said with a smile.

"Ms. McCabe, must you subject every employee at the hospital to your crassness?"

Kelli grinned. "Yes, yes I do. Besides, that was a celebratory fuck." She paused and cringed at the implied meaning of her words. "You know what I mean," she mumbled.

Nora's face reddened anyway. It made Kelli grin even harder.

"Good morning, Nora." Kelli inched forward. She grunted again as she lowered herself into the wheelchair. It felt good to move again. She glanced at Dan. "You want me to wheel myself to the training room too?"

Dan laughed. "No, I'll handle that part."

Kelli stared pointedly at Nora. "I *said* good morning, Nora."

Nora's lips twitched. "Good morning to you too, Ms. McCabe. It's good to see you up and about."

"Did it almost make you smile?" Kelli asked. She'd seen it, the twinkle in Nora's golden-brown eyes and slight curl of her lips. Kelli was starting to consider it a challenge. Before she left this hospital, she was going to make Nora smile.

Nora sighed. "I should leave you to your therapy."

Kelli didn't want her to go. "You're a little late this morning." It had gotten to the point, in a very short period of time, that her mornings didn't feel right without a visit from Nora.

Nora cleared her throat. "I had rounds to attend to, and today it took longer than usual."

"I'll forgive you if you go to PT with me." Kelli offered a compromise.

"I don't think—" Nora started.

Dan shrugged. "That's okay with me."

"Besides, I like your voice a hell of a lot better than his."

Dan coughed to cover up his laughter.

Nora turned yet another adorable shade of red. It made Kelli's stomach tighten in a very interesting way. She didn't want this little moment to end, so she pushed on. "See? Now, lead on MacDuff." Kelli waited a few seconds for Nora to correct her Shakespearian fuck-up. Kelli hated *Macbeth*, but *Taming of the Shrew* wasn't half bad.

As they left the room, she heard Nora scoff. "I do b[e] MacDuff.'"

"I knew that. Just trying to make sure you're paying attenti[on.]"

⁂

Kelli tossed the medicine ball back to Dan. Her muscles burned, but it was a good feeling. She glanced in Nora's direction. She sat discreetly in the far corner, looking as prim and proper as ever. Kelli was grateful for her presence, but she wanted more. "Talk to me, doc."

Nora's gaze strayed toward Kelli then back to Dan.

Kelli smirked. She felt special. When they were alone, Nora was pretty much an open book, and Kelli ended up spilling her guts as well.

She had to find an easy, everyday topic since they had company. "Any pets?"

"Yes, Phineas."

"Dog?" Kelli asked.

"No."

"Cat?"

"Kunekune." Nora finally answered.

Kelli blinked and almost missed the dense leather ball coming at her face. She caught it just in time. "Say what now?"

"A…domesticated pig…with fur."

Kelli dropped the medicine ball to her lap. The laughter that stirred in her chest tapered off when she realized Nora wasn't teasing. "You're serious?"

"I am."

Curious, Kelli asked, "You keep him in the house?"

Nora stared at her for several seconds.

Kelli held her gaze. "What?"

"I expected laughter. I can imagine it sounded odd."

Kelli shrugged. "I find it more interesting than funny."

Nora stood and moved toward her. "He's approximately 217 pounds."

"Oh, he's a big fu—"

"Ms. McCabe." Nora made a scolding *tsk* sound.

"Big one. I meant to say big one."

"He has a habitat in the backyard, but he has his own entrance into the house. He visits often." Nora paused. "Do you have pets?"

"Had a cat named Evil. Wouldn't let me touch him, pick him up, or anything. Damn thing disappeared months ago. He was always trying to escape."

"I'm sorry."

Kelli snorted. "I'm not. I was sure it was going to kill me in my sleep one night."

Nora's lips lifted at the corners.

That feeling in Kelli's stomach came back full force.

"May I ask you something?"

"Sure." Kelli shrugged.

"How long have you been with the police department?"

"Twelve years…detective for almost eight. Let me guess? You want to know why I chose to be a cop?" Kelli didn't wait for an answer. "I wanted to be a superhero when I was a kid. This seemed like the next best thing."

Nora gave her a pointed look. "Are you—"

"Serious? Nope. Not at all." Kelli grinned.

Dan cleared his throat.

Kelli jumped in surprise. She forgot that they weren't alone.

Dan stepped into view. "Let's do the bar and finish with some stretches."

Kelli nodded. She glanced at Nora, only to find her back in her seat.

Kelli ignored the sweat dribbling into her eyes. She growled in pain as she took step after step. Needing a distraction, Kelli glanced in Nora's direction. "It's great…that you're here, but I'm not keeping you from anything am I?"

"I have surgery scheduled in forty-five minutes."

"You need to go now?"

"Normally, I like to prepare up to an hour ahead…" Nora's voice trailed off.

Their gazes met and held. Kelli saw it. Nora didn't stay because Kelli asked her to. She stayed because she wanted to. "Thank you."

Nora simply nodded.

Kelli shifted gears to Travis. "The specialist is here…for Travis. I mean, I knew he was coming today." Since Nora was his doctor, it made sense for her to consult with the neurologist. Kelli continued, "You had to meet with him. That's why you were late."

Nora looked surprised.

"Travis told me about it, and he signed a release, too, for me and the rest of the family."

"Yes, I'm aware of that. The neurosurgeon decided on a highly experimental procedure. It's scheduled for tomorrow morning. He didn't see a reason to wait since Mr. Travis is stable."

Kelli licked her lips and could not fight the sudden weakness in her legs. She held onto the bar until the moment passed. None of this was fair. It wasn't fucking fair.

"I can make sure I'm there to…observe." Nora's tone was gentle, hesitant.

Kelli sucked in a breath. Her sense of relief was overpowering. Maybe she couldn't be there for Travis, but Nora could. That Nora would offer to do this for her…it meant a lot, and Kelli had no idea what she did to deserve it. This was too much. Kelli fought back the tears and glanced at Nora. Her expression was the softest Kelli had ever seen it. "You'd…do that for me?"

Nora stood again.

"Why?" Kelli asked. Yes, they'd connected, but Nora was still pretty much a stranger. Before the thought finished forming, Kelli knew it was complete bullshit. Kelli would never tell a stranger the things she'd told Nora, and she sure as hell wouldn't have let her see the things she had.

"I'm…I don't know." Nora looked just as confused.

"Okay…okay." Kelli nodded and leaned heavily against the equipment.

Their gazes met.

The door burst open, letting in laughter and a small group of people. Dan was already there, dealing with them. Distracted, Kelli looked toward the entrance. Then, her gaze found Nora's again.

"Thank you," Kelli whispered.

Nora moved closer. When she was within arm's length, Kelli barely resisted the urge to reach out to her. She had never been a touchy-feely person, but for some reason, with Nora she wanted to be.

"Kelli, I—"

"You only use my first name when you think I'm stressed." Kelli interrupted.

"It seems to calm the situation."

Kelli smiled. "It does."

"Sorry. Residents. They thought it would be fun to check out areas they'd never been in," Dan said.

Kelli ignored him. Nora was way more interesting. Nora looked down at her watch. For Kelli, it was just another clue, another piece of the puzzle. "You're a stickler for time."

Nora glanced upward. "I am, yes. I think routine makes things much more productive."

"I'm part of your routine?" Kelli already knew the answer. She just wanted to hear her say it.

For the umpteenth time, Nora blushed. "Yes, I suppose."

Well, hell. The tightening in her stomach turned into a hard tug. "That's why I've been seeing you at the same time the past few days."

"If that seems strange—"

"No, it doesn't, not at all. I like it."

Nora quirked a brow as she looked at Kelli expectantly.

Kelli smirked. "What? Does that make *me* strange?"

"Possibly." Nora's lips twitched.

Kelli shrugged. "Been called a lot of things. We can just add that to the pile." Kelli glanced at the wall clock. "You'd better get to your surgery. I'll see you at one o'clock."

Nora backed away. She held Kelli's eyes for a few seconds before finally turning to leave. Kelli stared at the door. Dan cleared his throat. He just had to ruin the fucking moment.

"Yesss?"

Dan laughed. "I was just thinking. We should bottle whatever it is you have and make sure Dr. Whitmore gets a daily dose of it. From the buzz I get from around here, the residents would be more than grateful."

Kelli snorted, but it was true. Nora was different around her. Hell, they were different around each other. This friendship or whatever they were working toward was about ten shades of weird, but for whatever reason it worked.

When Nora entered the operating room, several members of her team looked her way. She was not late, but this group was used to her being present several minutes before any procedure. She nodded. It was her way of telling them to proceed.

The jazz music piping through the sound system transitioned from dulcet tones to a heady crescendo of trumpet and saxophone. It reminded her of Kelli. She had the capacity for stillness. However, more often than not, she hummed with unreleased energy that affected the others around her, and Nora was drawn in as well. This wasn't the time for this. Focus. She needed to focus.

"Ten blade."

Nora pressed into the exposed skin of the abdomen. Blood welled around the incision and spilled over to flood the peritoneum.

"Suction."

Once the field was clear, she peered up at the resident assisting her—Dr. Lang—and asked, "What do you see?"

"Spleen is enlarged to twice its normal size denoting possible infection. Liver is bleeding profusely."

Nora waited.

"Is that…should we take a look at the small intestines as well? There seems to be inflammation."

"Very good. We may even find necrotic tissue."

She looked at Nora in surprise.

"Is there a problem Dr. Lang?" Nora asked.

"No, I just didn't expect…" She faded out.

Nora sighed. She hadn't expected the compliment. Honestly, Nora hadn't either. After each interaction with Kelli, she felt softened somehow. Was that wrong? It didn't feel wrong. A splinter of fear made its way into her chest anyway, but it was immediately followed by a flood of excitement. Kelli brought change, indeed, but there was so much more. "Proceed."

After the surgery, Nora removed her gloves, surgical cap, and let her hair down before washing and drying her hands. Laughter wafted around her. She turned as others entered the prep room.

Patricia, one of the surgical nurses on her team, smiled, and Nora was instantly uncomfortable. She stepped away from the group. It was an odd dichotomy. Her level of comfort with Kelli was rising, but with others, it stayed generally the same.

The nurse yanked the blood pressure cuff from Kelli's right arm.

"Really? I'm sure you don't have to be so rough."

The nurse rolled her eyes.

"I saw that," Kelli said.

"I'm sure you did." The nurse held up a piece of equipment. "This…is a pulse oximeter. It should look familiar to you, just like the blood pressure cuff, so you know it won't hurt. Should I call your mother just to be sure?" The woman smiled as she clipped the monitor on Kelli's finger.

Shit, the nurse was getting better with her snark. Kelli was going to have to step it up. "No, but you sitting in my lap might help." Sexual innuendo was always great to throw people, especially strangers, off their game.

The nurse reddened. The pulse…whatever the fuck it was beeped, and she left so fast that Kelli thought she saw wisps of smoke behind her. Kelli grinned. What she said was twenty different types of wrong, but she couldn't argue with the end result.

As the nurse left, Tony stumbled in.

"Oh shit, she was hot. Maybe I need to get shot." Tony laughed at his own joke.

It really wasn't funny. Kelli studied him. His face was pale, sweaty. She got a sinking feeling in her stomach.

Their mother walked in. "Did you see Ton—" Carina huffed and glared. "There you are. Why did you take off running?"

Tony sniffed and shrugged. "What's the big fucking deal?"

"Whoa, hold on. You have to be so disrespectful?" Kelli asked. "What's wrong with you?"

Instead of answering, Tony started laughing again.

Kelli looked at her mother, who rolled her eyes.

"She's right. Watch your mouth. Look at you. It looks like you've lost ten pounds since I last saw you, and I can tell you're not sleeping. You have luggage. You work too hard. Tell Kelli about your new job." Carina smiled at Kelli. "He's working nights."

"Yeah," Tony mumbled. He focused on picking the sore on his forearm.

"Antony." Carina said his name loud enough for the people down the hall to hear.

His head whipped toward her. "Yeah, nights. Construction." Tony glanced at Kelli and smiled before he found something else more interesting to focus on.

"No, that was your last job, remember? You're doing security," their mother said.

The sinking feeling went to being swallowed whole. The hairs on the back of Kelli's neck stood up. Tony's eyes were red, and his pupils were dilated. What in the purple fuck? Kelli knew. She knew something wasn't right with him, but she didn't want it to be this. All the signs were there. Tony was using again. And it was bad enough that he didn't give a damn that he was lit up like a Christmas tree in front of his mother.

Anger came for Kelli first, and sadness was right behind it. Hopelessness was late to the game, but it was a strong chaser.

"Oh shit! Check this out." He pulled on the string that controlled the blinds. The slats opened and closed. "It's like cartoons. If I do it real fast…the people. Spongebob. And the cars. They move so fast."

He wasn't making any sense at all.

"I gotta go see. Kelli…you do the blinds. Watch me. It's like cartoons." This time when he laughed, it was high pitched and scary. The laughter got louder as he ran out the room.

Kelli looked at her mother and waited.

Carina shook her head and sighed. "That boy. I told him not to drink all that coffee."

And there it was. Denial. Anything Kelli had to say right now was going to be called bullshit.

She glanced at Kelli. "I brought you a bear claw. There's a decent-looking bakery a few streets over." Carina sat the white paper bag on the nightstand. Kelli stared at it. She didn't see it before. Her focus was on Tony.

"Mom?" Kelli's voice cracked. She couldn't help it.

"I'm sorry. I better go find him. I'm his ride, and I'll be late if I wait for him to come to me." She brushed Kelli's hair back off her forehead and gave her a quick kiss.

Kelli closed her eyes and let it happen. When she opened them again, Carina was looking at her strangely.

"I'll, uh, give you a call later."

Kelli nodded and watched her go.

It only took a few seconds for all the emotions she was holding back to explode outward. With a violent swing of her arm, Kelli swiped everything off the night stand including the white paper bag.

Kelli welcomed the jolt of pain in her chest. She couldn't hurt any worse right now. What the hell was she going to tell Sean? Her insides clenched suddenly. After everything that just happened, Kelli's mind was a little clunky, but she was quick enough to figure out that if she knew something smelled shitty, Sean could smell it too. Why hadn't he said anything?

She only *thought* it couldn't hurt more, but she was wrong. It was one thing for Tony to be strung out. He was an addict. But to know Sean kept it from her? On top of keeping Travis's condition a secret? That was far worse. She needed to talk to Sean now. Kelli grabbed a crutch from the other side of the bed and used it to pull the phone toward her. When the phone was close enough, she bent over and grabbed it, ignoring her discomfort. Her hand shook as she dialed Sean's number.

"McCabe." He sounded tired.

"Tony was here. No more secrets, Sean. We need to talk." It took all she had not to yell, but she didn't try to mask the anger in her voice.

Sean was so quiet that Kelli could hear broken voices coming from the police radio.

"I'll be there in fifteen minutes," Sean whispered. "Kel, I—"

"No, just no." Kelli stopped him. She couldn't hear anymore until she had a chance to breathe. She had to pull herself together. Tearing Sean another asshole wasn't going to make the situation better.

Sean got there in ten. His face was sweaty just like Tony's had been, but it had nothing to do with meth. He stood a few feet from her bed. Despite the river of crap he was swimming in, Sean looked her in the eye. He was scared. She saw it. She saw regret too.

"He was in fucking outer space. What the fuck is wrong with me? I knew something was up." Kelli shook her head and stared. "How long?"

"I hated keeping it from you, but I wanted to give him a chance to clean himself up on his own. I know I should have told you."

"How long?" Kelli growled. She had no patience left.

Sean looked away. "About a month."

"Fuck," she whispered. "Fuck!" This time it was much louder. "You should have told me. At least you're not in denial like Mom. That's the only good thing to come out of this shit."

Sean hung his head. Seeing him like this took her back to when they were kids. He never could take it when she yelled at him even when there was good reason.

"I thought I was doing the right thing. Nothing else has worked. He has to buy in. He has to want to get better. I thought…I could help him see that. I'm sorry, Kelli." Sean moved closer to the bed. He reached out for her.

"Don't." Kelli murmured. What he said made sense, but he was pushing it. Sean jerked his hand away.

"This can't be about us, no matter what I feel right now." Kelli could barely look at him.

Sean agreed weakly. "Yeah, we need a plan."

Unable to help herself, Kelli glanced up only to see that they were not alone. Nora stood in the doorway. The shocked expression on her face was all the evidence Kelli needed to know that she'd heard plenty.

"I was trying to wait until you finished. I can return later if—" Nora said.

"No." Sean interrupted her. "I should probably go anyway. We can't fix it all today." He looked at Kelli. His eyes were sad, pleading, but he stood tall. "We'll figure this out."

"Yeah," Kelli agreed. She hoped to God he was right. "I think I can understand why you did it but it was still the wrong call."

Sean nodded slightly. "Later," he mumbled as he left.

Kelli watched her brother leave. She knew her response hurt him, but his secrets hurt her too. What the fuck was up with people keeping shit from her? There had to be a bigger word than overwhelmed, because whatever the fuck it was, that was her right now. It felt as though somebody had punched her in the face, and she was watching everything float in the air above her while she lay there like dead weight. The messed up part was that she had no idea how she was going to get up.

Nora walked toward her slowly. Her expression was gentle but unsure.

Tears burned Kelli's eyes. She closed them. It didn't help. They fell anyway. When she opened her eyes again, Nora was closer. There was so much Kelli wanted to say, but the words refused to come out.

"Kelli, I'm here."

Kelli felt alone, isolated, and she didn't want to be. She reached out. She didn't know if Nora understood what she needed, but she took the chance. When Nora's hand slid into hers, it rocked her to the core. Kelli's stomach flipped, and Nora looked just as startled.

A loud chirp filled the air.

"I'm sorry," Nora whispered. She dug into the pocket of her lab coat and brought out her pager. "It's 9-1-1." She sounded disappointed.

"Not Travis?" It wasn't farfetched for Kelli to ask. After all shitty things happened in twenties.

"No, not him, but I have to go."

Kelli swallowed and nodded.

Nora looked at their linked hands, and Kelli realized she hadn't let go. She really didn't want to.

"I'll be back as soon as I can."

Nora's words were enough to get her muscles working again. Kelli pulled her hand free, but Nora didn't move for another moment. Then, a few seconds later, she was gone. Kelli was helpless, and to make matters worse, she was useless as well. Things were falling apart around her, and there wasn't a fucking thing she could do about it. Nora was outside of all the bullshit. When Kelli was around her, she was able to breathe a little easier. No one had ever had that effect on her before, and it was worth trying to keep. She had to have something to look forward to.

Kelli could finally use the crutches with only a tiny bit of pain. It was simpler getting to and from the toilet and gave her a lot more dignity. She flicked the bathroom light switch off, but the TV gave her just enough illumination to see her way back to bed. Someone was already standing there. It was obviously a woman. Her first thought was a nurse, but Kelli's heart went into overdrive when she realized who it was. "Nora, hey."

"I didn't intend to take so long. I had to perform emergency surgery."

"It's okay. Not your fault," Kelli told her. She made her way to the opposite side of the bed. The closer she got the more she could see. This was definitely not the Nora she was used to. The purple scrubs were gone. Instead, she wore a dark skirt that molded to her body, highlighting curves that had barely been visible before. The skirt stopped at the knee and showed legs that were long enough to wrap around some lucky bitch twice. The pinkish blouse showed off her delicate collarbone and hinted at cleavage that Kelli really wanted to see more of.

Kelli's damn throat was dry again, but she couldn't ignore the way her stomach dropped. She expected to look down and see it on the floor at her feet. With everything that was going on, it didn't make sense to feel this attraction now. Kelli wanted to laugh at the timing. This was fucking crazy. There was too much on her plate as it was. The connection forming between them could be a positive thing, but with all the shit in her life, even the good stuff could end up fucked. She couldn't think about Nora that way right now. There was no room. Instead, Kelli slid under the covers and took a minute to center herself.

"You're done for the day?" Kelli asked.

"Yes, I didn't want to leave without seeing you." Nora's voice was soft, concerned.

Kelli sighed. "I'm here, Nora, for the most part."

"I can't imagine what it's like being in your situation."

"Sometimes, I can't either. I don't even know where to begin with this one. Antony's been to rehab twice. He just lost it after Dad died. And he can't seem to pull it back together." Without thought, Kelli found herself yet again spilling her guts, and it felt as natural as breathing.

"I'm not sure what to say." Nora sounded uncertain. There was no hand-holding this time, and for now, Kelli was grateful for that. Tonight, she didn't need the extra zing that Nora's touch brought with it. Kelli wanted a minute when she wasn't so goddamned swamped by everything.

"You don't have to say anything."

Nora didn't. She just stood there, and Kelli found a moment of peace.

Kelli was groggy, but she wasn't deaf. Even if she wasn't a light sleeper, she'd be able to hear the ruckus going on at the foot of her bed. Did they really think they were whispering? Why would someone come in her room to argue? She wasn't up for this shit. Kelli was a step away from handing them their asses when she realized who *they* were. She opened her eyes slightly. The flickering light from the muted TV helped her to see Dr. Rader and the president of his fan club standing there. Kelli didn't have to strain to hear.

"You'd better be right about this," Dr. Fuller said with a hiss.

"I am. What are you worried about? Trust me. This will work, and you'll enjoy every minute of it."

Kelli hoped she wasn't hearing Rader as he tried to convince her to do some sort of nasty sex thing. She cringed. For some reason, her thoughts went to medical tools and equipment. Was it possible to wash her brain? It felt dirty.

"We can talk about it more later. Now isn't the time," Rader begged. "Let me check the nurse's final notation on her chart, and we can get out of here."

A few seconds later, he muttered, "Done. Let's go. Just remember nobody likes her anyway. Who's going to care?"

Kelli stayed still until they were gone. "What the actual fuck?" she whispered.

CHAPTER 9

Kelli exhaled noisily but could barely hear it over sound of the machines hooked to Travis. She closed her eyes, and hoped when she opened them, things would be different. Travis looked like he was trapped in some sort of torture device. It covered his chest and his neck and ended in a circle of metal around his head. The nurse called it a halo. It was a weird fucking name for a contraption that was drilled into his skull. He certainly didn't look like an angel. The equipment was supposed to keep him immobile and stop him from hurting himself.

Kelli imagined the pain was epic, and the medication kept him as numb as possible to the whole thing. Gerry wasn't a big guy. Still, she'd never seen him look so small. There was a thirty percent chance he would walk again. Thirty percent should have been good news, but the whole thing was a gamble as far as she was concerned. Travis could come out of it with nothing but a wheelchair strapped to his back.

Kelli didn't like the odds. She wanted to have faith, but it'd been too long since she'd faith in anything except herself. Unfortunately, this whole thing was beyond her control. She leaned on her crutches and moved closer. No one told her she couldn't touch him. Maybe it would give her a little hope. Something had to. She squeezed his arm at the elbow and tried to transmit a little of herself to him. He needed it, and she probably needed a little bit of him too.

There was a place in her chest that throbbed. Kelli rubbed at her breastbone. It didn't help because the pain was too deep. She took sedatives when she needed to calm the nightmares, but nothing could help reality. Her eyes wandered. His room was no different from hers. He had a lot more flowers and balloons than she did, but she always suspected that the assholes at SPD

Homicide liked him better. A few of the guys came to visit her, but she was sure the whole damn squad had been to see Gerry. Kelli almost smiled. She stared at a bouquet that still had the card sticking out. Kelli plucked it and read it out loud. She needed to hear something besides the machines.

"We know you'll be back soon giving us shit, and we can't wait."

Kelli didn't hold back her smile this time. The card made her think about what she had to look forward to. Two things came to mind—working with Travis again and Nora. It was funny. Here she was, wading through knee-high piles of shit, and the sight of that woman made her forget—at least for a while. Nora was getting under her skin.

She looked up when someone else entered the room, but it was just Sean.

"Hey," he whispered and lowered his head .

"Hey back." Kelli was glad to see him despite the tension between them.

"How is he?" Sean moved farther inside the room but away from her.

"The same. It helps though…to be here and know that he's in one piece."

"Yeah, I know the feeling. His father will be here tonight. Maybe that'll help…somehow." He paused. "Kelli, it's been two days, and you're leaving here on Wednesday."

"I know that." Kelli tried not to spit the words, but she didn't know if she succeeded.

"I know you're disappointed and mad at—"

"I'm not…I'm not mad. I get it. I just needed a minute to think."

"Mom knows something's not right between us."

"I know that, but we need to be able to sit her down and really get her to listen. Doesn't make sense to do it here. I wasn't kidding. She stood there while Tony went all Willy Wonka and blamed it on coffee. She's in big time denial."

Sean looked down at his shoes. "Maybe. I kinda was too. I mean, I thought I could fix it on my own and look where it got him. I just wanted to take some of the load off you. You know?" He sighed. "But I can't be you. I don't even know how you do it. Take on everybody's shit."

Hell, sometimes she didn't either. His words made it easier to understand his reasoning. "I get it. I do." Kelli needed him to move on to the real issue. "But…Tony." She shook her head. "It's hard not to be pissed at him, but what it all comes down to is he needs to know we're here fighting for him. I guess we need to plan another intervention…or something."

"Yeah, right."

Their eyes met.

"You sure we're okay?" Sean asked hesitantly.

Kelli walked toward him until they were close enough to touch. "The two of us, we have to hold things together. When I can't help, you have a lot to take on. You did the best you could with what you had."

His throat bobbed as he swallowed. "I just—"

"It's done, Sean." Kelli reached out and squeezed his arm just like she did with Travis. "We've got other shit to deal with."

When Nora arrived at the nurses' station, she heard snatches of conversation. The two nurses behind the desk had their backs to her.

"I heard she was coming out of Gagne's office. You think she was filing a complaint on Whitmore?"

"Where did you get that from? There are a million reasons she could have been there."

"Oh come on, look who we're talking about. Of course she went to go complain about something, and from what I heard, she whines about Whitmore on a daily basis."

"Well, yeah, but doesn't everybody? Name one person who doesn't think she's weird. I swear the woman has no human emotions."

"That's true. We could be completely wrong, though. Fuller says some nasty stuff about Rader too. The guy's a pervert. I don't blame her. He gives me the creeps, and have you seen the way he slobbers all over her? He needs to be reported."

The nurses laughed.

"Or maybe Dr. Gagne got a complaint about Fuller. You never know."

Nora tuned them out. The conversation was idle gossip, just like everything else concerning her. Taylor Fuller didn't have the audacity to report a lie to administration. There was no way.

Nora reached for a chart, and that's when she became aware of other hospital staff in the vicinity watching her. It was a tad disconcerting. The staring wasn't a new occurrence, but through Kelli, Nora had almost gotten used to being treated like a normal person.

Her pager vibrated. Nora fished it from her pocket and saw the number for the chief of surgery's office.

Nora glanced up at one of the nurses who was now facing her only to have her look away a second later. It was a bit irritating. "May I have the phone, please?"

The nurse blinked in response.

"The…phone. Please," Nora said slowly.

A second later, the nurse handed it to her.

She punched in the three-number extension and waited for the ring. "This is Dr. Whitmore for Dr. Gagne."

"She would like to see you," her personal assistant said pleasantly.

"I have a surgery sche—"

"Immediately, Dr. Whitmore." Her pleasant tone shifted and became firm.

"Yes, right away." Nora's stomach twisted in apprehension. Internally, she shuffled through several scenarios that might explain this impromptu and apparently urgent meeting but found none. Maybe the gossip wasn't as idle as she thought.

Nora placed the phone back on the counter and tried to brush all speculation aside. There was only one way to find out. Nora glanced up to find that she was being studied by the nurse behind the desk. Nora held her gaze until the woman took the phone and looked away. Nora stood at the nurses' station for a few more seconds to collect herself. No, she couldn't allow any of this to disrupt her day. She turned and made her way down the hall toward the elevator. Several seconds later, Nora pressed the down button and waited.

The elevator dinged and the doors released a metallic groan as they opened to the administrative floor. Nora stepped out and walked toward her destination. The hall was quiet, empty. There was something ominous about it. For a moment, her initial trepidation returned. Nora entered the office anyway.

"Go right in, Dr. Whitmore."

Even the personal assistant watched her as she strolled past. The door was open. Dr. Lisa Gagne sat behind her desk. She was leaning forward and talking with the two men sitting in the chairs in front of her. The conversation stopped as Nora entered.

"Good afternoon, Nora." Dr. Gagne smiled slightly. "Come on in and close the door." She spoke with a thick Southern accent.

Nora did as she was told. They stared at her. Nora gave them all a perfunctory nod.

"Have a seat, Nora."

The use of her first name set her on edge. Something was very wrong here. "I'd prefer to stand."

Dr. Gagne nodded. "Suit yourself." She turned to her visitors and pointed at the one with the garish lime-green tie. "This is one of the hospital's lawyers, Mr. Post, and this is—"

"Mr. Lane from Human Resources." Nora interrupted coolly.

"Would you like to sit down now, Nora?" Lisa asked.

"No, but I would like to be called Dr. Whitmore."

Gagne nodded. "Fair enough."

"Thank you." Nora responded. "Should I assume that a complaint of some type was filed against me?" She was tired of the subterfuge. It was time to see if the rumors were actually true.

Dr. Gagne leaned forward and rested her elbows on her desk. "Yes, but it goes a bit deeper than that I'm afraid. You're valued here, but the hospital must be protected at all costs."

Dazed, Nora asked, "Would you care to clarify?"

"There has been an accusation lodged against you regardin' sexual harassment of a female resident."

As Nora processed what she heard, she became lightheaded and her stomach roiled painfully. She didn't sit down but sank her fingers into the plush back of the closest chair. Even after what she'd overheard at the nurses' station, it was still the last thing she expected. "You must be joking." This had to be some elaborate attempt at a practical joke even though there was nothing remotely funny about it.

"Afraid not, Dr. Whitmore."

There was no need to ask who was responsible. "Taylor Fuller," Nora said it as a statement, not a question.

"Need I remind you that retaliation is extremely inappropriate and can lead to harsher measures?" Mr. Post asked.

"I'm aware." Nora nodded. Her movements felt stifled, almost disjointed.

"You are well within your rights to know about your accuser. You are correct, it's Dr. Fuller."

The fury that swept through Nora was acute, cloying, and aimed directly at the man no doubt responsible for this farce—James Rader. "This is ridiculous. How could you even entertain—"

Lisa interrupted. "Because we have to, no matter how much of a hindrance it is. You should think about hirin' an attorney. Things like this don't usually just go away. She's gonna come out guns blazin'. People always do in this type of situation."

Finally, Nora sank down into the chair. She focused on the firm pillows that still managed to provide the utmost comfort. It was an odd fixation, but necessary. She tensed her muscles and relaxed them in hopes it would help to alleviate the stress that was rapidly building inside her. Nora turned her thoughts to Kelli. She cycled through their interactions from amusing to intense. The memories provided warmth but offered little solace against this accusation.

"That's not all I'm afraid," Lisa added.

Nora looked up. What could possibly be worse than this? This hospital was her life, and her reputation provided the buffer to make each day more meaningful than the last. Without it, she felt instantly exposed and vulnerable.

"You're a great asset, Dr. Whitmore, but the board has agreed that you should take paid leave to protect yourself, as well as the hospital," Mr. Post said.

Nora's gaze swept toward him as he finished speaking. It landed on his tie. The color really was awful. His words crushed her. Nora willed herself to calm down, but her body refused to listen. Bile rose up her esophagus. It left a fetid taste in her mouth.

"You had a Whipple and a colon resection scheduled. They have already been reassigned, as have your patients." Dr. Gagne informed Nora.

Nora closed her eyes and turned away. Each word sank into her psyche and shredded her.

"Despite what's goin' on, you still have this hospital's respect. And mine. Leave under your own steam, but leave immediately. Can I trust you with that?" Dr. Gagne's voice softened.

"Yes." Nora swallowed down the acid in her throat and stood slowly. If it was Rader's and Taylor's plan to shatter her, for now, they'd succeeded.

Lisa nodded. "Take care, Dr. Whitmore."

Nora dipped her head in acknowledgement. The men were strangely quiet, but she figured that there was nothing else to say. When she re-entered the hallway, it was still eerily empty. Nora stepped into the elevator and checked her watch. It was well past one o'clock. Kelli would be wondering where she was. A lump formed in her throat and inched its way down into her stomach. Nora leaned heavily against the railing, which was the only thing holding her up. The thought of not seeing Kelli again left her bereft. It was irrational to feel that way, but then again this entire situation was beyond reason.

―――

Kelli checked the clock. The only thing that ever made Nora late was an emergency. She thought about Travis, and naturally feared the worst. Kelli sat up in bed and reached for the button to call a nurse.

"Is there something I can help you with Ms. McCabe?" Dr. Rader hovered in the door for a few seconds before walking in.

Kelli stared at him instead of answering. Nora didn't like him, but he would know where she was. Kelli decided to take a chance. "Nora's not here, and I wanted to check on Travis."

"He's resting comfortably."

Kelli relaxed a little. "Okay, good, but what about—"

Rader interrupted. "And Dr. Whitmore won't be here for the foreseeable future."

Her guts twisted and she actually got a chill. There was a glint in his eye, and Kelli saw the beginnings of a smug shit-eating grin. "What the fuck does that mean?"

"I'm not at liberty to say." His tone was teasing.

Son of a bitch. Kelli knew there was something rotten about him. She always could smell asshole a mile away. "You make my fucking skin crawl."

Rader's face reddened, but he still smiled. He looked even more douchey. "Well, I—"

"Shut up. I'm not done. Guys like you get what's coming to them. Remember that." Kelli growled and stared at him intently. He would be the first one to look away, dammit. Kelli wasn't disappointed.

Dr. Rader took a step back. "I'm not a nurse, Ms. McCabe—"

"No, you're a smug bastard who can get the fuck out of my room."

A muscle ticked in his jaw. "You can always request a different doctor if you are unsatisfied."

That was exactly what he wanted, she was sure, and she refused to give him the satisfaction. "I think it's a little late in the game for that. I'm outta here in a couple days. I think I'll stick with you." She bared her teeth in a pseudo-grin. After all, sometimes it was a really good idea to keep enemies close, especially the new, unpredictable ones.

Rader's expression hardened.

Kelli scoffed. "You can wipe that look off your face. You don't scare me."

He reddened even more.

"What are you waiting for? Get the fuck out."

Without another word, he did.

For a long time, she stared at the empty doorway, hoping Nora would breeze through it and prove him wrong. But it was past two o'clock. Obviously, she wasn't coming. This was complete bullshit, but the reality of the situation left her empty. More than that, though, Nora was in trouble. Kelli could feel it in her bones. She reached for the phone and dialed quickly. Kelli huffed with impatience when it rang for the fourth time.

Finally, he picked up. "Williams."

"I need you to get some information for me."

There was a noticeable pause before he responded. "McCabe? For a second, it sounded like you were on the job."

"Williams!" Kelli said in warning.

"Yeah, what do you need?"

"Address and phone number for Nora Whitmore."

CHAPTER 10

Nora woke unexpectedly. She blinked rapidly to give her eyes a chance to adjust to the morning light and looked around, bewildered. Within a few seconds, she realized she was in one of her guest rooms. Nora felt something heavy covering part of her torso. It was alarming to wake up with someone wrapped around her. She wasn't the cuddling type especially…no she just wasn't the cuddling type. Nora glanced down to see an arm draped across her stomach. Just like the person it belonged to, the limb was well formed and muscular. His chiseled good looks hinted at coiled strength and power, and he'd appeared more than capable of the challenge Nora had in mind when she'd brought him home last night. Unfortunately, he'd failed miserably.

Annoyed by his presence and his stilted performance the previous night, Nora brushed his arm aside, along with the possessiveness the embrace implied. She was stunned by her ability to sleep through the night with such an unwanted visitor. Nora glared at him. She couldn't remember his name, but decided quickly that it didn't matter.

Last night, she'd wanted to be decimated by the powerful, thrusting hips of someone secure enough to give orders and to take them. Nora needed to be quivering and broken in order to rebuild herself into someone stronger, someone completely resistant to the chaos creeping in through the freshly formed cracks of her armor. When he failed to deliver what she craved, Nora tried to take what she needed, but that hadn't worked either. She continued to stare at him as countless emotions assaulted her, ranging from anger to helplessness. Over the past couple of days, this barrage of feelings had become a normal occurrence, and Nora didn't know how to make it stop. So, she resorted to old habits, such as the man in her bed. It was easy…so very easy and yet quite dissatisfying.

The stranger blinked and opened his eyes. They were green, and she immediately thought of Kelli. Even that didn't improve matters. She wanted her mind blank, not filled with someone who could make the situation even more unbalanced. The man smiled, his lips curled upward in a way that probably made other women swoon.

"Nikki," he whispered.

"Please go," Nora said flatly.

His eyes widened, then softened. "You don't mean that."

"I do, and don't leave anything behind. There's no need for you to return."

He sat up and threw the covers away from his body. He smirked as he sat there fully exposed. Nora cringed at the sight.

"You're the one who's missing out, lady. I'm more potent in the morning."

"So you're acknowledging that was not the case last night?" Nora was unsure why she was wasting precious energy on him when she just wanted him to leave.

"I had too much wine!" His voice cracked.

"I'll call you a cab." Nora eased out of the bed, aware that his gaze followed her. He showed obvious signs of arousal. In keeping with her erratic emotional state, Nora changed her mind about his departure.

Slowly, she walked toward him and stopped barely an inch away. Nora refused to let Rader take everything, and pleasure was always her key to oblivion. She pulled him into a bruising kiss.

He moaned. Nora's thoughts jumbled and flashed on a different set of green eyes—Kelli's. Arousal slammed through her, and panic followed right behind it. She gasped at the feeling. She wrenched away and stepped back. Her heart raced, and her breathing was ragged. Nora took a few more steps back to compose herself. She needed to file these events away for later.

He glared. "Oh come on. I know you felt—"

She cut him off. "Don't forget your belongings."

His face reddened and his fists clenched. "Fucking bitch."

Nora studied him and thought of Rader, another man who thought he had the right to casually sling names and insults at her. Her insides heated for an entirely different reason—anger—but she refused to let the feeling over take her. It felt good to be in control of something. Nora turned and walked toward the door. Before leaving, she glanced over her shoulder and calmly informed him, "I'll call that cab now."

"Why the fuck do I always get the crazy ones?" he mumbled.

As she closed the door behind her, Nora heard every word but couldn't argue. Maybe he was right. She certainly felt a little crazy.

After he left, Nora sat on the couch and sipped her cooling cup of coffee. She swiped through the news stories on her tablet, but nothing grabbed her attention. She felt strange. Idleness did not suit her. She found it draining, and she hated her lack of energy. She stood and slowly paced in front of the sofa. There had to be a way to shake her emotions free, even for a short period of time.

Being alone had never been an issue, but the loneliness had become one. Something within her was missing. Nora wasn't sure if that had always been the case, or if it was a recent realization. Unintentionally, she thought of Kelli, and for the briefest of moments, that ache disappeared.

Nora sat back down and went to Google on her tablet. She typed in Kelli's name. The search returned several articles. Some had pictures, and Nora focused on those. She smiled. Kelli looked uncomfortable in the spotlight. Nora was amused by the pinched look on her face.

Kelli McCabe was a well-known and respected detective. Nora didn't find this shocking at all. From firsthand experience, she knew a sharp intellect and generous spirit existed behind Kelli's tactless exterior. She allowed recent memories to soothe her, but unless Nora pursued the nascent relationship forming between them, that comfort wouldn't last. Despite the bond forming between them, Nora dismissed the idea as sheer lunacy. She brushed the thought away and ignored the twinge of disappointment that followed. Kelli was not the solution.

Nora hit the home button on her tablet and lifted the coffee cup to her lips once more. Its contents were tepid and bitter. She finished it anyway. For a moment, she didn't feel lost, grounded in the routine of drinking coffee in the familiar setting of her home. The moment passed. Nora tried to single out and dissect her emotions. She didn't have the energy to go on like this. One moment she felt almost normal and then she was overwhelmed by a massive wave of anxiety. There was also anger. It seemed to always be there right underneath the surface. Regardless of Rader's attempts to ruin her, she knew who she was, or rather who she *used* to be. Nora had misplaced her confidence and self-assurance, substituting them with fear and listlessness. She was shaken, vulnerable, and needed to trace this mayhem back to its origins.

Without much thought, she knew what her first mistake was. She just didn't see the scope of the problem at the beginning, when her life was first thrust into disarray. Opening herself to Kelli was pivotal, and everything she experienced after was the inevitable fallout. Kelli's invasion wasn't greeted with open arms, and Nora had yet to understand how she got in far enough to wreak such havoc. None of this made sense, least of all the instant flash of arousal Nora experienced a few hours earlier that had Kelli as its epicenter. She was baffled by her reaction. Yes, Kelli was clearly attractive, but Nora didn't make a habit of objectifying her patients. The entire situation was just the result of all the turmoil around her. It had to be.

Nora turned her anger inward onto herself. In an attempt to hold back her emotions, she closed her hands into tight fists, as if preparing for a fight. Inadvertently, she dug her nails into her palms. Nora grimaced at the subsequent sting. The pain was preferable to the mess she found herself in. She glanced down and rubbed her thumb over the crescent marks left behind in her skin. The symbolism was not lost on her. Nora was responsible for her own agony, and Kelli was right in the middle of it. Her heart pounded against her chest. Then, she couldn't breathe. Why couldn't she breathe?

Rader, Kelli, and the suspension, Nora worried that she couldn't handle it all. She needed to dam herself up before she drowned. That thought alone set off alarms inside her. There was obviously some part of her that wanted this. She tried to ignore the internal blaring, but the sound grew louder. Nora stood. Finally, she was able to take some breaths. She shook her head to clear it, which helped a little.

Nora didn't recognize this rebellious portion of her psyche. There had been a few introductions as of late to hidden, buried pieces of herself, and she had eventually accepted them with ease. However, this opposition wasn't welcome at all. There was a chance dangling right in front of her, a possibility to return to her natural…no, her previous state of existence, and a huge part of her resisted the carrot.

Again, Nora closed her hand into a fist. This time, she ignored the discomfort. Nora was stronger than this. She was. She had to be. Otherwise, these constantly exposed weaknesses would be her downfall.

Kelli held her breath as Travis's eyes fluttered and opened. They were bloodshot and unfocused. She moved closer. There were other concerned people in the room, but Kelli wanted to be the first person he saw. It was a selfish act, sure, but that didn't matter.

Gerry groaned.

"Son?" Gerald Travis Sr. towered over Kelli's shoulder. He was a hulk of a man, but his voice cracked with worry.

Travis blinked, and his gaze met Kelli's. "Hey."

She felt so damn relieved she almost laughed. That probably wouldn't have gone over well. "Morning," she whispered instead. Kelli sensed someone coming up behind her. She turned slightly as Sean clapped her on the back. They grinned at each other.

"Did I…did I hear my dad?" Travis asked.

"Yeah, you did." Kelli shuffled to the side.

Gerald Sr. cleared his throat and took Travis's hand. "I'm here."

Kelli had met Travis's father before, but this was the first time that she saw him touch his son. Too bad it took something like paralysis for him to reach out to his kid. Good thing Gerry had a back-up family. Kelli swallowed the lump rising in her throat.

"Did it work?" Travis's voice was small but hopeful.

Gerald Sr. hesitated for a moment and then looked at Kelli.

"Won't know until the swelling goes down," Kelli said.

As he smiled, his eyes shining, Travis's father nodded.

Travis, himself, grimaced and exhaled shakily. "I'm so tired of this."

Kelli felt tears prickle her eyes. She tried to breathe through them. Angry with herself, Kelli stepped back and turned away to compose herself. He needed her to be positive. She had to keep it together. She didn't have the time to fall the hell apart.

"I'm sure you are, but we're here." Sean stepped forward.

"I know," Travis murmured. "What the hell is this thing they have me in?"

"The nurse said it was called a halo." Kelli told him.

"Well…it doesn't make me feel…angelic."

Kelli almost laughed. She thought the same thing not too long ago after seeing him strapped in for the first time. It was amazing how much they were in sync at times. His eyes drooped slowly. Then, his breathing evened out. Kelli didn't blame him. She was fucking exhausted, and she wasn't the one who had surgery.

Kelli leaned heavily on her new cane and watched Travis while he slept. Sean nudged her. "Mom just texted. She'll be here in a few minutes to talk to the doctor."

Kelli nodded. She didn't like that her freedom from this hospital came with discharge instructions, but she was just glad to be leaving. The fact that Travis was awake and in good hands was a bonus.

"She wanted to take the day off, but…you know how she is," Sean said.

"Yeah, I know. Let's go then." Kelli completed one mission and tried to mentally ready herself for the several more that waited for her. She paused in the doorway and turned. Right now her faith in herself was shaky, but Kelli had plenty in Gerry Travis Jr.

<hr>

Her mother was already there, rummaging through the empty drawers, when Kelli walked into her room.

"Mom, I got everything." She pointed to the duffle bag on the bed.

"I was just checking; you never know. Antony wanted to come, but he called. He's doing a double at work."

Kelli glanced at her brother. They communicated silently. It was one of his favorite lies, and they both knew it. "Yeah, okay."

Their mother smiled. "You look good for somebody who had two bullets in 'em."

Kelli snorted.

"Good morning, McCabes. I'm sure our detective is ready to get out of here."

Kelli glared at Dr. Rader as he entered the room. "Just save it and give me whatever I need to sign." What a fucking asshole. She was dying to rip him another one.

"Kelli!" Carina exclaimed. "Where are your manners? This man took good care of you."

Kelli glanced at her mother. "Sure he did." She turned her attention back to Dr. Rader, but he refused to meet her gaze. This made Kelli smile. "Prick," she mumbled under her breath.

"It's okay, Mrs. McCabe. She's a handful, but we're glad she's healthy again." Rader grinned.

Kelli controlled the urge to smack him with her cane…just barely. She imagined it instead, and the images in her head were so very satisfying.

Dr. Rader smirked, which added to his sliminess. "I'm sure Nora would have been here…if she could."

Kelli smiled. She made sure it was wide and showed all her teeth. He was sticking his face in shark-infested waters, and if he kept pushing, Kelli didn't have a problem biting his head clean off.

Dr. Rader's eyes widened, and he looked away.

"Where is Dr. Whitmore anyway?" Sean glanced around the room as if he thought maybe he'd missed her somehow.

"Who?" Carina looked thoughtful for a second. "Is that the weird, pretty one?"

Kelli continued to smile. It was a real one this time. "Yes, that would be her, but don't call her weird."

"I like her," Sean said.

"Me too," Kelli glared at Dr. Rader. He was looking down at his shoes.

Rader cleared his throat. "Well, Ms. McCabe you will need to continue the physical therapy and check in with me once more on an outpatient basis before returning to your regular doctor."

"Lovely," Kelli added.

Her mother sighed. "I'm sorry, doctor. Trust me, I didn't raise her to be like this. Can you also tell her that it would be better if she stayed with me until she can get around without the cane?"

"Mom! You got me the cane. Let me use it. I'll be fine at my own place." Kelli stared at Rader, daring him to disagree. If he did, there would be no holding back. She was definitely going to give him a nice swat with her cane. This fucker deserved it.

He licked his lips and swallowed audibly. "She's ambulatory. She should be fine," Dr. Rader said hastily.

Kelli bared her teeth at him. "See, Mom. Told you."

"Fine, fine, but I'm coming over after work. I'm sure you need groceries…"

"All right." Kelli conceded because her mother would show up anyway.

"Yes, well, a nurse should be in momentarily with discharge papers and further instructions." Dr. Rader made his exit.

Carina stared at Kelli. "What is wrong with you? First you terrorize the nurses and now you're on to doctors?"

Kelli rolled her eyes and waved her hand brushing the complaint away. "He deserves it. Guy's a douche. I've got evidence now."

"Was this Dr. Whitmore the only one you were nice to?"

Kelli shrugged. "Probably."

Sean chuckled. "Only because she's hot."

"It was not! There were some hot nurses too. I—" Kelli started to defend herself.

Carina threw her hands in the air. "Whatever! I'm just glad they can't sue you. I've got to get to work." She pulled Kelli into a hug before she could protest. "I'll see you tonight."

"Yeah, yeah."

As her mother left, a nurse arrived with a wheelchair and a clipboard.

"No…no. I'm not getting in one of those things. I'm in real clothes for the first time in weeks, and I'm gonna walk out of here," Kelli grumbled.

The nurse opened her mouth no doubt to fight with her. Instead, she thrust the clipboard in Kelli's direction. "Sign by the Xs, and I mean this, we are glad to see you go." Her smile was genuine.

Sean laughed.

Kelli glared. "Fine, whatever."

The sun was too bright. Kelli shielded her eyes and tried to adjust. She shifted back under the awning and waited for Sean to pick her up. There were a few low-hanging clouds but not many. Strange. It was April in Seattle. It should be pissing rain; instead there was a sky full of sunshine. Kelli inhaled the fresh air. It was humid but she welcomed the feeling, because it was real compared to the smell and feel of the hospital. She was free from that place, but she couldn't do what she wanted. Between the damn cane and her concerns about Tony and Nora, she couldn't enjoy her parole. She was too worried. Antony was clearly getting high and doing who knew what else. And she had no fucking clue what was up with Nora, but whatever it was made Dr. Rader disgustingly happy. She couldn't think clearly. There was too much coming at her, even though she tried to keep things separate. As soon as she started focusing on one fucked-up situation, the other needed her attention. Fucked-up shit all the way around.

The past couple of days, Kelli picked up the phone at least a hundred times to call Nora, but never had the balls to dial the number. Besides, a phone call wasn't enough. Kelli had to see her. Nothing else would do. This pull she felt toward Nora was weird as hell, but it worked. Why question it?

Sean pulled his cruiser in front of her. He jogged around and opened the passenger side door. Kelli stumbled slightly as she folded herself into the car. "Dammit."

"You okay?" Sean asked.

"I'm fine. Let's go."

"Okay. Do you need me to stop anywhere before I take you home?"

"Yeah." Kelli fished the folded paper out of her pocket and read off the address to one of the swankier parts of the city.

Sean whistled. "That's on West Mercer Island."

"I know." Kelli pushed away her nervousness. Nora might slam the door in her face. She was crossing a shit ton of boundaries with this visit. Kelli changed the subject. She needed to, even though the new topic was just as shitty. "Have you seen Antony?"

Sean sighed. "No, he's been laying low the past couple days. Maybe he knows that he fucked things up coming to the hospital high as a kite."

"Maybe. I just hope he doesn't disappear on us." Kelli did all she could for Travis at the moment, so Antony stayed at the top of her list. Then, there was Nora. "We need to talk to Mom as soon as possible before shit comes crashing in on us."

"I agree, but I don't think he's just using. He's making money somehow," Sean said.

"You think he's in bed with a dealer?" Kelli dreaded the answer.

"Nothing would surprise me at this point. I'll check his hangouts to make sure he's okay."

"It makes sense. You're probably right." Kelli sighed. And the shit just kept on coming.

The radio crackled. Kelli missed that sound. When she heard it, it meant she had a chance of helping someone. These days, she wasn't doing much of anything. Kelli looked out the window at Lake Washington as they crossed Murrow Memorial Bridge. There were boats all over the lake. She could barely see the water.

"So, who are you going to see?" Sean asked.

"Nora." Kelli stared straight ahead and hoped her brother would let it go without giving her crap about it.

"Dr. Whitmore?" Sean glanced at her. "Why would you…ohhhh." He smirked.

"It's not like that." Kelli pushed her attraction to Nora to the side. "She's in trouble. I don't know what's going on, but I know she is."

"Okay, so? Why would you care?"

"Because…she did. She cared…cares. About me." Kelli had no idea what was going to happen, and that messed with her head a little. If this was the end of…whatever, maybe she would at least be able to say goodbye. Kelli didn't like that option. It didn't feel right. Too much had happened between them to just let it go.

They stopped at a red light. Sean looked confused.

"Just drive." Kelli sighed.

"Does she know you're coming?"

"No."

"You're kidding?"

"No." Kelli's voice went up an octave.

"Are you crazy?"

Kelli glared.

"So, what? I'm just supposed to wait in the car?"

"Yes," Kelli said.

"Guess it's a good thing. She might think you're stalking her."

"Would you please just shut up?"

"What? What did I say?" Sean grinned.

Kelli stared at him, but she was glad he was able to find humor in this…able to smile. She was glad somebody could because Kelli didn't find it funny at all.

※

"Goddamn," Sean mumbled as the turned into Nora's neighborhood. "It's like we drove onto a movie set. Everything's all shiny and shit. I bet there's no pot holes around here." Sean shook his head. "I shoulda been a doctor."

"Mmm, no shit," Kelli said in agreement. She rubbed her suddenly sweaty, damp hands on her jeans. Obviously, Nora was from a completely different world than her. Her nervousness went up a notch, but she refused to let it hold her back. The connection they shared wasn't about the way Nora lived or how much money she had. They were just two people who happened to find each other. Simple as pie.

Silently, she peered out the window at the perfectly groomed lawns and houses that ranged in size from small to "holy shit you're kidding." Sean slowed and pulled into the driveway. She hoped Nora's car was in the garage. Otherwise this trip was for nothing.

"Okay, this is it. You sure about this? I feel kinda low rent." Sean glanced at her, eyes were wide. Clearly, he was uncomfortable with the situation.

Kelli nodded. "We're in a police cruiser. It should be fine."

"Yeah, didn't think about that. You need some help getting out?"

"I'll be fine." Slowly, she got out of the car and looked around. Nora's lawn was as well kept as the others. Her hedges were trimmed into cubes and oblong shapes, and the flower beds looked like Crayola had thrown up on them. The house itself was moderate in size, and there was really nothing to make it stand out compared to all the other white houses around them.

Her leg started to throb, but she could take it for now. Kelli limped up the walkway. She felt tingly as she got closer to the door. It had been days since she'd seen Nora, and time had gone by way too fucking slowly. She stared at the doorbell and listened. The house seemed quiet. She couldn't hear a damn thing. Kelli hit the button anyway and the chime echoed through the house. Minutes passed, but Nora didn't answer. Disappointed, Kelli turned and glanced at Sean. He shrugged in return.

Then, Kelli heard a soft *snick-click* of the lock, and the door opened. Nora stood there, dressed in dark slacks and a cream-colored shirt. Kelli's heart pounded so loud she could have sworn there was a drum circle in her head.

"What are you doing here?" Nora's tone was cold, crisp. Her face was red and her eyes were huge. She didn't look happy at all. A few seconds later, she was unreadable.

Well, fuck. What did she expect? Kelli licked her lips and said, "Hey."

Nora blinked. "How did you—"

"I'm a cop, Nora."

"Yes, well." Nora cleared her throat and looked away. When she glanced back again, her eyes and voice were even colder than before. At least the blank expression was gone. "That doesn't explain why you're here."

The way Nora looked at her definitely left Kelli feeling a little chilly. She didn't know what to say so she went with the first thing to pop in her head. "Because."

"Because? This is highly inappropriate. Not to mention, I never extended an invitation."

Kelli leaned on her cane. The pain was getting worse, but she needed to figure out what the hell was going on. "Look, I know this is a shock, but everything you just said was bullshit."

Nora gasped. "Excuse me?"

"You heard me." Kelli held Nora's gaze. She was damn well going to get through to her.

"I think you should leave." Nora looked mad as hell. Her face was red again and her lips were all mushed together. Nora glared, and if she were able to shoot lasers with her eyes, Kelli would be all kinds of melted. And not in a good way.

Kelli didn't understand this at all. "Why are you angry at me? It can't just be about me showing up here."

"Why are you here?" Nora refused to give.

"Because I saw Rader."

Nora shrank back. "He had no right to tell you anything."

"He didn't." Kelli started to sweat, and her fucking leg screamed at her to sit her ass down. "I get that you're angry, but can you yell at me inside? My leg is killing me. I need to stretch out."

Nora continued to stare, but her face softened. Finally, she stepped away from the door. Kelli hobbled inside. Making it to the sectional was her priority. She ignored everything else. She'd worry about the penny tour later.

Kelli sat down and rubbed at her thigh. Nora paced the floor. She crossed her arms in front of her chest as if she was trying to hold something in or maybe keep it out.

"He didn't tell me anything, Nora. He was gloating. Fucking rat bastard. That's how I knew he had to be involved. And I had to be here. Okay?"

Nora stopped and turned. She relaxed her shoulders and let her arms fall to the side. But, her eyes looked haunted.

"Why?" Nora's voice was thick with emotion.

"Because I know you don't have anybody else." Kelli wanted to say that she was there because Nora was important to her, and even if she had a thousand people to help her through whatever was going on, Kelli would still be here for her. Unfortunately something completely different came out.

"I don't need your pity. You don't know me!"

Clearly, Kelli said it the wrong way, and now Nora's walls went back up, stronger than ever.

Nora started to pace again. Despite the pain in her thigh, Kelli reached out and grabbed Nora's arm. Nora spun around. She stared at Kelli's hand before wrenching away from it.

Kelli stood then. This time, she grasped Nora by the shoulders and shook her. "I wanna know you! I thought we established that. Don't you get it?"

Nora stared at her. Kelli couldn't look away.

Kelli had no idea why she was fighting so hard to hold onto Nora, but her gut told her that coming here was the right thing to do. "Nora, I…missed you."

Nora started to tremble, and the sob that followed caught Kelli by surprise. As if she had done it a million times, she pulled Nora into a full body hug. Nora clung to her as she cried. Kelli held on tighter.

Tears dampened her neck, but Kelli ignored it. The pain in her leg forced her back onto the couch. Kelli sat down gracelessly and pulled Nora with her. She pressed her lips into Nora's hair and whispered what she hoped were words of comfort.

Long minutes later, Nora slowly pulled back. She wiped at her eyes and looked away. Kelli wasn't ready to put distance between them. She took Nora's hand and squeezed lightly. "Don't be embarrassed. It's just me."

"Kelli," Nora whispered.

Warmth filled Kelli's chest and trickled everywhere else. Kelli glommed onto that feeling. She let it push her. "Talk to me."

"I…I don't know where to start."

Kelli shrugged. "Wherever you want to."

"Isn't your ride…"

"Oh." Kelli had completely forgotten about Sean. She should call him, but her cell phone had been shot at and smashed all to hell along with Kelli. "Can I use your phone?"

Nora nodded and reached for the cordless on the table.

Kelli realized she hadn't let go of Nora's hand. And she didn't plan to any time soon either. Sean's phone rang.

"McCabe."

"It's me."

"Forget about me?" Sean asked.

"Kinda."

"Uh-huh." He sounded amused.

Kelli ignored his tone. "I'm gonna get a cab or something later."

"Or she could just take you."

"Hanging up now, Sean."

Kelli hit the end button and placed the phone between them. "Now, tell me."

Nora hesitated at first, but once she started, the words just kept coming.

Kelli went from disbelief to fury and then back again. She bit the inside of her cheek to keep from interrupting. Finally, Nora stopped speaking.

"I'm never wrong. I knew there was something shitty about that guy. Two million dollars for pain and suffering, my ass. Where did she get that figure? And what the hell is hindrance of the educational process?"

"Because of my sexual advances, I isolated her from the overall learning environment at the hospital," Nora said sarcastically. "Her lawyer works quickly. I was served two days after my suspension, but my attorney was able to arrange the deposition already to keep them from dragging this on."

"When does it start?"

"This Friday."

"I'm coming with you," Kelli said firmly.

Nora leaned back, distancing herself. "Kelli. I don't think—"

"I'm going. I'll be good." She didn't let Nora's gesture bother her. Nora might not admit it but she needed Kelli. She recognized self-preservation when she saw it.

Nora gave her a knowing look. Kelli couldn't help but grin at that. This woman was getting to know her pretty well.

"Promise." Kelli wanted to nudge Nora with her shoulder, tease her a little, but Nora didn't look like she was up for any more physical contact.

Nora sighed, but she curled her lips in a slight smile.

Despite everything that she learned the past week about Tony, Travis, and now this, Kelli was hopeful. She accomplished something today, so that was a start.

"So, do I get to meet this pig?"

"Kunekune."

"Phineas," Kelli said with her most charming smile.

Nora smiled wider.

That feeling in her stomach was back. She was starting to like the shit out of it.

CHAPTER 11

Kelli sat up in bed, and the covers pooled around her waist. The cool air felt good against her skin. She was sweating like she had been chasing a perp, and her heart thudded in her chest. Kelli wiped a trembling hand over her face and tried to forget the images of her nightmare. It didn't help, but eventually she had to get used to it. Kelli threw the blankets to the side and scooted to the edge of the bed. She flexed the large muscle groups in her legs and winced as she studied the raised red scar. It was lovely…just fucking lovely.

Kelli leaned forward and pushed a hand through her damp hair. She groaned tiredly as she took stock of her body. Everything hurt in one form or another, and Kelli knew it had more to do with stress than the actual trauma her body had been through. Her shoulders hurt the most. Understandable since they carried the heaviest weight. Her own demons perched their asses there, along with the ones circling her family and Travis. And Nora. Kelli wondered how much she could hold safely before she cracked under the pressure. She dismissed the thought. She would take on whatever was needed as long as there was room. It's what she did.

Slowly, she worked out the kinks in her neck. Kelli looked around her bedroom, hoping it would relax her further. It looked just as it always had—masculine and earthy, decorated in dark browns, black and green. Her walls were empty except for the mounted flat screen. The night stand held a digital clock and a lamp that matched the overall décor. The room was kind of bare except for the bed. She didn't have a lot of pillows, but the ones she owned were the most comfortable ones Kelli could find. The fluffy down comforter and the sheets were a luxury she had actually splurged on. This bed was her sanctuary. She worked here if she needed to and at other times it was her refuge for whatever crappy thing she needed a break from. On any given night, this room had everything she needed—a game, beer, and on occasion, a woman. It was easier that way. After trying the relationship *thing* a couple of times, Kelli learned that some women wanted a level of devotion she didn't think she was capable of.

The job came first.

Kelli glanced at the clock. It was two and a half hours until the deposition. She wanted to be early because Nora was avoiding her. All her phone calls went unanswered. Kelli wasn't happy, but she understood it. Nora had fallen apart in her arms, and she knew that Nora liked to play it cool. Kelli was honored to be there to help, but she remembered when the shoe was on the other foot. Kelli had been embarrassed and very cautious after the whole thing. It wasn't a good feeling.

Kelli refused to take Nora's lack of contact as a message to leave her the fuck alone. Kelli knew better. She needed to be there, but most of all, Kelli wanted to be there even if Nora was being stubborn about the whole thing. There were times, like their last meeting, when Nora's actions and her words didn't match.

Kelli swallowed and released a long breath as she remembered the softness and the heat of Nora's body, and the way Nora fit perfectly against her. Kelli felt a familiar tug at her stomach. Her feelings for Nora were growing despite all the shit going on around her. Kelli had to remind herself that this wasn't the time or the place to focus on the attraction she was feeling. She pushed the notion aside. Kelli got out of bed, pulled the ratty tank top over her head, and threw it on the floor. She yawned, stretched, and pushed boxers down her legs to the floor next to her T-shirt. Naked, Kelli headed for the bathroom.

Droplets of soothing, hot water rained on her from above. Nora lifted her head toward the spray. She wanted the shower to do far more than cleanse her of dying epithelial cells. She hoped to rid herself of the weariness. The final suds washed down her body and into the drain. Unfortunately, all she felt was clean.

Despite her intention to put herself back on even footing, nothing had changed. Hurricane Kelli came in and swept her up yet again. How dare she?

Better yet, how…why did it keep happening? Instead of detaching herself from Kelli, Nora opened up even more, letting Kelli into places no one had ever been. The whole thing left her drained and overstimulated. Each tantalizing interaction peeled back new layers of herself. After their last meeting, her very core was starting to bleed through. In truth, Nora was terrified to learn what lay at the heart of her. Where had all this warmth come from? And she had never needed anyone. She liked being alone. Now she wanted more, and Nora wasn't prepared to feel, to need, or to want. She wasn't prepared for any of it. Nora leaned heavily against the heated shower wall and closed her eyes.

Her emotions were in disarray, which only added to the turmoil she was already facing. Nora didn't sleep much, and when she did, she experienced nightmares. They were always the same. She was drowning, slowly, and when she took her last breath, she'd wake up gasping. Sheer resolve kept Nora from picking up the phone to call Kelli—the person who put her in dangerous waters in the first place—and beg her to pull her free.

Despite the heat of the shower, Nora shivered. She couldn't hide in here forever. As soon as she stepped out, life would still be there waiting for her. It didn't matter if she answered Kelli's calls or not. She would be at the deposition. Kelli promised, and Nora saw the conviction in her eyes. She opened the stall door and stepped out of her makeshift cocoon.

She wrapped herself in a bath sheet, but water still dripped on the floor as she walked toward the sink. Nora wiped away the condensation from the mirror. She blinked, not liking the vulnerability reflected back at her. The dark circles beneath her eyes looked like bruises. Exhaustion and stress creased her forehead and caused lines around her mouth. Nora found the sight disturbing, as was the burning ache in her chest. No matter how hard she fought against the forces bombarding her, she ended up losing the battle. She had no choice except to try and hold on to what remained of the woman she knew. The only problem was she had no idea how to avoid the strengthening connection with Kelli.

Nora attempted to refocus her thoughts to the deposition, which threatened everything she knew, but for Nora, it was a more manageable situation. Drs. Rader and Fuller proved their ability to hurt her with their lies and thinking about them sparked a deep-seated anger inside her. They could taint her career, but Nora was sure that she would recover eventually. Kelli was a threat in a class all her own.

Kelli leaned heavily on her cane and waited patiently in reception at Thomas, Young, and Associates. The receptionist smiled in greeting as she hung up the phone.

"How can I help you?"

"I'm here for the Whitmore deposition."

"Name?" She peered at her computer.

"Kelli McCabe. You won't find my name on the list. I'm here for moral support," Kelli glanced at the receptionist's name plate: "Judy."

Judy blinked, and her brow furrowed.

Kelli smiled. "I know I can't talk to her lawyer or sit in on any meetings. I just want to wait in your lounge. It's important she knows I'm here. If I could get some coffee and the paper, it'll be like I'm invisible." She deepened her grin. A little flirting never hurt.

Judy sighed. "Okay, I suppose that's benign enough. How do you take your coffee?"

All right then. Score. "I was kinda kidding about the coffee, but if you're game, I am too. Black with two sugars. Can you point me toward your waiting area?"

"Sure. It's through those big double-glass doors in front of you. It's well stocked."

"Great. When Nora gets here, will you let her know where I am?"

"Well, you're not asking for much, are you, Ms. McCabe?"

Kelli chuckled. "Message received."

Kelli grabbed a copy of *The New York Times* and eased into a seat. She checked out the espresso maker and array of breads and fruits, but decided to leave it all for the paying customers. The lounge looked like it had been decorated by a cyborg or something. Everything was black, white, and gray except two oversized red vases that were big enough for Kelli to climb inside of.

As the minutes ticked by, she glanced again at the expensive-ass coffeemaker and wrinkled her nose. She didn't like to chew her coffee or go through froth to get to it. She glanced up as the door swung open.

Judy grinned and handed Kelli a Styrofoam cup filled to the brim. Her fingers brushed against Kelli's hand. "You'll be glad you waited. I make great coffee."

Obviously, the flirting hit its mark. Kelli pulled her hand away. She cleared her throat and uttered a simple "Thank you."

Judy's smile dimmed a bit. "I'll be sure to let Ms. Whitmore know that you're here." At least she kept on being nice.

Kelli nodded.

Alone again, Kelli jumped slightly when her phone vibrated in her pocket. She fished it out and read the texts.

I think Tony's about to run 4 it. Found him at one of his girls' places. He's been camped out there the past 2 days. Lots of traffic in and out btw. Somebody is planning something. Gotta get things goin tonite. Might have 2 be creative 2 get him out.

Kelli leaned forward. The weight on her shoulders seemed to physically increase, and shit was just getting started. She sighed and typed out her reply.

Yeah we waited long enough. I'll make a couple of calls and get something lined up.

Sean responded almost immediately.

Ok keep in touch.

Kelli lifted the cup to her lips and took a small sip. Tony, Travis, Rader, and Fuller…she was tending to a big pile of shit that was just getting nastier by the minute. Just the thought of it all left her hollow. She swallowed down more coffee to fill the hole.

Kelli moved to a seat on the other side of the lounge. There was plenty of room. The other chair gave her the perfect view of the lobby. At least that damned part was easy. As she sat down, the door swished open and Nora walked in. Kelli smiled even though Nora didn't.

"Hey," Kelli greeted her.

"Kelli." Nora's tone was freeze-Kelli's-ass-off cold. It went perfectly with her grey pencil skirt and snow-white blouse. Nora looked like a librarian…a very hot one.

Kelli forgot to breathe for a second. She was still getting used to Nora saying her name. It didn't matter how she said it. "You knew I'd be here."

"I did." Nora nodded.

Kelli held Nora's gaze and added, "You were tempted to just leave me sitting here."

Something shifted in the Nora's eyes. "I was."

"But you didn't."

"No…I didn't."

This was turning out to be just peachy.

"I'm here because I wanna be, Nora. There's no ulterior motive. I don't want anything from you."

"Yes, you do."

A man cleared his throat.

Kelli forgot they weren't alone.

They stared at each other.

Nora turned and left the lounge. Kelli followed Nora to an empty conference room. Now that they had privacy, she didn't waste any time. "Is that why you didn't answer any of my calls? You think I want something from you?"

"You said—" Nora started.

"I said I wanted to be your friend." Kelli finished for her.

Nora looked so prim and proper sitting there, back straight, hands on the table. Kelli knew better. There was something behind the hoity-toity thing Nora had going on. Kelli had seen it, felt it.

"Yes…that's something I don't think I can do. I'm not equipped for this."

Kelli stepped forward. "You coulda fooled me."

Nora's eyes widened. Her face flushed. "What do you mean?"

"Do you think that asshole Rader would have done what you've done for me?"

"Well, no," Nora answered.

"Damn straight. Why did you do it?"

"I'm not sure. It…felt—"

"Yeah, I know. You saw me at my worst, Nora. And you came back. You weren't my doctor. You didn't have to, but I'm glad you did. I wanted you to." Kelli took a deep breath. Her heart was racing, and she was trying like hell to catch up to it.

Nora's expression softened. "May I finish a statement before this conversation is over?"

Kelli smirked. "Yeah, sure. Sorry."

Several seconds passed as she waited for Nora to speak, but Kelli didn't mind. She was happy just to look at her.

"I'm not sure what to say. I have no idea what I'm doing with you…or anything else, for that matter."

Kelli sat down on the opposite side of the table and fought the urge to touch Nora. Kelli would do anything to make that lost look on Nora's face go away.

"Just remember that I'm not the enemy. You don't have to fight me so hard. Save it for Rader and his tag-along twat—"

"Kelli."

Nora didn't really sound upset, but Kelli decided to humor her.

"Bitch." She held out her hands placatingly. "I meant bitch."

Nora sighed.

Kelli continued to stare at her. She couldn't look away.

Nora dropped her gaze. "My hesitation and lack of experience with all of this must be tiring for you."

"You mean, why aren't I screaming and running the other way?"

Nora nodded.

"First of all, I can't run." Kelli gestured toward her leg.

Nora smiled slightly.

"Second, no, I'm not tired," Kelli said softly.

Nora's eyes widened, and Kelli noticed a distinct hitch in her breathing. It was a full minute before she responded. "You will be."

Nora spoke with confidence so Kelli took the statement as a challenge. "No, I won't."

Nora turned red and looked away.

There it was again—that urge to touch. It made Kelli's palms itch.

"I can't make you any promises about this…about us, but I'll try this…friendship," Nora said.

The door to the office opened. A tall man with white hair peeked in. "It's time."

Nora stood gracefully. "Thank you, Tom."

Kelli smiled. "They're full of shit. You're gonna beat this."

Nora nodded.

When the door closed, Kelli felt like she could breathe again. The more Nora pulled away, the harder Kelli pushed. It was worth it. She didn't mind putting in the extra work. Kelli had a feeling that it would pay off big time.

Nora walked beside her attorney. She listened as he talked.

"Remember, this is the first of what will likely be many depositions. Her lawyer will try to rattle you almost immediately just to see if she can."

"I understand." She tried to clear her head, but it was useless. Regardless of what she was about to walk into, she couldn't stop thinking about Kelli. Nora was torn more than ever. The constant push and pull that battled inside her throughout the whole "Kelli situation" was exhausting, but apparently, she wasn't tired enough to make a decision and stay with it.

"I'm only allowing an hour with this first meeting, so it shouldn't be too invasive. In the future, you don't have to attend a deposition if you're not testifying. The entire proceeding will be digitally recorded so I can go through the footage with you, as needed."

Nora didn't comment. As far as she was concerned, this whole thing was a disaster. Tom grasped her elbow. She pulled away, uncomfortable with being touched.

"Sorry, but you're passing the conference room."

As she stopped, Nora made an effort to concentrate on the matter at hand. She entered and sat quietly. Nora studied the woman across from her and assumed she was the opposing lawyer. She appeared to be in her mid-fifties and was attractive in a cosmetically enhanced way. Her smile was too perfect not to be veneers. It really was tragic what women did to themselves to keep from aging. There was probably a minute scar underneath the woman's chin and one hidden in her hair line. Nora fought the urge to ask about them and expose the lawyer's secrets. It seemed only fair, given what she was about to do to Nora.

"Ms. Whitmore. I'm Angela Perkins."

Instantly perturbed by the common use of her name, Nora corrected her. "Dr. Whitmore."

"Pardon?" The lawyer's smile faltered.

"I would prefer to be addressed as Dr. Whitmore."

Angela cleared her throat. "I see. Let's get started then. We are now on the record."

They all stated their names for the record, and Nora was sworn in.

Nora placed her hands in her lap and waited.

"You do understand, Dr. Whitmore, why you're here today?"

"Yes."

"You barter surgeries for sex."

Nora stared back unblinkingly. "That is incorr—"

"Would you care to rephrase, Ms. Perkins?" Tom asked.

"Fine. You are being sued for perpetuating a hostile workplace as well as sexual harassment. To clarify, you are here for soliciting sexual favors from a subordinate. Is that correct?"

"No, it's not correct. I've done nothing wrong despite Dr. Fuller's claims."

"They all say that, but let's move on. How many sexual relationships have you engaged in with residents since you've worked at Seattle Memorial?"

"Seven." Nora answered without hesitation.

Angela paused. "Uh, both male and female?"

"Five male, two female."

"And you would like us to believe that they were all consensual?"

"They were," Nora said.

"How many since you became an attending?"

"One."

"So, you've only had sex once since you became an attending?" The lawyer scoffed.

"No, I thought it prudent to exclusively seek partners outside the hospital."

"Why is that?"

"I wanted to prevent the appearance of impropriety," Nora said.

"I really don't think you succeeded with that one."

"Ms. Perkins. We will end this now if you continue along these lines." Tom tapped his fingers on the table with succinct precision, as if to punctuate his statement.

Nora turned to her lawyer. "I know what she's referring to. I think it's important that I address it."

"Are you sure, Nora?"

"Yes."

"Ms. Perkins, if you would care to repeat?" Tom said.

Angela nodded. "Do you think you managed the impropriety?"

"No. He, Dr. James Rader, had a difficult time accepting the end of our sexual involvement, but he has since moved on with your client."

The lawyer smiled. "You sound bitter. Is that why you went after her? To get back at him?"

"I am in no way interested in Dr. Fuller sexually."

"But you are interested?"

Nora waited for clarification.

"My client details incidents where you humiliated her in front of colleagues and patients."

"I've treated her no differently than I do the other residents when their performance and work ethic are subpar."

"Dr. Whitmore, I have a detailed list of eight different incidents when you humiliated her, culminating with your demand for sex in exchange for the opportunity to assist you during surgery."

The lawyer reviewed the list.

"I am aware of the allegations." Nora maintained her calm facade. She'd had a lifetime of practice at letting things roll off her.

"But what is your response?" Angela raised her voice.

"I believe I made that clear just a few minutes ago."

"You're dodging the question, *Ms*. Whitmore."

Nora remained quiet and unruffled despite the lawyer's vehemence. In her opinion, she answered the question already. It was all a lie.

"Do you have a conscience, Ms. Whitmore? It doesn't seem likely."

"All right, Ms. Perkins, our time is just about up for today." Tom stood.

Angela huffed. She gathered her things and left.

Tom cut the camera off. "You did great, Nora. Can you continue to rein in your emotions? I think it will help."

"That won't be a problem," Nora said, her voice held as tightly in check as her emotions.

"Do you still believe that Dr. Fuller and Rader are in collusion?"

"I do, but I suppose the burden of proof is on us?" Nora asked.

"It is. I'll ask you again. Can you think of any witnesses that have seen them together?"

"As I said before, I'm sure there are plenty, but I don't have a particular name to give. Talking to the residents may be a viable option or even the charge nurses, but I believe some of them are more interested in adding to the gossip pool." Nora recalled the words whispered at the nurses' station the day of her suspension and wondered if the nurse celebrated being correct in her assumptions about Fuller's complaint.

"Do you think any of them would be sympathetic to you?"

Nora took a moment. Throughout her time at the hospital, she responded to numerous attempts at friendships with disdain. After a while, the staff stopped trying and gave her a wide berth. Today, she regretted that decision. With hindsight, Nora speculated on what could have been. She couldn't change the past. If Kelli had entered her life earlier, her current existence would be completely different. Her days would be filled with laughter, warmth, and so much more, but she couldn't dwell on that. She needed to answer based on the current reality. "I'm not sure." Nora weighed the additional comments from the nurses and decided to inform Tom even if the information wasn't helpful. "Only that some think that Rader is capable of sexual harassment himself."

"I'm not sure if that's pertinent or not, but settling is still an option—"

Nora paid his firm too much money for him not to listen. "No." She cut him off. "I've done nothing wrong."

"Sometimes that doesn't matter." Tom's voice was a mix of sympathy and practiced cynicism.

"Are you insinuating they are going to win?" Nora asked brusquely.

"No, their case is weak, but they can drag us along for a while."

Nora stood. "Earn your retainer, Mr. Young."

"I usually have more to work with, Nora."

Exasperated by his implication, Nora said the first thing that came to mind. "I'm sure security has seen plenty as well."

"Would some of the guards be impartial—"

"Interactions with them have not been typical for me." Nora was done with this conversation, both emotionally and literally. "Have a good day, Mr. Young."

When Nora entered the lounge this time, she found Kelli leafing through a magazine. For several seconds, she simply watched her. Kelli seemed so free with her time, her friendship, and everything else, but Nora knew that wasn't the case. She considered the possibility that they brought out latent characteristics in each other. It was an interesting theory to say the least, but not one she wanted to dwell on at the moment.

As Nora stepped closer, Kelli glanced up. She gazed at Nora, her expression earnest, concerned. "You okay?"

Nora's heart stuttered. It was a peculiar feeling. There wasn't a person at the hospital who thought favorably of her, and it was strange to be face to face with someone on the other end of that spectrum. "I...I suppose."

"If you're done, I'll walk you to your car."

Nora nodded.

They stood close to each other in a nearly empty elevator. Kelli gazed at her. Nora could actually feel the heaviness of it. The elevator doors opened and other people disembarked. They were now alone.

"You're not okay. I can tell."

Warmth invaded Nora's chest. To have someone know her was intoxicating. No one took the time, nor did she allow such familiarity. "You were right."

"About?"

"About me not having anyone. I've wanted it that way." Nora looked at Kelli. She tried to figure out what it was about this woman.

"Do you still want that?" Kelli asked softly.

"I…I don't know."

The elevator stopped, and the doors opened to the parking garage.

The need to flee overwhelmed Nora. Before she made it out of the elevator, she was stopped, rather abruptly, when Kelli grabbed her arm. She felt burned by the touch and gasped in response. She met Kelli's gaze. Because of the gentleness in Kelli's eyes, Nora panicked even more. She couldn't breathe. Nora didn't believe in magic, but Kelli had to possess some kind of strange power to be able to do this to her.

"You said that you'd try," Kelli whispered.

"Well, would you look at this. The day just keeps getting better and better."

They both turned to find James Rader by the driver's side of his car. He moved toward them.

"Is that what it was, Nora? You like the ladies more?"

Nora instantly saw red. She stepped forward, but before she could speak, Kelli was in front of her.

"You can't be that stupid, you slimy piece of shit, to approach her in the parking garage of her lawyer's office."

Rader closed the distance between them.

"I take it back. Obviously, you are," Kelli said with a humorless laugh.

"You stay out of this!" He pointed at Kelli.

"You're pathetic, but come closer. I'm not sure what I'll do, but I'm sure it's gonna be fun."

Rader stopped and seemed to pale. "Are you threatening me?"

"I don't recall making a threat of any kind." Kelli tapped her cane against the concrete.

Nora watched the interaction. It mesmerized her. Heat coiled in her chest. Kelli was doing this all for *her*. No one had ever come to her defense before, not like this. Was this what people did when they cared?

"Just get the fuck out of our way, asshole."

Kelli brushed against her. Nora's stomach spiraled then dropped rapidly to the concrete below, leaving her even more breathless than before.

"I'm not—" Rader reddened and stepped back. He didn't seem to have as much bravado as he did minutes earlier.

"Really, this state isn't big enough for the two of us right now. Just get in your car and leave." Kelli gestured toward his vehicle.

Rader stared, but Kelli stared right back.

He was the first to look away. "Fuck you! Fuck both of you!"

Kelli waved and smiled. "No thank you."

A few seconds later, he sped away. Kelli turned and grasped Nora by the shoulder. Her hand slowly slid downward until it encircled her wrist. "You okay?"

An electric charge sizzled up Nora's arms and rushed over her skin. She blinked, completely blindsided by the jolt.

"Nora?" Kelli stepped closer to her.

Nora's belly twisted again. She stared helplessly into Kelli's eyes. She changed her mind. Magic…it was definitely sorcery of some kind.

"Are you okay?"

Nora needed to breathe. She needed to think. She pulled away from Kelli's grasp. "Yes, I—" She had no idea what to say.

Kelli's face colored. "Are you mad? Don't be mad. I know you can take care of yourself. I just…that guy pisses me off."

"I'm not mad." Nora walked away. She had to move. Nora could hear Kelli not far behind. They reached her car. She noticed that her hands were trembling as she searched her purse for keys.

"Then what are you?" Kelli whispered from behind.

Nora wanted to turn around but couldn't. "I…don't know." The truth fell from her lips. This situation and these feelings were too unfamiliar, too new.

"Nora?"

Nora closed her eyes. She could hear the uncertainty in Kelli's tone. Nora spoke but she had no idea where the words came from. "I'm trying, but right now, I need to leave."

Kelli didn't respond, but Nora took that as understanding. She unlocked the Mercedes and eased into the driver's seat. Nora could still feel Kelli's gaze on her. She glanced at her and found it very difficult to look away.

Kelli held up a hand and stepped back.

Nora started the car and fled.

Kelli shuffled into her mother's house. After the day she'd had so far, she didn't know if she was up for this, but she didn't have a choice. Her family needed her, and that meant she needed to concentrate on them now. She called out, "Mom!"

"I'm in the kitchen!"

"Can you come out here?"

Her mother wiped her hands on a towel as she walked into the living room. "What's going on? You okay? I can get some pillows so you can stretch that leg out."

"My leg is fine, Mom." Kelli lied. It hurt like a bitch.

"Then what is it?"

Kelli licked her lips and moved toward the couch. She waved her mother over. As soon as they sat down, Kelli said, "Sean's coming. He's bringing Antony with him."

Carina smiled. "Oh, that's good. Maybe we can have dinner. It's hard to get the three of you together like this nowadays."

Kelli's sighed. "I know, but look, I know you want him to be okay, but he's not. I need you to see that."

"Who? What are you talking about?" Her mother scrunched up her face and scooted away.

"Tony. C'mon, Mom. You see it. I know you don't want to, but you can't keep pretending everything's roses."

"It? What's it?"

"Tony's on meth again." Kelli decided to just spit it out.

"What? No, he's always been high strung. Why do you always have to think the worst about him?" Carina's face reddened, and her eyes were glassy.

Kelli knew this wasn't going to be easy. "Spongebob? You remember that? He was talking out the side of his head. Caffeine is a wonderful thing, but it doesn't make people do that. Think about it, Mom. All the signs are there. I know you know what I'm saying."

Carina started to cry. "I thought he was trying."

"I'm sure he was trying at first, but right now the drugs are stronger than he is."

Her mother covered her face and wept in earnest. "Oh God."

Kelli gently took her mother's hands and stared into her eyes. She had never been all that affectionate, especially as an adult, but it seemed like the time. "We have to help him."

"I don't know how anymore."

"Yeah, but we gotta try. I called in some favors and did an involuntary committal. The police should be here soon to take him to the hospital until we can get him to detox."

"What's this involuntary committal thing about?"

Kelli squeezed her mother's hands. She knew this wasn't going to go over well. Kelli started to feel the first pang of guilt, but she pushed it away. "I was able to put him on a seventy-two-hour psych hold, and we just have to hope a spot opens up in rehab before that time is over."

Her mother jerked away. "But…he's not crazy. You lied?"

"Mom," Kelli said wearily.

There was a thud at the door, and then it burst open.

Sean stumbled in, carrying a groaning Tony over his shoulder. With a loud grunt, Sean laid Tony on the loveseat and then bent over to try to catch his breath.

Tony smelled like he'd been rolling in piss and liquor, and Kelli's eyes watered from the stench. It had been a long time since she'd seen Tony like this. The sight broke her heart.

"What did you do to him?" Carina cried and rushed over to Tony.

Kelli saw the flash of hurt in Sean's eyes. She squeezed his shoulder to let him know he'd done well.

"What I had to," Sean finally said. "I followed him to an area known for meth distribution."

"What?" Carina asked, her face drawn tight with emotion.

Kelli glanced at Sean, and answered so he wouldn't have to. "Mom, we talked about this. Look at him."

"Maybe we can give him some time to get a handle on things." Carina swept the hair away from Tony's forehead and tried to shake him awake.

"I tried to do that. It didn't work," Sean said.

Antony groaned louder and started to move. Without warning, he lashed out and knocked their mother to the floor. "Get the fuck away from me!" He wiped snot from his nose and pushed himself up. He wobbled, but stayed on his feet.

Kelli glanced at her mother. Sean was already helping her up, which allowed Kelli to focus on Tony.

Kelli studied him closely, trying to get a handle on his next move. He was high, and that made him unpredictable and capable of anything. "Antony. You're home," she said calmly. "You're in a safe place."

"Fuck you!"

Kelli raised her hands in surrender. She didn't want to fight, and Tony needed to know that. "You're mad. I get that, but we did this to help you. We love you and want you to get better."

Antony laughed. "St. Kelli doesn't get shit!" He lunged for her.

Kelli tried to move, but she couldn't get out of the way in time. Her damn leg made it impossible. He tackled her to the floor. She cried out in pain as she tried to roll away, but her reflexes were shot. She was already getting tired. Tony's closed his hands around her neck.

Sean wrapped his arms around Antony's torso and tried to pull him away.

Tony growled like a wild animal. He was definitely homicidal. Maybe the psych hold wasn't a reach after all.

Sean's face was red, but he managed to overpower Tony.

Antony shouted, his eyes wide and bloodshot, his nostrils flaring, and a line of spit dripped from his mouth.

Carina screamed in the background.

Kelli pushed against Tony until she was able to wriggle free. She scooted backward until she hit the wall. She closed her eyes as blackness swam up to meet her.

The buzzer was loud, and it pulled Kelli back to consciousness. Her mother stumbled toward the door.

Kelli didn't recognize the two uniformed cops who entered. They jerked Antony up and cuffed him in a matter of seconds. Sean sagged against the couch, and Carina stood by the open door crying quietly. Antony squirmed, but the officers pulled him out of the living room and toward the door with no problem. "Seattle General is the only place with room in adult psych," one of the uniforms said.

Kelli stood slowly, keeping her back to the wall.

"I fucking hate you for this." Tony glared at her.

The officers nodded at Sean and Kelli and closed the door behind them.

Then they were alone.

Carefully, Sean helped her to the couch.

They sat in silence.

CHAPTER 12

The Cuisinart hissed and dribbled coffee into the pot. Impatiently, Kelli glared and willed it to go faster. She looked around the kitchen. There wasn't anything else to do for the moment, and she thanked God for that, given the way the past forty-eight hours had gone. The walls were painted a soft yellow, set off by the bright white cabinets and light gray granite countertops. Nothing had changed in the past fifteen years or so. Kelli felt a sense of comfort wash over her. *Home.* It was warm, familiar, and reminded her of better times. Currently, those times seemed few and far between. Kelli tried to shake free of her thoughts. She yawned and scratched the back of her neck. The coffee needed to hurry the hell up. Kelli was already on the other side of exhaustion…wherever that was.

She peered at the clock. It was barely seven-thirty and Kelli was up earlier than usual for physical therapy and her final doctor's appointment. In other words, it was going to be the best motherfucking day ever. Not. The stairs leading to the living room creaked loudly. Kelli tilted her head toward the noise and listened carefully. When she heard a definite sniffle, she closed her eyes. She was worried about her mother and didn't expect her to quit crying anytime soon. It wasn't every day that Tony was dragged from the house in handcuffs.

Kelli curled a hand around her throat. Tony didn't get a chance to get a good hold on her, and she didn't bruise easily. Thank Christ, because those kind of marks would have been hard to explain. Kelli wanted to forget that part ever happened. She did her best to clear her head and waited quietly for her mother to make an appearance.

"Oh hey, honey." Carina tried to sound cheerful as she wiped at her eyes.

The sight nearly gutted Kelli. "Mom, it's okay to cry as much as you want," Kelli reminded her.

"I know. I'm just tired of it. Seems like I've been crying for years. I thought I was all dried up."

Nodding, Kelli poured her mother a cup of coffee with a crapload of cream, just the way Carina liked it.

"He's gotta make it this time. Isn't that what rehab is for? I don't understand why it doesn't work for him."

Leaning against the counter instead of her cane, Kelli answered her mother the best she knew how. "He has to *want* it to work, Mom. Maybe this time will be different."

Carina shook her head and took a sip from her mug. "I look at you and Sean… I just don't get it. We raised all of you the same, with a lot of love. There's even a business waiting for whoever wants to take it over. What made his life so terrible?" Distracted, she sat the cup on the counter.

Kelli sighed. She'd wondered the same thing for years and came to the conclusion that some people were just cursed with addictive personalities. "I don't know. I wish I did."

"Maybe he has mental health stuff? I mean, maybe he's not responsible or in control of what he does…" Carina didn't even finish.

Heart dropping to her stomach, Kelli swallowed. "Mom, don't. It's possible. It's not an excuse. Just don't lie to yourself like that. Not anymore."

They stared at each other.

Carina's eyes were filled with resentment and pain. When she blinked, the emotions were gone, and the tears came back full force. Her mother fell into her arms. Kelli stiffened for a second as she always did with physical contact. Her breath caught in her throat, and she tried like hell to swallow down the anxiety threatening to drown her. The broken, helpless sound coming from her mother made it impossible. Kelli held her tightly, and let her own tears fall too.

Her mom sniffled as she pulled back. "I got us both going. I'm sorry. I know that you try to be strong for everybody."

Kelli swallowed and stayed quiet. It was the truth.

"We're just going to be hopeful. That's all we can do, right?" Carina asked. Her voice was a long way from sounding even remotely hopeful.

Still, Kelli nodded and wiped at her own cheeks. Her mom needed to believe for a little while, and Kelli wouldn't deny her that.

"I love you. You know that, right? I just wanted to let you know that it's okay for you to cry too. Things affect you deeply. They always have. You're just better at handling crap than most people."

Well, she was *trying* to handle everything, but it wasn't working out too well. At least nobody could see that. Kelli looked down at her bare feet. A touch on her chin encouraged her to glance upward.

"Thank you for staying with me. Go home, baby. It's okay."

Her mother obviously needed some space. Kelli had gotten her over the hump, and it was time to move forward. "Alright," she agreed.

Carina gave her a watery smile. "I've got to get to work. Give Gerry a kiss for me. I expect you to be gone when I come home."

Kelli chuckled at her mother's bluntness. It was a trait that definitely trickled down to her. "Okay."

Kelli found herself alone in the kitchen again. She sat at the counter, drained the remainder of her mother's coffee, and thought back on the last couple of days. The person that Sean dragged in wasn't really Antony. Sure, it looked like him on the outside, but the inside sure as fuck wasn't her brother. It was as if he was…possessed. There was no other way to describe it. His drug usage was bad before, but she had never seen him like this. Kelli hated the way that shit fucked with people and ripped apart their families, friendships, and everything else that mattered. Her mother had brought up hope, but it was hard considering what she'd seen.

Using her cane, Kelli made her way to the living room. She eased down on the couch and hiked her shorts up over the almost healed wound on her thigh. It was jagged and slightly repulsive. The thing looked like an ugly-ass caterpillar had attached itself to her leg. Kelli touched the scar. It barely hurt at all anymore. There was just an uncomfortable pulling sensation when she flexed the muscle.

Kelli smirked, but her humor came from a dark place. Strange how the pain on the outside was going away, and the shit on the inside just kept growing. Sometimes, she hated her life. Luckily, that feeling usually only lasted for a couple of minutes. Instead of wallowing, Kelli reached for her phone and went to N in the contacts. She touched Nora's name and just barely stopped herself from hitting send. Given what happened after the deposition, Nora obviously needed some time to herself. This time Kelli was trying to let her have it.

Physical therapy left Kelli weak and jittery, but she welcomed the feeling. She was ready to kick the world in its ass. Well, not really, but she was definitely healing. Kelli smiled sheepishly at the nurses as she made her way to Travis's room. Kelli needed to cheer the fuck up before seeing Rader because tearing out his liver probably wouldn't help Nora's case. When she walked in his room, Travis wasn't alone.

Williams glanced up and grinned. "Well, smack my ass. Look who just walked in."

Kelli stared at him. "I don't need that kind of imagery."

"What? Isn't that what you kids are saying these days?"

"No, we kids don't say shit like that." Travis shook his head, a disgusted look on his face.

"Regardless, it's good to see you two together." Williams shrugged, seemingly oblivious to having grossed them both out.

Kelli sat down in a chair near Travis's bed. It was good to see him smiling. She pointed toward his beard. "You really are serious about it. At least you look better than before. The grizzly serial killer look isn't for you." Kelly poked at Travis knowing there was no way he was going to let that one fly. No way in hell.

"No, it'll be a while before he looks anything like *Grizzly Adams*." Williams said the words as if they made perfect sense. So far, his two cents had been worth a lot less in Kelli's opinion.

Instead of saying anything, Travis glanced at Kelli, and they both looked at Williams and waited.

"You know? The guy who lived in the forest. With that bear," Williams said.

"No, just no. That doesn't even go with what I just said." Kelli shook her head. It was good to have this back. Kelli missed their little…discussions.

"Your ass is old and a little senile. How did you go from serial killers to some guy who liked bears?" Travis asked.

Williams sighed. "It's a good show. You could probably find it on the you tube."

Kelli looked at him again and noticed the twinkle in his eyes. Williams was so full of shit, but it was the good kind. The kind that distracted from the bad shit like paralysis and drug addiction. "Not on Netflix yet?" Kelli asked with a smirk.

Williams shrugged. "Not entirely sure what that is."

Travis snorted. "It's a new porn site."

"Then why the hell would *Grizzly Adams* be on there?"

Gerry looked thoughtful. "Sounds like a porn title to me. Bestiality is in with us young folk. You haven't heard?"

Williams gave him the stink eye. "I'm not going there with you."

"What? Nothing about *Little House on the Prairie*?" Kelli asked teasingly.

"Those are two completely different things. How the hell do you know one and not the other?" Williams grumbled.

Kelli shrugged. "The you tube?" She purposefully mispronounced YouTube by stretching it into two words as Williams had.

Travis chuckled, but it died quickly. "I'm a cop," he whispered. "I'm the fucking murder police. It's all I wanted to do, and in a few days, I might not be able to do that, or any goddamned thing, ever again."

The elephant in the room fucking roared.

"Kid, you made a name for yourself. The higher-ups won't take that lightly." Williams sounded hopeful.

Travis looked at Kelli. "I might not walk again." He completely ignored Williams.

Kelli met his gaze. She could see how strong he was, but he was waiting for something. It took her a second, but she finally realized he wanted her to be straight with him. "Yeah, that's true. You might not."

Gerry flinched. Then, he nodded. "I don't know if I could deal with being half a cop stuck at some desk in front of a computer all day."

"I'm sorry, kid. I wasn't trying to be insensitive. I just thought it would help." Williams patted Travis's leg.

"I know, old man."

"I can understand. You may not be the desk jockey type, but, hey?" Kelli asked.

"What?"

"You know I'm not a beacon of hope or whatever, but you gotta remember that you could actually walk out of here."

For a long time, Travis was quiet. "That's true."

Kelli took a breath and nodded. She had to be ready for whatever came. It was the only way to help him.

Kelli pressed the button on the wall. A few minutes later, the elevator opened. She stepped on and turned around to see Williams walking toward her. She held the door for him and watched him warily. The man had a way of making her spill her guts all over the place. It didn't matter that there were three other people standing there with them.

"Why are you looking at me like that?" Williams asked.

"Just bracing myself for your usual interrogation," Kelli answered.

He chuckled. "All I was going to ask is how you're doing."

"Bullshit." Kelli smirked and glared.

"Seriously, I'm not pushing. Your choice. Give me the short version—say you're fine and tell me to fuck off—or give me the long version." He grinned. "So, how are you doing?"

She continued to stare. Some people got on the elevator and some got off.

He leaned against the railing and waited.

Williams offered her a special kind of absolution. He always had been able to pull things out of her with a few well-placed questions, but his methods sometimes felt like a full-scale assault. A perfect example was him getting her to admit to the nightmares. She took a minute. She'd known Williams forever, but it was still hard as hell to talk with him about the real shit in her life, but Nora—a woman she just met—the whole talking thing wasn't hard with her at all. The words just flowed. But comparing Williams to Nora was like comparing apples to planets. Even though he would understand where she was coming from, Kelli needed *something* to be simple and uncomplicated. There was only one place she could find that, and it wasn't here. Kelli glanced at Williams. "Short version."

He met her gaze and studied her. Kelli wasn't sure what he saw, but he smiled like he knew some secret.

Kelli scooted back on the exam room table. Nothing would make these damn things comfortable. The white paper liner crunched in protest. She was in a strange mood. It was a combination of weariness and a heightened state of readiness for just about anything, even this dickhead.

Rader opened the door and walked in. At least he didn't try to give her one of those car salesmen smiles. She probably would have punched him, but he didn't even bother to look at her. His face was planted in a chart.

Kelli snorted.

A nurse came in right behind him, and she had a big old goofy grin. Apparently, she hadn't talked with the other nurses recently.

"Is that your protection?" Kelli pointed at the nurse.

"She's here to protect us both…considering," Rader answered.

"Mmm hmm."

He stood on the same side as her injured leg. Rader reached out but stopped abruptly. His hand shook.

Kelli took advantage. She remembered something on her way to the hospital, and she was damn well going to use it. "You really aren't too spry without your girlfriend. I guess it's a good thing that I'm a light sleeper. Good for Nora, I mean, and here I thought you two were talking about some kind of weird sex stuff. Turns out, it was something a whole lot more interesting." She was pushing him, but what the hell. She didn't do things halfway. His boat needed to be rocked. Kelli leaned forward. "You're gonna crack, and when you do, everything is gonna fall apart around you."

The nurse gasped.

"I don't know what you're talking about. Can you expose the wound please?" Rader asked. His voice was monotone, and still, he refused to meet her gaze.

"Sure." Kelli moved the gown out of the way. "Nora must really be something to reduce you to this. You know this isn't the kind of lie you walk away from?"

"This…conversation is being wit—"

"She's a witness. I get it." Kelli smiled at the nurse and flexed the large muscle groups in her leg as Rader poked at her. "I am so okay with that. Are you?"

Rader cleared his throat. "I'm going to need you to disrobe so I can—"

Before he could finish, Kelli had her tits to the wind.

"Um, shortness of breath?" He pressed around the wound.

"No," Kelli answered.

"Any aberrant pain?" Rader continued. "Take a deep breath, please."

"Nope, not really." Kelli inhaled and reminded herself that, no matter how much he made her skin crawl, she couldn't get all violent when he touched her.

"Good."

"Uh-huh."

"Your, uh, blood work was clean as well. You can follow up with your regular doctor from this point on. Maybe we won't have to see each other again."

Kelli chuckled darkly. "I'm sure you'd like that, but I'll be seeing you soon."

Rader looked at her then. His gaze was hard, cold. He stood tall, seemingly confident. The prick actually thought he had a chance to win. "I guess so. Goodbye for now, Ms. McCabe."

Kelli left the hospital feeling more out of sorts than ever, and she didn't want the day to go on with Rader on the brain. Nora came to mind. Automatically, she reached for her cell phone again. She pulled up Nora's number for the umpteenth time in the past few days and looked at the digits. Her belly fluttered as she replayed their last meeting. There was a connection between them. Kelli knew that already, but now there was an ache too. Kelli liked who she was around Nora. She was sharper in some places and softer in others. The parking garage was a perfect example.

When Rader approached them, something awakened in Kelli. Something raw, and she loved every second of it. The situation, the way Nora looked, and the way Nora felt all left her weirdly turned on. And then Nora ran. Kelli's gut screamed for her to follow, but her head encouraged her to wait. She was still waiting and didn't know how much longer she was going to last. The phone screen went dark. She put her cell away again with a sigh, and slid the key into the ignition.

Nora brought the grocery cart to a standstill and perused the aisle for her usual brand of granola. Having the other patrons around her, even if they were strangers, made her feel a little less isolated. At home, she had nowhere to go except inside her head, and that wasn't a pleasant place to be. Her thoughts were churning, twisted, and confused. It was a complex equation where new information was inadvertently added constantly. This current turn of events with Kelli represented yet another part pushing her closer to the brink of overload.

She grabbed an organic brand of granola and read the list of ingredients on the back. Grocery shopping was not something she engaged in on a regular basis. The concept was very low on the list compared to work and the hospital, but today it was a small indulgence, a distraction from everything.

A loud peel of laughter caught her attention simply because it was too close to ignore. Nora turned to see a young couple chatting near the cereal. They stood extremely close to each other. Even though she couldn't hear what they were saying, the look in the man's eyes captured her attention. His expression was a combination of softness and—

Before she could figure out more, they kissed. Nora looked away hurriedly and threw the unknown brand of granola into her cart. She felt uncomfortable, but her response was so much more. Her chest tightened, and Nora couldn't deny the loneliness that had taken root inside her. She thought of Kelli, and

Nora's body filled with a familiar heat. Her insides curled pleasantly. She was far from inexperienced and knew the signs of attraction. In the past, the awareness had always been fleeting, and the connection usually ended as soon as she was satiated. This time, Nora felt a more visceral pull that left her smoldering. Trying to outrun her feelings, Nora moved quickly. She abandoned the aisle and anything else she might want there.

Three days had passed since they last spoke. Nora hadn't called Kelli, and Kelli hadn't called her either. This newfound attraction was a frightening concept, but combined with the friendship between them, Nora was hungrier than ever for the smallest interaction. Nora knew how to fix it—a phone call or a text. But after their last encounter, Nora had no idea if Kelli would even respond.

As she turned the corner, Nora went from anxiety to anger, and there was helplessness as well. She was tired of the inactivity that paved the way for this constant deluge of emotions. Even if the change was only temporary, Nora wished to be carefree, and maybe, in spite of all the turmoil around her, to find some peace.

It was just past midday when Nora arrived home. She uncorked a bottle of Roar 2010 Sierra Mar chardonnay and set it on the kitchen counter to let it breathe while she put the groceries away. By the time she was done, the wine bottle still held a pleasant chill. Eager to relax and unwind, she filled her glass, releasing the crisp tang of fruit into the air. She took a tentative sip, and the flavors burst on her tongue. Nora closed her eyes to savor it and found a moment of solace in the simple pleasure.

She heard her phone ring from the coffee table where she'd left it earlier. Nora walked toward it, leaving the kitchen for the living area. Nora picked up her cell, and Kelli's name flashed across the screen. Anticipation raced through her, and she shivered. She didn't give herself enough time to overthink before she accepted the call.

"Hello?"

"Hey."

The familiar husk of Kelli's voice increased the wave of awareness to a searing flash of lightning. Nora swallowed and brought the wine glass to her lips.

"You answered your phone."

"Yes." Nora cleared her throat.

"I suppose I didn't expect you to. I wasn't sure—"

"Kelli?"

"Uh, yeah?"

"I apologize for ignoring you last week." Nora wasn't sure if this was what she wanted to say, but there was no taking it back now.

"I'm sorry for steamrolling over you."

For some reason, the statement made Nora smile. "No, you're not."

Kelli chuckled. "You're right, I'm not, but it sounded good, didn't it?"

"I'm going to consider that rhetorical."

"You do that then."

The seconds ticked by before Kelli spoke again. "I wanted to call this weekend, but I figured you needed space. I tried to be patient, but I just couldn't wait anymore."

Kelli's tone was apologetic, and it made Nora feel selfish. There was so much more going on in Kelli's life. Nora needed to at least try to equal Kelli's efforts toward their friendship. "Your brother?"

Kelli chuckled darkly. "You pay attention, and, yeah, my brother. I pulled some pretty heavy strings to get him detained. He's going back to rehab. I just hope they can convince him to stay."

"Are you o—" Nora let the question fall from her lips even though she knew it was trite.

"No, I'm not okay." Kelli interrupted. "My mother can't stop crying. Travis is a mess, and to top it off, I had to see Rader today. I really don't know how I stopped myself from punching him. I *really* wanted to, but I pissed him off instead. I don't get what you saw in that guy. I mean, he's pretty, but in that creepy, oily way."

"I'm not at all sure what that means, but my encounter with him was an error in judgment." That was the only way to explain the Rader situation, but the most important part was Kelli's fierce desire to keep her safe. It gave Nora a pleasant tingle low in her belly. Being cared for by Kelli meant she fell under her circle of protection, and that was a heady feeling.

"You have enough going on. I'm not trying to overload you with my shit, but it's like as soon as I talk to you, it all just comes out."

"It's okay. I just don't know how to respond sometimes."

"You could…let me in."

For a brief moment, Nora was confused by Kelli's request. Then, she understood. Her heart accelerated, and heat enveloped her. She whispered, "You're outside."

"Yeah, I didn't want to show up without calling."

"But—"

"Semantics, Nora. You gonna let me in?"

"Yes," she answered breathlessly.

"Okay."

The line went dead.

Nora returned the phone to the table and picked up her iPad. After inputting her code, she stared at the security feed, considering what Kelli's arrival at her house meant for their relationship. Seconds later, Kelli came into view. Nora watched in silent contemplation until the doorbell rang and galvanized her into action.

When she opened the door, Kelli smiled crookedly at her while leaning on her cane. Nora was not prepared for her reaction to seeing Kelli in the flesh after a few days absence.

Something inside her stopped, dropped, and roared to life again in the span of seconds. Whatever it was shook her, but the ingrained lessons in etiquette enabled her to seamlessly usher Kelli inside.

Kelli's brow wrinkled. She moved closer and reached out, but she stopped short of touching Nora. "You okay?"

Evidently, she didn't hide her emotions as well as she thought. Nora stepped away. The panic that had momentarily flooded her ebbed away, but the warmth remained. "Yes, thank you."

Nora made her way toward the couch, and the glass of wine beckoned to her with the sweet promise of alcohol-induced serenity. She reached for it and took a huge gulp. She glanced back to find Kelli's gaze intensely focused on her, which alarmed and comforted her at the same time. "You're no longer on narcotics?"

Kelli shook her head and walked toward the couch. "As needed, but not since Friday."

"Would you like a glass of wine?"

Kelli scrunched her nose in distaste. "I'm more of a beer girl. I won't spit it out, will I?"

"Not if you wish to remain in my home."

Kelli's eyes widened, and she burst out laughing. "Noted."

Nora reentered the kitchen. She needed a minute to regain some equilibrium. She set a new glass on the counter. Her hands trembled slightly so she took another pull from the chardonnay to steady them.

When Nora returned to the living area, Kelli was seated. Nora joined her on the couch, but kept a respectable distance between them.

"Where's Phineas?"

"Around I suppose."

"Frolicking?" Kelli asked with a smirk.

"Undoubtedly."

"I don't have a saddle, but I swear to God when I'm done with PT, I'm gonna ride him."

At the imagery alone, Nora felt something light and warm bubble in her chest. She glared at Kelli and got a big smile in return. The feeling in her chest intensified, and she did something she hadn't done in ages. Nora chuckled. She covered her mouth with her hand.

Kelli's eyes darkened, and she smiled even wider. "Well I'll be damned. I should get a plaque or something." She reached for her wine.

Nora continued to smile and filed the moment away with the plan to never forget it.

"Whoa, this is good."

"I'm glad you approve," Nora said sarcastically.

"Uh-huh." Kelli made a show of inspecting the house. "So, do I get the nickel—or should I say ten-dollar tour?"

Nora nodded, and before she knew it, they were wandering from room to room. Kelli was silent for the most part, save a long, low whistle here and there.

Eventually, they found themselves back in the living room.

"I know doctors make a lot of money, Nora, but—"

"I have an inheritance."

"Oh," Kelli said.

Nora glanced at her. "Does it bother you?"

Kelli shrugged. "I'm not judging, but what's the point of working?"

Nora took a few seconds to think about her answer. She wanted to do what felt right. Nora wanted to take a step forward with Kelli, even if she couldn't maintain the momentum—a distinct possibility given her emotional state. "I'm not the jet-setting socialite type, and I assumed it would be no different from when I was growing up. I imagine being taunted by adults and the gossip columns would have been even less enjoyable. Medicine is…who I am, and the money isn't."

Their gazes met.

"Yeah, I get that."

Nora saw genuine understanding in Kelli's eyes, but she also felt herself sinking deeper into them. She tore her gaze away and searched for something else to say. "I'm sorry about your brother."

Kelli exhaled forcefully. "Me too, but I did what had to be done, I guess. Seems like I always do. I'm sure I'm gonna pay for it one way or another."

"I wish there was some way I could help," Nora said. "I mean that. I know I haven't exactly been very present so far."

Kelli looked away and was quiet for several seconds. "This is gonna sound… hell, I don't know how it sounds, but all I could think about was getting over here. I had to see you. I tried to stay away. Give you some space, but, yeah, that didn't work out."

Nora tried to breathe, but couldn't quite remember how. She looked everywhere except for where she was being pulled. Their gazes met anyway. Nora expected to see sparks in the air around them.

"More wine?" Nora's voice was high, strained.

Kelli nodded vehemently. "Yes, please."

Kelli closed her eyes and leaned against her door as a combination of feelings washed over her. She was tired, but Kelli had become very used to that. It was the other stuff—the stuff with Nora—that left her hot, tingly, and craving more. Hell, with Nora, she always wanted more, but Kelli had no idea what to do about it. A loud knock rattled the door and scared the shit out of her. She moved away and turned toward the sound.

"Yeah?"

"Kelli McCabe?" the man asked.

"What do you want?"

"Delivery. I need you to sign for it."

Kelli cracked the door open and stared at him. A shaggy looking young man stared back. He held up an envelope and his clipboard for her to see. She was confused, but she widened the door anyway.

"You've been served."

Son of a bitch. Kelli accepted the clipboard and signed. After he handed her the envelope, she slammed the door in his face. It wasn't his fault, but it sure as hell was satisfying. The summons was too quick to have anything to do with the fun time she had with Rader today. If she did, in fact, have to testify, Kelli decided that the ride wasn't going to be easy, at least for them. "Dumbasses," she grumbled.

CHAPTER 13

Nora sniffed at the contents of her coffee cup. The scent was bold, rich, and pungent, just as Columbian coffee should be. She took a sip, but didn't enjoy it like she usually did. Her life, hued in monochrome and unwavering routine, was something she used to find comfort in. Now, she longed for a splash of color. She took another sip and admitted to herself that Kelli brought the color with her. When Kelli visited, the walls that surrounded Nora burst with life. Without Kelli, Nora's home was quiet. So very quiet.

Nora no longer cared for the silence.

The air burned between her and Kelli, but there was so much more—acceptance, warmth, humor, and an easiness that grew with each encounter. All of these things were new constructs and frightening unknowns, but it would be a lie to say she wasn't drawn to them anyway, even though part of her continued to recoil from the emotional messiness that came with that level of human connection. Somehow, the previous day's visit turned to drinks, drinks became lunch, and lunch led into a light dinner. Just ten hours ago, her day was more full and enjoyable than it had ever been before. When Kelli first arrived, they hesitated briefly at the awkwardness that was still present between them. The feeling dissipated quickly and left behind a familiarity that shouldn't have been possible.

Kelli made her laugh, and Nora was equal parts shocked and titillated by Kelli's ability to do so. She was learning that Kelli was very adept at provoking both feelings within her. Nora's stomach tightened just thinking about it. Nora was sure that the attraction she felt would dwindle in time, but the other things Kelli offered—friendship, laughter and understanding—were things Nora wanted to hang onto. Nora glanced at her phone and wondered if she should continue moving at a snail's pace. Or was it more prudent to let Kelli know her presence, and all she brought with it, was welcome?

Nora made her decision quickly.

Kelli's cell phone rang loudly. She groaned, turned over, and threw the covers over her head. She'd finally fallen asleep a couple hours ago and was ready to kill whoever was calling for waking her up. The phone stopped and started ringing again. Kelli grunted and kicked the comforter away. For a second or two, she stared bleary eyed at the ceiling before reaching blindly for her cell phone.

"'Lo?"

"I woke you."

Every single nerve in Kelli's body jumped to attention all at once. Except, of course, the one leading to her voice box. Kelli sat up in the bed and knocked her pillow to the floor as she fumbled to make her mouth work. "Uh."

"I can call back later."

"No! No, it's fine. I was up…kinda."

"Liar." Nora called her bluff.

Kelli blinked. Nora sounded *almost* playful. "Who is…*this*?"

Nora sighed. "You're being facetious."

"I am a little, but not really. I can't be on all the time. You're calling me. This…is just unexpected. I guess pod people really do exist."

"Was that some sort of pop culture reference?" Nora asked.

"It was." Kelli chuckled. It amazed her how naïve Nora was about some things.

"Would you care to elaborate?"

Kelli chuckled again. "You're calling me. It doesn't seem like something you'd normally let yourself do."

"How did you come to that conclusion? You don't know me that well."

"I know you well enough, Nora."

There was a brief moment of quiet, but there was still something sexy about it. Kelli loved that she had the ability to throw Nora off balance.

"I suppose that's accurate," Nora agreed.

"It is," Kelli said softly.

"Well, I wanted to call. Should I assume that you want to know why?"

"Yeah, please do."

"I—" Nora started but stopped suddenly.

"It's okay." Kelli reassured. "It's hard for me to talk about things too, remember?"

"We don't seem to have that issue with each other."

"Then this should be easy." Kelli knew it wasn't, but she wanted it to be.

"In theory—"

"And in practice," Kelli said firmly.

"I…" Nora cleared her throat. "I enjoy our conversations." She finished the sentence in a rush.

"I do—" Kelli started.

"I'm not done."

"Oh, sorry." Kelli apologized and found herself smiling.

"I've been alone most of my life, and I've always been the one to temporarily amend the situation when necessary. I enjoy…your company, Kelli. I thought it important that you know that our *friendship* is reciprocated."

Kelli felt as if she was wrapped in warmth, and the feeling settled in the places that got cold at night. She welcomed what Nora was saying, but for some reason, the message also made her feel a little too vulnerable. So, she fell back onto her oldest habit—humor. "So in other words, I grew on you."

"Yes."

"Like a fungus," Kelli said with a grin.

"You really are insufferable. But I expected your answer, so I guess I know you well enough too."

"What's that supposed to mean?"

"Draw your own conclusions, detective."

With that statement, Kelli found herself even more intrigued by this woman.

"Now, if you could open the door before your neighbors report me for stalking…"

Nora was outside. Here. Outside her apartment. It took a moment or two for Kelli to remember how to inhale. "What…how did—?"

"The Internet is a wonderful invention, even if it can be an invasion to a person's privacy. Thirty-fifth Avenue is a prime location. You can see the Cascades and Mt. Rainier from here." Nora explained. "Plus, I brought breakfast and a very good French Roast, but if I'm intruding—"

"No! No, I'm just a slow ass. You caught me by surprise. That's twice now, Nora. You're gonna have to pay for that." Kelli scrambled out of bed and searched for something resembling pants.

"I look forward to it."

Kelli swallowed down the sudden lump in her throat. That sounded dangerously close to flirting, and it threw Kelli all out of whack. It's not as if she were a fumbling teenager, but this was *Nora*. She meant something. More than Kelli was ready to admit. "Um…"

"I meant that I look forward to your…continued company." Nora corrected. She sounded a little breathless.

"Yeah, just let me put on pants."

"You don't have to put on pants for me."

Sweet. God. Kelli actually took the phone from her ear and stared at it for a moment before responding. "Uh…wha—?" Jesus, what was it about Nora that turned Kelli into a mumbling idiot?

"I was trying to relay—" Nora said at the same time.

Kelli laughed. Every time they met, things got more interesting and entertaining. She hoped their exchanges stayed that way. Kelli found her jeans on the floor and pulled them on.

"Yes, well, maybe you should hurry so I won't say anything else seemingly inappropriate," Nora muttered.

"I wonder what you woulda said if I just got out of the shower." Kelli said as if they talked—hell, flirted—like this all the time.

"Kelli!"

"Yes?" She smiled and let a little tease filter into her tone.

"These are the best cinnamon rolls in the city. They need to be fresh to be truly appreciated."

"Zipping up as we speak. Be with you in a sec." Kelli ended the call. Her leg was stiff so she limped lightly toward the bathroom. Her cane was propped against the open door. She glanced at the mirror. She looked like a cow had been licking her head. Kelli ran her hands through her hair. The quick styling could only be an improvement.

Kelli walked into the living room and the first thing she saw was the subpoena on the coffee table. "Fuck." She'd almost forgotten about it. Kelli had made her peace with the stupid thing. If Fuller and her lawyer thought she could be manipulated or tricked, they were in for a rude-ass awakening. Nora was a different story. She was either going to look at the whole thing logically or be pissed the hell off. Kelli wanted to be ready for whatever happened.

Kelli opened her door only to see her neighbor's door opened as well. "It's okay Mrs. Landau. She's a friend."

Mrs. Landau looked at them for a few more seconds and then disappeared from view.

Kelli gave Nora her full attention. She tried to swallow down the golf ball sized lump in her throat. Nora really was breathtaking. It was hard not to tell her. Kelli was sure that conversation would send Nora screaming the other way. Instead, Kelli smiled. "Hey, come in."

Nora smiled slightly as she walked in. "I told you that your neighbor thought I was up to something."

"Mrs. Landau. She's my self-appointed guardian angel. Nice old lady."

When Nora stepped into the living room, Kelli suddenly became self-conscious. "It's not much, so don't look too close."

Nora glanced around the room and then back at Kelli. "Minimalism fits you. I think you have good taste."

Kelli's gaze swept the area, taking in the clean lines of the mission-style furniture. Her face flushed with heat at Nora's appraisal. "I don't spend a lot of time in here."

Nora sat the bag and coffee tray on the table. "Ten-dollar tour?" she asked.

Nora's golden-brown eyes were soft and free of judgment, but held a hint of nervousness. For some reason, Kelli relaxed. "Yeah, if you don't mind the unmade bed."

"I don't."

Kelli nodded and led her toward the eat-in kitchen. They stopped at the entrance. Kelli assumed that Nora would ease past her to get a better look. The warmth at her back told a different story all together. She peered over Kelli's shoulder. Nora was close enough to smell and feel. Kelli tried to ignore the heat that blasted her. She took a deep breath and willed her body to relax.

"Do you cook?"

"Minimally." Kelli answered with a smirk.

Nora curled her lips into a smile.

They made their way to the bedroom. "This is where you spend your time."

"Yeah."

Nora scanned the room, but Kelli didn't miss the redness in Nora's face when her gaze stopped at the bed. Without thinking, Kelli put her hand at the small of the Nora's back. "You okay?"

Nora jumped in surprise. Her whole body stiffened, which only made Kelli move closer. "Nora?"

Nora glanced at her, but looked away quickly. "Yes, I'm fine. I'm…" She licked her lips. "I'm still not used to being touched."

Kelli pulled her hand away but missed the heat instantly. "I'm sorry. I don't know why I did that."

"It's okay. I suppose I have to get used to being around someone so demonstrative."

Kelli shook her head and smirked. Nora's honesty fueled her own. "That's the thing. I'm really not."

"Strange," Nora whispered.

"It is, but I guess it fits." Kelli backed away from the doorway to get some distance from Nora. "Cinnamon rolls?"

Nora nodded. "They should still be warm."

"Good. After, we need to talk."

※

Kelli waited and watched anxiously as Nora skimmed the documents. She hated to fuck up their progress, but it wasn't as if she could avoid showing her the subpoena either. Nora's expression went from shock to anger.

"What could she hope to gain from this?"

"Don't know. Only thing I can think of is, I was in the room that time you sent her running."

Nora gasped. "When I insinuated a relationship between her and Rader?"

"Yeah."

"Surely that's not enough—"

"Sounds like they are trying to establish a pattern of behavior."

"There isn't one. I haven't treated her differently!" Nora said in outrage.

"Calm down. I'm a cop. They messed up. She's not gonna get anything usable from me. If anything, I could hurt them. Rader is an ass, and he's smug, but they are gonna dig themselves into a hole. In fact, I guess with all the other shit I had going on, I didn't think about this until you told me about this whole lawsuit crap, but I'm almost sure I overheard them planning the whole damn thing…right there at the foot of my bed. They're sloppy, Nora, and this shit is gonna roll over on them sooner or later."

"That's a relief, but I just can't believe they're actually doing this. Why go through all the trouble?"

Kelli reached out to touch her. At the last second, she stopped herself.

"It's okay. Maybe I need it," Nora said.

Kelli didn't have to be told twice. She covered Nora's hand with her own and squeezed.

Nora looked at their clasped hands. Her lips parted, and the flush Kelli was quickly becoming addicted to came back with a vengeance.

"Maybe your lawyer will be able to do something with what I just told you."

Nora closed her eyes. She looked so tired. "I want this all to be over. I don't know what I've done—"

"You think it's you? There are some screwed-up people in this world, Nora. Rader is definitely one of them. I could smell it all over him. The guy gave me goosebumps even when I first met him. As for Dr. Fuller…people like that find each other."

Nora's lips thinned, and her eyes flashed. "Then how did I miss it?"

"I'm trained to notice, and you, you distance yourself from people. So, how could you see something you're trying to avoid?"

Nora stared at their joined hands. "I haven't…from you."

Kelli grinned crookedly. "Maybe I'm special."

Nora gave her a small grin in return. It was followed by a blush. "Possibly."

With her free hand, Kelli cupped Nora's cheek. She wasn't sure when she moved. Apparently, some of her body parts had a mind of their own. Her fingertips brushed against Nora's smooth skin where the redness lingered. The softness she found there made it hard to pull away. "I must be to keep causing this."

Nora opened her eyes wide, and they grew darker by the second. "I don't know what—"

"You're flustered. You seem to always be around me."

For the moment, Kelli didn't have anything else to say, but she couldn't look away. Even though she couldn't see it, the air around them had to be on fire because something powerful was responsible for the heat growing between them.

"I think I've become accustomed to it," Nora whispered.

Kelli smiled and cleared her throat. "Good. I think." She knew there was going to be a reaction to the subpoena, but she never expected to find herself pulled deeper into Nora.

"And maybe…I like it," Nora said.

Something warm unraveled itself in Kelli's chest and slipped into her belly. When it got there, it was a heavy molten ball that threatened to burn her from the inside out. "Even better."

CHAPTER 14

After two beers, Kelli was finally able to doze. The alcohol didn't keep the heavy shit off her mind and she still worried about Travis, her family, and everything else. Those worries helped to clear the cobwebs when she heard her phone ringing. There were two possible callers who Kelli wouldn't allow herself to miss—Nora or someone in her family. Kelli reached for it. The number was unfamiliar, but she answered the call anyway.

"Hello?" Kelli mumbled.

"What? Early night, sis?"

Kelli sat straight up in bed. "Antony?"

"The one and fuckin' only." Tony sounded sober. Angry, but sober.

"How did you—"

"I can make calls."

This wasn't going to be a social call. Kelli could already tell that by his tone. Kelli sat up and mentally prepared herself for the shit he was about to fling. "Then you should be calling, Mom. I'm—"

"Don't you worry about me and Mom. I got rights, Kelli, even if you don't think I do." Tony interrupted. "I know what you did. I'm not homicidal, and I sure as hell don't wanna kill myself. Did you think I was stupid? Like I wouldn't find out?" His voice was cold.

True, when Kelli arranged the involuntary committal, she hadn't known what his state of mind was. But by the time the officers picked him up, he was in a blind, homicidal rage. Hearing his voice reminded her of how his hands felt around her neck. Kelli clasped the phone tightly. That was shots one and two. He had more. She was sure of it. Guilt made her guts churn, but she had to put it away for now. Kelli knew there were going to be consequences for what she did. If she was lucky, it would just be her brother yelling at her. "Look, I—"

"You know what? Fuck you. I'm your brother, and you just throw me away like a piece of trash!"

"How many times have we been here, Antony? How many chances have you had? You *are* my brother. That's why I want you to get better, but I'm fucking tired. Sean is too. If you won't help yourself, we gotta take care of each other." A hard knot filled with all her fear, and weariness settled at the bottom of Kelli's stomach.

"Yeah, that's what his fists keep sayin'." Antony paused. "St. Kelli. You were always the favorite. You never fuck up." He chuckled, but there was something mean about the way he sounded. "Until you almost got your partner killed."

"You don't know what the fuck you're talking about." Kelli countered. That knot in her stomach turned to lead. She wanted to hang up, to stop Antony from saying all these things to her, but she couldn't. He was her brother. Despite his accusation that she abandoned him, she owed it to him to listen. That's what family meant to her.

"How does it feel? You ain't perfect after all. But when you screw up, everyone jumps in your corner. When I screw up, I get dragged away in handcuffs."

"Take responsibility for your own shit," Kelli shouted.

"I fuckin' hate you. Ever since Pop died, you and Sean have been treating me like shit." His voice shook.

Kelli understood where Antony was going with this. He felt betrayed. That's the only way he could see it, but she still hated how fucking weak he was, pushing the responsibility for his fuck-ups onto her and Sean. Kelli took a deep breath and said, "That's not true, and you know it. You're always looking for a shortcut to get what you *think* everybody else has, and if you can't hack it, you get high. I did what I thought was right. Someday, I hope you see that."

"Whatever. I just want you to know you're gonna pay for this, and I'm gonna make sure it fucking hurts."

"We all do what we have to." Kelli refused to take the bait. She let Tony make his threats, but she knew they were empty. After what the cops witnessed at her mom's house, there was nothing to come back and bite her on the ass. She did what she had to do.

"Yeah, well. I coulda left a couple days ago, but I ain't stayin' in this shithole because of you. I'm doin' it because Mom begged me to."

"Yeah? I'm glad. I don't care what the reason is. Mom doesn't know you never made it through the other programs," Kelli whispered. She didn't try to hide the emotion in her voice. Why couldn't he see? She would do just about anything to make sure he was all right, but she was so tired and running out of options. Kelli hated strung-out Antony, but she loved the man he was underneath all the drugs.

"So? She don't need to know, and that don't matter right now," Tony said.

"Yeah, it does. Sean and me never told her, but I don't think I can protect you anymore. I don't have it in me." Kelli felt actual pain in her chest as though someone punched her right in the fucking heart. "But I lo…" Kelli let the words die in her throat. It hurt to say them because she knew he wouldn't believe her.

Tony didn't respond for a moment, then he snorted. "Well then, I guess it don't matter if I fuck up again."

"So you're…gonna break her heart?" Kelli asked softly. He was slipping through her fingers. She could feel it, but didn't know how to stop it. She nearly choked on the helplessness that swamped her senses and made it impossible to think properly. She was the one with the plan. The one who acted. The one who protected those she loved. And she was the one who failed Antony.

"That's between me and Mom. You ain't nothing to me no more."

And then he hung up, leaving her with nothing but a deafening buzz of the dial tone and an ache in her heart the size of a fucking bus.

Kelli couldn't catch her breath, and the pain in her chest spread just about everywhere. She tried to breathe through the feeling. At times like these, she missed her father so much that it felt like a physical thing. She missed him so much, she couldn't stand to be alone with her own guilt and the inability to fix this. She dialed Nora's number without thinking.

It rang and rang.

"This is Dr. Nora Whitmore. Please leave a message."

Kelli closed her eyes. Just hearing her voice helped. She ended the call and got out of bed. So much for fucking sleeping tonight.

Kelli felt as though her eyes were filled with the gritty graphite residue left in the barrel of her gun after a day at the range, and they burned with exhaustion. Since Antony's late-night ambush, her emotions went from regret to reluctant understanding. She was still just as raw as she was when he hung up on her. In order to feel somewhere close to human, Kelli poured her third cup of coffee. She felt like she was on the job but…not.

Morning crept up on her. She opened the doors to the balcony and watched the sky behind Mt. Rainier lighten and catch fire as the sun rose. After a few minutes, Kelli shuffled back toward her bedroom. There had to be something sports related on. The knock on the door put a slight wrinkle in things. It had to be her mother, and Kelli didn't know if she could talk about things right now. Antony probably called her first, and she most certainly would want to talk about all the shittiness that occurred. A phone call wouldn't be good enough. Kelli didn't want to hear "I told you so." She wasn't up to it, but she didn't really have a choice. This was her mother, and Carina wouldn't forget about the conversation. Whatever she needed to say would build inside her and burst out much bigger when she finally cornered Kelli.

Besides, Carina had a key. If Kelli didn't answer, she'd come in anyway. Kelli sat her mug on the coffee table and headed toward the door. She disengaged the locks and opened it without checking the peephole.

Her ex-girlfriend—or fuckbuddy, the terms were interchangeable in this case—stood at the door, and she was the last person Kelli expected to see.

The tiny brunette launched herself at Kelli, pulling her into a tight hug. Kelli stiffened and kept her arms to her sides, even though the weakness in her leg made her stumble a bit.

Kelli glanced at Mrs. Landau who was scowling at Ashley. She mouthed "Sorry" and closed the door.

"Ashley, what the hell?"

Ashley smiled. Kelli didn't. She ended the embrace but still stood way too close. It made Kelli uncomfortable. She took a step back.

"That old lady is still creepy by the way. She just gapes at me," Ashley said. "I heard you were out of the hospital."

"How would you know that? And Mrs. Landau does that because she doesn't like you. Never has."

Ashley narrowed her eyes. There was a time when those eyes did things to Kelli's insides. Now, she didn't feel anything, and Kelli could smell the fight brewing a mile away.

"Cops talk, especially at bars. I had to work up the nerve to come. I would have called, but I figured you would have brushed me off."

She was right. Kelli just stared. She didn't know what else to do.

"I would have thought you'd contact me," Ashley said accusingly.

Kelli snorted. "It's been over two months, and we didn't end things on a friendly note."

Ashley stepped closer. She reached out and traced her fingertips over Kelli's collar bone. "That didn't keep you out of my bed that first week after we broke up."

"Well, that was a mistake." Kelli deadpanned and brushed Ashley's touch away.

"I...I still care about you. I'm not sure why. You were never in our relationship to begin with. It was more like you came to visit for sex. But hearing about you being hurt reminded me that sometimes it was good. Really good."

Kelli softened a little. For a person to put herself out there like this was a big deal, especially when there was a chance of getting hurt. Not to mention, Ashley was right. What they had was never a relationship. Kelli had approached the whole thing as a decent, reliable lay. The clingier Ashley got, the more standoffish Kelli became. Kelli thought separating herself was the easiest way to keep her feelings from being a factor. Did that make her selfish? Kelli knew the answer was yes, and she accepted it. "I'm still a cop. Getting shot doesn't change that," she reminded her gently.

"We never even had a chance to see what we could be. We could start over. You could request a desk job." Ashley sounded hopeful.

Kelli went back to staring. "Really? That's what you're going with? I was miserable, and you…you wanted me to be somebody I wasn't."

"I just wanted more time with you!"

"I didn't have it to give! You knew my job came first. Did you think I was kidding when I told you? I couldn't be everything to you then, and I sure as hell won't try now." Kelli threw her hands in the air. "This argument is stupid. You're the one that broke it off. In a text message."

"Do you have to be so mean? You know it didn't bother you one damn bit."

Kelli's glared. "I'm not trying to be mean. Look, I have enough to deal with right now, believe me."

"God, I forgot how big an asshole you are."

Kelli smiled. Being an asshole was easy. "Glad I could remind you."

Kelli's home phone rang. She groaned. It couldn't be good news, not at this point. She snatched the cordless from the receiver and continued to glare at her unwanted guest.

"What?"

There was a brief pause.

"Kelli? I tried your cell."

Nora's voice at the other end was unexpected and took Kelli's breath away. "Nora."

"Mine was on vibrate. Why didn't you call my home phone when you tried to reach me last night?"

All the leftover emotion from her conversation with Antony rushed up to meet her, and she swallowed hard. She turned away, putting her back to the past so she could keep the present moment to herself. Nora got her full attention. Everything else disappeared. "I figured—"

"Are you all right?" Nora interrupted.

The concern in Nora's voice was hard to miss, and Kelli's insides went all gooey. "No." She wanted to tell Nora everything, and even if she had nothing to offer in return, Kelli would feel better.

"Will I still see you later? These past few days I've gotten…" Nora words trailed off.

Kelli exhaled noisily. "I probably won't be good company. We're finding out about Travis, and this crap with my family. I won't be cracking jokes, that's for sure."

"I know. Come anyway."

Kelli warmed at Nora's words. "Okay."

Ashley cleared her throat. Kelli turned around in surprise. She'd forgotten she wasn't alone.

Ashley glared.

Kelli ignored the laser beam shooting her way. "I'll see you then." She ended the call and looked at Ashley. "Time to go, Ash."

"Who was that?"

"None of your business. Please don't do this again."

"You never talked to me that way. Not even on our first date. She obviously doesn't know you and the jerk you can be."

Kelli sighed and wondered what she ever saw in this woman. "Look, I'm sorry." She pointed at Ashley then back to herself. "This, us, wasn't happening then, and it's not now. Please go."

Ashley's face flushed with anger, but she turned and moved toward the door. "You're going to disappear on her too," she said over her shoulder.

Kelli met her gaze. This was different. *Nora* was different. "No, I won't."

Ashley slammed the door.

Kelli stood in the middle of her living room and wondered at her final words to Ashley. They were true, and she knew it. Nora had earned her loyalty and so much more. Her feelings for Nora were new and scary as fuck, but now she had to admit that she didn't want them to stop despite the shittastic timing.

Nora sat her phone on the coffee table near an array of colorful swatches. Picking out a new paint color for the kitchen became a distant thought compared to the missed call and distraught tone in Kelli's voice. All Nora knew was that she had to do something to make Kelli feel better. She still couldn't figure out when Kelli had become so important. She just…was. Nora had no idea she had the ability to care within her, but she knew who was responsible for uncovering it. Nora was just more when Kelli was with her, and Nora was starting to enjoy the experience.

Then, there was her growing attraction to Kelli. With every visit, phone call, and thought, those feelings increased, and her emotions swirled together in the back of her mind like a slow boiling pot. Nora was certain that if she covered her feelings with a tight lid, this pull toward Kelli would die down eventually, just like liquid when removed from the heat. It was a nice visual, and deep down, Nora knew that's all it was. A visual.

In reality, if she covered her feelings, the pressure would build until she exploded, and the mess would be a thousand times worse than it already was.

Concerned about Kelli's behavior, Nora pushed the thoughts aside. She had a choice. She could wait for Kelli to come to her, or she could meet the situation head on. She didn't weigh the pros and cons. She didn't analyze the details. In a very un-Nora-like fashion, she went with the feeling lodged in her chest and let it guide her. She grabbed her cell phone, keys, and purse and hurried out of her house.

Nora knocked on Kelli's door and waited. The loud creek coming from the neighbor's doorway didn't surprise her. She didn't look in Mrs. Landau's direction, but the soft snick of the door shutting told her she'd been accepted. She was friend, not foe.

Nora heard Kelli grumbling through the closed door. When it opened, Kelli's eyes widened in surprise and a small smile curved her lips. But her expression fell quickly.

"Hey," Kelli said flatly, but there was something in her voice and her eyes that said Nora had made the right choice by coming here.

"Morning."

Kelli stepped aside to let Nora enter.

"You are the last person I expected to see. I sounded that bad?"

"Maybe I'm just able to pick up subtle intonations in your voice now."

Kelli smiled again. "So, that's a yes."

Nora nodded. "It is."

Kelli sat on the couch. Nora followed, sitting a respectable distance away. She watched quietly.

Kelli pushed a hand through her hair, making it stand up even more than normal. "I swear to God, I should become the heartless bitch that some people think I am. I can't be fuckin' perfect. I just do what my gut tells me is right." Kelli's jaw clenched as if she were chewing her words. "I didn't shoot drugs into Antony's vein, and I'm sure as hell not gonna go back to a woman who didn't understand me in the first place." She threw her hands up for emphasis. "I mean, I knew the involuntary committal was going to make some waves, and I do feel guilty about it. But he had to go. My mom doesn't know this, but the other times, he didn't stay. That would kill her if she knew. Things are bad enough. Hell, me, Sean, and even Tony, all agree on that one way or another. Rehab is where he needs to be. That's all that matters when it comes down to it, and I think—I hope to God—he stays this time."

Kelli's expression made Nora's chest ache. She looked so lost. Her eyes were glassy with dark smudges underneath, and she was pale. Their gazes met, and the urge to reach out to Kelli and physically comfort her was overwhelming. She made a fist, but it did nothing to lessen the impulse. The longer she waited, the more ridiculous it seemed to resist. Nora moved closer and trailed her fingers over Kelli's hand. She tried to calculate her next move. Finally, her instincts took over for her. She covered Kelli's hand with her own and squeezed. Kelli did the same in return. Warmth radiated up her arm and moved through her body.

"I'm glad you're here."

"Me too," Nora whispered. She paused and chose her words carefully. Nora wanted to help, not compare their circumstances. This was impossible anyway. "As the attending, my job is to teach residents and push them to be first rate. I've not made the best decisions in the recent past, but I can't be responsible for other people's shortcomings," she said. "Neither can you."

Kelli huffed and smiled tremulously. "Yeah. Damn. I can't tell you how long I've been trying to tell myself that."

A little unsure about Kelli's response, Nora said, "This is new territory for me. I've never given advice that wasn't medical in nature—"

Kelli's thumb brushed over her knuckles and interrupted her speech and thought process. Nora swallowed as the warmth, still present from an innocent touch, became prickles of heat.

"Nora, you're right. I can't keep throwing these pity parties for myself." Kelli pulled her hand away, ending the moment.

Nora looked at her hand. She could still feel the imprint. She realized Kelli had continued talking and renewed her focus.

"I mean, I can't wallow in all this. Travis needs me probably more today than ever." Kelli rubbed a hand over her face.

Need. Nora wondered if she needed Kelli as well or was starting to. She put the thought away for another time. "You're very protective and present for those you care about."

Kelli shrugged. "Just the way I am, I guess."

Nora allowed another thought to take hold, and before she could decipher and weigh it, she spoke. "Am I one of those people?" Nora's face flushed with heat as she finished.

Kelli's smile was wide, unrestrained. "Yeah, you are."

Nora experienced an intense flash of excitement that left her speechless. "I…I…"

"That shouldn't be a surprise." Kelli's forehead wrinkled, and she drew her eyebrows together.

Thoroughly embarrassed by her reaction, Nora cleared her throat and said, "No one has—"

Kelli interrupted. "Well, I'll say it again—it's their fucking loss."

Nora faced a different kind of excitement that puddled low in her belly.

Kelli stood. "Do I still get to see you later? I need to get ready to go to the hospital."

"Yes," Nora answered thickly.

"Is it okay if I come to you?"

"Yes," Nora said again, unable to think of another response.

A slow smile formed on Kelli's lips. "You're discombobulated."

Nora stared, but then, she returned Kelli's smile with one of her own. "Yes." She felt the tension inside her loosen slightly.

"Since you're yessing everything, can I have a million dollars? I should, just for using that word. Discombobulate. Bet you were surprised to hear that come out of my mouth."

"No. And yes."

Kelli snorted. "Such a fun sponge." She sobered seconds later. "If it's bad news, I need to apologize now for anything I might say or do."

Their gazes met.

"Come anyway," Nora repeated.

As the elevator moved closer to Travis's floor, Kelli grew more nervous and nauseated. She ignored the people surrounding her to concentrate on breathing. Travis needed her calm, collected, and he was going to get that, no matter what she had to do to make it happen.

On the next ding, Kelli glanced at the flashing red numbers. Her stop was next. She muttered an "excuse me" and used her cane to clear a path to the front. The elevator stopped. Kelli took a deep breath and stepped out after the doors opened.

The hallways in ICU were almost empty. Kelli was thankful. The last thing she needed was to run into a nurse with a grudge. On her way to Travis's room, she found her two favorite people at the nurses' station. Kelli snorted and decided to take a second to stir this pot. Messing with these two assholes would probably give her the edge she needed to face whatever was around the corner.

As she got closer, Kelli sensed some weird tension between them. And she was about to add to it. Kelli stopped behind them and cleared her throat. The doctors spun around comically. Their eyes were wide, their faces flushed.

Kelli had to stifle a laugh. She flashed a grin instead. "Ladies."

Rader scowled, but he didn't say a word.

Fuller's eyes narrowed. She pursed her lips as if she was struggling to keep them shut.

"Got your little invitation to the party. Can't wait." Kelli winked. She didn't stay for their reaction. She had more important things going on. Kelli was right about her encounter with Rader. It gave her some much needed bluster and a surge of adrenaline.

The door to Travis's room was closed. Kelli stood outside for a second before walking in. Williams, Sean, her mother, and Gerald Sr. stood around Travis's bed. They all turned to acknowledge Kelli's arrival.

Kelli caught her mother's gaze. They shared a moment and silently agreed that any discussion about Tony would have to wait.

"What's up, sis. Thought I was gonna have to call you."

"My place had a damn revolving door for a while, but there was a good part. Nora came over."

Sean's eyebrows shot to his forehead, and his lips curled slightly.

"I'm so not going there with you," Kelli said as a warning.

"Going where?" Travis and Williams asked simultaneously.

Kelli glared at her brother. "You see what you did?"

"I didn't say a thing! You did it to yourself." Sean laughed.

"Whatever." Kelli shot Williams a look. He threw his hands up and grinned. She moved closer to Travis and smirked. "You know Sean is full of shit."

Travis grinned crookedly. "It's a McCabe trai—" Travis cut himself off and looked at Kelli's mom. "I didn't mean that the way it sounded, Mrs. McCabe."

Kelli and Sean chuckled.

Carina brushed it off with a wave of her hand. "Eh, we're all full of shit at one time or another."

They all laughed, even if it was a little forced.

Kelli studied Travis. She wondered if he was ready to hear what the doctor had to say. Were any of them? Kelli saw fear in his eyes, but there was also determination. His slight nod gave her the answer she needed, and the sudden flash of his smile was just cake. That's what it all came down to in this whole crappy situation—he was doing his best to be ready no matter what the news.

"If your mother were alive, she'd be tickled at the family you've made here." Gerald Sr. stood tall and powerful, but his voice was as soft as she'd ever heard it.

"You think that's because we're white and Irish?" Sean asked.

Kelli swatted at him in return, cuffing his shoulder. "That's stupid. You're saying she'd be racist."

Sean rubbed his upper arm. "Owww, what? I was just kidding. Everybody knows I was kidding?"

Gerald Sr. chuckled. Probably more at their antics than the bad joke. Kelli's attention went back to Travis. He continued to smile, but it was a little more wobbly.

"No, it's because you're white…and crazy," Gerald Sr. said.

Travis cut through everyone's laughter just as it started again.

"If it's bad news, it's not your fault Kelli. I mean it."

Kelli was moved by his words. She looked away, hiding her face from him, from everyone. There were too many people seeing parts of her that were not approved for public scrutiny.

"Look at me. Please."

Kelli exhaled noisily and slowly met Travis's gaze.

"It's not your fault. You can't save everybody, and you can't be everywhere," Travis said.

"I know," she whispered. A touch at the small of her back startled her. She stiffened and turned to find Sean smiling gently at her. She allowed the contact for a minute, but then shook it off. This was about Travis, not her.

"You can't worry about me. This is about you." Kelli glanced over her shoulder when she felt another presence. Sean stood on her right and Williams on the left. Despite the situation, it almost felt like the team was together again.

"I know," Travis whispered in return.

There were no more jokes.

"It's the elephant in the room. Can't ignore it, and I don't want to," Travis said.

"Son, we're not—"

The door swished open. "Good afternoon, everyone. I didn't mean to keep you waiting." The neurologist greeted them.

"It's okay, Dr. Randolph," Travis said.

The doctor nodded. "Well, I won't keep you all waiting any longer."

Kelli held her breath and reached blindly for Travis's hand. He squeezed hard enough to hurt. She was more than okay with the pain.

"According to the latest MRI, it appears as though we were able to remove the majority of the scar tissue that the bullet caused. You should have some tingling in your extremities once all the residual swelling is gone. Then, after you've healed enough for it to be safe, you'll start physical therapy. We are looking at up to a six-month recovery time, but I have every reason to believe that it will be full one."

When she heard roaring in her ears, Kelli assumed it was her heart thundering against her ribcage, but actually everyone else in the room was cheering. She licked her lips and tasted salt. Kelli wiped her cheeks, and her fingers came away wet. Somewhere along the line, she'd started to cry, and for once, she didn't try to stop herself. She was still holding Travis's hand. Tears streamed down his face, but he smiled big enough for the patient in the next room to see it.

Kelli sobbed. She couldn't wait to share this with Nora.

"Thank you! Thank you." Gerald Sr. smiled and shook Dr. Randolph's hand.

He laughed. "I'm glad I could help. All of you take care."

The room exploded as everyone tried to talk at once.

"You have to come stay with me. You can have Sean's old room."

"I'll make sure you have the best home care." Gerald Sr. said as he wiped at his eyes.

"I knew you could do it, kid," Williams said.

Kelli took it all in quietly and continued to hold her partner's hand.

Nora taped a swatch to the living room wall. She stepped back and visualized the color encompassing the whole room. The hue was bold, and a far cry from her current color palette, but the modification seemed to fit her emotional metamorphosis. She decided to carry the wave of change she was riding from the kitchen to other areas of the house.

Change was past due.

The doorbell rang. Then it rang again and again, forming a recognizable pattern. Nora sighed, but not in exasperation. She loved Kelli's playful side. Obviously, this meant good news.

When she opened the door, Kelli stood there, and her smile was dazzling. Her face was flushed, and her eyes had a spark Nora hadn't seen before. This Kelli was completely different from the one she'd seen earlier in the day. She didn't wait to be greeted or invited in. Kelli swept Nora into a hug and carried her into the living room. Her cane fell to the floor with a clatter.

She laughed happily. "He's gonna be okay."

Kelli tightened her embrace, and Nora's heart raced. Nora hugged her back. Initially, she felt awkward, but it passed quickly. Nora savored Kelli's distinctive, earthy scent, as well as the solid feel of her body.

The press of Kelli's lips against her hair startled Nora, and her breath caught in her throat.

"I can hardly believe it." Kelli mumbled. Nora had never seen Kelli so happy, and she was thankful to be a part of it.

Kelli sifted her hand through Nora's hair, then splayed her fingers possessively at the nape of her neck, massaging gently. Nora shivered and tipped her head back to meet Kelli's gaze.

She was captured by the intensity in Kelli's eyes, and a bolt of arousal spread through her body, searing her from within.

"Nora," Kelli whispered.

Kelli said her name with such reverence that Nora closed her eyes against the surge of emotions. She wanted to run, but there was nowhere to go. Kelli trailed her fingertips from Nora's cheek to her lips. Unable to help herself, Nora leaned into the touch. She fisted her hands into the back of Kelli's shirt and held on as if her life depended on it.

When Kelli's lips brushed hers, Nora gasped at the gentleness in the kiss. She felt Kelli's joy, and she basked in her hope. Before she could respond, Kelli ended the caress. Nora's eyes fluttered open. She stopped breathing and simply met Kelli's burning gaze.

"I'm not sorry for this," Kelli said softly.

Kelli dipped her head once more. This time, when Kelli kissed her, there was unchecked hunger. She ran her tongue along Nora's lips and slipped seamlessly inside her mouth. As Kelli moaned, Nora whimpered. The sound escaped without permission, and little pinpricks of heat became a raging fire that spread through her quickly as Kelli's tongue slid across her own. Nora clutched at Kelli's shoulders, desperate to give as much as she was taking. Ultimately, she surrendered and lost herself in Kelli's kiss. Her mind went blank and nothing else existed, save this.

As they moved deeper into the living room, Nora bumped into something, lost her balance, and tumbled to the floor. She gasped in surprise and pain. Phineas gave a loud grunt of acknowledgment and moved on without a care in the world. Nora touched her lips and peered up at Kelli.

Kelli blinked, and her startled expression transformed into a satisfied smirk. "Whole new meaning of knocking a woman off her feet, huh?"

CHAPTER 15

Nora took a long sip of her coffee and then continued to stare blankly at the far wall. Kelli was a hazardous addition to her life. This had become her mantra over the past few days. The knowledge wasn't new, but the threat level had increased radically.

In the past, she tried to apply logic to her reaction to Kelli with the hope of understanding how one woman could cause such… Nora wasn't sure there was a word that adequately described the overall situation. But logic didn't work. Nora even tried to isolate herself, and all it took was a text, a call, a visit—a smile—and her defenses buckled like wet paper.

Nora licked the remnants of her French Roast and sweet cream from her lips. They tingled with the memory of Kelli's kiss. Nora wasn't a novice when it came to kissing, but with Kelli it was so different from all her other experiences. She lost herself in the moment—in Kelli's touch, taste, and the woman herself. Her self-control deserted her the moment their lips touched. The feelings were both freeing and frightening, and Nora continued to struggle to handle them.

As a surgeon, she was used to delicate procedures. She should have the ability to separate and contain heated emotions, just as she did with necrotic tissue from viable organs, allowing their friendship to thrive just as a patient would. It wasn't a well-thought-out plan, but it was an illusion to think she had some degree of control over this.

Kelli hadn't brought up what had happened, which gave Nora a small reprieve. However, when Kelli looked at her now, there was something different in her gaze, and whatever that was called to Nora. To add fuel to an already powerful blaze, Kelli touched her with ever-increasing frequency. It felt as though Kelli was merely lying in wait.

Nora's stomach quivered and then clenched into hard knots as a reminder of what her body wanted, what she craved. The feeling was a primitive reaction that scattered her senses every time it happened. Her body spoke one language, while the rest of her spoke another. Her mind flashed red in warning, but the alarm did not screech as loud as it did before. That, in itself, was unsettling.

Nora took a deep breath and tried to alleviate the ball of emotion steadily growing inside her. She checked her watch, and her heart sped up when she saw the time. Kelli would be here soon for their appointment with Nora's lawyer. Her body filled with a strange combination of anticipation and the still simmering anger at Dr. Rader and Dr. Fuller. Nevertheless, Nora was ready for the deposition phase to be over so she could return to some semblance of a normal life.

Before, Nora had some doubts about her ability to win the lawsuit despite her innocence. Now, Rader and Fuller were as insignificant as flies and just as irritating. She wasn't alone in this battle, and Kelli's friendship gave her hope that she could get past this mess. As if it were common and an accepted practice, her thoughts centered on Kelli. Today, the compartmentalization of Kelli McCabe was just as ineffective as all her other attempts had been. Nora's continued failure to keep herself in check shook her. She wiped suddenly clammy hands on her slacks.

She could still run. Nora inhaled deeply and dismissed the idea as soon as it formed. It didn't work before, and Kelli deserved better. And Nora knew she deserved better too. The thought of going back to who she was—to *where* she was—held little appeal, however, moving forward terrified her. She was frightened by her own unpredictability, her own needs. Nora closed her eyes and accepted that she was just as lost as she was days ago, but for some reason, Kelli appeared more confident than ever. Despite her fears and reluctance, Nora gravitated toward the assurance Kelli offered. It was just one more contradiction to add to the ever-growing pile.

As she neared her Chevy Impala, Kelli pressed the key fob to deactivate the alarm and unlock the car. She lifted her shoulder to bring the phone closer to her ear.

"I talked to Antony last night. He sounded positive, but I know he's struggling. He's still mad at you and Sean, but I think it'll pass. He just needs somebody to blame." Carina told her.

"Yeah, maybe, but I wouldn't hold my breath. He was pretty pissed when I talked to him the other day, remember? But I don't care what he said as long as he takes this seriously," Kelli said.

"What he said has to still hurt." Carina's voice was gentle and full of concern.

Kelli swallowed past the thickness in her throat. "Mom, I'm fine. Really. I'm making my peace with it."

"Fine." Carina sighed, but she didn't push. "I'll see you at dinner, then?"

"I don't know if I'll be there. I have some things I need to take care of. Can't we just play it by ear?" Kelli asked.

"Let me guess. This has something to do with that doctor you're seeing? Just bring her too."

"I'm not seeing her. We're just friends." Kelli cringed. The words didn't even sound believable to her own ears.

"But you want more than that? Sean said—"

"Sean needs to find a woman of his own. Maybe then he won't be so nosy."

"Is she nicer than that Ashley girl?" Carina asked as if Kelli hadn't said a word in denial.

Kelli groaned. The Ashley thing was definitely something she wanted to forget. "Mom—"

"Or what was her name? Dina? She was pretty, but kinda cold."

"How would you know, Mom? You met them both once." Finally able to walk without her cane, Kelli appreciated how easy it was to open the door and get in her car.

Carina scoffed. "I've only met all of them once. That's a good thing."

Kelli sighed. "Anyway. Like I said. I don't know about dinner."

"Like *I* said. Bring her." Her mother reinforced her offer.

"I don't think she's ready for that, and neither am I."

"You must really like this one," Carina said.

Kelli tiptoed around the trap her mother was trying to lay. "She's a friend, and I'm just trying to help her. That's all. Besides, she will probably cook when we get back to her place."

Carina hummed. "Oh, really?"

"Yeah."

"She any good?"

Kelly smiled. "Yes, and she is one of those people who pairs wine with food too."

"Is that right?" Carina asked innocently.

"It is." Kelli knew it was just another tactic to fish for information, but she answered anyway.

"We've been through a lot these past couple months, but I still know when you're full of it. You like her. She must be something to get you to drink wine."

Kelli rolled her eyes and cursed her mother's ability to sniff out even the smallest clues. "I'm not doing this. I'm a grown woman."

"So, that's a yes?"

It was a *hell yes*. Kelli bit her lip to keep the grin from returning. In the past, with other women, Kelli had walked freely into relationships that had all the symptoms of failure. She always saw the end coming a mile before impact but indulged herself while it lasted. It wasn't the best decision, but it was often the easiest. This…situation with Nora was hard to read, and most of the time Kelli found herself overwhelmed by her feelings. It was different and scary as fuck, but Kelli couldn't resist.

Kelli saved subtlety for police work. With everything else, she steamrolled her way through. At times, stuff actually worked out, and this *thing* with Nora was definitely one of them. Even though Nora looked as though she might run at any moment, she still answered Kelli's calls and allowed Kelli's touch. Thank Christ, because Kelli couldn't keep herself from touching Nora if she tried. It seemed as if nothing had changed, but Kelli could almost smell Nora's fear and knowing she was scared had held her in check over the past few days. But that would only last so long. Kelli knew what she wanted, and the kiss only solidified that fact. All of this had the potential to be messy, but that didn't matter. Kelli learned something from what Travis went through—sometimes things worked out. She let the thought fuel her desire for Nora Whitmore.

"She's kinda weird Kelli. I don't know." Her mother sounded wary.

"She's just a little standoffish, but once you get to know her—"

"So, you know her?"

"Dammit." Kelly was trying to avoid one trap and got caught by a different one altogether. Carina's hesitance was just part of the game. This whole thing with Nora needed to belong to just her right now. It was too big and precious to share. "Hanging up now, Mom. I'll call you later."

Thirty minutes later, Kelli shoved the phone in the pocket of her jeans as she exited her car. With only a slight limp, she made her way up the sidewalk. Kelli pressed the doorbell and decided on "Jingle Bells" or as close as she could get to it.

Nora opened the door and glared. "It is nowhere near the holidays."

Kelli smirked. "Christmas lives in my heart."

Nora bit her bottom lip, but couldn't hold back her smile. She stepped back and let Kelli inside. "No cane today?"

"I'm convinced that it made me a little too bitchtastic at times."

"I'm sure that only happened with Dr. Rader," Nora said dryly.

"Possibly." Kelli chuckled. She brushed by Nora, barely touching her. The potential heat between made her insides sweat, but Kelli ignored it. She sat down on the sectional. "Coffee, scones, or hell, I'll even take some of that nasty yogurt you like."

"That is one of the best Greek yogurts—"

"It makes my mouth feel like it's wearing a coat, Nora."

Nora scoffed. "Then why did you ask for it?"

Kelli grinned. "Because even after all this time, it's easy to get a rise out of you."

Right on cue, Nora blushed a bright crimson. She glanced away and murmured, "The coffee is fresh. I will—"

Kelli saw Nora's anxiety. Instead of letting her escape, as she walked past, Kelli reached for Nora's hand. Nora gasped at the contact, but she still covered Kelli's fingers with her own.

Kelli squeezed. She smiled at the tingle the touch caused, as well as Nora's helpless response to it. "Sit," she murmured huskily. "I'll get it."

Nora opened her mouth, presumably to protest.

"I won't break anything. I promise." Kelli stopped her.

The color in Nora's face returned to normal, and a smile came with it. "All right."

As Nora sat, Kelli stood. "You want anything?"

Nora shook her head and said breathlessly, "No. More caffeine probably isn't the best of ideas."

Kelli found the statement peculiar. Not the words, but the way Nora said it as if there was more to it. Silently, she stared at Nora for a few seconds, but she refused to meet her gaze. Kelli walked toward the kitchen and a weird prickly sensation at the back of her neck made her stop. She was being watched. She glanced over her shoulder. Caught, Nora's eyes widened, but this time she didn't look away. Kelli saw hunger, confusion, and a bunch of other indecipherable things.

"I have bacon scones," Nora whispered.

"What?" Kelli wasn't sure if she heard correctly. It was such an odd thing to say at the moment. Then again, it was so very Nora.

"Bacon scones. I was sure you would like them."

Kelli smirked. "Hell yeah. Fat is tasty, especially bacon fat."

"I'm sure." Nora's eyes twinkled.

Kelli turned and made her way into the kitchen.

❦

Kelli groaned in pleasure and swallowed the last bite. "My God, that was—" She groaned again.

"So, I was correct?" Nora asked.

"I think the answer's pretty clear. Did you make those?"

"No, I got them from the bakery not far from here. I'm sure I could. A maple glaze would probably complement the saltiness—"

"Please stop. I think my mother is getting jealous of you as it is."

Nora's eyebrows shot upward. "I'm sorry?"

Kelli grinned. "She's a great cook. She asked me about your—"

"Your mother?" Nora asked.

"Yeah? That loud, tiny, nosy, dark-haired lady with green eyes?"

"I'm familiar. I just don't understand why she would ask about me."

Kelli shrugged. "Sean runs his mouth a lot, and, apparently, I need to keep mine shut."

Nora looked dumbfounded. "You…you talk about me?"

"I guess." Kelli paused. "That's not weird. I mean, is it?"

"You're asking me?"

Kelli chuckled. "Well, I usually don't…about anybody. Talk, that is. I think that's why they're both being so catty about it. I need to go back to my old policy."

"Why? I'm not sure I understand."

"I just don't want to share you." Kelli said the words before thinking about their impact.

Kelli swore she could see the exact moment when Nora stopped breathing. Nora's mouth fell open, and her eyes grew dark and filled with a lush heat.

"Oh…I…" Nora mumbled. For a few seconds, she stayed perfectly still and didn't speak. The temperature around them spiked a few degrees. Nora clenched her hands into fists, and Kelli wondered what she was stopping herself from doing.

Nora averted her eyes and brought the moment to a screeching halt. "Maybe…" She cleared her throat. "Maybe more coffee is just what I need." Nora stood.

Kelli did as well. She refused to let Nora off that easily. Quietly, she followed her into the kitchen.

Kelli leaned against the counter. "Nervous?"

Nora glanced her way. "Excuse me?"

Kelli didn't even try to control her smirk. "About the meeting. What did you think I was talking about?"

Nora licked her lips before answering. "Without some sort of segue, I wasn't sure what you were referring to."

"Mmm." Everything started to crackle around them again. Kelli loved the feeling.

"To answer your question, no. Not in the least. It's a step closer to ending all this nonsense." Nora lifted the coffee cup to her lips, and her hand shook. It only increased the electricity in the air.

As if pulled by an invisible thread, Kelli slowly closed the distance between them. Nora set the cup back on the counter and stepped away toward the door.

"We should probably go," Nora said airily.

Nora moved quickly, but Kelli was faster. She grasped Nora's forearm and brought them to a standstill.

"We have time," Kelli said.

Nora's gaze dropped from Kelli's eyes to her mouth and back again. Her breathing hitched, and the sound nearly sent Kelli's stomach to the floor.

"I didn't forget about what happened between us," Kelli whispered. "Just because I haven't said anything about it doesn't mean I forgot. I can't." She took a step closer, and the sparks between them became flames. "You're scared, I get that, but I'm not gonna stop this." She leaned in and brushed her lips against Nora's forehead.

Nora whimpered softly.

"I don't think you want me to," Kelli added. This was Nora. She needed to be gentle despite her body screaming at her to do the opposite. Kelli kissed her tenderly. Their lips clung to each other as they shared the same breath. Nora fingertips dug into Kelli's arms. Afraid to let her go or afraid to pull her closer? Kelli couldn't tell.

Nora didn't say a word in response, but she didn't need to.

When Kelli placed her hand at the small of her back, Nora stiffened slightly. It was a gesture meant to reassure. Still, the contact also denoted possession.

Her mind whirled with questions. Hadn't Kelli possessed her with her words, her kiss? Nora knew the answer, and she was defenseless against it. She relaxed and allowed her resistance to melt away. Her senses tingled, and she was so much more aware of the things around her. It was a strange sensation, but then again, all of this was.

They walked into the lobby of Thomas, Young, and Associates and stopped at the front desk. The receptionist smiled brightly at Kelli, but her expression seemed to dim when she noticed Nora.

"Nora!" Tom Young stepped away from the small group surrounding him. "Early as always. Don't move. I'll be right with you."

"Now that's what I call service," Kelli whispered.

"Indeed," Nora peered over her shoulder and caught Kelli's gaze.

Kelli smiled. "What?"

"Nothing. I'm just glad you're here."

"It was either this or daytime television." Kelli stepped closer. "You're a lot more stimulating."

Nora looked down and tried to hide her flushing features. However, she could do nothing against the surge of heat.

Tom reappeared. "Ladies, please follow me."

Tom leaned back in his chair and watched them expectantly. "Due to your existing friendship, I'm sure Ms. Fuller's lawyer will have you labeled as hostile. Regardless, I'm confused as to her reasons behind this."

Kelli shrugged. "I'm sure they are trying to establish pattern of behavior. I was a patient in the hospital and witnessed a conversation between them."

"Was it something volatile?"

"She commented on Dr. Fuller being on Rader's service."

The lawyer blinked. "That's all?"

Kelli smirked. "She was bitchy about it. It wasn't any different than she was with some of her other residents."

"So, you're saying that from what you saw, Dr. Whitmore treated all the residents the same?"

"Yeah, but she was also hinting that they were sleeping together. She just didn't come out and say it until I asked directly."

"I believe that was common knowledge," the lawyer said.

"It was." Nora agreed.

"Did she sound jealous or hurt by this?"

Kelli snorted. "I'm a cop. I've seen plenty of jealous lovers. This wasn't it. She said that sleeping with him had been a big mistake. Seems to me, Rader has the problem with letting go."

"What do you mean?" Tom asked.

Nora glanced at Kelli. Her expression was serious.

"Well, I overheard Rader and Fuller talking in my room one night. They thought I was sleeping. I'm pretty sure they were talking about setting Nora up. Fuller sounded like she was ready to back out, but Rader told her that it would work out and whatever they were planning was worth it. Plus, since they brought me in, maybe we need to establish our own little pattern. I'm gonna assume you guys have video surveillance of the building? Entrances, exits, even the garage?"

"Interesting but that's pure conjecture. Did either of them use her name?"

"No, unfortunately."

"Too bad but if I wait until the right moment, I may be able to use that. They're sloppy, I'm sure we'll find a smoking gun soon. As for surveillance, yes, we do. Complete with audio too. You'd be astonished how much help *that* is at times."

"Good, pull the files from the day of the first deposition. You'll see what I mean."

"All of this sounds extremely promising. It could put some exploitable cracks in their case. Thank you, Detective McCabe. Now, if you would excuse us. I have some things to discuss with—"

"I'd prefer for her to stay." Nora interrupted.

Kelli peered in her direction, grinning. "She's the boss."

In response, Nora smiled.

Tom cleared his throat. "That she is. I just wanted to let you know where we are. Our investigators are still interviewing security personnel, but so far we've gotten nothing. I think that just means we've been asking the wrong questions. We need to concentrate on the day the accusations were made, as well as a few days before and after. As far as the security footage goes, we hit some red tape. If we get some answers from personnel, that may help clarify things. I was able to get the medical records for Gerald Travis Jr. as you suggested. It will go a long way to show cause and weaken their argument that you pressuring her sexually excluded her from your surgeries."

Nora nodded and experienced a renewed sense of hope.

Kelli buckled her seatbelt and glanced at Nora. "All that made me kinda hungry."

Nora started her Mercedes. "Really? It's only been two and a half hours since you had scones."

"Yes, well talking burns calories. What can I say? Besides, things are looking up. Shouldn't we celebrate? There's a food truck farther downtown that serves the best carnitas tacos I've ever tasted."

Nora pulled out of the parking garage. "From the back of a truck?" She asked hesitantly.

Kelli smirked. "Well, welcome to my world. We celebrate with meat and beer, even if it's from the back of a truck. Now c'mon." Kelli begged. "Live a little."

Nora scrunched up her face, and Kelli laughed. Without looking at Kelli, Nora said, "As a doctor, I'm uncomfortable with that practice."

"I guess you'll just have to trust me." Kelli pointed at the turn she wanted Nora to make. "Make a right up here. And, sorry, they don't usually sell the type of wine you drink at these things. Maybe box of wine."

"Why on earth would someone do that? Is beer ever sold in a box?"

Kelli felt nauseated. How could Nora say something so…disturbing? "Hell no. That'd be nasty."

"Precisely." Nora's face crinkled again. She looked ten kinds of disgusted. It was fucking precious.

"Well, get ready, because you can't have a taco without beer. That's just sacrilegious."

"I'll take it under advisement."

"You do that. Hang a left on the next block, then an immediate right on Fourth Street, then get on Yesler's Way. The truck is usually near Pioneer Square." Kelli enjoyed the banter, and she didn't want it to stop. Plus, Nora's skittishness from earlier seemed to have disappeared. "I've had your wine, you know. So, it's only fair that you try beer. I wouldn't make you drink the bad shit. Some of the most popular beers in America taste like moose piss."

"I don't understand."

"Diluted moose piss. That's all you need to know. Again, trust me."

"That doesn't sound encouraging." Nora shook her head.

"Beer is just like wine. There's the good stuff, which is pretty much anything produced by Founder's brewery and a few other ones. There is the middle of the road beer, like Abita, and then there's utter crap."

"America's favorite," Nora said.

"Quick study."

"Thank you." Nora's voice was laced with sarcasm.

Kelli smiled and then turned to scan for traffic and parking. "Pull in here." She pointed at an empty spot in front of one of the local credit unions. "I thought we were gonna have to walk back down. I'm surprised there's parking." Kelli was far too excited, and she wasn't sure why. But she was content to just go with the flow.

When Kelli got out of the car, she circled around to the driver's side to open Nora's door. Nora stood and stared across the street toward their destination.

Wondering why Nora hesitated, Kelli offered some encouragement. "There's always a crowd, but they're fast."

"The Dirty Cat?" Nora murmured.

Kelli peered at the bold red lettering on the yellow food truck and laughed. "Yeah, it's not easy to forget. Travis loves this place." Just like that, Kelli understood her excitement. She was sharing yet another piece of herself. It was a small one, but it was a piece wrapped in good memories instead of the crap she pushed her way through now.

"*The Dirty Cat.*" Nora emphasized the words. The disgusted look was back, and, yeah, it was still adorable.

"Don't let the name fool you. Trust me." Kelli said again and put her hand on Nora's back. She gave her a little push forward. "Watch out for traffic."

Nora stopped and glanced over her shoulder. "I do."

Kelli didn't remove her hand. She slid it downward to the small of Nora's back. "You do what?" She asked, a little distracted.

"Trust you." There was a flash of fear in Nora's gaze. Maybe she was scared to admit it? Maybe she expected the sky to fall? But the look quickly changed to one of warmth.

Kelli felt her heart stop for a moment and then sputter back to life, beating ten times stronger and faster. Was she smiling? Because her face felt like it was about to split in two. "Best thing I've heard all day."

On cue, Nora blushed.

The line moved fast as promised. "I guess I should've asked, but do you like spicy? I'm pretty sure they use serranos."

Nora looked at her. "Is there anything else you want to tell me before we reach the front of the line?" She smiled slightly.

"Negra Modelo." Kelli smirked.

"Pardon?"

"Dark beer and very easy to drink. I think you'll like it."

"We'll see," Nora challenged.

Kelli's stomach did that thing where it flipped upside down. "We sure will." She stepped up to the window.

"What's up, McCabe?"

"Stopping in for a bite. How you been, Julio?" She grinned at him. He was a big man, both tall and wide.

"You know, eating too much." He rubbed his belly. "Drinking too much. My story doesn't change, but I heard about what happened. Good to see you out and about." Julio glanced at Nora briefly. "Where's Travis?"

"He's still in the hospital."

"Damn. He's good, though, right?"

"Yeah, it's just gonna be a while," Kelli told him.

"Well, I tell you what. Stop by here before you go visit him from now on. His food is on the house."

"Really?" Kelli was touched and a little surprised.

"Yup."

Kelli inched closer to Nora. "I brought you a new customer. Isn't that worth something?"

Julio snorted. "Undying gratitude?"

Kelli glared at him, but out of her periphery, she saw the smile on Nora's face. People always told her she was entertaining and making Nora smile was a huge bonus. "Thanks a lot. Appreciate it," she added sarcastically. "We'll have four carnitas tacos and two Negra Modelos."

"Sorry, man. It's a no-go on the beer and fountain drinks. I got a guy coming to check out my set-up within the hour."

Kelli deflated a little. "You don't have anything in a can?"

"Coke in a bottle, water, and Te—"

"Ugh don't even say it." Kelli paused. "Really?"

Julio nodded.

"What's wrong with that one?" Nora asked.

Kelli did everything she could to keep from going on another beer tirade.

"Nothing. She's a beer snob. It's a popular brand in California and Mexico," Julio said.

Kelli gave him the stink eye.

He smiled.

"What's your point?" Nora looked at Kelli.

Kelli leaned over and whispered in her ear. "Moose piss."

"It can't be that bad." In spite of their earlier discussion, Nora looked unconvinced.

"I thought you said you trusted me." Kelli teased.

Nora lowered her gaze, but she had a slight grin in place.

Amused by the display, Kelli decided to play a little. "Give the lady what she wants. A can of beer, two cups, and a couple waters, please. We're holding up the line." A majority of the people in their line had moved to the other side of the window, but there were still quite a few behind them.

A couple of minutes later, and with food in hand, Kelli steered them toward one of the tiny tables that sported a giant yellow umbrella in the same shade as the truck, and they sat down.

"I forgot to get a fork," Nora said.

Kelli chuckled. "You're cute. It's okay to get your hands dirty. I promise."

And there it was again—the blush.

Kelli opened the beer and poured a little in each plastic cup. "Let's get this out of the way first, and you'll never doubt me again." She placed the cup in front of Nora and picked up her own. "Cheers." She knocked the beer back, cringing as it went down. She smacked her lips and chugged a half bottle of water. She looked at Nora and waited, but Kelli couldn't keep the smirk off her face.

"You didn't seem that affected."

Kelli shrugged. "Drink up. It might be better if you do it like a shot. This definitely isn't a sipping beer."

Nora stared at her.

Kelli traded her smirk for a smile.

Nora brought the cup to her lips and took a giant gulp. Her eyes widened and her cheeks puffed out.

Kelli reared back in laughter. "Don't forget to swallow."

Nora glared at her, but there was a warm glint in her eyes as well. She swallowed and gasped. "That was—"

"Say it with me now—moose piss."

"Somewhat disgusting," Nora said instead.

"Mmm hmm. Eat your food before it gets cold."

Nora coughed. "Obviously, you take beer seriously."

Kelli opened a tiny plastic container full of red sauce and poured it on her taco. "Damn right I do. If I have beer and jelly in my fridge, I'm happy." She took a bite.

"Is that some sort of additional condiment?" Nora pointed at the half filled container.

Holding up a finger, Kelli finished chewing before she answered. "It's a garlic habanero thing. Spices things up quite a bit."

"I didn't get any."

"You have to ask for it, but I've been here enough. Julio knows what I like."

Nora twisted the top off her water. "May I have some of yours then."

Kelli stared at her for a moment then asked. "You sure?"

Nora nodded. "Completely."

Kelli pushed the habanero sauce Nora's way. Their fingers touched in the exchange, and Kelli wasn't sure if it was the peppers or Nora that made her feel so warm inside.

Nora lifted the corner of her mouth. "Thank you," she said softly.

Well, that settled things. The peppers had absolutely nothing to do with the jolt of heat.

Kelli took another bite of her food and watched as Nora did the same.

Nora didn't even flinch.

Hot damn. That was sexy. Kelli couldn't look away—a normal occurrence when she was with Nora.

Nora chewed slowly and met Kelli's gaze. She picked up a napkin to wipe her mouth. "Is there something—"

"On your face?" Kelli finished for her.

Nora nodded.

"No, it's perfect." Kelli continued to stare. When Nora's eyes widened, Kelli realized what she'd said. "I meant…" She stopped talking and slowly let her gaze wander over every part of Nora's face, from her porcelain skin, her intriguing, whiskey-colored eyes, delicate features, and her full lips. Kelli knew what Nora's skin felt like. She knew how her lips tasted. In Kelli's mind, there were no other word that could describe her. "I meant what I said the first time," she said softly. "You look perfect."

Nora opened her mouth, but she closed it a few seconds later. Her face blushed bright red, and her pulsed pounded at the base of her throat. Her eyes grew dark, her expression vulnerable. "No, I…Kelli…" Her voice trailed off. She took a deep breath and closed her eyes. When she opened them again, Nora looked utterly confused. "What you see when you look at me, it's not who I am."

For several seconds, Kelli remained quiet. She wanted her next words to have an impact. She chose them carefully. "Yes, you are. You just haven't gotten to know her yet."

If possible, Nora's expression became even more vulnerable than it had been a minute ago, but Kelli also saw fear creep back into her eyes. "How do… who *are* you?" Her voice shook. Nora looked at Kelli as if she had never seen anything—anyone—like her before.

Kelli smiled and ate the rest of her taco.

CHAPTER 16

Under her own power, Kelli walked into Seattle Memorial and made her way to ICU. As she passed the nurses' station, Kelli was a little disappointed that her favorite doctors weren't hanging around. She chuckled quietly, confident that the scales would tip Nora's way soon.

She knocked twice and then entered Travis's room without invitation. She stopped abruptly to take in the sight of Gerald Travis Jr. with a white face. It took a few moments for her brain to catch up with the image and for her to realize that it was shaving cream. Or he'd developed some sort of skin disorder.

"At first, I thought you were wearing makeup."

Travis wiped his hands on a towel and rolled his eyes. "Trust me. I have no desire to be white," he said as he picked up his razor and mirror from his lap.

"Do you have to make it sound like the worst thing in the world?" Kelli smirked.

Travis snorted. "I can moonwalk. What can you do, white girl?"

Kelli groaned. "Too soon! It's only been like ten years since he died. I'm still learning."

Travis turned his head slightly and pressed the razor to the right side of his face.

"Why are you getting rid of the whiskers?" Kelli asked.

"Because I look like somebody pasted them on?"

Kelli snickered. "It was starting to fill out…a little."

Travis glared. "Friends tell friends when they look ugly. Don't get me started on my hair."

"What? The curly bush thing works for you. Makes you look mysterious. Very Fu Manchu."

He glared harder at her. "I can't believe you just said that. I don't even know what that means. Plus, I'm not Chinese. I'm half Korean, remember?"

Kelli smirked. "Yes, but you're one hundred percent easy to fuck with."

"Riiight. You still could have said something."

Kelli murmured, "Considering what's been going on, there was nothing wrong with a little white lie."

His gaze softened. "Yeah, true." He held up the mirror.

Quietly, Kelli watched him. The moment felt almost normal, as if she were waiting because they were running late for work. She missed the smell of the station—stale coffee and too much Old Spice. She missed teasing him about the tie he wore, but she did not miss the way his arm started to tremble.

"Fuck, my muscles are like jelly." Travis plucked at the crisp white T-shirt covering his chest. "At least I'm able to get this on by myself."

Kelli eased into the chair by his bed. "Isn't that normal? The weakness I mean?"

"I guess. Can't sit here looking like this, though." Travis looked uncomfortable. "I guess I could get one of the nurses to do it. Sean's already been by, but maybe my dad won't be too weirded out."

"I'll do it." Without pretense, Kelli stood.

Travis grinned crookedly. "You ever done this before?"

"Nope. Saw this movie once, where shaving someone was some kind of exercise in trust."

"Yeah, sexy too."

"Ew." Kelli took the razor from him and dipped it into the cup of water before she sat on the bed.

Travis pursed his lips and batted his eyelashes. "What? You don't think I'm sexy?"

"Fuck you," Kelli laughed. "Now, give me instructions."

Travis smirked. "Shave with the grain."

"Say what now?"

"The direction of the hair growth."

"Oh, gotcha." With a steady hand, Kelli started where he left off.

He watched her quietly. "Things cool off between you and Sean, I take it?"

Kelli nodded. "I had to get over the whole lie-of-omission thing. Not gonna say it was easy, but there's no way we could have handled Tony separately."

"True. You know, you never said if it bothered you that Sean talked to me about Tony."

Kelli shrugged and stuck the razor in the water to clean it off. "Not enough. I didn't know about it until later. He had to tell somebody. I'm sure dealing with Tony alone was eating him up inside." She grasped his chin and turned his face to the side. "I don't get it, really."

"Get what?"

"You're a lot younger than me."

Travis rolled his eyes. "Six years, for fuck's sake."

"That's a lot like dog years."

"Whatever. What's your point?"

"You're the go-to guy. For both of us, obviously. How the fuck did you get so wise?"

Travis chuckled. "Confucius say—"

Kelli stopped and stared at him. "Don't even go there. I swear to God, I'll cut you."

Travis grinned. "Fine. We all have our roles, I guess. Yours is protector or asshole, depending on the day."

Kelli laughed. "Shut it. Tilt your head up."

They didn't talk for a few minutes, but the quiet between them was comfortable as always.

"So…" Travis's voice went up an octave or two.

"Mmm?"

"I hear you've been seeing Dr. Whitmore."

Kelli took her hand away and glared at him. She wasn't ready to discuss anything concerning Nora. "Really?" She grumbled.

Travis quirked an eyebrow. "Have I had anything to do besides gossip?"

"That doesn't excuse it."

"Yes, it does." He countered.

"Whatever. You might not want to upset me right now."

He laughed. "Your threat didn't hold water a minute ago, and it still doesn't. It's not a straight razor."

"Still, I'd hate for that baby face to be littered with toilet paper." Kelli grinned.

"You'd do all that to protect your secret?"

"I don't have a secret." Kelli sighed wearily. This was the last thing she expected to talk about with him or anyone.

"Uh-huh." Travis looked totally unconvinced.

She dipped the razor in water and pressed it to his face once more. "We're just—"

"Don't even go there. I do not deserve to be poo-pooed."

Cringing, Kelli muttered, "You do just for saying it."

"Don't be such a dry box. I see right through you."

Kelli did a double take. "A what?"

"Does shriveled sound better?" Travis asked innocently.

"How bout we not talk about my box at all?"

"Well, if you insist."

"I do, dammit. I do," Kelli said.

Travis held up a finger, and she pulled back. "But, I think the conversation is directly related to your box, so there's no avoiding it."

Kelli sighed. "You irritate the shit out of me sometimes."

"I'm aware." Travis chuckled and settled into a soft smile. "I've been out of touch. I want to know what's going on with you."

Now, she just felt shitty. This was Travis, and maybe, she was feeling a little generous today. They stared at each other for a few seconds, and that was enough to convince her that whatever was said here would stay here. "Yeah, we're kinda seeing each other."

"Kinda?" Travis looked confused.

"It's…complicated. She's scared."

"Straight gir—"

"No, it's not that." Kelli shut him down.

His gaze continued, but she could see when realization hit him. "Oh, she's one of those commitment-phobic people. Wait, you are too. Do you know what you're doing?"

Kelli smiled. "No clue."

Travis shook his head as he laughed. "You're in trouble."

"Yeah, kinda." She started shaving underneath his chin.

He learned what he needed to know, so Travis didn't ask a million more questions about Nora. He didn't work that way, and he knew she didn't either.

"Kelli?" His expression was soft, wistful.

"Hmm?" Kelli replied.

Seconds went by.

"I'm starting to feel prickles in my legs."

Kelli stared at him. "Prickles?"

"Yeah, kinda."

Kelli laughed.

Nora was surrounded by a paint crew, and her kitchen was essentially hidden underneath protective drop cloths and plastic. It felt good to move forward even with the small things like getting her house interior painted.

"Ms. Whitmore?"

She turned toward the voice. The man who spoke was tall and muscular with decidedly rugged good looks. His features were further highlighted when he smiled. She returned his smile to be polite, but it was only a slight lift of the corners of her mouth. "It's Dr. Whitmore."

"I won't forget that next time," he said.

"Thank you."

He continued to stare. Clearly he was attracted to her, but she didn't feel the least bit interested. Intellectually, she appreciated him aesthetically, but her libido didn't seem to notice. "You wanted to ask me a question?" she asked crisply.

His smile dimmed. "I just wanted you to know that the kitchen shouldn't take more than a couple of hours, then we'll get to your living room."

Nora nodded. "I'm aware. Your crew chief already informed me. It's why I hired him."

He took a step back. "Uh, I was just making sure."

"Thank you." Now able to smell fresh paint, Nora pressed a finger underneath her nostrils.

The man turned and rejoined his crew.

Unable to stand the fumes any longer, Nora left the kitchen and made a beeline for her bedroom.

The interaction disturbed her. Not because of anything he said, but because of her reaction. Or rather her lack of one. She decided not to overthink it. Her last attempt at casual sexual release wasn't the least bit satisfying. Maybe her non-response was her body's way saving her from disappointment.

As was her new normal, her thoughts inevitably turned to Kelli. This explanation made sense in regard to the painter, but it had nothing to do with Kelli. Her body came to life when she was around. Nora felt familiar stirrings in her stomach and so she searched her room for a distraction.

She picked up the remaining paint swatches and evaluated her bedroom walls by holding up several shades of red. The color would be a bold change from sage, but maybe it was time. She pressed a tiny square against the wall that had a more pinkish hue than the others. She pictured Kelli rolling her eyes and saying something snarky about Pepto Bismol. Nora sighed at her inability to keep her thoughts from drifting to Kelli. They saw each other every day and even talked on the phone. Nora was immersed in Kelli.

Her cell phone rang. Nora picked the phone up and stared at the caller ID. Apparently, thinking about Kelli invoked her presence in some form or fashion. Something in the back of her mind encouraged her to ignore the call. Despite that, Nora answered anyway.

"Hey. I thought I was gonna have to leave you a message. Glad you answered."

"Hello to you as well, Kelli." Nora smiled. She couldn't help herself.

Kelli chuckled. "Always so proper. I can't wait to see the day when you're not. I'm gonna take video and put it on YouTube."

Even though she was sure that Kelli meant nothing sexual, the statement made her stomach clench. "Well, that, I'm sure, will be the first sign of the apocalypse."

Kelli didn't respond for a moment, then finally said, "Did you…did you just make a joke of some kind? I mean, it's been a while."

Nora was surprised herself. "I'm not sure. Did I?"

Kelli released a bark of laughter. "Well, I'll be damned."

"Quite possibly." Nora blinked. She felt strange but warm at the same time.

Kelli laughed harder. "Holy shit! I'm corrupting you."

Nora waited for the prickle of unease that was usually a part of talking to Kelli, but it never came. "Obviously."

"This day is just getting better and better. Spent my morning shaving Travis's beard, and talked like old times. Now, Nora Whitmore is making jokes. Can't top that."

"Are you being facetious?"

"Not in the least. Maybe before the day is over with, I'll have you laughing again."

"Maybe." Nora looked forward to the possibility.

"I have PT in fifteen. What are you up to?"

"Hiding away from the paint fumes, and I've decided to have the master bedroom painted as well."

"Oh yeah? What color?"

Nora's lips twitched. She wasn't at all sure what had gotten into her. "A derivation of pink."

"Ugh, you mean like Pepto pink?"

Nora smiled. Kelli had yet to disappoint her.

"I know you're joking. So, moving on. If the paint fumes are bothering you, just go to my place. Might as well get a jump start on relaxing before Monday's deposition. You're coming later anyway."

This time the warmth in her chest was much more than a flutter. "I'm not sure," Nora said nervously.

"I don't bite." Kelli teased.

The comment hung in the air. It was nothing like her statement about taking video. This time there was something in Kelli's tone. This one had definite erotic intent. Nora pictured Kelli's sweat-soaked body moving on top of hers.

"Uh, you know what I mean." Kelli's voice dropped an octave. She was clearly affected as well. "Besides, shouldn't be an issue since I'm not there anyway."

"I'll consider it."

"Mrs. Landau has a key."

There was a pause. Nora could hear conversation in the background.

"I'm gonna go. Just walked into Williams. See you later?"

"Yes."

Nora ended the call. She peered down at her cell phone and tried to figure out when she had gained the kind of social skills she had just utilized. This particular change was delicate, unassuming, and not like anything she'd experienced so far. Perhaps that was why it was so easy to acknowledge. On the heels of this epiphany, Nora decided to take Kelli up on her offer.

Nora walked hurriedly down the corridor, balancing an array of grocery bags that were growing heavier by the minute. It had become commonplace for her to bring food to cook when she came to Kelli's. Otherwise they'd end up eating take out. She neared Mrs. Landau's door but paused when she heard loud music coming from Kelli's apartment. Intrigued, Nora knocked on the door rather than getting the key from the neighbor. She waited an appropriate amount of time, adjusted the bags, and knocked again. There was still no answer. Mildly irritated, she tried the knob and the door opened.

The music was nothing more than electric guitars, drums, and a man screeching at the top of his lungs. She cringed and moved farther inside. Sean McCabe stood in the kitchen with his head thrown back, guzzling a beer. He wiped his mouth with the back of hand and bobbed his head to the music, oblivious to Nora's presence. The bobbing quickly changed to thrashing, and then he began jumping around as if he were caught in the throes of a seizure.

Nora wondered if she could slip out unnoticed. The handle on one of the bags tore, and a wheel of Gouda, an onion, and a couple of red peppers fell out. Thankfully, there were no breakable items. Nora placed the rest of the bags on the floor and picked up the runaway cheese and produce. When she looked up, Sean was staring at her in disbelief.

"Dr. Whitmore?"

She could not hear him over the music but was able to read his lips. Nora pointed at her ear.

Sean nodded and turned off the stereo. Finally, the noise stopped. Nora picked up the bags to take them to the kitchen. Sean intercepted her and took them for her.

"Let me get those." He glanced at her warily. "How long have you been here?"

Nora didn't respond. She simply stared.

A slight blush tinged his cheeks. "That long, huh?"

She followed him to the kitchen.

"I didn't expect Kelli to have company. It's my day off, and sometimes I come here."

Nora scanned her surroundings, and noticed his sneakers and socks on the floor in the living room, along with a number of empty snack packages. Kelli's prized and usually mounted flat screen TV was centered on a flimsy stand. Cartoon images raced across the screen. "I see."

His face flushed. "I got the spare key from Mrs. L. because Kelli has a better TV for…video games. I'll clean it all up before she gets home." He sounded contrite.

Nora simply nodded and continued to stare.

"Don't call her. I only do this like once every blue moon."

"Mr. McCabe—"

"Sean. I think you can call me Sean now."

"Sean. I agree that you probably need to clean up, but I see no need to resort to a phone call."

He grinned and released a deep breath. In that smirk, Nora could see the family resemblance just as clear as day. She found herself smiling in return.

Sean began digging through the bags. "So you're the one who stocks her fridge? I was wondering why there's more than beer, jelly, and leftover Chinese." He watched her speculatively as if he was expecting something more.

Nora returned his gaze.

"Kelli's definitely moving up in the world."

"We share meals. Sometimes at my place and other times here. I've learned that it's usually a good idea to bring a few things."

He smirked again. "Uh-huh." He held up his bottle of beer. "You responsible for Dirty Bastard too?"

"Yes, Whole Foods has quite the selection of Founder's products."

"Mmm, you know I'm a firm believer in the trickle-down theory." Sean's tone and gaze were playful.

"What does economic policy have to do with our conversation?"

"Because what's good for one McCabe is good for another. If you're gonna bring her shit, don't be shy about bringing it to me as well." Except for the teasing glint in his eyes, he looked completely serious.

Nora glared, but Sean's expression didn't change. It's what got her in the end. Her lips quivered with the effort to keep herself from smiling. "Charming."

Sean's smile was bright and full of dimples. "That's part of trickle-down too." He waited a second. "You know? Charm trickles down to each McCabe."

"I see." Nora grinned.

He laughed. "Think of it as a public service announcement."

"Maybe I will."

Sean turned and put the rest of the groceries away. In the quiet, Nora realized that she just had a very entertaining conversation with someone she barely knew *without* feeling uncomfortable. At first, she assumed that it was just because he was Kelli's brother, but she discarded that idea because he was still, in essence, a stranger. She wasn't sure how she felt about this. So, Nora decided to retreat.

"I should leave you to your music and games." Nora backed up a step.

Sean glanced over his shoulder. "Metallica and *Mass Effect 2*."

"Pardon?"

"The music and video games. Don't make yourself scarce on my account. I can just use her bedroom."

Nora glared at him again.

A corner of his mouth curled upward. "You know her that well? Then, maybe not."

"Wise choice," Nora muttered.

"You still don't have to go. Stay. Supervise the clean-up?"

"I don't think—"

"Look, I'm not exactly sure what's going on with your job, but I know two things. Kelli is trying to help, and she wants you here. So, stay. Putter around in the kitchen. I'll clean up. Okay? You won't even know I'm here."

Reluctantly, Nora gave in with a nod. She waited until he left the area completely before pulling out the cutting board and a knife. The simplicity of preparing food was strangely soothing.

Several minutes passed before Sean returned.

"My God, what is that smell? I just wanna stick my face in it."

Nora glanced up from the sizzling sauté pan full of mushrooms, onions, and peppers.

He gave her a lopsided smirk. "I wasn't trying to disturb you. Just couldn't help myself. What are you making?"

"A veggie and cheese frittata."

"A what now? Kelli eats that?"

Amused, Nora said, "She does."

Sean snorted. "Well, she does like cheese."

Nora turned toward the other counter and began cracking eggs. She could feel Sean's gaze on her back.

He mumbled something.

"I'm sorry. I didn't hear you," Nora said.

"Just thinking out loud, but I guess it's worth saying."

Assuming he needed her full attention, Nora gave it to him.

"Kelli doesn't do this."

"Do what?"

"What you're doing. You must really be something."

He was alluding to her growing relationship with Kelli, and Nora's chest tightened with panic. She tried to breathe through it. Suddenly, she wasn't sure she wanted to be that level of *something* to Kelli. Not that it mattered because Nora couldn't stay away.

"Just don't—" He started.

The door opened, halting their conversation.

Kelli glanced at her brother for a few seconds before her look turned into a glare. "I better have beer left."

Sean rolled his eyes. "Nora brought more."

Kelli's gaze softened. She smiled, and it was big enough to encompass the room. Nora's uncertainty dissipated. There was freedom in letting go. Nora had already walked forward two steps before she realized she was moving, but Kelli noticed. Her eyes darkened accordingly.

Kelli cleared her throat and pointed at her brother. "He didn't bother you, did he?"

The moment ended and seamlessly developed into another.

"Hey!" Sean protested.

Nora looked at him. He pleaded silently with his eyes, and she said, "No, he didn't bother me at all."

"Uh-huh." Kelli sounded vaguely suspicious. She narrowed her eyes. Then, her expression changed completely. "My God. What is that smell?"

Nora rinsed the dishes and placed them in the dishwasher. On the other side of the kitchen, Kelli wiped the stove and countertops. The lack of conversation wasn't unusual or awkward, but rather it was a part of the growing comfort between them.

Nora glanced over her shoulder. "Your brother is interesting."

Kelli snorted. "Careful now. He's just in the living room. He might hear you and get a bigger head." She paused. "You're not gonna say he's the male version of me, are you?"

Instantly amused, Nora asked, "Heard that before, have you?"

"Ugh, Travis, Williams, and even my mother."

Nora bent slightly over the dishwasher to put the silverware in the tray. Kelli brushed against her. In response, Nora stiffened and straightened. Kelli touched her lower back and Nora turned her head only to come face to face with Kelli herself.

Kelli closed the open cabinet behind Nora's head. Their eyes met, and Kelli cleared her throat. "I had to put the spices up." Her eyes darkened and strayed downward to Nora's lips.

Nora's stomach tightened, and a deep, powerful pull of arousal surged through her. She was equal parts panicked and lured by the feeling. Within a few seconds, her anxiety tipped the scales. Nora pulled back abruptly. She remembered Sean's words. *Kelli doesn't do this.* Nora had free reign over Kelli's home. Kelli discussed Nora with her friends and family. Nora put it all together, and obviously, she meant a lot to Kelli, more than she thought, and that was a tremendous responsibility. Did she have the ability to take that on? It was certainly something she needed to think about. What if she couldn't give Kelli what she wanted? What if—

"Whoa." Kelli held up her hands. Her voice was a whisper. "You thought I was gonna kiss you?"

Nora swallowed and averted her gaze. Still, Kelli was close enough to smell, to feel, and to touch. She didn't know what to say.

"Nora?"

There was something about the way Kelli said her name that set her nerves on fire. Nora was helpless against it. Analyzing it wasn't going to change that fact. They continued to stare at each other, and the flames burning between them grew. She opened her mouth to speak, but no words came out.

"Did you want me to?" Kelli asked throatily.

Nora's stomach dropped, and her body flooded with need.

Kelli stepped closer. Her pupils were nearly black, her breathing ragged. "Did you?"

Nora took a deep breath in an effort to center herself, and it wasn't helpful in the slightest. Dear god, she wanted to kiss her. The need bordered on compulsion, and part of her still ran from it. "Your…brother is in—"

"Then, I guess you'd better hurry and decide." Kelli reached out to trail a fingertip over Nora's nose and onto her bottom lip.

Whatever control Nora thought she possessed fled in that instance. She swiped Kelli's fingertip with her tongue, then parted her lips, and sucked it into her mouth.

Kelli moaned. Nora was captivated by the sound. She pulled Kelli in deeper.

"Fuck," Kelli whispered.

Arousal bolted through Nora. That one word—dirty and vulgar—was her complete undoing. Nora gasped. Then, before she could take another breath, Kelli swooped in. Their lips met, and Kelli kissed her ravenously. She grasped Nora's hips, and the touch made her shudder. Hard. Nora clutched the back of Kelli's neck, desperate to hang on. Kelli continued to press forward, backing Nora into the counter. Nora used the leverage to push herself harder against Kelli's body. As Kelli licked at her bottom lip, Nora moaned and opened her mouth to let her inside.

A throat cleared, distinctly masculine in nature followed by a whistle. "Well," Sean said. He sounded amused.

"That's not what I do on the counters in my kitchen," Carina said teasingly.

Kelli pulled away abruptly. Nora's face flushed with heat, and the urge to hide was overwhelming. Kelli touched her elbow. Their gazes met. There was humor in Kelli's eyes along with reassurance. Nora drew from that.

"Mom! What—"

"You missed dinner this week, so I thought I'd make up for it by fixing something here." Carina held up the grocery bags and pursed her lips, but nothing could hide her smirk. "Not seeing her, my ass. Looks like you're doing a lot more than that."

Nora was sure she was going to pass out from embarrassment.

Sean grinned.

"Mom!" Kelli said.

"What? What'd I say?"

CHAPTER 17

Kelli passed Safeco Plaza and turned on Second Street to get on Marion. The chatter on the radio seemed loud. Otherwise, it was quiet. Too damn quiet. Kelli didn't like it at all. She glanced quickly at Nora before cutting her eyes back to the road. Nora sat there with perfect posture and stared out the windshield. There was a weird sort of tension surrounding them. Kind of like the scene in a horror movie before everything goes to hell. Kelli swallowed the lump in her throat and wondered if she had pushed way too much and way too hard. She had no fucking clue what to do so Kelli went with what she knew—humor. It had to get them to a better place than they were right now. Right?

Stopping at a red light, she looked at Nora again and said, "You know, I just noticed something. I'm usually the one who drives us everywhere. I think it should be considered an audition of sorts, leading up to the Mercedes."

Nora turned slightly and raised a brow in response.

Kelli's grip on the steering wheel tightened, and the light turned green. Well, she was wrong on both counts. Her statement got them nowhere, and humor was definitely not the right way to go. A flaming bag of shit probably would have been better received. Nora had been like this all weekend. The only good thing was that she didn't freeze Kelli out completely, but maybe freeze was the wrong word. They talked. They spent time together, but something wasn't right. The easiness wasn't there, and that hurt. It wasn't a full on beating. More like tiny little needles poking at Kelli's skin. Kelli didn't know where she found the willpower to not say anything, but she was afraid if she waited any longer to speak her mind, an even greater distance would form between them.

"You're even quieter than you were this weekend." Kelli said.

The radio droned on. Nora didn't say a word.

Kelli sighed as the needle went in a little deeper. "Was it dealing with my family or that kiss that caused this?"

Nora's shoulders seemed to straighten even more, and Kelli could almost hear her thinking.

"We've kissed be—"

"Not like that." Kelli interrupted as she remembered the raw need that pretty much kicked her in the stomach. She came to another red light. Kelli looked at Nora, and she made a point to hold her gaze. Nora glanced away, but not before Kelli saw agreement in her eyes. "Just because they saw us doesn't mean there's a label on us or anything." She was grasping at straws. Kelli was sure she sounded a tad bit desperate, but it would be an icy day in hell before she let them go down like this.

The traffic signal changed and Kelli hit the gas.

"I don't do things like this. It makes matters more complex. Our… friendship has already—" Nora started.

"Complicated your life?" Kelli asked

"Yes, but I've accepted it." She hurried. "I appreciate it, especially with all that's happening." Nora paused. "I'm not trying to be insensitive, and I'm certainly not trying to hurt you."

"I know." Kelli nodded as she merged into the next lane.

"I'm used to being alone, Kelli."

"I know that too, but you're not anymore."

"I don't know how to do this." Nora whispered, and she sounded so helpless. "My way has been easier."

Nora's way. Kelli learned what that meant a few weeks ago. Nora had been so matter-of-fact and detached while explaining her views on sex, as well as her lifestyle, as she sipped on a glass of chardonnay. That life was easier. Hell, Kelli'd even lived some of it herself, but that kind of existence had to be lonely.

"You're scared. I know that already," Kelli said. They were clearing the air, finally.

"I like order. It's served me well, and there's been nothing else. That, in no way, describes you."

Kelli smirked even though her stomach just tied into about a hundred knots not the good kind either. All of a sudden, she really didn't like where this seemed to be going. "Hurricane Kelli strikes again, huh?"

"She did," Nora said softly.

Those needles? They were becoming a very dull blade just hacking away. Kelli tried to steel herself against the pain as she asked, "Is this the 'let's just be fiends' speech, then?"

"No…I…" Nora faltered. "I'm not sure, actually."

For some reason, Nora's lack of conviction made Kelli hopeful, and she capitalized on the emotion. "You want this, though. I know it."

Nora exhaled loudly, but whispered, "Yes. I don't know what *this* is, but yes."

As they came to yet another red light, Kelli gave Nora her full attention. She understood Nora's hesitation and could actually identify with it. Kelli was no expert on feelings, on women, or on relationships, but this connection with Nora was powerful enough that none of that other stuff mattered. She was wide open and unguarded. Kelli flinched mentally. If all of this ended shitty, she was heading toward a world of hurt.

Knowing this didn't keep her from watching Nora, studying her. Nora's hands were sitting in her lap. They were clasped together and white at the knuckle, but Kelli could see the fine tremor.

"I just don't know if I can do this." Nora's tone was apologetic.

"You're warning me." Kelli stated it as a fact.

"Yes," Nora murmured.

"Would you run? Cut me off completely, if it got to be too much?" Kelli asked. She had to know the answer. It wouldn't change what she wanted or how she felt, but she had to know.

A horn blared, but Kelli held Nora's gaze. She could see Nora's confusion and fear.

"I don't know."

Kelli turned away and gunned the engine. The car lurched forward, but it smoothed out quickly. The voices on the radio argued about the state of the Mariners. The smart thing to do was to cut her losses now and run the other way, but just thinking about that made Kelli sick as fuck to the stomach. Ending this just didn't seem like the right decision. She could feel it in her gut. Yeah, there could be a shit ton of pain coming her way, but the possible pay-off didn't even compare. "I'm a big girl, Nora."

"Kelli." Nora sounded vulnerable, small.

"I mean it." This was her choice. Kelli was in too far now. She had no idea when that happened or what it meant.

Nora went back to looking out the windshield.

The radio commentators started discussing the Seahawks.

They walked toward the elevator in the Thomas, Young, and Associates parking garage. Kelli scanned the vicinity and kept herself on guard for the possibility of another Rader sighting. Out of need, out of habit, her hand pressed into the small of Nora's back. Seconds later, Kelli realized her mistake, and pulled away. She didn't want to make things any more awkward between them. Nora stopped and turned toward Kelli. The puzzled look was back, but there was something else too. Kelli wasn't sure what it was.

"It's okay," Nora whispered.

Kelli reached out again. Touching Nora felt natural no matter what was going on between them. Still, the look in Nora's eyes shook her, and Kelli wondered if it were possible to kiss away Nora's confusion and make things better again.

"Ladies." Tom Young greeted them with an overly-practiced smile and led the way to his office.

They sat down and peered at him from the other side of his large oak desk. Kelli glanced at Nora to look for signs of nervousness. She was still in the middle of a lawsuit, after all. Nora held her gaze, and for the moment, it was almost clear. Kelli smiled and tried to communicate some confidence and everything else she couldn't say right now.

Nora responded with a slight curl of her lips, and that was enough.

Tom cleared his throat, and when Kelli looked at him, his smile was bright and wide. "The day is looking good, thanks to your suggestions, Detective. We got what we needed late Friday, and our investigators spent most of the weekend sorting through it. I had to change my entire approach. Angela, Dr. Fuller's lawyer, is starting with you this morning, Detective McCabe. This is going to be a little different than what you're used to. Be casual and confident. This isn't court. Pay attention to her questions. Some of them may seem irrelevant. They are not, but if she leaves holes, fill them. You're going to be considered hostile anyway. We want enough information in our favor on the record to make them withdraw, not end up in settlement. After you, she's going to question Dr. Rader. I'm going to end the day with him, hopefully shake them up for next time."

Kelli leaned forward. She could practically see the certainty rolling off him. Like on the job, she could smell it. Things were coming together nicely. "You're about to nail them, aren't you?"

Tom Young smirked. "Yes, I am."

Kelli glanced at Nora and her expression was full of surprise and hope. Then, she turned back to the lawyer and asked, "Really? Do tell."

Kelli sat down in front of the video camera to be sworn in. She smiled winningly at Angela Perkins, who stared at her like she'd grown another head.

"Can you state your name and occupation for the record, please?" Angela asked.

"Kelli McCabe. Homicide Detective, SPD."

"Thank you, Ms. McCabe. While this witness is for the plaintiff, I would like her entered as hostile."

Tom nodded. "No objection."

Angela paused. Her eyes narrowed before she trudged on. "Ms. McCabe, what is your relationship with Dr. Nora Whitmore?"

"We're friends," Kelli said simply.

"Did that happen after your discharge from the hospital?"

"No. It started while I was still a patient." Kelli leaned back in the chair, getting comfortable and looking like she didn't give a shit.

"Are you lovers?" Angela barked out the question. So much for finesse.

"No." Kelli didn't even blink.

"Are you aware that Dr. Whitmore is sexual with both men and women?"

"I am." Kelli shrugged. It was no big deal despite what this lawyer wanted her to think.

"Are you aware of the situation involving this case?"

"I am."

"Dr. Whitmore comes from a wealthy family. She's more than likely used to getting what she wants. Does she seem like the type?" Angela continued to hammer ineffectively at Nora's character. Obviously, this woman didn't know Nora at all.

Kelli chuckled. "You mean a spoiled little rich girl? No, she's not."

"I see, and would it surprise you to learn that she has engaged in sexual relationships with several residents at the hospital?"

"No, it would not."

"A woman who changes lovers like she changes clothes? That doesn't sound spoiled or entitled to you?"

Kelli shrugged. "Sounds like somebody who enjoys sex."

Angela cleared her throat and grinned as if she had a secret. "You are a lesbian. Is that correct, Ms. McCabe?"

"It is common knowledge."

"Dr. Whitmore is a beautiful woman. I'm sure individuals of either sex would say or do anything if it led to some kind of favorable involvement with her. Are you one of those people?"

"Nope."

"And how do we know this?"

Kelli grinned. "I guess you'll just have to take my word for it." The lawyer's questions jumped randomly from subject to subject. Kelli knew that she was trying to throw her off balance. It was a tactic she was more than familiar with.

"Remember, you are under oath."

"This isn't my first trip to the movies lady," Kelli added irritably, but it was more than enough to make the lawyer smile.

"You are familiar with my client, Taylor Fuller?"

"Not really. I know who she is, but we never had a conversation while I was a patient. She usually just stood there, hanging off Rader's arm."

Angela sighed. "I'm instructing the witness to save her commentary unless she's asked for it."

Kelli resisted the urge to roll her eyes.

"So, you have no opinion on Taylor Fuller?"

"Do you mean before or after this mess?" Kelli wanted to make sure she answered the right question, especially considering how vastly different the before and after opinions were.

"Before."

"No, I did not."

"So, on the morning of April seventeenth, Dr. Fuller was making her rounds with Dr. Rader, and they entered your room. Is that correct?" Angela asked.

"I don't remember the exact date, but okay."

"Do you recall what transpired?"

"Are you asking for commentary now?" Kelli smiled.

Angela's lips thinned. "Yes, I am."

"They came in. I wasn't in the best of moods, and I didn't really feel like talking. Dr. Fuller kind of insulted me, but I ignored it."

"What do you mean by insulted?"

"She asked if I was lucid because I didn't respond to them," Kelli said.

"How is that an insult?"

"She had a snide tone," Kelli emphasized.

"Continue, Ms. McCabe."

"Dr. Whitmore came to see me. They looked shocked by that fact. Dr. Rader seemed angry. Dr. Whitmore made a comment about Dr. Fuller still being on Rader's service, and she stormed out. Dr. Rader left not long after that." Kelli offered the bare-bones summary of events.

"Since you were gracious enough, Ms. McCabe, to bring up tone of voice, how was Dr. Whitmore's when she addressed Dr. Fuller?"

Kelli blinked. This woman was going to have to do much better than that. "She sounded aggravated and disappointed, like she usually did around residents."

Angela Perkins's head jerked up from her notes. She stared at Kelli with obvious irritation.

Kelli grinned. "You asked for commentary."

The lawyer licked her lips and flicked through the collection of papers for several seconds. She cleared her throat. "So, you wouldn't categorize Dr. Whitmore's tone, as envious and malicious?"

"No, not at all."

"You are aware that Dr. Whitmore and Dr. Rader used to have sex on occasion?"

"I am, and she thought the whole thing was a mistake."

"I want that stricken. It's hearsay. There was no one else to witness this conversation," Angela stressed vehemently.

"Objection. Dr. Whitmore stipulated in her deposition that she ended that relationship. The stenographer can read it back if you like. Your request doesn't make sense, neither does this line of questioning, but she's your witness." Tom's smile was apparent in his tone even if it didn't show on his face.

"Yes, she is." Angela hissed.

"Using your own judgment, do you believe that Dr. Whitmore had an alternate meaning to her statement?"

"Yeah, she was implying that they were sleeping together," Kelli said.

"So, this implication made Dr. Fuller flee the room?"

"Yes, I'd say that," Kelli agreed.

"So, Dr. Whitmore's words embarrassed her?"

"Yes. No different than most of those kids. None of them look comfortable around her. Dr. Whitmore, I mean."

Angela glared, but then, she smiled slowly. "Why do you think that is?"

Kelli returned the grin. "She pushes them to be better, and from what I've seen, she's not afraid to call them out if they're wrong."

An hour and half later, Kelli was still being asked the same set of questions in different ways. Finally, Angela Perkins stood and began placing the stack of folders back into her bag.

"Are you done with this witness, Ms. Perkins?" Tom asked.

"I am." She looked up at them. "Thank you, Ms. McCabe." She gave Kelli a tight smile.

Kelli nodded and gave her a huge grin in return. She had to rub it in just a little bit. Angela Perkins hadn't planned on her. She was no help to them at all.

Tom stood as well. "I'm reserving the right to recall Ms. McCabe if I deem it necessary later in the proceedings. We'll continue in an hour."

"Agreed," Angela mumbled.

Nora stared at the cup of espresso in her hand. She was sure it was impressive, but her interest in being even more caffeinated had waned. She scanned the private waiting area. It was clean, colorless, and screamed affluence. The furniture looked familiar. She recognized it as top of the line, pleasing to the eye, but far from comfortable. She sat anyway. The deposition was just starting, and she was sure it would take a while.

After smoothing the wrinkles in her skirt, Nora crossed her legs and maintained her posture even though she was the only one present. She spied a wide range of magazines that included well-known medical journals like the *American Journal of Surgical Pathology*. It almost made her smile that they would go to such lengths to make her comfortable. There was nothing left to do but wait. For Nora, inactivity almost always led to introspection, but she fought against it. Over the past couple of days, she had been drowning in her thoughts in an effort to come up with a plausible way to keep her churning emotions at bay. Nothing came of it. She was being pulled in two directions—both toward Kelli and away from her at the same time. Self-preservation seemed to be her only recourse. Her instincts screamed for Nora to save herself in any way possible, regardless of the fallout. As a result, when Kelli had brought up their relationship, Nora was painfully blunt in her reply. Words can hurt. Nora knew that now more than ever. Kelli deserved honesty, but not the heartache that came with it.

Closing her eyes, Nora took a long cleansing breath in hopes it would somehow provide even a few seconds of clarity. Kelli seemed so clear on what she wanted: Nora, plain and simple. She was awed by Kelli's determination and patience and found herself drawn to her even more. If this were surgery, there would be no question as to Nora's abilities and the path she needed to take for the best outcome. However, it was not, and her aptitude in the emotions department was sorely lacking. Kelli's willingness to endure pain for a chance with her should have inspired confidence. It did not.

Nora mentally traced the evolution of their relationship. There seemed to always be a pattern of resistance that was followed by an awakening. The harder she fought against Kelli's intrusion, the more she learned about herself. Nora centered her thoughts on the intimacies they shared. Each kiss increased in intensity, ripping her open even more. She knew what it was to be a woman in charge of her own body, her own pleasure, but with Kelli, her body screamed its needs on a constant basis. As a lover, Nora had no doubt that Kelli would be passionate and commanding, requiring everything that Nora had to give and more. In a few kisses, Nora had immersed herself in pleasure instead of trying to regulate it like she had done with others. That kind of loss of control was unprecedented.

Frightened by what she was feeling, Nora was also lured by it. As she recalled each special moment with Kelli, her body responded viscerally. Her breathing hitched, her stomach twisted, and the hard pull between her legs was synonymous with a powerful rush of arousal. Yet, Kelli McCabe wasn't even in the vicinity. Nora reached for the espresso. Her hand shook slightly. If it was only attraction, if it was only awareness, the entire situation would be simpler, but there was tenderness. There was respect, and so much more.

I'm a big girl, Nora. Kelli's words echoed in her head, and Nora wondered if she had the ability to be a *big girl* too. When Nora was sure an eternity had passed, the office door opened. Kelli filled the room. Her gaze was steady, but her smile and her steps forward were hesitant. Nora felt a stab of guilt. With just a few words, she put distance between them, and Nora had no idea how to fix it. That was certainly a tragedy.

"Hey," Kelli greeted her.

Nora returned the smile with one of her own. For right now, it would have to do.

Kelli's grin reverted to her customary smirk. "I think they're gonna regret serving that subpoena."

It was good news, and she was grateful to hear it.

Nora was aware of Kelli's attention on her as the elevator descended. It dinged loudly as they reached the parking garage.

"Ask me." Nora had created this space between them with words, and she decided that she would try to fix it with them as well. Nora caught her gaze and waited.

For a few seconds, Kelli said nothing. "Ask you what?"

"You seem like you have a question."

Kelli smirked lazily. "It should bug me that you know me like that, but it doesn't. It's all kinds of sexy."

Nora faltered for a moment and enjoyed the warmth that infused her at the compliment. She was relieved. This was an improvement on their earlier interactions, but it wasn't the same. She waited for more instead of responding right away.

"You didn't want to stay? See how things with Rader went?"

"I pay this firm enough for them to handle it, and at this point, I'm certain that all this will work out," Nora answered.

"Yeah, but it's your career."

"It is." Nora hesitated, choosing her words carefully. "I think I would be more worried if you weren't here."

Kelli smiled as they got into the car.

Guitars and drums serenaded them from the stereo speakers as they left the parking garage. They passed an ambulance a block away. Its cacophonous wail drowned out the music.

Nora glanced at Kelli several times before her gaze stayed on her. The guilt she felt earlier reared its head. After stopping at a red light, Kelli turned to look at her.

"Ask me."

Despite the heaviness around them, Nora smiled, but the momentary lightness she felt didn't last. "It's more of an observation. I hurt you with what I said."

A muscle ticked in Kelli's jaw. "Was it the truth?"

"Yes."

"Then it had to be said." Kelli paused. "I care about you, and that's not going away. I sure as hell don't wanna send you running in the other direction or go backwards. Even with what you said, I don't think you do either. So, I guess we find a happy medium."

That sounded…interesting. Intrigued by the prospect, Nora asked, "And that is?"

Kelli chuckled. "Don't know, but if it ends up anything like Friday before my family interrupted us, I'm gonna enjoy the hell out of it."

CHAPTER 18

Kelli's yawn was wide enough to swallow her entire head. She brought the cup of coffee to her lips as she padded her way back to the bedroom.

The doorbell rang.

Kelli stared at the door. She hadn't had good luck with visitors as of late. She sure as hell didn't want to tempt fate. She definitely wouldn't come out on top.

"I saw your car, and I know your ass isn't asleep."

Kelli rolled her eyes and smirked. She opened the door, and Williams grinned back at her.

"They have these things now called cell phones." Kelli moved to the side to let him in.

"Cancer sticks, all of them." He waved dismissively.

Kelli chuckled and walked back toward the kitchen. Glancing over her shoulder, she asked, "Coffee?"

He crinkled his nose. "I've tasted your coffee."

Kelli opened the cabinet to get another mug. "My coffee has changed." She nearly laughed at the understatement. Everything, including her coffee, had changed.

"No more instant?" Williams asked.

"Nope. Using my coffeemaker nowadays. Got this French Roast…" Her voice trailed off, and Kelli looked up at Williams.

His eyes narrowed, and his mouth opened.

"Don't even start!" Kelli headed him off at the pass.

Williams laughed. "What? I was just gonna say you seem different."

"Uh-huh." The mug made a thump when she set it on the counter in front of him. Kelli filled it to the brim.

"Well, you do." He muttered before taking his first sip. "Oh sweet God…" He moaned.

Kelli snickered. "No, it's chicory. This is a New Orleans blend. Nora turned—" Her mouth snapped closed. Well, shit.

That look in Williams's eyes came back. "The doctor you're dating?"

Kelli sighed. "I swear to God, all the men in my life gossip like old hens."

Williams grinned. "So, it's true?"

"I plead the fifth. Is that why you came over here?"

"Nah, Lieutenant Cooper has been griping about you. It's his way of saying he cares and wants you back." He took another sip of coffee, humming in delight. "You think you're ready to face the psych eval? After a couple weeks' desk duty, obviously."

Kelli finished her coffee quietly, but she didn't take her eyes from him. She stared him down. Kelli felt ten feet tall. "I look ready?"

"Mmm," Williams held her gaze.

"To be honest, I haven't really thought about the job. Haven't had time to with everything that's going on, but it'll be good to be back. I'll probably drive everybody crazy until I get back in the field."

"That I'm sure of. Still having nightmares?"

She nodded. Kelli could at least share that. "I've gotten used to them. I sleep through the night. Some of my reality is shittier these days."

Williams nodded. "Travis won't be there."

Kelli swallowed already feeling an emptiness in her stomach. "I know that, but it's only temporary."

"Six months to a year, Kelli." Williams added, forever the voice of reason.

"I know that too. So, it's either you or a temp."

"Yeah. Think about it. You want someone who knows all your nooks and crannies? Or someone who doesn't know shit?" Williams asked.

"You make it so appealing when you put it like that."

"I won't sleep with your mother again." His brows cast a deep "V" on his forehead. He looked thoughtful.

Kelli sighed. At that time, it felt a lot like betrayal. "I'm over that, seriously, but when it happened—"

"Your father's death was still fresh. I know."

Kelli refilled her coffee cup. She studied Williams. It wasn't a hard decision to make. "We're good. I'll probably be cleared for desk duty by Friday after my last PT session."

Williams's smile grew even larger. He tapped Kelli's mug with his own. "Good to hear. So, more deposition today?"

"Nosy son of a bitch. All of you need to get a life. Mine isn't all that exciting."

Williams snorted. "I've seen your doctor. Now *that's* exciting."

Kelli had to fight her smile. "Whatever."

"You didn't answer the question."

Kelli grumbled. "Not really. We're viewing a recording from the other day."

"I hate those civil things, long and boring. Should be able to get right to the part where things explode into a Springer episode and somebody goes home crying."

Kelli laughed outright. "I think we're there. When Nora's lawyer called last night, he made it sound like shit's about to hit the fan."

Alone, Kelli turned the coffeepot off and leaned against the counter. She pushed a hand through her hair as she ventured deeper into her thoughts. Almost all the sharp edges in her life were smoothed over and that probably had a lot to do with Nora and Travis. Some of them could still cut her deep. She thought about Antony, but she hoped that sooner or later, that situation would work out too. A smile pulled at her lips. After the shooting, Kelli knew nothing would be the same. The pain both inside and out had damn near pulled her under, but it didn't. Now, her life was richer, fuller than she ever thought was possible.

For several minutes, Kelli wondered how all of this would affect her job. Would she still have that edge and the emotional distance she needed? Kelli didn't dwell on it. Right now, there was no point. She thought about Nora instead, and the warmth that burst in her chest started to take over completely. She had definitely come out of this whole thing with more than she'd bargained for.

Nora gathered her purse, cell phone, and keys as she prepared to leave. She paused and looked around at her living room. The area used to be sterile, bordering on cold. No more. The warmth that had been lacking was now in abundance with the help of a bold coat of paint and some design changes. Nora wasn't one for metaphors, but she was standing right in the middle of one. That had been her once—frosty and pragmatic, with clearly defined borders. Now, she was muddled, softened, and her lines were blurred.

After her parents' death, Nora lived a life of restraint with no impressive highs or lows. As of late, her existence had changed dramatically, but now things finally seemed to be coming together, at least professionally. Nora never pictured herself as a victim. Yet, she almost was. Thanks to James Rader and Taylor Fuller.

With the end of the deposition in sight, Nora's former life dangled in front of her, but even if the prize presented itself, Nora was torn between her past, present, and the uncertainty of the future. Kelli came to mind, as she often did. Their relationship was hanging in the balance, and it was further complicated by the unrelenting heat between them. Part of her wished for a middle road with fewer complications, but she didn't think that was possible. Nora opened the front door. At least there was hope that something positive would come out of the day. Then, soon, she'd be a practicing surgeon again. If that cloud was lifted, maybe Nora could see everything else around her more clearly.

Nora exited her Mercedes and left it idling. Kelli was already making her way down the walkway. She had obviously been waiting for her. Was it normal for such a small act to make her stomach twist like that? Nora shouldn't be surprised by anything her body did when she was anywhere near Kelli.

Kelli smiled as they met on the sidewalk. "Hey, I figured, with everything happening, you'd want to get there a little early."

Nora smiled back. "Possibly."

Kelli rolled her eyes. "You're excited, I can see it. It's written all over your face."

Nora swallowed. She felt her belly twisted again. "Really?"

Kelli smirked. "Yep."

Was she that easy to read? Or maybe she was, for Kelli.

Kelli brushed by her and headed toward the car. Her heat and scent lingered for Nora to enjoy, and so she did. It was nice to stop and savor something so simple.

"Kelli," Nora called to her.

Kelli turned. "Yeah?"

"Would you like to drive?" Nora asked breathlessly.

"Shit yes!" Kelli left the driver's side door ajar and moved quickly to the other side to hold the door open for Nora. Nora expected her to start jumping up and down like a small child. She did a little bounce, and her smile was huge. It was an endearing sight.

A few seconds later, Kelli pulled away from the curb.

"So, what did I do to earn this?"

"You asked," Nora answered. "I know it was a little while ago."

Their gazes met briefly. Nora was the first to look away.

"You'll give me anything I ask for?" Kelli's voice was low, husky.

The feeling in Nora's stomach doubled. Instead of answering, she released a long, trembling breath. That definitely wasn't an example of a happy medium. It was way too potent to be.

"Should I apologize for taking it there? I really don't think I want to," Kelli added softly.

"No," Nora answered. She took another deep breath and tried to calm the erratic beat of her heart.

"You liked it." Kelli did not pose it as a question.

"Yes." Somehow, Nora was breathless again.

For a moment, the air in the car disappeared and left behind a thick molten heat.

Kelli stopped at a red light, which seemed to strengthen the current buzzing between them. Nora shifted. She uncrossed and re-crossed her legs. She was aware of Kelli's gaze. It made her burn. Nora swallowed. Unable to resist, Nora met Kelli's gaze again. Her usually sparkling green eyes were dark and beckoning. Nora's awareness of Kelli quickly morphed into arousal.

Music blared loudly, accompanied by bone-rattling bass from a passing car. The sounds startled Nora and pulled her from the moment. Then, they were moving again. Nora tried to take a deep breath but found that she couldn't.

"I am in so much trouble," Kelli mumbled.

"Excuse me?" Nora asked. Trouble? Yes, she could consider this a whole new level of trouble.

"Nothing. Just something Travis told me."

"I see."

"So do I," Kelli said. The smile in her voice was obvious.

"Pardon?" Nora asked.

"Nothing."

"Something else Travis told you?" Nora, stimulated by Kelli's words, as well as her presence, she didn't want this feeling to end.

"Nope. Figured it out on my own. I am a detective, you know."

"Mmm, I'm curious. What else have you figured out?" Nora knew she was skirting a line, but she always did with Kelli.

Kelli laughed. It was deep, raspy. "Maybe I'll save that one for later." She cleared her throat. "Speaking of detecting, maybe both of us will be back at work soon. I'll be pushing papers for a while."

Nora accepted the change of subject that Kelli offered. It gave her time to gather herself. "That won't be pleasant for you, I imagine."

"Not at all. Neither will seeing the department psych, but I'll be there. That's what counts, I suppose." Kelli paused. "I bet you can't wait to get work again either. Has to be something holding all that life in your hands."

The thought of going back to work was exhilarating, but Nora attempted to be practical as well. "I'm confident the suit will be dropped, but discussing it may be a bit premature. The deposition could go on long—"

Kelli snorted. "No, it won't. Three more meetings, maximum, and we're done. Wanna bet?"

"I don't thi—"

Kelli interrupted her. "Oh come on! Live a little."

And just like that the flutter in Nora's stomach was back. "What are the terms?"

"Holy shit! You're serious?" Kelli stared at her before turning back to the road.

"You asked."

Kelli groaned. "Dear God, don't start that again."

Nora could not help herself. She smiled.

"I don't know what my terms are yet. What do you want?" Kelli asked her.

That was a loaded question if Nora had ever heard one. There were many places she could go with it. "Dinner at my favorite restaurant."

"Hmm." Kelli fell silent. "Is it the kind of place that has a million little forks and I'm supposed to know when to use—"

"Yes." Nora interrupted. This was an odd discussion to say the least.

"Let's just hope that I win, then."

Tom Young entered the conference room with a laptop under his arm. Nora tried to read his expression, but he gave nothing away. Nora glanced at Kelli. As if she could feel Nora's gaze, Kelli looked up. She closed the *Sports Illustrated* magazine and threw it back on the table.

Kelli gave her a tentative smile.

Tom sat down, peering at them both. "Pity you didn't sit in. It was a thing of beauty. I think we have them. We had to end things early with Dr. Rader because…" He chuckled. "You'll see." Tom opened the laptop and hit a few keys before turning it toward them. "I don't think I need to call him back. I gave them forty-eight hours to stew in it, and if Dr. Fuller doesn't withdraw, I'll tear into her as well. I definitely think you should be present for that."

Nora's attention went from her lawyer to the laptop and back again. She nodded, but her heart roared in her ears. This really was almost over. Her gaze turned to Kelli. She was smirking.

"Told you so," Kelli teased.

That smirk and those words were exasperating and exhilarating all at once—just like Kelli herself. Nora reached for Kelli's hand. She entwined their fingers, making the touch all the more intimate. Nora smiled and for once let herself enjoy the connection between them unfettered. "Yes, you did," Nora agreed. "You may proceed, Mr. Young."

Tom reached around the laptop and clicked the mouse.

After being sworn in, Radar stated his full name.

Angela Perkins smiled at him. "Thank you for being here today, Dr. Rader. Dr. Fuller is grateful for your help."

Rader nodded, but he looked clammy and pale.

"Is there a question in there somewhere?" Tom asked.

"Let's move on," Angela said. "You are a mentor of sorts to Dr. Fuller, as well as her lover, correct?"

"Yes."

"She came to you with these allegations, and you encouraged her to take action?"

"Yes. Her demeanor had changed over the course of the past couple of months. I knew something was wrong. I never guessed it would be this."

Even though Rader's words were meant to be accusatory, his tone didn't hit the mark. He squirmed in his seat and adjusted his tie. Not for the first time, Nora wondered what in the world had attracted her to this man in the first place.

Kelli snorted and shook her head. "He sounds like he's in a soap opera."

Nora shushed her but smiled as she diverted her attention back to the computer screen.

"So, you encouraged your current lover to reveal these things about your former lover?" Angela asked.

"Yes, I'm aware of how it sounds, but it was the right thing to do. It's sickening really, because until recently, Dr. Whitmore was still coming after me."

"Dr. Whitmore stipulates that she ended your relationship. Do you have a different account?" Angela continued.

"I was engaged at the time, when she first started pursuing me. I had to break it off with Nora and try to save my relationship. It didn't help, but that's beside the point."

"So, Dr. Whitmore was not at all agreeable to ending the affair?"

"No, she wasn't," Rader answered.

"Were you seeing Dr. Fuller and Dr. Whitmore simultaneously?"

"No, Taylor came later."

Nora stared at the screen and very nearly rolled her eyes. "He's such a reprehensible human being and an atrocious liar. He looks like he's about to pass out."

Kelli chuckled. "Well, that would certainly add to the whole soap opera feel. Now, shush." She squeezed Nora's hand affectionately.

"Tell me about the rumor mill at the hospital," Angela asked.

"There are no secrets." Rader shrugged.

"What do you deduce from that?"

"That Nora learned I was sleeping with Taylor."

"To your knowledge, how did Dr. Whitmore treat Dr. Fuller overall?"

Rader licked his lips. "She was hard on her, but it was no different from everyone else. Taylor seemed to accept it. All the residents had a running joke about Nora. I think they called her Ice Queen or something to that effect. Since the first day I met Taylor, she was outgoing and well liked, so the changes in her behavior were obvious."

"Did Dr. Fuller work well with the more experienced residents and doctors?"

"She rotated regularly on everybody's service, even Nora's until she was cut off."

"Clarify that, please."

"She no longer engaged in surgeries with Dr. Whitmore, so I put her on my service to pick up the slack."

"Did you find that odd?" Angela asked.

"Not for Dr. Whitmore, no. She has her favorites, I suppose."

"Thank you, Dr. Rader." Angela shuffled some papers and flipped through a legal pad. "Were you witness to any hostile behavior toward Dr. Fuller by Dr. Whitmore?"

Rader nodded. "Yes the most recent was the morning of April 17th. In front of a patient, Dr. Whitmore alluded to the sexual relationship between Dr. Fuller and me. It was inappropriate and embarrassing."

"Tell me about her demeanor," Angela said.

"She looked at her like she hated her. It seemed very malicious to me. I'd never seen her like that. Jealousy doesn't look good on anyone, I suppose."

"When Dr. Fuller told you about Dr. Whitmore's proposition toward her, did it all make sense?"

"It did," Rader answered.

"Very good, thank you." Angela grinned. "Dr. Rader, the defendant would have us believe that you coached Dr. Fuller to make up this story to get back at her for the demise of your sexual relationship. Is that true?"

Rader laughed this time, loud and full. Then, he stopped abruptly. "Sorry. No, it's not true. That wouldn't make any sense."

"Ugh, the guy is creepy. He's like a cartoon villain and not one of the good ones. Elmer Fudd or something." Kelli sounded disgusted.

"Who?" Nora asked, but she had to agree. He wasn't very good at any of this.

Kelli sighed. "Oh dear God. Bugs Bunny?"

Nora glanced at Kelli and grinned slightly. "I'm sure you'll educate me sooner or later." When Nora looked back at the computer, Tom was questioning Rader.

"Do you need anything, Dr. Rader? Water? Coffee?"

"No, I'm fine, thank you." Rader smiled, but it was weak, pitiful.

"Then let's get started." Tom smiled back. "Let me get straight to the point, Dr. Rader. You stipulated that Dr. Whitmore refused to include Dr. Fuller in her surgeries out of jealousy and spite, correct?"

"Yes."

"It wasn't because Dr. Fuller missed a liver laceration that nearly killed a patient?"

Rader shifted in his seat. "Uh, not to my knowledge."

"To your knowledge, Dr. Whitmore didn't correct that error or bring it to your attention afterward?" Tom asked.

"Not to my knowledge."

"May I remind you that you are under oath."

"I am aware, thank you," Rader said.

Tom shuffled through some files in front of him, pulling out a single piece of paper. "This is a release signed by Gerald Travis Jr., giving access to his medical records." He paused and reached for more documents. "These notes show that he had a second surgery to repair a liver laceration within forty-eight hours of his first one, which was to remove the bullet and repair subsequent damage. The initial surgery was performed by Dr. Fuller, accompanied by a Dr. Simmons. What conclusions could you draw from that, Dr. Rader?"

"Objection! I wasn't informed about this. Let the record reflect—" Angela intervened.

"You can question him again. I'm nowhere near done. This is a deposition, Angela, not open court. This whole thing is about discovery."

Rader's pallor grayed.

"Isn't it true that Dr. Whitmore refused to include Dr. Fuller in her surgeries because of her sloppiness, not out of pettiness or jealousy, as was suggested?"

"I—I'm not sure," Radar answered.

"You stated that you did not have a conversation with Dr. Whitmore about this. Is that still accurate?" Tom continued to press.

"I didn't discuss this with Dr. Whitmore." Rader shook his head.

"Somebody is lying here, Dr. Rader, and I don't think it's my client. Again, after what's been revealed, you still consider your statements to be accurate?"

"Asked and answered. Let's move on!" Angela interrupted.

Instead of acknowledging her, Tom walked toward the door. When he returned, he had the same kind of laptop that Nora and Kelli were now watching.

"Dr. Rader, you also stated that Dr. Whitmore was bitter after you ended your sexual relationship, which is why her alleged behavior centered on Dr. Fuller. Correct?"

Rader cleared his throat and began to fidget even more. "Yes, she wouldn't let go."

Tom pressed a button and the video started for Rader. "That's not what you indicated in the parking garage."

"Is that what it was, Nora? You like the ladies more?"

"I renew my objection!" Angela banged her hand on the table.

"This is a deposition. It's what your client requested, so here we are." Tom turned toward Rader. "Do you need that water now, Dr. Rader?"

Rader glared at Tom, but it looked to be more of a grimace.

"Does this altercation indicate that Dr. Whitmore is jealous or bitter, Dr. Rader?"

Rader looked away. He didn't answer.

"Or does it sound as though you're the jealous one?"

Rader loosened his tie some more. "Where…how…" He sputtered.

Tom stopped the video and removed the disc. He replaced it with another one. "Maybe this will help you make sense of this, Dr. Rader."

The video didn't have sound, but the scene was very familiar to Nora. It was one of their many run-ins at the hospital, but this time Rader threatened her with retaliation. Now, here they were entangled in this ridiculous lawsuit. Nora continued to watch as Rader stepped into her personal space.

"Son of a bitch! I should have beat his ass when I had my cane, but I'm sure pistol whipping hurts a lot worse," Kelli said through gritted teeth. She turned to Nora. "You told me he was a total dick to you, but I didn't think he'd have the balls to get in your face like that. Just wait—"

Nora squeezed Kelli's hand, interrupting her tirade. "No one has ever defended me before, and that's how many times you've done that now?"

Kelli valued her, as an individual and as a human being. It was surreal to watch on video how the other people in her life did not.

Kelli blinked. "Uh, I don't know? That's so not the point."

"Yes, it is."

Kelli closed her mouth and stared. Her gaze softened. She brought Nora's hands to her lips and kissed it. Nora's pulse quickened, and she could feel the heat rushing to her face. She glanced at Tom. She had almost forgotten he was there. He raised a brow and smiled. Nora looked away quickly and refocused her attention to the laptop.

"Dr. Rader, isn't it true that you and Dr. Fuller are in collusion because of *your* inability to let go? Isn't this your attempt to get back at Dr. Whitmore?"

James clawed at his tie and pulled it completely loose. He looked like he was having trouble breathing.

"Dr. Rader, do you need me to repeat the questions?" Tom pushed.

"Look at him. We need to end this. He's turning blue. Obviously, this man needs help!"

"Fine, I will recall him next time, after I'm done with your client." Tom added.

James Rader slid from his chair to the floor.

"Oh my God! He fainted! Call an ambulance!" Angela cried.

Kelli laughed. "Serves him right."

Nora was shocked. "That was…I don't think I can adequately describe what I just saw. Excellent work, Tom." The shock transformed to relief. This farce was nearly over.

Tom nodded and smiled. "I'll let you know how this proceeds. I really think they will concede. It's not rational to go on with this, and if they do, I'll be ready."

With their hands still clasped, Nora stood. Kelli did as well. "We'll be ready too."

Kelli took a long swig of her beer. Studying the label, she realized she didn't recognize the brand, *Hoppyisum, IPA*. "This is good. I'm making you my official beer shopper."

"A title I'm sure many have vied for," Nora murmured.

Kelli chuckled and popped another piece of cheese into her mouth and damned near spit it out again. "Ew, that's nasty. What's this one?" She pointed at the pieces with dark rind.

"Drunken goat."

"They should have kept him sober." Kelli took another pull from her beer.

Nora cleared her throat but she looked amused. "I'm sure if you write them a strongly worded letter…"

Kelli glared.

Nora grinned, slightly.

Kelli continued to stare. Nora looked very much at ease. That sad, worried glint in her eyes was gone. It was good to see her like this. "You look happy."

Nora finished her wine and set the empty glass on the table. "I do?" Nora turned, and their knees touched.

"You do."

Nora's brow wrinkled. "I suppose I am. This is all going to be over soon."

Kelli leaned back into the couch cushion, but she didn't look away. Nora Whitmore was a beautiful woman, but right now, she was a lot more than that. "It looks good on you." As expected, Nora blushed. Kelli enjoyed every second of it. "We should have gone out for this pre-celebration celebration."

"I don't think I have the energy. It's only early afternoon, and I'm exhausted."

Well, that let a little air out of her balloon. "You want me to go so you can get some rest?"

"No," Nora answered quickly. "Don't. You don't have to."

"Good, I didn't want to," Kelli said honestly.

"It's still hard at times to believe that you actually enjoy my company."

"I could probably say the same." Kelli wanted to reach out, to take Nora's hand.

"It's not the same. You have friends and family. I have—"

"Me." Kelli interrupted. She saw and heard the catch in Nora's breathing. The warmth that was always just underneath her skin when Nora was around started to simmer and turn into something hotter. Goddamn. She loved that feeling. "You have me," she said it again, making the words as solid as possible.

"Yes, I have a…friend." Nora obviously tried to choose a nice, *safe* word.

Kelli smirked. "We're more than that, and you know it."

"I'm aware. What would you call us at this point?"

Kelli turned and threw her arm over the back of the couch. She gave Nora her full, undivided attention. "Complicated."

"Yes, that does seem to fit," Nora agreed in a whisper.

"It doesn't have to be." Like it was the most natural thing in the world, Kelli moved closer and tangled her hand in Nora's hair. It was just as soft as she remembered. Nora gasped and leaned into the caress. Her eyes widened and darkened in the span of seconds. Suddenly, it seemed like forever since they touched this way. Kelli pulled her hand away slowly, but she held on to a honeyed strand, twirling it around her finger. An ache formed in her chest and settled into her stomach as a hard twist. That feeling needed to be bottled. Someone would make a fucking fortune.

Kelli was chasing a woman who had no idea if she wanted to be caught. She should have backed off a long time ago, but she couldn't. She just wanted more. The twist in her belly turned into a hard clench that ended with a delicious pull between her legs. No, she was wrong. It was *that* feeling. Shit could be sold by the gallon. Her fingertips trailed down the side of Nora's neck. She stopped and traced over the base of Nora's throat where her pulse was literally throbbing. Then, she found her way to soft lips and could not pull away.

Kelli's chest burned. She couldn't breathe worth a damn. Kelli leaned forward bringing their bodies closer. She wound her hand in Nora's hair again. The spike in heat around them was almost more than she could stand. Just a little taste. That couldn't hurt, right?

"I need pre-payment. On our bet," Kelli husked.

"What do you wa—" Nora's question ended with a whimper. Kelli captured the sound with her lips. Her tongue slipped inside Nora's mouth, intent on drawing even more noises from her. Nora moaned loudly. This time, the sound was incendiary. Kelli could feel fire crackling over her skin, and she groaned in response. Why the fuck did this have to be so good? Before Kelli could get used to one feeling, she was assaulted by another. In a flurry of movement, Nora straddled Kelli's thighs, and she was literally surrounded by softness and scorching heat. Nora's breasts, larger and heavier, pressed against her own. It was erotic as hell. A second later, Kelli changed her mind as Nora's hips began to roll against her. Shit, what was this? The death of her, that's what this was.

Nora made desperate needy sounds, and her nails crawled into Kelli's shoulders. Kelli was getting drunk on it all—the way Nora smelled, sounded, felt, and tasted. Kelli was completely overwhelmed. She didn't really need to breathe. Did she? Yes, yes she did. Kelli grasped Nora's hips and whispered Nora's name into her open mouth.

Nora whimpered and pulled away slightly, ending the kiss. Their foreheads touched. Kelli closed her eyes. She couldn't look at her right now, or she would be deep inside Nora in two seconds flat. Nora played with the sensitive hairs at the nape of Kelli's neck. Kelli shivered appreciatively. She tried to calm her ragged breathing, but it was damn near impossible.

"Kelli," Nora murmured. She tried to move away, but Kelli wouldn't let her. She needed to hold onto something. Why not her hips? They wouldn't stop moving a second ago.

Finally, their gazes met. Nora's eyes were cloudy, unfocused. Her lips were wet, red, and swollen. Kelli felt heat flare up inside her again. "We're both in really big trouble, aren't we?"

"Yes, we are."

CHAPTER 19

The past two days seemed to drag on forever. In fact, Nora was sure that if Kelli hadn't been present for most of it, she'd be right on the cusp of insanity or very close to it. Still, she slathered her croissant with marmalade as if it was an average day. Nora could feel Kelli's gaze from across the table. She glanced upward.

Kelli peered at her over the rim of a coffee cup. She took a sip and set it on the table. "Stop."

Nora put her knife down and brought the pastry to her lips. She chewed slowly, thoughtfully, and she was completely aware that her lack of response exasperated Kelli.

Kelli leaned back in her chair and crossed her arms. She continued to stare. When Nora looked at her again, there was definitely irritation in her eyes, but there was affection as well.

She put her croissant back on the saucer and brought a napkin to her lips. "I didn't do or say anything," Nora finally responded.

"You don't have to. I can tell you're over there wallowing in your orange jelly."

And there it was. Hiding herself and her emotions from Kelli just wasn't possible anymore. "I don't wallow, and it's marmalade."

Kelli rolled her eyes. "You're worrying, then."

"Yes, somewhat. I want this whole fiasco to hurry up and be over. Too much time has been spent on it already."

"True, but the deposition is just a couple hours away. I can't believe Fuller didn't drop the suit. Suppose some people just need their asses handed to them. And you…you're usually more patient, but you've been antsy the past couple days. I thought you were gonna come out of your skin. Please don't do that. I like your skin."

Nora smiled slightly. It was impossible not to do so around this woman.

"So, just hold your horses. Is worrying about it making time go by faster?"

Nora picked up her coffee and drained it. She added cream to her now empty cup and reached for the French press.

"That wasn't rhetorical, but I'm sure you knew that," Kelli growled playfully.

Nora bit the inside of her cheek to keep from grinning. "I'm aware, but I'm sure you know my answer. I didn't see a need to respond."

Kelli shook her head and laughed. "I don't even know what to say to that."

"Mmm," Nora murmured. She loved the interplay between them. It was stimulating, and she was always left wanting more.

Kelli smirked. "I'm on to you."

Nora felt heat flood her face. "Really?"

"Uh-huh, really. There's something sexy about the way we talk to each other."

Nora took a quick scan around the cafe before her gaze found Kelli's again. "Yes, I have to agree."

Kelli looked back at her teasingly. "Still worried?"

She was not. Kelli worked her special brand of magic. "Well—"

"No, it's okay. I know the answer to that one too." Kelli interrupted.

Nora didn't hold back her smile.

"Don't let the fact that she hasn't withdrawn the suit bother you," Tom said. "It's not all that unusual. Sometimes there needs to be a clear loser before common sense prevails."

"That's pretty much what I told her a little while ago…in my own words of course," Kelli agreed.

"Yes, the similarities are astounding," Nora said dryly. She glanced at Kelli who looked back at her with a sparkle in her eyes.

Kelli shrugged and grinned. "Tomat-o, tomat-o."

Nora pressed her lips together and wondered if Kelli ever turned off the charm.

Tom chuckled and stood. "Okay, I'm going to get you guys set up in here for the live feed. You can always just sit in, you know. Sometimes it's more intimidating, especially near the end."

"Nora can, but it's probably better for their health if I don't. Thanks," Kelli said flatly.

"This is fine. It gives me a little distance. I think I need that at this point to start putting all of this behind me," Nora said.

"Understood." Tom turned his laptop toward them. "Adjust the volume at your convenience." He nodded and exited his office.

The camera was already on. Rader sat on the other side of the table from Taylor. He glared at her, but she didn't shrink from his gaze. She met it head on.

Kelli whistled. "That tension is thick. This should be interesting."

Kelli was right. Nora could practically feel the volatility between them. "Very."

Nora took a deep breath as Tom entered the conference room. She was ready to watch the pieces of her life slide back into place.

Tom smiled. "Morning, everyone." He stopped and talked to Rader. "Good to see you're feeling better, Dr. Rader."

Rader cleared his throat and looked away.

"Let's get started. Water, tea, or coffee, Dr. Fuller? You might need it." Tom sat down.

"Get on with it, Tom." Angela hissed.

Taylor nearly jumped out of her chair when Angela reached out to touch her. "It's okay. Just relax. He's just trying to intimidate you."

Tom snorted while he puttered with the computer he brought in. "Okay, we're ready." He cleared his throat. "I'm sure you've been made aware of the videos shown to Dr. Rader, as well as his reaction to them. How do you explain that, Dr. Fuller? It seemed to me that he was guilty of something."

"I—I didn't believe it either, that he was over her, and she was the one chasing him. She's a beautiful woman. I think those videos show that he still cares. I suspected it. He lied to me about it to keep from hurting me. He's a good man like that." Taylor's voice was shaky and sounded vulnerable.

"I'm going to give you a few seconds to re-think your answer. I know you're nervous," Tom said.

"My god, she is so full of shit. That's some horrible acting, and I mean like scripted reality show bad," Kelli interjected. "Maybe she's one of those people who thinks everyone else is stupid…when it's really been her all along. Know what I mean?" She glanced at Nora.

"I'm not familiar with reality TV, but I do understand what you're saying."

"Really? How can you not know about reality TV?"

"Put it on the list," Nora insisted.

"At least you know who Justin Bieber is now."

Yes, unfortunately she did. "Kelli."

"What?"

"Shhh!"

"Yeah, sorry," Kelli whispered.

Nora smiled fondly and turned back to the laptop.

"I'm telling the truth." Taylor stayed firm after a few seconds of silence.

"I don't know if I believe that, Dr. Fuller. The man on the security footage seemed angry, bitter, and even vengeful. Watch."

They were all subjected to the video once more.

With a click, Tom paused the digital feed at the altercation in the garage. "Look at his face, Dr. Fuller."

Rader's face was red and his mouth was open. His expression was contorted, and eerily evil looking.

"Now, which assessment sounds more feasible? Mine or yours?" Tom asked.

"Mine. She turned on him by coming after me. I'm sure it hurts him."

"Okay, let's connect the dots. He's hurt, and he wants to hurt Dr. Whitmore in return. What better way to do it than to use her sexuality and her love of medicine against her? What better way than to paint her as the hospital whore and get her out of the operating room?"

Taylor chuckled, but she didn't really sound amused. "That sounds like something from a movie."

"It does, doesn't it? So tell me, what usually happens in the movies when people create these kinds of schemes?"

Taylor shrugged.

"You need to answer, Dr. Fuller." Tom pressed for a response.

"Not sure. I'm not a big movie watcher."

"They get caught, Dr. Fuller. This is a civil suit. The settlement phase, if we get there, could be very lucrative for you. Dr. Rader gets to shame a spurned lover, and you get a pile of cash. It's a win-win. Isn't that correct, Dr. Fuller?" Tom asked.

"We're not working together. This isn't some lie that we cooked up. Dr. Whitmore made me feel like I was nothing!"

"Was this before or after you botched that surgery?" Tom continued.

"I wasn't the only doctor in that room, but that doesn't even matter. She just treats everyone like crap!"

"So maybe you wanted a little revenge for yourself as well, Dr. Fuller?" Tom asked.

"No, I just wanted to be a doctor." Taylor started to cry.

Nora could not turn away. It was like watching a train wreck. She had to see the carnage even though the proceedings were chilling to watch. "I find it hard to believe that people that manipulative exist."

Kelli snorted. "I wouldn't have a job if they didn't."

"I suppose you're right." Nora leaned closer. She didn't want to miss a thing.

"You're stipulating that you and Dr. Rader are not in collusion?" Tom pushed on.

"Asked and answered in about twenty ways, Tom," Angela retorted.

"Yes, that's what I'm saying," Taylor added anyway.

"Funny. I can—and I will—call Detective McCabe back to testify that you and Dr. Rader discussed nearly the entire ordeal at the foot of her bed when you thought she was sleeping," Tom said.

Taylor laughed, but she sounded very nervous. "I—I don't know what you're talking about."

"I strongly object to this. You're just fishing," Angela said, her voice somewhere between speaking and shouting.

Tom ignored her and began tinkering with the computer again. "If that's not enough to sway you, can you tell me what's going on here?"

Everyone in the room was mesmerized by the video. Taylor came out of the Chief of Surgery's office and scanned the area before walking quickly down the hallway and entering another room.

"I don't understand. What's the big deal?" Fuller asked.

"It's somewhat suspicious behavior don't you think? Especially after the yarn you spun to the Chief of Surgery that day."

"Objection! You're reaching! I renew my objection to these videos as well!"

"Noted." Tom inclined his head.

"It's…just a closet. I needed a break from everything. I mean…I just—"

Rader started pulling at his tie.

"Needed Dr. Rader?" Tom asked.

The footage continued. Taylor left the room first, and a few minutes later, Rader did the same.

Taylor stood and shouted. "Yes, he was the only one who supported me!"

"In a closet, Dr. Fuller? Why didn't he sit in the waiting area? Why the need to hide? Does that seem like something innocent people would do?"

Taylor's chest was heaving. Her gaze was centered on Rader, and her hands were clenched into fists.

"Sit down and answer the question, Dr. Fuller," Tom insisted.

James Rader jumped to his feet. His face looked extremely pale as he stumbled toward the door.

Taylor's expression was murderous. Her face was blotchy red, and she screeched like some wild animal before launching herself in his direction. "You don't get to run from this you son of a bitch!"

Someone in the room gasped in surprise.

Nora decided that train wreck wasn't a strong enough description for what she was seeing, but she didn't take the time to think of one. As she continued to watch, Nora's heart jumped to her throat and then plummeted to her stomach. Pure elation bubbled up from somewhere deep inside her. It was an odd sensation, but it was a feeling she could definitely learn to enjoy.

"Je-sus Christ," Kelli muttered.

Nora reached out blindly. She wanted to share this moment, and Kelli just wasn't close enough. Their fingers intertwined.

Taylor slapped Rader. Hard. The sound of skin connecting reverberated through the room. "I told you this wasn't going to work! You're going to fucking pay for this. My goddamn life is over thanks to you." She continued to rant.

Tom reached for the phone, but his words were drowned out.

Rader pushed her away. He turned and lunged for the door. She jumped on his back and wrapped an arm around his throat. "Stupid…spineless…"

Rader coughed and sputtered. "Get off me. You went along with it. Don't…don't put this all on me." He twirled around as he tried to dislodge her. A few seconds later, he backed her into the wall.

Security burst through the door. Two rather large men ripped them apart from each other. Taylor went for Rader again, but she was thwarted by the wall of muscle between them.

"We're not done," Taylor shouted in Rader's direction. She flailed uselessly in the security guard's arms.

Tom stood. "Thanks, guys."

One of the men nodded.

Tom adjusted his tie and looked down at Angela Perkins. Her mouth was open, and her face was flushed. He smiled. "Well, should we take a break?"

Angela sneered at him and threw her pen on the table.

Nora rose from her chair. Her vision tunneled. All she could see was the computer screen. It was…over. An exhilarating sense of relief flooded her chest. She heard a sound and realized that the noise came from her own mouth. There it was again. A sob. Nora covered her mouth with the back of her hand. Then, Kelli was there. She pulled Nora into her arms.

"It's over. You got your life back," Kelli whispered.

"I know." Nora pressed her face into Kelli's neck, basking in her scent and warmth.

Kelli held on tighter.

CHAPTER 20

Nora stared at her cell phone. It danced on the coffee table as it continued to vibrate. The number that flashed was one she hadn't seen in some time. There went that happy, bubbly feeling again. After the fourth ring, Nora answered.

"This is Dr. Whitmore."

There was a distinct pause.

"Yes, it is." The Chief of Surgery's Southern drawl was as distinctive as ever.

Nora felt anticipation shoot through her. She stood to give it some room to grow. "Good morning, Dr. Gagne."

"That it is, especially when things work out the way I like them. Yesterday was very satisfyin', but today is a lot better. The Board has made its decision. I'm gonna cut to the chase, Dr. Whitmore. You have been reinstated and may return to the hospital whenever you see fit. Let's put these unfortunate events firmly behind us. Wouldn't you agree?"

"Yes. Yes, I would." Nora didn't hesitate.

"Good. I had a feelin' you'd say that. Glad to have you back. Make sure you make an appointment to see me for continuity's sake by the end of the week because I'm assumin' you'll be gracin' these walls by tomorrow."

"That's highly likely," Nora said breathlessly.

"Have a good day, Dr. Whitmore."

"You too," Nora murmured. Unfortunately, Dr. Gagne had already hung up.

Within seconds, Nora was calling Kelli. It was her first instinct to share the news with someone who thought she mattered. After the third ring, Kelli mumbled, "'Lo?"

The sound of Kelli's sleepy rasp made her shiver. "I woke you." Nora could hear the covers rustle.

"So? You're allowed," Kelli said, sounding more alert. "What's up?"

"The hospital called." As she said the words out loud, her excitement level shot upward.

"Yeah? And?"

"I can go back tomorrow if that's what I want." Nora smiled as she finished speaking.

"Ho-ly shit!"

"Yes, that's exactly what I was thinking," Nora said sarcastically.

Kelli chuckled. "Aren't you about to explode? What am I saying? Of course you are."

"I am, I suppose." Nora felt tingly, and she suddenly had more energy than she knew what to do with.

"I wanna see it for myself. I'll be there in about an hour."

Usually, Kelli would have just walked in, but Nora didn't think to unlock the door. So the ringing of the doorbell became a musical interlude. Nora rushed to stop it.

"I wasn't finished, but hey." Kelli greeted her with a smile.

Those few words, and Kelli's proximity were all it took for her body to react. Nora felt sparks rake over her skin. She stepped back to allow Kelli room to enter.

Kelli moved forward and closed the distance between them. Without delay or permission, Kelli slipped a hand around Nora's neck and tangled it in her hair. Before Nora could take another breath, Kelli took it from her completely. Kelli's lips moved over her own gently like they had all the time in the world. The moment was profoundly sweet, and it shook her, bones and all.

Nora whimpered as the embrace ended. Her attention remained on Kelli's kiss-swollen lips. She traced them with trembling fingertips. Electricity arced down Nora's arm into her chest.

Finally, their gazes met. Kelli looked amused. She smiled. "So, that's what it looks like." Kelli cupped Nora's cheek, and her thumb brushed over still-heated skin.

Nora leaned into the touch, but she was confused. She opened her mouth to ask for clarification.

Kelli laughed. "The conversation we had earlier? About you being all giddy?"

Nora's face heated. She really had forgotten.

Kelli smirked. "Me kissing you does all that, huh?"

A smile tugged at Nora's lips. "Maybe."

Kelli kept them close. Nora wasn't ready to end the embrace anyway.

"Mmm hmm, good to know." Kelli cleared her throat. "I have an idea to run past you. Feel free to say no regardless. I know we had our little pre-celebration celebration, but there hasn't really been a real one. Plus, I won the bet."

"I'm aware. So, what do you want?"

Kelli's answering chuckle sounded very dirty. It made Nora shudder. "I could write pages, but I'll settle for dinner with my family Thursday. Well, tomorrow night. I know it's short notice."

Nora swallowed. Dinner. With the family. It was a huge step, and it meant labels, assumptions, and awkwardness. Could she do this? In the scope of all Kelli had done for her, dinner did not seem like much.

Nora felt the stiffness in Kelli's muscles and saw the nervousness in her eyes. Her smirk dimmed. Nora had waited too long to give her answer. "Yes, I think I can do that."

Kelli exhaled slowly. "Don't do this out of some obligation to me. If you're not ready—"

"I am. I'm ready." Nora knew that, if she felt herself floating away during it all, Kelli would be her anchor.

The time was six-thirty, and most of Nora's morning ablutions were complete.

A simple phone call had restored a vast piece of her existence. Without restraint, she smiled as she washed her now empty breakfast dishes. Smiling was frighteningly easy and commonplace. Her lips curled upward even more as she thought about Kelli. Before, Nora didn't know what it was like to have someone in her corner, and now, she couldn't imagine a time when there wasn't. One thing she learned over the past few months was that Kelli McCabe was a force of nature. She radiated warmth and fiercely protected those she cared about, which in turn earned their loyalty. Reluctant at first, Nora had ultimately become a willing follower.

She allowed her thoughts to become sensual, prurient. Nora's body responded accordingly with a slight shiver. Of course she'd known attraction before, but at this level, the pull seemed fathomless. It would be easy to lapse into a sexual relationship with Kelli; however, she had no desire to treat her like all the others. The air heated around them when they were close, and a glance from Kelli only sharpened her appetite for more. Unfortunately, when they were apart, Nora's brain took over, which gave her too much time to think and rationalize reasons to back away. Thankfully, that voice was now a whisper.

So very much had changed, and all those changes were walking into the hospital with her. What was that going to be like? She brushed a nervous hand over the jacket of her gray Armani pantsuit. Her attire was over the top, but provided her the level of professionalism she needed as a buffer for whatever awaited her at the hospital. A string of butterflies tumbled around in her stomach. Nora glanced at her watch, and frowned. It was past seven o'clock. She was going to be late her first day back, and it was all Kelli McCabe's fault. Instead of being frustrated, Nora smiled.

As she made it to the front door, her cell phone chirped. Nora fished it out of her COACH handbag. She continued smiling when she saw the caller ID.

"Good morning," Nora murmured.

Kelli groaned. "I'm not really up, but since I might have to start waking up at this ungodly hour again in a few days, I thought I'd practice."

"Thoughtful."

"Yes, I know." The amusement in Kelli's voice was obvious. "Nervous?"

"A little," Nora answered. The words rushed out of her. It felt good to be able to talk to someone about it.

"You don't have anything to worry about, you know?"

"Maybe," Nora said.

"You're not stressing over the wonder twins are you?"

Nora waited. She would get an explanation soon enough.

Kelli's initial sigh turned into a chuckle. "They were probably two of the lamest superheroes in creation. Seemed to fit Rader and Fuller."

"No, I doubt they'll show up at the hospital, and if they do, I'm sure I'll have no problem—"

"I'm sure you could deal with them, but I'm gonna ask anyway," Kelli interrupted. "Maybe I'll see you later? I have PT, and I need to see Travis."

Nora smiled even though no one was there to see it. "Okay."

"Knock 'em dead."

Nora chuckled. "That's not preferred."

She could almost hear Kelli's eyes roll. "You know what I mean."

"I do. Thank you."

"Trust me. You're very welcome." Kelli's voice lowered an octave. The words were drawn out teasingly.

Nora felt a tingle as goosebumps prickled her skin. "Kelli…" Nora had no idea what to say.

"What?"

She heard Kelli shifting in bed but continued to say nothing.

"It's okay."

For a second, Nora closed her eyes. She wasn't sure what "it" encompassed. Their relationship? The mess that just ended? Her constantly changing emotions? Regardless, Kelli's reassurance eased her somewhat. "Is it?"

"Yeah."

Kelli sat in a chair in the far corner of the room. She tucked her hands underneath her thighs to keep them to her damn self. Kelli gritted her teeth as she watched Travis struggle. She wanted to help him. Hell, she would carry him on her back if she needed to, but learning to walk again was something *he* needed to do. Knowing all that didn't keep the ache out of her chest. Travis was covered in sweat, and his face was all screwed up in obvious pain. But the determined glint in his eye was a thing of beauty. He took two more steps forward.

Dan, the physical therapist, offered encouragement. "I know it hurts. That means you're doing it right."

Travis groaned. "I want to but…I need to stop." His chest heaved as he fought for breath.

"Two more steps, and then I'll rub you down."

Travis chuckled then wheezed. "That's not an incentive.

Dan laughed. "Good. Keep that sense of humor."

The conversation made Kelli think. She reached deep into her bag of tricks and pulled something out of her ass that was sure to catch his attention. "Saw Williams naked."

The room was so quiet the words could have echoed.

Travis looked at her. "Say what?"

"You heard me. Naked and swinging in the wind."

"Ew, was it with your mom? You woulda told me about that by now."

Kelli bit the side of her cheek. "Disgusting, now you've gone too far," She deadpanned.

"And we're done! Good job Gerry," Dan announced.

Travis looked confused. "Wha?"

"You made it," Dan said.

Travis glanced at the physical therapist. Then, his gaze moved to Kelli. His thanks shined in his eyes. "Bitch."

Kelli laughed. "Next time think about him chasing you. It might help."

His grimace curled into a slight grin. "You're still a bitch."

Kelli nodded. "I know."

⁓

Later, Kelli didn't even break a sweat in her own PT session. She tried not to think about the differences in her and Travis's experiences as she walked deeper into the ICU. Kelli looked around in hopes to getting a glimpse of Nora. She hadn't seen her yet, but the place wasn't that damn big. When she got close to Travis's door, she heard laughter and recognized her brother's voice right away.

Sean smiled at her as she walked in. Kelli quirked an eyebrow in greeting. He rolled his eyes.

"Looks like she's almost back to normal. Gotta love the strong, silent types," Sean said just to fuck with her.

"Silent? Who the fuck are you talking about?" Travis chimed in.

"Me. I don't run my mouth half as much as you two." Kelli pulled up a chair and straddled it.

"Maybe we're just in touch with our feminine sides," Sean countered.

"Fuck that. I'm a metrosexual," Travis muttered.

"Isn't that the same thing?" Kelli asked.

Sean's expression turned thoughtful. "So, what does that make you?"

"A woman," Kelli answered.

Travis and Sean burst into laughter. "I'm calling bullshit!" Sean added.

"Careful." Kelli growled even though she was enjoying herself. She had to keep her little brother on his toes.

"I'm not scared of y—"

Kelli glared.

"Well, not really." Sean cleared his throat.

Travis snickered.

"What am I, then?" Kelli asked.

"Butch," Travis answered. "I think I'm gonna start calling you Serpico."

Sean doubled over in his chair, squealing like a little girl.

Kelli rolled her eyes. "Fuck the both of you, and how do you even know who that is? That movie is older than you."

"It's a classic cop movie. Of course I know what it is," Travis answered.

"Really? That's the best you can do? That's your comeback?" Sean glanced at her. His face was still red from laughing.

"Give me time. It'll come," Kelli said.

"Dr. Whitmore must have you tied in all kinds of knots. You're losing your touch, partner," Travis said.

Kelli stared at him. He had no idea.

"Ooooh. Trust me when I say that you don't scare me at all," Travis said.

Kelli turned her gaze to her brother. "You better not be an ass tonight."

His face was all scrunched up when he looked at her. "What? Why?"

"Because Nora's coming to dinner."

Sean's eyes widened. "No shit? You've never invited anybody over for family dinner."

Kelli sniffed and shrugged her shoulders. "First time for everything." He didn't need to know how deep she had fallen into Nora. "I'm sure she's nervous about it, so be on your best behavior, or I'll yank your underwear so far up your crotch you'll be tasting your own piss."

Travis snorted. "Damn, that's what I call abusive."

Sean rolled his eyes. "I'll try." He glanced at the door and shushed them.

"What's wro—" Kelli turned to see what caught his attention. Nora stood in the doorway. Their gazes met. Kelli felt like all the oxygen was sucked out of her lungs all at once. She swallowed and stood. Even in purple scrubs, Kelli found it hard as hell to look away. So, she didn't bother. Nora walked toward them.

"I didn't mean to interrupt," Nora said. Her gaze stayed on Kelli.

"You didn't. We were just being stupid," Sean said.

Nora glanced his way for a second before finding Kelli again. It was getting kind of hard to breathe. Dammit how could she be this whipped already?

"Nice to have you back, Dr. Whitmore." Travis waved to get her attention.

Finally, Nora's eyes strayed for more than a second. She smiled slightly in Travis's direction. "Thank you. It's the reason I stopped by actually, to thank you for releasing your records. I'm sure Kelli's told you that it helped tremendously."

"You're welcome. It was the least I could do. It wasn't much. You had Serp—"

Kelli looked at him and tried to sew his lips shut with her thoughts.

Travis just grinned. "Kelli…in your corner, after all."

Nora nodded and began backing away.

Before she could stop herself, Kelli took several steps in her direction. There was a flash of something in Nora's eyes. Whatever it was sent a red hot bolt of heat right to the pit of Kelli's stomach. It took everything Kelli had not to pounce on her like some sex-starved teenage boy.

"Later?" Kelli croaked.

"Yes," Nora whispered. She turned and left the room.

Kelli stared at the empty space. She expected to see smoke. Or something.

"Holy fuck. I couldn't breathe for a second," Sean muttered.

"For real. Me either," Travis agreed.

Kelli ignored their comments and went back to her chair and sank into it. They were staring at her. Kelli took a deep breath and prepared herself. They were going to tease the piss out of her. She just knew it.

"Jesus Christ, I want somebody to look at me like that," Sean said instead.

Kelli glanced at him.

He held up his hands in surrender. "I'm not kidding."

Kelli looked at Travis.

He shrugged. "Just remember to wrap up your junk."

Kelli rolled her eyes.

"So moving on to something just as uncomfortable. Heard you saw Williams naked? When the hell was this? Better yet, where was it?" Sean asked.

Kelli grinned. "I was just kidding. You really think I could look him in the eye after that?"

Travis snorted. "I knew it, but it doesn't hurt to ask."

"True," Kelli agreed. She was a little less wound up now that Nora was gone, but she put those feelings on the back burner to let them simmer. Perfect time to change the subject. "I might be on desk duty starting Monday. I'll know for sure by tomorrow."

Travis's eyebrows shot upward. "No shit?"

Kelli looked him in the eyes. He seemed sad, but he smiled anyway. "No shit," she repeated.

"Williams better be watching your back when you get out in the field, right?" Travis asked. His words were firm.

Kelli smirked. "Yeah, he is."

"Good, knowing some newbie was on your ass would probably keep me up at night."

"Me too." Kelli nodded.

※

Kelli was a woman on a mission—a very urgent one. She'd wanted other women before, but not like this. Some switch had been activated, with the dial set on Nora. Kelli headed straight for the nurses' station and tapped the desk until someone paid attention.

"Do you know where Dr. Whitmore went?"

"No, I didn't even see her. She probably just took the elevator back down to her office." One of the nurse's answered.

"Where's that?"

"Three floors down."

Kelli nodded her head in thanks.

Minutes later, the elevator opened, and Kelli pushed her way past the crowd of people. She looked down one end of the hall and then the other. There were too damn many doors, and she didn't have the patience right now to peek into every one. Kelli took out her cellphone. It rang twice.

"Where are you?" Kelli didn't even give Nora a chance to say hello.

"In my office," Nora answered.

"Poke your head out."

"You're…" Nora paused. "Okay," she finished breathlessly.

Kelli hung up. Her nerves were practically sizzling with anticipation. To the left near the end of the hallway, Nora stood. Kelli didn't wait. She moved toward Nora like the devil was chasing her.

Kelli stopped in the doorway. They stared at each other, and it was as if someone lit a match. Kelli's insides were actually burning. Nora stepped back, but she only allowed a small space for entry. Kelli brushed past her, and the temperature shot up another ten degrees.

Nora had barely closed the door when Kelli pushed her against it. Kelli couldn't breathe, and she loved the fact that Nora's chest was heaving too.

"Hey," Kelli said, her voice a deep burr. Her mouth hovered over Nora's.

Nora licked her lips. "Hello again."

Their bodies lined up perfectly torso to hip, but it wasn't enough. Kelli was starting to think being inside this woman's skin wouldn't be close enough. She stretched the moment between them further. It was getting downright painful.

Nora whimpered, and Kelli wasn't sure what the hell for. She was the one that was dying.

"Don't." Nora whispered, but she didn't push Kelli away.

What. The. Actual. Fuck? Surely, she didn't hear her right. "Uh…what?"

Nora tightened her arms around Kelli's neck, and her fingertips played with the hairs on the back of her head.

Kelli shivered. "Don't touch me like that if you don't want me to—"

"I do, but it can't…be here. I need to be able to function. It's my first day back—"

Kelli got it. "Okay, I understand. You need to be on your toes, not distracted." Nora's words should have cooled her off, but knowing that she had that kind of effect on Nora just made her hotter.

Nora continued to look at her. Her expression was hungry but soft as well. "I knew you would."

"Yeah, but you have to stop looking at me like that, or you're gonna make me out to be a liar because I won't be able to promise shit."

Nora gasped and nodded. She closed her eyes and tilted her head back against the door. The movement put a little distance between them. Kelli looked down the see the slight line of Nora's cleavage. She looked farther still, and she saw Nora's hardened nipples poking against her scrub top.

Sweet merciful God. Hot lava. It was as if hot lava was seeping through her body. She couldn't be good all the time. She just couldn't, goddammit. Kelli wanted to touch skin, but she would take what she could get. Kelli dragged her thumb across Nora's right nipple.

The most amazing thing happened.

Nora cried out and arched toward her.

Breathing… She just wasn't going to be able to do it around Nora. Kelli covered Nora's breast with her hand and squeezed.

"Kel—"

Kelli trailed her lips across Nora's cheek and whispered in her ear. "I'm here."

"Please." Nora pleaded. She covered Kelli's hand with her own.

That word possibly meant so many different things. Please kiss me. Please fuck me. Please don't ever leave me. Who was she kidding? She knew what it meant, but sooner or later something had to give. All patience aside, she was damn near ready to explode. Somehow, Kelli was able to step back. "God," she whispered and tried to catch her breath.

When Nora opened her eyes. They were dark. "I'm sorry," Nora mumbled.

"I get it. Really. Just…for future reference, my desk will never be off limits."

Nora blinked. Then, she laughed.

Kelli watched for a few seconds and smirked.

Nora stopped laughing but her gaze held wonder. "What's happening between us?"

Kelli had questions of her own. She certainly didn't have answers for that one, so she went with the explanation that seemed to fit. "It's complic—"

"No." Nora interrupted. "I meant that I know that much." She paused. "You don't know either."

"No, not really, but I think for now, that's okay." Kelli moved forward. She reached out and swiped her thumb over Nora's cheek before leaning in to kiss her forehead. She kept her lips pressed there, just enjoying the hell out of the contact. "Have a good first day and don't let the worries pile up about tonight. I'll call you later."

"Okay, please do."

That word…that word out of Nora's mouth was going to do all kinds of crazy things to Kelli from now on. She was kind of looking forward to it.

⁓⁓⁓

Alone for some time, Nora found herself staring at the far wall as she felt the first stirrings of anxiety. She took a deep breath to center herself. After several more, she noticed a difference. She peered down at the chart. It was the last one. Nora was officially caught up on her patients. It was a relief to know that they all fared well in her absence. Life in the hospital went on without her, it seemed. This should have given her pause, yet Nora knew she was just one cog in a well-oiled machine. She was an important piece, but just a piece nonetheless.

Nora skimmed the chart and looked over vitals and nurses reports. She finished it in record time. Her stomach fluttered. So far this morning, she had managed to avoid nearly everyone. When she arrived, she had made a beeline for the records room to get what she needed. Nora wasn't sure if it was fear that facilitated this behavior or just a need to re-acclimate herself. She stood. No more delays, even though some of them had been rather stimulating. Time to make rounds.

She waited in front of the elevator. When it opened, the car was full of hospital personnel. Nora was aware of their stares. Instead of being malicious, her co-workers merely looked curious. There were no grumbles or whispers, and this was a welcome relief. When the elevator stopped at her floor, Nora gently pushed past the remaining people. She walked quickly and carried herself with confidence and purpose. Residents teemed around the nurses' station, peering at the white board.

The sound of her name wafted toward her as she moved closer.

"Ah, shit. Dr. Whitmore is back."

The statement actually brought a smile to her face. She wasn't sure why. It remained when she called out particular names. "Drs. Crowder, Simpson, Ford, and Willows, you are with me."

They stared at her slack-jawed.

Annoyance unfurled. Instead of expressing it, Nora asked, "Will any of you have a problem with being on my service today?"

They continued to stare as if she was one of those pod people Kelli made reference to from time to time. Nora almost laughed, but that would have been completely inappropriate. Her smile did feel bigger, however. Obviously, this was not the Dr. Whitmore they were expecting.

"Speak up, please," Nora said.

Mumbling started. Then, one by one they moved closer.

"Thank you."

Dr. Crowder looked stricken.

Was she really never cordial? Nora felt more at ease with herself than she ever had. She was stunned by this, and everyone else seemed to be as well, judging by the way they were staring at her.

Nora cleared her throat. "Follow me."

As she passed the nurses' station, Nora heard snatches of conversation.

"Maybe she's sick."

"Nah, something's changed."

That nurse was right, but more than ever, Nora felt like she was home. If she could conquer this, dinner with Kelli's family would be simple.

※

Kelli maneuvered the car into the next lane so she could reach the exit going toward Beacon Hill. She glanced over at Nora for probably the hundredth time in the past twenty minutes. She looked nice in her blue skirt and strappy heels. Those legs she was convinced went on forever, but that wasn't why she was staring. Kelli saw a smile curl Nora's lips.

"I'm fine."

"I can see that. Then, why the hell am I a mess?" Kelli asked.

"Because you've never done this before?" Nora smiled.

"Neither have you." Kelli reminded her.

"Rader just tried to destroy my life. Dinner with your family doesn't make me nearly as nervous."

For whatever reason, Nora's admission made Kelli feel better. "Okay, I can work with that."

"What an odd thing to say."

"Did you ever hear me claim to be normal?" Kelli chuckled.

"Well…no."

"There you have it, then." Kelli took a deep breath as another wave of nerves hit.

"I see."

She had to warn Nora. Sean turned into a teenager when they were at home together, and her mother…well, her mother was going to put her on the hot seat no matter what Kelli said or did. Maybe this wasn't the best of ideas. Nora wasn't ready. Hell, Kelli wasn't ready.

"I can feel you panicking from over here," Nora said.

Kelli turned so damn fast she almost wrenched her neck. "I can't help it. I know them. I *know* what they are capable of." She swallowed and got to the heart of the matter. "I thought it was important for you to get to know them and vice versa, but now that it's happening, I just don't want them to scare you away."

Kelli felt as if her insides were dangling on a clothes line. Nora was skittish. Bringing it up only drew even more attention to that fact. Kelli looked Nora's way. She was staring out the window. "Look, I'm sorry I even said anything."

"No, you have valid reasons," Nora whispered and looked at Kelli. "I wish I could offer you some kind of reassurance for the future. Presently, I'm here, and I want to be."

Nora's words would have to do, and Kelli was starting to think that she needed to make the most out of right now. She didn't even want to think about whatever was coming. "Okay…okay."

Since the driveway was full, Kelli parked on the curb. She turned off the car and released a long breath. "Okay, let me just apologize for anything they do right now. They can't help it. This is just the way they are."

Nora stared. "Do you mean to make things sound so ominous?"

"Yes, I do."

Nora eyes widened, and for the first time tonight, she really looked nervous.

Kelli chuckled. "Now that I've got your attention. You've seen an abbreviated version of my mom before at the hospital, but the woman has no censor."

"So, just like you?" Nora asked and grinned.

Kelli glared but she smiled at the same time. "You just had to bring that to my attention?"

"Yes, I most certainly did." Nora answered playfully.

Kelli shook her head, and she couldn't stop grinning like a fucking idiot. Could she be worried for nothing? "Get out of my car."

Nora laughed. "It's my car."

She was cute. "And?"

"I was just stating the obvious." Nora opened the passenger side door.

"Hey?"

Nora turned.

"C'mere." Kelli crooked her finger.

Nora moved closer, her smile was still firmly in place. "Yes?"

In a very smooth move, Kelli unbuckled her seatbelt, leaned forward, and captured Nora's lips in a brief kiss that she filled with gratitude and gentleness. When Kelli pulled back, Nora still had her eyes closed, her face was flushed, and her mouth hung open slightly. She blinked slowly and revealed a wondrous look something like a kid on Christmas morning.

"What was that f—"

"Because you're here, and you want to be."

Nora entered the McCabe home and looked around. The television blared, and the living room was decorated in cream and soft pastels. However, the smell that filled the house got the majority of Nora's attention, and it was divine. The air was heavy with the tang of tomato sauce, garlic, and fresh herbs. "What is—"

"I know, right? Between the two of you, I'm surprised I can fit in my pants."

Nora smiled and continued to try to figure out what was making her mouth water. It all came together. "Lasagna."

Kelli smirked. "Very good." Then she turned away and yelled, "Mom! We're here."

Nora jumped slightly. She didn't expect Kelli to be so loud. Raised voices were never allowed in her home, especially during an event as formal as dinner.

"She knows." Sean popped up from the couch and started grinning. "You're a couple minutes late, so she had me peek. Told her the windows looked fogged up." His grin widened. "So, I didn't wanna come out to bother you." He glanced at his sister then back at Nora. "Hey, Nora."

Nora blinked.

"And don't start that Mr. McCabe crap. It's just Sean, remember? I ate your food, drank your beer, and saw you make out with my sister. I think we're familiar."

Kelli sighed. "And here we go."

Yes, all of that was true. She didn't need to be reminded of such an embarrassing—yet stimulating—moment. "Hello, Sean." This dinner was going to be memorable in one way or another. Nora just knew it. She cleared her throat. "Maybe I can go help in the kitchen?"

Kelli nodded, but she was glaring at her brother. She turned and pointed toward the door past the dining area. "Kitchen is through there. I'll be just a second."

Kelli wanted her to go in there alone? Nora felt a small zip of panic. Did Kelli forget her mother was in there?

"Promise," Kelli said as if she'd read her mind.

Nora moved slowly toward the kitchen door. A cry of pain made her look over her shoulder.

Sean was holding his head and laughing while Kelli tried to hit him.

Nora found herself smiling at the display. She imagined that, within these walls, there had been a lot of horse play between Kelli and her brothers. Growing up, Nora had the nanny and the maid, and she couldn't remember ever playing anything with them, hugging them or even laughing. It was strange and slightly uncomfortable to witness such things and realize the impact of what she never had. That was the past. Now, there was playfulness in her life, along with humor. Perhaps Nora should do whatever she could to hold onto it. She pushed the door open and stepped inside.

Carina glanced up and smirked. "Well, hey. My daughter sent you in here alone? That's brave." She placed a large pan of lasagna on the counter and removed her oven mitts.

Very memorable.

The kitchen door whooshed open. "What's brave?" Kelli asked.

"You sending your girlfriend into the lion's den by herself," Carina answered.

Kelli's mouth dropped open, and Nora had never seen her blush before. Kelli was beet red. "Mom!"

"What? It's the truth, isn't it?" Carina shrugged.

Girlfriend. That was definitely a label, but the word didn't cause as much anxiety as Nora thought it would. Her stomach and heart fluttered a little before she settled again, but Kelli looked like she was floundering. Nora's first instinct was to help. She reached out and took Kelli's hand. "It's okay."

Kelli gazed at Nora like she was searching for something. Apparently, she found it. Kelli smiled slightly and squeezed Nora's hand.

"Kelli tells me you're a cook," Carina said.

Nora cleared her throat again. She could do this. She could. "Yes, I dabble."

"Nothing wrong with that." Carina motioned Nora over. "Come over here. I tried something a little different. Lasagna is lasagna, you know? I wanted to give it more zing."

Nora released Kelli's hand and moved forward. "Sure." Nora could picture Kelli sitting on one of the stools that lined the island to do her homework and watch her mother cook. She was never really allowed in the kitchen. Her mother didn't do such things. Nora was an adult now, but there was something surreal in Carina McCabe's request to come in to taste her lasagna that caused a pleasant tingle to shoot down Nora's spine.

"It's not poisoned is it? I don't wanna end up on one of those Discovery shows about mothers who commit murder," Kelli asked teasingly.

It was nice to have Kelli back to making jokes again, even if they were her way of dealing with uncomfortable situations. Or maybe because of it.

Carina glared at her daughter. "You just hush and go toss the salad or something since you can't burn it." She dug into the lasagna with a spatula and placed a tiny bit on a plate. "The cooking gene just past right over her. My boys have some of it, but maybe she's just saving it for my grandchildren."

Nora actually gulped.

Carina laughed. "I'm just kidding. Right now, anyway. The look on your face…"

"Mom!" Kelli exclaimed.

"Shush." Carina gave Nora the plate and put a fork on it. "Go on."

Nora did as she was told. She felt Kelli come up behind her. Nora glanced at Kelli, and her gaze was warm, affectionate, just as always. Nora returned her attention to the food and dug in. The lasagna was bursting with flavor, and there was a delightful spiciness. "Roasted red peppers and cayenne?"

Carina smiled. "Very good. I'm impressed." She looked at her daughter. "I'm glad you never brought that Ashley girl over here. She looked like she couldn't tell an onion from a tomato."

Nora was relieved. Without a doubt, she'd just passed a test of some sort.

Kelli rolled her eyes. "Whatever. Can I get a taste?"

"Yeah, when we eat in ten minutes." Her mother answered. "The garlic bread will be done by then. You still haven't fixed the salad, and when you get done with that, you two can set the table." Carina shooed her daughter away. "So, did your mother teach you to cook?"

The question saddened Nora, and she was reminded of how empty her life had been. "No, I…I learned mostly through trial and error, but I did take classes some years ago," she answered honestly.

Carina studied her. "I'm sorry to hear that." She responded softly. "If Kelli doesn't run you off, I'd be happy to teach you a few tricks with Italian food. You'll have this one…" She pointed at Kelli. "…following you around like a puppy."

"Thank you. I think I would like that." Nora felt a spark of anticipation.

Kelli had her head in the refrigerator, her hands full of ingredients for salad. "Hey, you know I heard everything you said, Mom."

"And you know I didn't whisper," her mother countered.

Nora smiled at the banter. She wasn't sad anymore.

A few minutes later, Nora placed the salad bowls in the proper place for an informal dinner, to the left of the forks. She could feel Kelli's gaze on her. When she looked, Kelli was smiling, and there was a dazed look on her face. Nora tilted her head. "Are you all right?"

Kelli's smile dimmed to a smirk, but her expression remained. "Yeah, you're just…" Kelli laughed. "You're something else."

Nora let the compliment wash over her. It felt stupendous.

"They sucked," Kelli insisted. "They were grown men in the NBA with the ball-handling skills of a grade school team, especially near the end. Not to mention the pissy coaching and management. I'm glad they're gone." She dipped her bread in red sauce and popped the piece into her mouth.

"They used to hold their own with the big boys," Sean said.

Kelli snorted. "Whatever. We don't need a professional men's team. I like the Storm, and they are doing just fine."

"This is a stupid argument. If they brought them back, it wouldn't be the same players or management." Sean said.

"Oh yeah? I'm sure there's some fat cat somewhere waiting in the wings from before."

"Uh-huh, admit it. You just like Seattle Storm because there's some hot women on that team. I've seen your DVR. Why else would you record the games?" Sean challenged with a smirk.

"Uh, because I work," Kelli answered.

"No, you rewind so you get to see tit—"

"Hey!" Kelli cut him off. She glanced in Nora's direction.

Sean rolled his eyes. "She likes tits too. Hell, we all do. Except for Mom." He pointed his fork in his mother's direction. "Isn't that right Nora?" Then he pointed it at her.

"Jesus Christ, are you twelve? Show some damn manners," Kelli yelled at her brother.

He shrugged. "Nora will get used to it." Sean continued to wave his fork around. "Won't you, Nora? I mean, you got used to this potty mouth right here." He shook his utensil at Kelli.

"Oh, fuck you." Kelli rolled her eyes and grinned.

"See? See what I mean?" Sean laughed.

Nora put her own fork down and waited. "Am I allowed to speak now?"

Kelli snorted.

Sean smiled. "I like her. Did I tell you that before?" He glanced at Kelli.

"Probably, but don't you think she needs to hear it?" Kelli asked him.

The fork was back and Sean's smile widened. "I like you."

He was accepting her into their circle. Nora had never fit in before, but she could here, if she wanted to. Did she want to?

"What?" He looked at Nora expectantly. "I don't get anything back? Not even a 'Sean you're great?'"

Nora laughed. She liked him too. "Sean you're—"

"An asshole." Kelli finished.

"Hey! I learned from the best, sis," Sean said.

Nora watched them bicker for a few more seconds before glancing at their mother. Carina was smiling and shaking her head. She looked Nora's way. Nora held her breath. She wasn't sure why. Maybe she wanted to see acceptance in her gaze as well. Instead, Carina rolled her eyes and pantomimed her children's argument.

"I don't know how you put up with her." Carina mouthed and pointed.

Nora felt heat rush to her face. She glanced at Kelli. She smiled, and Nora grinned in return before Sean pulled her back into their discussion. Nora's gaze found Carina again. She peered at Nora over the rim of her glass and winked.

Nora experienced a warmth she couldn't explain, but she just went with it. If this was a fraction of what family was supposed to be like, then she had missed out on a lot, but she was eager to try to make up for it.

"Since we were talking about tits, TV, and lesbians, I have a question. You're with Kelli now. I'm gonna assume you're done with men? I've seen a video or two. There are a lot of things women can do to each other in the bedroom, so there's no way to get bored." Carina eyes stayed on Nora as she spoke.

Well, that was unexpected. No censor, indeed. This was obviously another test. Even though there was a smirk on Carina's face, Nora knew she was serious.

All conversation stopped.

"Did you just say you watched porn?" Sean asked, his mouth hanging open.

"Oh my God! What the hell?" Kelli looked as if she was about to faint.

Somehow, Nora pushed through her embarrassment and growing trepidation and searched for an answer. Her palms felt sweaty, and her stomach was suddenly jittery. There was no safe response. Carina McCabe was protective of her children. Lion's den was an apropos description. She had no idea if she was going to be with another man again or if she and Kelli were going to last. She decided to go with the first thing that came to mind. She had to say something. "Based on what I've gleaned from the Internet, lesbian erotic fiction is considered more stimulating."

The dinner area was quieter than it was a minute ago.

Nora didn't dare look at Kelli. She found the wherewithal to seek Carina's gaze.

Carina continued to study her. Her face was blank, but Nora started to see her lips quiver as she fought her smile. Carina McCabe lost the battle. A huge smile spread across her face. "I like this, and when Tony gets home, it's gonna be even better."

There it was…the acceptance Nora was hoping for.

Nora felt the previous warmth creep back. She glanced at Kelli to see that her dazed look had returned. Truth be told, Nora was astonished by her own behavior, pleasantly so, but Kelli's expression made the moments of discomfort worth it.

Nora opened the bathroom door to see Kelli leaning against the opposite wall. Kelli grinned. "I'm not stalking, just wanted to show you something since you were back here."

"Okay." Curiosity got the better of Nora.

Kelli made her way down the hall and motioned for Nora to follow. They stopped. "This used to be my room. I still crash here from time to time." Kelli opened the door.

Nora stepped inside.

"It looks a little more adult now without all the posters and crap." The color palette was similar to Kelli's bedroom in her own home, except for the full-sized bed and desk. Kelli pointed at the wall near the entrance. "I used to have a life-sized cut out of Boy George taped there."

Nora bit the inside of her cheek and remained quiet. The name sounded familiar.

Kelli sighed. "I'll just add him to the list." She smirked. "That changed to posters of Corey Hart and then Metallica. I don't know how I went from pop to metal."

"Maybe you'll develop an appreciation of jazz in time as well."

Kelli shrugged. "Anything is possible."

"Yes, I'm learning that." Nora sat down on the chair in front of Kelli's desk. The chair squeaked. "So, this is where you grew up, and this is your family."

"For better or worse, yeah. What you see is what you get." Kelli sat on the bed, but they were only a few inches apart. She looked hesitant and hopeful at the same time.

"You're very lucky." Nora paused. "I never…" Her voice trailed off as she remembered the emptiness of her childhood.

"I know," Kelli said gently. She covered Nora's hand with her own.

"And they made me…they made me feel." Nora's thoughts were scattered, and her words came out the same way. "I laughed. Your brother likes me. And your mother…" Nora didn't know what to say about Carina.

Nora wasn't sure how she ended up in Kelli's arms, but she liked being there. Kelli chuckled. "My mom likes you too. We're a mess, but it's a package deal. If you want it."

That was a lot to think about.

"Oh, hey, there you guys are." Sean stood in the doorway. He leaned back and yelled down the hall. "I found them, Mom! They were making out in Kelli's old bedroom."

"Goddammit, Sean!" Kelli exclaimed.

Nora laughed.

Kelli jiggled Nora's car keys in her hand. The night was over, and she didn't want it to be. So many good things happened in a row. After all the up-and-down crap of the past couple of months, Kelli wanted to hang onto those moments. She looked at Nora. "Come in for a little while? I know you have work but do it anyway."

Nora smiled and reached for her keys. She slid her palm over Kelli's as she took them. The touch left Kelli's hand all tingly.

"Okay."

Shit really does work out sometimes. "Good, you left wine in my refrigerator. We can drink the rest of it."

Nora nodded. "Yes, it would be a travesty to waste it." She grinned as she climbed out of the car.

Kelli had to jog a little to catch up, which was cool. She didn't mind running behind Nora at all. When they reached the entrance, Kelli pressed her hand in the small of Nora's back and guided her away as some guy exited. Kelli caught the door in time to keep from using her card key. "Was that the only reason?"

Nora pressed the button on the elevator. It opened almost immediately. Several people got off. "Only reason for…?" She asked as she pressed her back against the railing.

"Coming up." Kelli reminded her.

Nora stared. There was no fear in her eyes. She didn't look as if she was about to run, but there was a shitload of intensity in her gaze. Kelli felt her stomach tie in all kinds of knots because of it.

"No, it wasn't. I just don't want to stop feeling this way," Nora whispered.

Damn, Kelli was sure that her heart stopped beating for a second. "What way?"

"Happy, accepted. Wanted."

Kelli smiled. "Yeah, all those things."

Nora glanced away for a second. When their gazes met again, Kelli's stomach crashed to the floor of the elevator.

"I'm aware that you want me," Nora said.

That look was back—the one from the hospital earlier today—and there went Kelli's ability to breathe. "I never hid that from you, but it's more than that." Kelli walked toward her, and she didn't stop until they were touching. She braced her arms on either side of Nora's head and leaned in. She needed Nora to hear what she was about to say. She needed her to feel it too. "The way you are you're incredible. I can't help it."

Nora slid her hands up and around Kelli's torso, and it felt so goddamned good.

"You say these things, and you make me believe them," Nora said.

Kelli welcomed the explosion of heat in her chest. It was a good pain, and she wanted more of it. Just one more kiss, she promised herself. Just one, and this night would be perfect. Before Kelli could put actual thoughts to action, Nora's lips brushed against hers.

So soft. The connection was fragile, delicate.

Nora mumbled something and wrapped her arms around Kelli's neck.

Kelli felt like she was being ripped apart. Everything inside her spilled out, and the funny thing was, she didn't fucking mind at all.

Ding.

The world stopped and started moving again. Someone cleared his throat. Distracted by the ass standing next to them, Kelli ended the kiss, but fuck him. Kelli didn't move away. She pressed her forehead against Nora's and wrapped her arms around her.

Nora was too energized to sit still. She got up from the couch and walked toward the kitchen and the sound of clinking glasses. Kelli stood at the counter. She had a package of grapes dangling from her mouth and an earnest look on her face as she cut pieces of what appeared to be sharp cheddar. She abandoned the cheese to put the grapes on a plate. Kelli glanced at Nora.

"What? Was I taking too long?"

"Yes, you were." Nora meant for it to sound as if she were joking, but she was completely serious. She didn't want to be away from Kelli right now.

"Sorry. I figured you'd want something to go with the wine. I've never seen you just drink it straight."

"I would have tonight. Here. Let me help." Nora's shoulder brushed Kelli's as they stood side by side.

"Okay. There's some Gouda in the fridge too," Kelli said.

"This is fine." Nora cut an apple into slices.

"We gotta have more than one cheese. You taught me that," Kelli said playfully.

Nora grinned. "It's nice to know you're listening, but I don't want Gouda."

Kelli turned to Nora. There was no teasing in her gaze. "What do you want then?"

The question wrapped around her. Nora's body—something deep inside—reacted viscerally to Kelli's words. On pure instinct, Nora closed the gap between them. She didn't want to think. For once, she just wanted to feel. Nora leaned in. Kelli's eyes darkened, and her breathing was already labored. Nora's stomach coiled into hard knots. Her mouth grazed Kelli's, then immediately, claimed her thoroughly, and Kelli was eager to give in return.

Need slithered like molten lead through Nora's body.

She nipped Kelli's bottom lip and found her answers inside Kelli's mouth.

This…she wanted this feeling…this hunger. This woman.

Nora pressed Kelli into the counter. They stumbled slightly. Kelli's hands tightened around Nora's waist. Then they dipped lower and slipped underneath Nora's skirt, palming and squeezing her gluteal muscles. Nora moaned as a wave of arousal slammed into her.

Kelli pulled back slightly, but their lips continued to cling. "You like being on top, don't you?"

Instead of answering, Nora whimpered.

Apparently, that answer was sufficient for Kelli. "Maybe next time," she muttered before kissing Nora again.

The remaining wall around Nora collapsed completely. The heat that suddenly blasted her left her insides singed. The meaning behind Kelli's words were clear. Nora was safe.

Then, they were moving. Slowly but surely, Kelli was walking them toward the living area.

Kelli's lips trailed over her chin to Nora's neck. Initially, she was gentle, just dragging her mouth across sensitized skin, but that changed as Nora felt the sting of teeth.

Flashes of pleasure shot down Nora's spine. She tilted her head back silently demanding more.

Suddenly, she was against a wall. Nora didn't care where she was, so long as Kelli was touching her, kissing her. Their lips met again hungrily. Nora put everything into each glide of her tongue. When the caress ended abruptly, she murmured in protest and reached out for more only to see Kelli yanking her shirt and bra over her head.

There was so much skin. Nora didn't wait to touch. She pressed her hands flat against Kelli's stomach. Hard. Soft. And so very warm. Kelli's abdominals twitched in response. Nora's hands slid upward over brown-tipped breasts.

Kelli shuddered and moaned.

This wasn't enough.

Nora dipped her head and pulled a nipple deep into her mouth.

"Fuuu…" Kelli cried out.

Nora's body clenched in excitement.

Still, this wasn't enough.

She unbuttoned Kelli's jeans and yanked the zipper free before sliding her hand inside. The heat that awaited her there was staggering.

"Jesus!" Kelli exclaimed.

In a flurry of movement, Kelli pressed Nora's hands against the wall high above their heads.

Their gazes met. And it was like a flame devouring dry wood.

Kelli surged forward, and this time when their lips collided, colors exploded behind Nora's eyes as every synapse in her body ruptured.

They were moving again.

Kelli struggled with the buttons on Nora's shirt. She cursed and gave up. Seconds later the material was being pulled over her head.

The next thing Nora was cognizant of was falling into bed with Kelli on top of her, and Kelli's tongue sliding over her left nipple which was abruptly replaced by her entire mouth. Nora arched upward and whimpered with each firm suck.

Kelli's hands were everywhere gliding down her torso and over her still clothed hips. Nora felt a cool rush of air as Kelli slid her underwear over her thighs. Nora wiggled and kicked them free. It was followed by her skirt.

Realizing her heels were still on, Nora pushed one foot into the other until she was able to shake both shoes free.

The material of Kelli's jeans felt rough against her naked thighs, but the friction the texture created was glorious. Nora rolled her hips seeking more contact. More everything. She wasn't sure if she wanted to soothe the mounting pressure between her legs or strengthen it.

Kelli decided for her as she met Nora thrust for thrust.

Nora moaned, but the sound was swallowed by Kelli's kiss. The caress was brief but intense. Kelli's tongue left a wet trail between Nora's breasts and she continued to move lower.

No. She needed…Nora tangled her hand in Kelli's hair and pulled. She wanted to feel her strong and sure against her. Kelli glanced upward. Her face was flushed, and her eyes were darker than she'd ever seen them.

"I need…"

Nora never finished. Fingertips teased her clit before sliding home.

"Kel-li!"

"Yesss," Kelli whispered.

Nora shivered at the feeling of fullness, and then she was empty again. She whimpered and then cried out helplessly as Kelli thrusted into her slow and deep. This became the center of Nora's universe. Pleasure careened through her body, obliterating her senses. When Kelli's fingertips curled inside her, Nora lost herself. Her hips rolled frantically. She dug her nails into Kelli's back, but Kelli refused to be rushed.

"Please," she murmured. Kelli moaned loudly as she covered Nora's lips with her own. She grasped Nora's leg and pulled it upward.

Nora saw stars and planets alike as Kelli glided in deeper. They all burst open in a blinding array of light that seeped into Nora and tore her apart.

Minutes later, Nora was still floating on a cloud of sensation. Kelli's lips brushed over her cheek. Her eyes fluttered open, and Kelli came into sharp focus.

Her face was red. Her breathing labored. She was grinding her hips softly against Nora's thigh, and there was hunger in Kelli's eyes.

Nora's stomach tightened. Urgently, she pushed at Kelli's jeans in an effort to get them off as quickly as possible. Before Kelli had a chance to protest, Nora had flipped them over. She straddled Kelli's thighs and looked down at her. Kelli was powerful, majestic, and helplessly aroused.

Nora grazed the hardened tips of Kelli's breasts with her fingers. She cried out, and her hips surged upward. Nora's heart jumped to her throat. To have this kind of power over Kelli made her dizzy.

So she did it again and again.

Kelli rasped, "I'm gonna…I can't stop…"

Kelli grabbed Nora around the waist, holding her still as Kelli's hips took on a mind of their own. Nora groaned. She had to feel it. She just had to, and there it was. Kelli's release rushing over her fingertips.

Kelli blinked and opened her eyes slowly. She'd been fighting the urge to get up and pee for some time. She was way too cozy and warm to move, so she just lay there with Nora tucked against her side and breathing all over her neck. Kelli smiled. She wouldn't have it any other way. Kelli had never been a snuggler, but there was a first time for everything.

Nora murmured in her sleep, and suddenly Kelli felt wet lips against her throat that sent a tingle all the way to her toes and then…nothing. False alarm. Nora fidgeted and stilled once more.

Damn. Because last night and early this morning was…damn. Kelli couldn't wipe the smirk off her face. She had no regrets, and she hoped to God that Nora didn't either. Sex with Nora? Yeah, Kelli planned on doing that with her. *A lot*. Funny thing, though, in the past she used to be an expert at slipping out in the morning or way before dawn. Hell, she was even able to convince a few women to leave under their own steam. No fuss. No muss. Right now, none of that mattered because she was where she wanted to be. It was more than a little frightening to abruptly realize how *much* she had changed. She refused to focus on that particular feeling, however.

Kelli gently lifted the covers and looked at all the naked skin hidden underneath. They looked so fucking hot all tangled up together like that.

"What are you doing?" Nora mumbled.

And, suddenly, Kelli felt like a pervert. "Uh…" Kelli moved back an inch or two until she could look Nora in the face and completely forgot what she was about to say.

Nora was free of makeup, and her hair was beyond messy. Not to mention the sleepy look in her eyes. In the light of day, this was the sexiest thing she'd ever seen. "You. I was looking at you."

Nora moved away slightly. Her expression cleared, and she was starting to look apprehensive. Kelli hoped it wasn't the beginning of morning-after awkwardness. She had to do or say something to keep the ease between them. Kelli pulled her close again. "It's nothing bad," she whispered.

"Then what?" Nora asked hesitantly.

"You." Kelli slid her hand down Nora's naked back and savored the softness of her skin. "Me. Us. This. All of it. It's so fucking good." Kelli decided putting her feelings out there front and center was the best way to go.

Nora's mouth opened but nothing came out. Her face was flushed red, and she looked startled. Her expression softened. She reached out to touch Kelli's face with her fingertips. "Yes. That doesn't…scare you?"

Kelli chuckled, but her heart was beating a mile a minute. "Scares me shitless. Let's keep doing it anyway."

Nora's eyes widened, and she had never looked so open before. Her lips curled upward in a slight smile. "Yes," she whispered and leaned in for a kiss. "Yes."

CHAPTER 21

The sound of saxophones reached a swelling climax as Nora pushed aside the man's large intestines to get toward the bleed underneath. Her gloves were coated with bodily fluids, which ensured that everything she touched slithered through her fingers. "Flush the cavity. I need a better view." She expected to hear the music start again but it didn't. Someone had forgotten to put it on repeat.

Without a word, the resident did as she was told and more as she suctioned the area as well. Minutes later, blood filled Mr. Brown's abdomen again.

"BP is dropping. We need to close him, Dr. Whitmore," Dr. Ford said, her voice firm.

Feeling hassled but determined, Nora glared at the resident. Dr. Ford was right. Nora was impressed that she'd attempted to stand up to her. "Just a few more seconds. I know I'm close," Nora insisted.

Machines blared suddenly.

"Dr. Whitmore!"

"I found it. Clamp please." Nora said, relieved.

"BP is rising," Dr. Ford relayed with enthusiasm.

"And Mr. Brown gets to see another day. Would you like to close, Dr. Ford?" Nora peered at her and waited.

"Was that rhetorical?" Dr. Ford asked warily.

"Not at all. A 'yes' or 'no' will do."

"Hell yes!"

The resident's eagerness was almost endearing. Dr. Ford's eyes widened. "You're gonna stay though, right?"

"This team is more than competent, but if that's what you need, I will," Nora said.

All eyes turned toward Nora. They all looked surprised. She cleared her throat. "I give praise when it's due, but all of you deserve it. Consistently."

And…they just kept staring.

Decidedly uncomfortable, Nora murmured, "Mr. Brown is waiting."

The statement snapped everyone back to attention. Nora observed the remainder of the surgery and endured the continued gazes of her team. Their stares didn't feel invasive. They seemed more inquisitive. Nora knew she was as proficient as ever as a doctor, but the wall she kept around herself wasn't nearly as high as it used to be. Obviously, people were starting to notice, and that felt surprisingly good.

Less than an hour later, Nora was removing soiled gloves and other protective gear. The surgical nurses and tech were laughing when they entered the room. She had her back to them. Out of habit, Nora stiffened, but she relaxed within seconds. Nora turned slightly and one of the nurses, Patricia, caught her gaze. She smiled tentatively at Nora.

Nora smiled back. Maybe it was time to give people a chance. She did with Kelli, and look what she got in return.

※

Nora unlocked her office door. As she walked in, a white envelope slid across the room after she inadvertently kicked it. Nora embraced the giddy sense of anticipation that filled her. She picked the envelope up, and put her charts on the desk. For the moment, the note in her hand held more importance. How could it not? It was from Kelli. Carefully, Nora opened it. She skimmed the words quickly then read at a slower pace. She welcomed a familiar heat to her face, and her heart constricted as well. They were just words written on a piece of paper, but they had tremendous power. Nora was even more moved today than she was when she got the first one. Unable to resist, she opened her desk drawer and pulled out the initial correspondence. Reading it again made her smile just as wide.

Hey,

I'm not a romantic. If I was, I would have done this when you first came back to work or had your office overrun with flowers. To tell the truth, I don't know why I'm doing it now. Actually, yeah, I do. I got used to spending the day with you. Don't get me wrong. I'm happy you're back at work. It's where you belong, but I think you belong with me too. Don't forget that. I guess what I'm trying to say is that I miss you already. Look! It only took me about forty words to say it! I'm growing... or something. Let me add a caveat. Or should I have done that at the beginning? Are you impressed? It's a sexy word, caveat. Anyway, I'm warning you, if you tell anybody about this...mainly Travis or my brother (they have their ways), there will be no more tongue or any kind of other action for you. Okay, I'm lying about that part, so sue me. Haha...is it too soon? If I don't see you until tonight, you'll have this. It's kinda like talking.

Later,
Kelli

Nora refolded the note and stared at the new one. It was short but no less poignant. *I can't stop thinking about you.* Nora was in awe. Kelli was always giving to those who needed her, but Nora was sure that she had a special piece that no one else got to touch. She was extremely grateful for that caliber of gift. Then, there was the myriad of little things that Kelli did that always seemed to add up to something gargantuan. Like the notes. Nora was starting to wonder if she was adequately returning the gesture. She shared her body. She let her mind wander for a second, recalling what Kelli tasted like, felt like, and sounded like. She closed her eyes and enjoyed the sizzle of electricity that flashed over her nerve endings. For the first time, Nora had no qualms about Kelli, about their relationship. She wanted to move forward. It was time to accept who she had become. Nora pulled herself away from recent memories with some difficulty. Yes, she shared her body and provided comfort when Kelli needed it. But had she given enough of herself? Nora glanced at the letter once more and hoped that Kelli would never find her to be a disappointment in that department. Giving was a process, and Nora was in the novice stage. She looked at her watch. An idea struck. Nora stood and made her way out the door.

As she entered the PT room, Nora spotted Kelli and Dan talking and laughing. The physical therapist nodded in her direction. Kelli turned, and the smile that graced her face was dazzling. All of Nora's thought processes scattered, and her heart started to race. Amazing what one look could do. She had no idea what her expression held, but Kelli's eyes darkened. Nora's stomach tensed in reaction.

Dan cleared his throat. "Well, good to have you back, Dr. Whitmore."

Nora briefly met his gaze. "Thank you."

Kelli moved toward her. She stopped when they were mere inches apart, demanding all of Nora's attention.

"Hey, not that I don't love it, but what are you doing here?" She reached out, intent on touching Nora. At the last second, her hand fell away.

If Dan wasn't there, Nora would have allowed the caress. She needed it. "It's your last day. I wanted to show my support," Nora told her.

"That it is. You came to give me a…sendoff?" Kelli asked teasingly.

Only Kelli McCabe could make a seemingly harmless word salacious. Amused, Nora grinned. "Maybe."

"Mmm, did you get my note?" Kelli asked. Their bodies brushed. Nora felt hot and cold at the same time.

"I did," Nora answered. She resisted the urge to close the small gap between them….just barely.

A door closed. Nora glanced around the room only to find that they were alone. It momentarily diffused the haze forming between them.

"That's sweet of you to come here. I know you need to keep us separate from the hospital." Obviously unable to help herself, Kelli trailed a finger down Nora's forearm.

And that was all it took for sparks to ignite. Nora melted inside, and Kelli looked as though she would pounce at any minute. The air charged around them.

"I loved the way you looked at me when you first walked in," Kelli whispered in Nora's ear. Having Kelli so close sent tiny pinpricks of sensation throughout her body that settled with a jolt between her legs.

Nora's mouth went dry. "How did I—"

"Like you were completely rattled. I'm the only one that's ever done that to you." It was far from a question. Kelli said it with confidence. "I'm so fucking proud of that." Kelli's lips grazed her cheek.

"Yes," Nora said even though no question was asked. Yes, she wanted Kelli to touch her, and yes, being next to her eclipsed everything else. Her insides whorled violently. She turned toward the sound of Kelli's voice. Their lips made soft contact. Nora's breath caught and escaped as a whimper.

Kelli stepped away and ended the exchange before it really had a chance to start. Her chest heaved. Kelli was stiff, tense, and her eyes held enough heat to set the room ablaze. "I don't think you have any idea how much I want you right now."

That was far from the truth. Nora knew because she wanted Kelli too. She could feel it circling between them like a desire-laden feedback loop.

A man coughed and cleared his throat.

They both turned to see Dan. He scratched the back of his neck and gave them a sheepish grin. "I'm sorry. I hate to interrupt—"

The sound of Nora's pager stopped his apology. Shaken, she nodded in his general direction before leaving the room. How on earth could she want Kelli more than she did before? This was going to take some getting used to.

"Don't be mad." Kelli had followed her. Nora knew she would. She turned toward her.

"I didn't mean to start anything back there. You just…do something to me," Kelli said.

Nora whispered, "I'm not upset believe me, but I do have to go. I'm sorry."

"I know. It meant a lot, you coming down here."

Nora stepped closer and grasped Kelli's hand. She held on tightly. She searched for the right words to go with her actions. "You give…you just give, and I want to make sure I'm giving back. I need to be there for you"

"Nora, you are. I don't need—"

"I can't stop thinking about you either, and I don't want to. If my actions haven't been enough, I want to make sure you know that."

Kelli's smile was even more radiant than it was a few minutes earlier.

Kelli flexed her bicep and made a fist. The feeling was returning to her arm after the blood pressure cuff was removed. She looked at her family doctor hopefully.

"Your blood pressure is a little high."

Kelli chuckled. Being around a woman like Nora would certainly keep it up there. "Still?" Kelli fidgeted. Her paper gown rasped against the protective tissue covering the examination table. Thank God this was her last doctor's visit. She was tired as hell of being poked and prodded in these little rooms.

Dr. Emily Rainer stared and waited.

"Sorry, private joke," Kelli said.

"Mmm hmm." The doctor notated something in the chart. "Well, considering what you've been through, you've healed quickly. There is excellent mobility in your leg. According to the latest scans, there is minimal scarring in your lung. Let's chalk it up to clean living and you being relatively young."

Kelli smirked. "Gee, thanks."

Dr. Rainer smiled, making the heavy lines around her eyes crinkle. "You're welcome, smartass."

"Mmm, I didn't think I'd see you. I expected the nurse practitioner for something like this."

"Considering you probably won't need an appointment for a while, I thought I'd take over today."

"Okay, so what's the verdict?" Kelli held her breath. Dammit she wanted this. It would be shit if she had to wait after setting her sights on Monday.

"I'm releasing you to desk duty. A week tops. I see no reason to keep you out of the field any longer than that."

Kelli grinned. "Wooo. I was sure you were gonna say two."

Dr. Rainer pursed her lips and looked at Kelli teasingly. "I still can, you know."

Kelli held up a hand in surrender. "No, no that's fine. Let's go with your first instinct."

Dr. Rainer laughed. "Good, now how's your family?"

"Mom's still working her ass off. I'm sure she hasn't been in to see you for a while."

"You might be surprised." The doctor smiled.

"Good to know," Kelli said.

"I didn't say anything."

"Uh-huh, and Sean is well…Sean. Antony—" Kelli stopped and shot some positive vibes into the universe. It had better fucking listen. No matter how they left things, he was still her brother. "He's in rehab."

Dr. Rainer sighed and patted Kelli's knee. "Yeah, third time isn't it?"

"Something like that." Kelli answered. "Travis is up doing PT now. Six months, a year tops. I'm sure of it. I know you don't know him, but—"

She squeezed Kelli's knee before pulling away. "Family is relative. Anything else interesting going on?" Dr. Rainer looked at her expectantly.

Kelli glared. "I don't believe that's part of the exam."

The doctor smirked. "I've known you for a long time, Kelli. Your mother longer. I can ask whatever the hell I want."

Kelli laughed. "So, Mom has been here, and she's been running her mouth."

"I didn't say that. To confirm anything would be a HIPAA violation." Emily Rainer grinned.

Kelli continued to glare.

"A doctor, huh?"

Groaning, Kelli covered her face with her hands.

"That sounds like something interesting," Dr. Rainer said.

"There are way too many fingers in my pie." Kelli folded her arms over her chest.

Dr. Rainer snorted. "Was that a lesbian joke?"

"Oh God."

"She must be something to make you blush like that."

"It's called embarrassment," Kelli snarked.

"It's called people who care looking out for you," Dr. Rainer said gently, the teasing tone still coloring her voice.

Feeling properly admonished, Kelli met the doctor's gaze. "Yeah, I know."

They stared at each other for a few seconds. The doctor continued to look at her expectantly.

Amused, Kelli bit her bottom lip to keep from smirking.

"You're not going to tell me anything are y—"

"Nope." Kelli interrupted.

"Fine. I at least know she's pretty."

Kelli softened. That really wasn't a strong enough word. She felt blood rush to her face. "She's…" Her mouth opened but nothing else came out.

"Is she now?"

Kelli nodded.

Dr. Rainer chuckled. "I'll leave you to get dressed."

Kelli pulled her shirt over her head and smiled. No woman had ever made her speechless before, but she was starting to think it was a good thing.

Kelli fiddled with the holster on her belt to make sure it was secure. It felt good to wear it again, even though she was going to be sitting at a damn desk all day. The Glock was heavy on her hip, but Kelli had always liked the weight of it. She was dressed to sit on her ass in jeans and a button down shirt. Kelli glanced in the mirror. Her hair was perfect—not in the way, just how she liked it. She was ready to go. She picked up her towel and threw it toward the open hamper. It went in, for the most part. Kelli shrugged.

She reached for the door and opened it slowly. Damn thing had a tendency to creak, and Kelli didn't want to wake Nora. They'd been up half the night, and it wasn't just sex. They talked and laughed. Kelli smiled just thinking about it. She could get used to things being all comfortable and domestic. Anyway, she was up way too early, but she couldn't help herself. She was fucking excited. Yeah, she had desk duty. She would still be in the thick of things where she could hear the guys grouse about their cases and their wives, and feel the excitement when a perp was collared. Some of the guys would welcome her back warmly with a pat on the back and others didn't give a fuck.

There had better not be balloons and shit on her desk.

Kelli stepped into her bedroom and glanced at the bed. Damn thing was empty. So there was probably a naked Nora running around.

No, not probably. There *was* a naked Nora running around. That sounded way better than the coffee she was now smelling. Kelli went in search of both. When she got to the living room, she could tell Nora was nowhere near naked, but maybe later. She had on one of Kelli's T-shirts—Metallica, Master of Puppets. "I was trying to be quiet. It's not time for you to get up yet."

"I don't think it's time for you to get up either." Nora yawned and brought a cup to her lips.

"Well…no, but early bird and all that shit." Kelli paused and grinned. "Plus, I'm excited as hell."

"Obviously." Nora smiled. "I made coffee."

"Obviously," Kelli said. This was a nice gesture, and it made her feel all fuzzy inside. "You didn't have to get up or anything."

"I'm aware of that. Can't I just do something for you sometimes?" Nora asked softly.

Kelli was just a regular fucking Casanova. She walked toward Nora, took the coffee cup from her, and pulled her close. "Yeah, you can. I really wasn't trying to be an ungrateful ass, I'm just not used to having somebody around who wants to take care of me."

Nora's eyes widened. "And I am?"

Kelli smirked. "Huh, you have a point."

"Yes, I'm aware of that." Nora smiled in return.

Kelli leaned in and brushed her lips. Nora's smile widened. Kelli could feel it. She pulled back. "Thank you for the coffee and the send-off. But—" Kelli paused for effect.

"But what?"

Kelli grinned. "It woulda been better if you were naked."

Nora blinked. Then, she laughed.

Kelli pushed her way through the crowded elevator to get to the number pad, only to see that her floor was already lit up. She glanced around to check for familiar faces. There were some staring right at her.

"Holy fuck! The bitch is back."

Two men, one burly and rough looking, the other tall with the disposition of a scarecrow, elbowed their way toward her. Kelli got her pats on the back.

"And a good morning to you too," she said.

"Williams didn't say a damn thing. If I'd known you were coming back today, I woulda baked you a damn cake," the scarecrow told her with a straight face.

Kelli smirked. "Uh-huh."

He smiled and it didn't help his ass at all. "Welcome back. We do lunch orders at ten-thirty."

Kelli glared.

Finn, the burly one, shouldered his partner. "Nice little reunion and all, but we need to stop and talk to somebody in DEU. Remember?"

"Oh shit, yeah." Coleman said. "Our floor is coming then. Since that's your old stomping ground, McCabe, I'll let everybody know you're back."

The elevator opened.

"Later." Coleman nodded as they exited.

Kelli nodded right back. Two more floors to go for her. She thought about Williams. He knew she wouldn't want any pomp and circumstance. Kelli was lucky to have him as a friend and a temporary partner. The elevator dinged. She glanced up at the red numbers. This was her floor. Kelli walked out into the hallway. She stopped and looked into the squad room. It was everything that she remembered. Several detectives were front and center already. Some sat at their desks pecking at their computers. Others stood in front of an evidence board going over their findings. Only a select few had commandeered the overall computer system and peered up at the large monitor that lowered from the ceiling. And there was that smell—aftershave and burnt coffee. Kelli stood there and took it all in. A couple months ago, she was fighting to stay alive, and her life was fractured, broken. The pieces were coming together…Tony, Nora, Travis, and now this. For once, shit was damn near perfect.

Someone swatted her on the back, nearly sending her ass over teakettle. "You waiting for a goddamn parade or something?" Williams asked.

Kelli glanced over her shoulder at him and smirked. "Fuck you, old man."

Williams snorted. "Good to have you back, McCabe."

###

EXCERPT
CROSSING LINES

by KD Williamson

Kelli watched Taylor's car disappear further up the road. After a few more seconds, she turned back toward the door. When she opened it. Nora was there. The soft look in her eyes made Kelli's heart turn over in her chest. "I'm not sure if we need to watch out for her or not, but I didn't want her to ruin—"

Nora interrupted her with a kiss.

Kelli smiled and pulled Nora closer to deepen the caress. Slowly, they parted.

"I can go smack around a few more people if that's what it gets me," Kelli said teasingly.

Nora grinned and whispered, "Dinner's ready."

"Mmm, don't know if it's gonna be this tasty," Kelli mumbled and nibbled on Nora's neck.

Nora laughed even as she turned her head to the side to give greater access. "Did you just say—"

Kelli groaned and steered them toward the kitchen. At least she could help with plating…maybe. "Yes, I did. Who knew I was so goddamned corny?" What was next poetry? Maybe a dirty limerick?

"It's not the first time, but I won't complain," Nora said.

"Good to know. What's for dinner? Because that smell—"

"Flank steak with chimichurri sauce, fingerling potatoes, and honey glazed carrots."

"I have no idea what a chimi-what's-it is but you had me at steak and potatoes."

"I knew I would."

Nora had her even if she'd made gruel.

About KD Williamson

KD is a Southerner and a former nomad, taking up residence in the Mid-West, east coast, and New Orleans over the years. She is also a Hurricane Katrina survivor. Displaced to the mountains of North Carolina, she found her way back to New Orleans, where she lives with her partner of ten years and the strangest dogs and cats in existence.

KD enjoys all things geek, from video games to super heroes. She is a veteran in the mental health field working with children and their families for over ten years. She found that she had a talent for writing as a teenager, and through fits and starts, fostered it over the years.

CONNECT WITH THIS AUTHOR:

Blog: kdwilliamsonfiction.wordpress.com
E-Mail: Williamson_kd@yahoo.com

Other Books from Ylva Publishing

www.ylva-publishing.com

The Red Files

Lee Winter

ISBN: 978-3-95533-330-0
Length: 365 pages (103,000 words)

Ambitious journalist Lauren King is stuck reporting on the vapid LA social scene's gala events while sparring with her rival—icy ex-Washington correspondent Catherine Ayers. Then a curious story unfolds before their eyes, involving a business launch, thirty-four prostitutes, and a pallet of missing pink champagne. Can the warring pair join together to unravel an incredible story?

Conflict of Interest

(2nd revised edition)
Portland Police Bureau Series—Book #1

Jae

ISBN: 978-3-95533-109-2
Length: 466 pages (135,000 words)

Detective Aiden Carlisle isn't looking for love, especially not at a law enforcement seminar, but the first lecturer isn't what she expected.

After a failed relationship, psychologist Dawn Kinsley swore to never get involved with another cop, but she immediately feels a connection to Aiden.

Can Aiden keep from crossing the line when Dawn becomes the victim of a brutal crime?

Driving Me Mad

L.T. Smith

ISBN: 978-3-95533-290-7
Length: 348 pages (107,000 words)

After becoming lost on her way to a works convention, Rebecca Gibson stops to ask for help at an isolated house. Progressively, her life becomes more entangled with the mysterious happenings of the house and its inhabitants.

With the help of Clare Davies, can Rebecca solve a mystery that has been haunting a family for over sixty years? Can she put the ghosts and the demons of the past to rest?

All the Little Moments

G Benson

ISBN: 978-3-95533-341-6
Length: 350 pages (132,000 words)

Anna is focused on her career as an anaesthetist. When a tragic accident leaves her responsible for her young niece and nephew, her life changes abruptly. Completely overwhelmed, Anna barely has time to brush her teeth in the morning let alone date a woman. But then she collides with a long-legged stranger…

Coming from Ylva Publishing

www.ylva-publishing.com

Crossing Lines

Cops and Docs-Book #2

KD Williamson

Despite all the upheaval around them, Nora Whitmore and Kelli McCabe found their way…together. Unfortunately, little by little, things fall apart around them. Can they navigate through seemingly impassable obstacles? Or will the lines they cross keep them part?

Collide-O-Scope

Andrea Bramhall

One unidentified dead body. One tiny fishing village. Forty residents and everyone's a suspect. Where do you start? Newly promoted Detective Sergeant Kate Brannon and Kings Lynn's CID have to answer that question and more as they untangle the web of lies wrapped around the tiny village of Brandale Stiathe Harbour to capture the killer of Connie Wells.

Blurred Lines
© 2016 by KD Williamson

ISBN: 978-3-95533-493-2

Also available as e-book.

Published by Ylva Publishing, legal entity of Ylva Verlag, e.Kfr.
Ylva Verlag, e.Kfr.
Owner: Astrid Ohletz
Am Kirschgarten 2
65830 Kriftel
Germany

www.ylva-publishing.com

First edition: 2016

No part of this book may be reproduced, scanned, or distributed in any printed or electronic form without permission. Please do not participate in or encourage piracy of copyrighted materials in violation of the author's rights. Thank you for respecting the hard work of this author.

This is a work of fiction. Names, characters, places, and incidents either are a product of the author's imagination or are used fictitiously, and any resemblance to locales, events, business establishments, or actual persons—living or dead—is entirely coincidental.

Credits
Edited by Jove Belle
Cover Design by Streetlight Graphics

Printed in Germany
by Amazon Distribution
GmbH, Leipzig